DESIRING AN ANGEL

MISSING LINK 3

LYNN BURKE

Editor: Kat McIntyre

Cover Artist: Golden Czermak

Photographer: Wander Aguiar

Visit my website at authorlynnburke.com

DESIRING AN ANGEL

I've been called a ray of sunshine but can't get my head out of the clouds, and I sure as hell can't carry on an intelligent conversation.

What I do excel at? Cooking, cleaning, and caring for children.

But I'm no 1950s housewife looking for a husband. Independent and driven, I want to fulfill my daydreams of having two men love me until I breathe my last.

Missing Link provides me with the opportunity to fulfill my desires with Rhett and Ashton, long-time partners who are looking for an angel to share in their life. When unforeseen circumstances leave me homeless, Ashton offers me my greatest fantasy come to life which places me in close proximity to the two hot men.

The problem?

Reservations and impenetrable stoicism keep me from winning Rhett's heart.

But tragedy brings crippling emotions, forcing a battle of the wills. Can Rhett find the strength to be vulnerable, or will Ashton be the only person whose love he'll trust in?

1

───────

PROLOGUE

RHETT

Darkness lay outside the large windows of my new bedroom, and silence had long since fallen throughout the rest of the house.

Ten-thirty, my alarm clock read, much too late for a twelve-year-old to be up according to Mom.

She and Dad slept in the master suite on the floor below me while I sat cross-legged on my bed, unable to relax after a day of lugging boxes up three flights of stairs.

My parents had moved us three towns south the day after I'd finished the seventh grade, and I missed the comfort of my old bedroom, the safe place I could hide in to ensure I didn't disappoint them.

The four walls of my supposed new escape surrounding me didn't put me at ease. Rather, they seemed to push inward, threatening the stoicism that had been ingrained in my head at too young of an age.

Instead of thinking about the strange, unsettled feeling inside my stomach, I forced my mind toward easing my tension...and a way to flee from the disquiet of a bedroom that didn't feel like home.

A plan formed in my head, giving me something to focus on, and I snagged hold of it.

Stomach tight and hands clammy, I hopped up, tugged on my sneakers, and quietly crept into the hallway. No lights shone from the stairwell, so I slipped down a flight and held my breath.

My parents didn't make a peep from behind their closed bedroom door.

One last scurry down another set of stairs, and I stood in the massive house's entryway.

Dad had already quizzed me on the alarm system, so I snuck outside into the warm night air with no one the wiser, filling my lungs for what seemed like the first time in months since I'd learned we were moving closer to Boston.

Dad's new job came with a lot more money, and even though neither of my parents showed much emotion, both seemed quite pleased to have climbed higher in the ladder.

Me? Not so much. I didn't care about money, cars, and *being* someone. I just wanted peace and quiet—but more than the fake kind that had always lay over our house.

Sure, with only the three of us, home had always been on the silent side. But peace? I didn't understand the word and hadn't felt anything but restless for as long as I could remember.

Unless I'd been closed up in my old bedroom.

"And now I don't even have that anymore," I muttered to myself, yanking my bike off the ground from where one of the movers had left it alongside the garage.

Settled on the narrow seat, I pedaled down the driveway, intent on getting away from the scene of my newfound misery. Without knowing the neighborhood, I chose left and just kept riding since we'd come into town by that route earlier in the day.

Trees and houses lined the dimly lit road, eventually giving way to thicker woods I remembered that had spread out eastward beyond a large cemetery.

My legs burned after the long hours of climbing stairs with box after box, but I kept pushing until I couldn't go any further. Heart thundering, I slowed alongside a wrought-iron fence separating me from the graveyard. My pants for air sounded loud in the still night, broken only by a lonely owl somewhere in the distance.

Moonlight shone through the towering maple trees to my left, touching headstones like creepy ghost fingers, but I felt no need to flee.

My insides simply wanted to fold in on themselves.

Crying never solved anything, Dad had always claimed, *so be strong and take control over your emotions.*

It is what it is, Mom had declared the last time I'd had her arms around me at age seven when I'd buried my puppy that had been hit by a car.

One final tear had escaped my eye that day, and I'd been nothing but stoic and proper since then, which pleased both my parents.

A hiccupped sob sounded in the night, and I held my breath, straining my ears in the darkness.

Another soft cry turned my focus back toward the cemetery, and I slowly pedaled forward, my tires near silent on the cracked sidewalk beneath them. A break in the trees revealed a wide expanse of open field dotted with dark stones, some tall and monstrous, others short and leaning from age.

The crying grew louder as I approached the entrance. A double gate sat closed and locked, flanked on either side by towering stone pillars.

A bike leaned on its kickstand in front, the paved

driveway on the other side leading deep into the cemetery's gloom.

I parked my bike alongside the one that stood the exact height as mine and pressed my face to the cool bars of the gate, scanning the area beyond.

Someone huddled with their back to me in front of a headstone off to the right. Arms wrapped around their legs, and head bowed, they shivered, their shoulders shaking as cries reached for me like a magnet to my ironclad heart.

A strange ache moved over my chest, and I rubbed at my shirt, trying to soothe it away.

Frowning, I tilted my head back and eyed the gate in front of me.

It stood too tall to climb.

But the fence beyond, the tree alongside where the person's bike sat—its branches crept over into the graveyard just as creepily as the beams of moonlight reaching through the leaves.

The boy's sniffles continued, pulling my focus back on him.

Boy, I had decided, because no middle school aged girl I knew would ever go into such a place alone after dark when everyone else slept.

I eyed the tree. Glanced at the crying boy. Rubbed at my chest for a second time, my feet itching to move closer.

He had gone to see that grave by himself, but I felt he shouldn't be alone. He needed someone strong beside him while weakness held control over his emotions.

Mind made up, I set a plan in motion that had me scaling the tree, shimmying along a branch until I hovered over green grass, and dropping to the ground.

The boy turned at the thump of my feet behind him but didn't jump up in startled fear like I'd expected.

Definitely brave...or perhaps he'd already heard me coming.

"Hey." I moved closer as he swiped his arm over his eyes. I wasn't about to ask him if he was okay. That would have been a waste of words.

Instead, I stopped beside him, reading the name etched in granite in front of him.

Archer Blackwood.

A quick calculation let me know he'd been dead three years to the day—and that he would have been twelve if he still lived.

I sank onto the hard ground, breathing in the scent of soil, fresh cut grass, and flowers.

The boy beside me sniffled. "He was my brother," he whispered, sending that weird twinge through my heart again. "My twin."

Our elbows brushed, sliding a shiver down my arm.

"I'm sorry for your loss," I murmured, looking over at the boy.

Wetness still filled his eyes that appeared as red as his nose in the moonlight shining on us. "Thanks," he whispered, his voice breaking. He didn't seem embarrassed by his tears or the show of emotion like I would have been.

But I wasn't about to put him down like Dad used to do with me all the time.

"I'm Rhett," I told him but didn't offer my hand since his clasped around his knees—and I didn't want either of us moving and breaking the magnetic contact between our bodies.

"Ashton," he replied quietly.

"What happened to him?" I asked, picking at the grass between our thighs so I wouldn't grab hold of him like I wanted to and hug his sadness away.

"Leukemia. It's been three years, and Mom and my therapist tell me that healing will come, but they didn't have their other half ripped away from them." He wiped his nose on his T-shirt at his shoulder, leaving a smear of wetness that should have grossed me out but didn't. "Even my dad and four older sisters don't understand."

I had no clue what it was like to have a twin—or even a sibling.

Heck, not even a close friend since I'd never allowed my emotions free so someone could get to know me beyond the hard shell I hid inside.

That owl hooted again, pulling my gaze off the cold stone for the cemetery's darkness beyond. The paved road wound through shrubs and what looked like a small chapel in the distance.

A new beginning lay before me like the path that disappeared into the unknown. A new life...

And the family-rich boy beside me seemed just as lost and lonely as I felt deep inside where I smothered all my feelings.

"This and our birthday are the only two days I can't live in denial he's gone," Ashton whispered. "It's just so much easier pretending he never got sick and died. He was my sunshine, my shoulder to lean on." The boy released a shuddered sigh and sagged even more like he wanted to sink into the soil and join his twin.

I rarely smiled, so I couldn't fill up that first part of him he'd lost with his brother. But I sure as hell could offer the second.

"I just moved here, and even though I could never take Archer's place in your life, I'd like to be your friend," I suggested quietly. "And I promise you can lean on me whenever you want."

Ashton turned and threw his arms around me, clinging to me like he had decided I was his tower of strength.

Warmth flooded through my body, and my eyes stung for the first time since I'd buried my puppy. My throat went tight, and I allowed myself to touch him like I'd longed to do. Hugging him close, I leaned my cheek onto the top of his head as he started to cry again.

He smelled like sweat and dirt, the outdoors...and *home*.

I closed my eyes and filled my senses with all things Ashton Blackwood, calmness I'd been missing since leaving my old town settling into my bones.

I *would* be Ashton's rock, be the stability he needed, I decided in that moment as sure as the breath in my lungs.

And he would be my best friend until we too lay beneath soil and moonlight with nothing but a lonely owl keeping our spirits company.

2

———

ASHTON

For once, I woke before Rhett, and I soaked in the pleasure of watching him in a state of slumber, the only place vulnerability owned his mind.

His dark hair stuck up from my running my fingers through it while he'd loved on me the night before. No furrow lined the skin between his thick eyebrows. His lips parted, slack and peaceful in slumber where he rested his cheek on navy satin sheets.

I wondered if he dreamed, and if so, what images filled his mind as the sunrise began to bathe the beach outside our bedroom window.

Once his eyes opened, that brain of his would fire on all cylinders, going through his plans for the day even though Saturday lay before us.

My favorite day.

No work, just hours spent with my lover in the peaceful silence of our oceanfront home.

Smiling, I ghosted my fingertips over his smooth brow and sharp cheekbones, down the bridge of his nose to the perfect bow of his upper lip I wanted to taste.

Rhett Stirling had drawn me in from his first "Hey" when I'd been crying my eyes out by my brother's grave. Without knowing who the heck he was, I'd thrown myself into his arms since fate had sent him there to help fill the hole Archer's death had torn open in my soul.

Twenty-three years together, and Rhett was still the one I clung to when my emotions overran and bled for the world to see.

Rhett stirred, his strong arm wrapping around my waist and easing me closer against his hard chest. He hummed under his breath, peeked an eyelid open to reveal orbs as dark as luscious chocolate, and zoned in on my mouth.

Smiling, I closed the distance and pressed my lips against his.

"Zing," I whispered what I had the first time we'd kissed back in eleventh grade.

"Still?" he murmured, a hint of a smile lifting the corner of his mouth as he slowly blinked the sleep from his eyes.

"Always." I snuggled against his body and soaked in the warmth and solidity of him. "I love you."

"Love you too, baby." He kissed the top of my head, his hand starting its trail up and down my spine.

"So, is coffee, a shower, or fucking first on your agenda for the day?" I asked, since there was no way his brain lay as serene as our limbs.

"Let's cook breakfast together, I'll fuck you over the kitchen island once we finish eating, then I'll wash you from head to toe, paying extra attention to every crack and crevice on your body."

My dick twitched to life at his rumbling tone and the promise of a good time. Rhett Stirling was a book boyfriend come to life, and I couldn't get enough.

"I fucking love Saturdays," I groaned and untangled

from his body, ready to get on with the day even while wanting it to last forever and keep the following workweek from coming.

My smile faded as I pulled on the lounge pants I'd left draped over the foot of our bed.

Don't waste the life you've been gifted. Carry on the family name...

The memory of my dad's face etched with grief flashed in my mind as it always did when the anniversary of my brother's death loomed mere days away.

My father was the only son of an only son—four generations back. Having twins, he had accomplished more than his ancestors, but that feat had crumbled down when my brother had fallen sick and a man instead of a woman had stolen my heart.

But there had been no stopping what had started that late night in the cemetery. Best friends connected at the hip, Rhett and I were both attracted to boys *and* girls...but our hearts had chosen each other.

I'd overheard my dad sharing his grief with mom later on the night I'd told them that Rhett was my future until death parted us.

While neither of my parents were homophobic, I'd been unable to keep my dad's reaction from haunting my mind throughout the following years.

Rhett hadn't been too keen on the idea of having children, but four years earlier, we finally sat down to discuss creating a family. His first idea had been surrogacy, but I desired more and had pushed for it—

"Maeve won't be here until seven tonight," Rhett said while climbing off the bed, pulling my mind back to the present, "so we have the day to ourselves."

Maeve being our latest match on Missing Link, the

polyamorous dating app Rhett and I had created after that conversation.

I kept my fingers crossed that she would possess the same sunshiny personality as Archer to balance my own, darker nature but also would be someone who would help Rhett express emotion, because after twenty-three years together, he struggled to reveal most of his inner workings to anyone.

Myself included.

While we had been content with each other, there were parts of us the other couldn't fulfill. Fuck knew we'd enjoyed our fair share of hookups throughout our years together while searching out the perfect woman to include in our household, but we'd yet to meet the *one*.

We'd spoken with the latest, Maeve, via FaceTime twice, and she checked off what we had listed in our ML profile to a T.

If only those wants input when we'd created our profile had been my desires rather than Rhett's.

Maeve seemed polished and proper, her character more in tune with my stoic partner's than what I desired for my children's mother. I hoped for someone full of happiness and positivity—since neither Rhett nor I could claim those traits, and I wanted that for our future children.

We had yet to find a woman we agreed on, one that clicked at first call or meeting, one that made my insides zing yet rest with that sense of rightness I had only ever experienced with him.

Hundreds of men and women had joined the Missing Link community in the first two days of its release into the world. Three years later, and thousands had uploaded profiles, seeking fulfillment of their dreams and fantasies.

Rhett and I fell into the category of looking for relationships rather than hookups, but sifting through women hoping for the same as we did had become more laborious than fun like it had been in the beginning.

Unfortunately, Maeve proved just as disappointing as the rest.

Even though Rhett and I both found her attractive enough, the woman writhing between us later that night felt...wrong.

No, no, no...

I wanted to deny yet another failure, but her breath panting over my face hinting at sweet cherries from wine shared over dinner didn't entice me to kiss her or drink down her moans.

I kept my eyes on Rhett behind her, his parted lips, the lust in his dark eyes doing more for me than the wet pussy clutching at my dick. Our gazes clashed, and I imagined it was my ass he took rather than the woman between us.

Love you so damn much, I told him with my steady gaze, my heart breaking, and his eyes promised me the same without a word.

"Oh..." Maeve shuddered and came, her core clasping tight around my girth.

"Ash..." Rhett's jaw clenched, and his tone, the need in his stare over her shoulder, took me to the edge. We fell together like we always did.

We left her boneless on our bed a few minutes later, both of us going to the bathroom to clean up.

"She's not it," I whispered, tying off my condom and tossing it into the trash with a little more force than necessary.

Rhett hugged me from behind, his sweaty, hard body relaxing the tension riding me. I sagged into his familiar, comfortable hold. "We'll find her." He kissed my shoulder, his lips warm and sure.

I clasped my hand over his atop my heart, twining our fingers together.

"Promise." Rhett kissed me again, and my back grew cool while he retrieved a wet towel for the woman we'd left sprawled in our bed. "I'll take care of Maeve and send her on her way," he whispered.

A heavy exhale caved my chest as he exited the bathroom.

She was far from the first to come between us. She wasn't the first Rhett would see out the door while I showered either. But he'd always been better with letting people down, the confrontations I didn't handle well, so I left him to it and accepted the fact we would have to continue our search.

I stepped into the spray, tilting my face into the pelting, hot water. The scent of rose perfume, sweat, and cum, swirled down the drain. While my balls had emptied, I hadn't found anything satisfying about sex with Maeve outside of sensing Rhett's dick a membrane apart from mine, his focus on me, and the connection I'd felt since that night he'd found me crying by Archer's grave.

Rhett had been the one to give my life worth, value, when I'd thought I should have been buried six feet under instead of Archer—

The glass shower door opened, and Rhett stepped in to join me, his allaying presence enough to ease my disappointment over our latest failed match and the swamping sense of worthlessness that always attacked whenever I thought too hard on my brother's death.

Rhett wrapped me up in his arms again, and I melted into his chest, my head tipping back to his shoulder. "Sorry," he whispered, his scruff scraping across mine and sending shivers down my spine.

"Nothing to be sorry for." I reached around behind me, palming his ass, holding his groin tight against my backside.

"I chose her when you weren't that interested," he murmured against my ear, his breath warmer than the water hitting my chest.

"If there's a match that catches your eye, I'm not going to say no just because I don't feel it after a few emails and video calls. It's like my sister always says," I reminded him for at least the fiftieth time, "just because you don't like a dress on the hanger doesn't mean you won't rock the shit out of it."

Rhett chuckled and kissed my cheek. "Which sister?"

"All four," I muttered.

He lightly laughed again, and I turned.

"Love you so damn much it hurts," I murmured and gave him my mouth before he could reply. Tasting him—hot male, heady and intoxicating—trickled life back to my groin. My body had always been insatiable when it came to him, but he pulled away before my dick thickened fully.

"Let me take care of you, baby," he murmured, reaching for the bodywash.

I went pliant as he washed me from head to toe like he'd done as promised earlier that morning, cleaning all trace of the woman from my skin. He massaged shampoo, then conditioner into my scalp until my eyelids fluttered closed, my entire body blissed out from having his attentive hands on my body.

When Rhett finished, he tugged me against his chest, his firm touch grounding. "Are you okay?" he murmured.

His question came as it always did after a waste-of-time

date, but I knew he referred to more. The edge of concern lacing his voice was a telling, rare sentiment.

The following week I would experience the pain of an anniversary I despised. The one that had left me feeling incomplete and reminded me that denying death didn't reverse its effects. Even though Rhett coming into my life had lessened those emotions, I still struggled with my grief and survivor's guilt.

Losing a twin was devastating, especially if they were the happy sort, the one with light in their eyes regardless of circumstance. Always joking and laughing, thinking the best, and expecting great outcomes.

The sunny opposite of what I couldn't help but be—

"Hey." Rhett's firm tone stopped my thoughts, his dark eyes peering into mine as he lifted my cheek from his shoulder, hands cradling my face.

I attempted a smile while he rubbed his thumb over my lower lip. "Yeah, I'm okay."

A lie, one Rhett could read on my face, expected after twenty-plus years of being partners, but he wouldn't refute.

We crawled into a freshly-made bed a few minutes later and came together like magnets, front to front. Shared breath, arms wrapped around one another. I rubbed my cheek against his chest, shuddering as a sigh rippled through me.

Rhett had always been home to me, even when we had lived apart, beneath the care of our parents.

"I love you," Rhett stated quietly against my damp hair, and I closed my eyes, trusting his embrace, his words, same as I did gravity to keep my feet firmly planted on the earth.

"You're my rock," I murmured against his warm skin what I'd told him hundreds of times over the years, "my knight in shining armor. No one has cared for my well-being like you do."

He squeezed me tighter.

Maybe it was time to face the truth that no woman would ever fit between me and Rhett in the way I dreamed of.

My heart had been so set on finding someone happy like Archer and my own mother. Someone who would be content as a stay-at-home mom and take an active part in parenting alongside us. Giving our children sunshine and happiness that came from positive energy neither Rhett nor I possessed.

I couldn't imagine raising children in a somber household, especially when one of the dads never really wanted kids to begin with, especially of his blood.

But it seemed I'd been left with no choice. Fate hadn't intervened like she had when bringing Rhett into my life.

"Do you still have all that information you printed out on surrogacy?" I asked, my eyes closed and voice quiet.

Rhett's soothing hand on my back stilled. "Yes."

I released an unsteady exhale, setting my mind on a new course, one he had already mapped out and waited for my consent. "I'm thinking about plan B."

Tension I hadn't realized ran through him eased, relaxing his body along mine, hard muscle and soft skin I'd memorized by sight and feel from forehead to foot. "You're sure?" he murmured, his tone soft.

No.

"Yeah." My throat tightened.

Swallowing against the tears welling behind my clenched eyelids, I clung to Rhett harder and told myself it was time to face reality.

3

RHETT

Fucking finally.

We had invested so much of our time in creating the Missing Link app to find a mother for the children Ash wanted when an easier answer, the most direct course of action to achieve his dreams, only cost money.

Something we had plenty of.

Years earlier, I had suggested finding a surrogate mother for the offspring he dreamed about fathering to carry on the Blackwood name, but he wanted more. Someone, he claimed, to add to our lives, someone full of sunshine to balance his melancholy and my stoic nature.

I had no wish for kids, but I also didn't need a woman coming between us unless she climaxed. That, I could handle. Even enjoyed immensely. Sharing Ash emotionally when he was the only one I sometimes allowed to see the real me?

Not so much.

But Ash owned my heart, and there wasn't anything I wouldn't do to help fulfill his dreams, especially about carrying out his father's desire—hell, *command*—for grandsons.

Even if his bastard father didn't deserve it. Jerry Blackwood didn't outright portray homophobic tendencies, but I'd caught the disappointment in his eyes when Ash and I had sat down together with his parents back in high school to tell them we were dating.

In Jerry's eyes, I wasn't good enough for his Ash. I couldn't personally give him what he hoped to get from his only surviving son.

But I'd tried in the one way I could with Missing Link.

"I'm sorry our idea didn't work for you," I murmured against his hair while hugging him close and sliding one of my legs between his.

His exhale heated my chest where he snuggled like always, and not for the first time, I wished he could burrow beneath my skin and take up permanent residence. "No you're not."

I wasn't going to argue, engage in the way he wanted just to take his mind off the week ahead and the sure grief to unearth like it always did on the anniversary of Archer's death.

"Tomorrow we can go over the surrogacy paperwork," I said instead, focusing on the plan, the course of action to get the ball rolling. "We'll take the next steps in making this happen. Together."

Ash pushed up onto an elbow, meeting my gaze. "And if we can't find the right fit, someone who will agree to remain in our child's life after they're born?"

He dreamed of a mother like his own, constantly available with warm hugs, open ears, and loving smooches on boo-boos. He also wanted someone like his brother had been—happy and full of life until his had gotten snuffed out.

I preferred quiet and reserved, a lady. One who wouldn't bring drama to our future and co-parent from a distance, just like our dating app profile showed we searched for.

"We'll find her," I promised.

"That's what you said about our app."

I bit my tongue, but Ash read my stiffened body like an open book.

"Sorry. That was uncalled for," he whispered to soothe away the sting his words had caused. "I shouldn't take my disappointment out on you. Maybe it's just not meant to be." He laid back down, his cheek on my chest where it always was when we cuddled in bed while awake.

I kissed the top of his head, letting him know I forgave him, and he settled in without another word.

My mind continued to move as though hyped on caffeine, keeping me awake long after he slept.

Meant to be, he'd murmured.

Ash had used those words the first time we'd kissed, that day my dreams of playing football on the iron grid lay in shatters. Literally. I'd been taken down by three guys, my lower leg snapping in more than one place.

Ash had snuck into my bedroom, in the middle of the night, wrapping me in his arms while I sprawled out stiff and unmoving, refusing to break down in weakness.

His warmth had breathed life back inside my chest, and I'd eventually leaned into him, drew strength from him for the first time in our friendship.

His close presence had always tingled awareness through my body, but it wasn't until he had pressed his lips to my cheek that I recognized what he stirred inside me.

Desire. Longing for more than mere friendship.

"*Rhett*," he had whispered, his voice thick as though experiencing the same thing making every inch of my body begin to burn with need.

I'd pulled back to see him in the light of my bedside lamp, desperate to observe, to *know*.

Hazel eyes welling, he had studied my face, stalling out on my mouth.

Raw, hot arousal had shot through me like a well-aimed spiraling football, ripping the air from my lungs.

We'd moved as though of the same mind, magnets as always.

Our first kiss, the crush of lips, the sharing of air—one of the most profound and real moments in my entire life.

"*Zing*," he had murmured against my mouth, making me snicker. "*We were meant to be, Rhett Stirling. Forever.*"

I hadn't argued since he'd beautifully vocalized the feelings coursing inside me, something I still struggled to do.

My insides a churning mess, I stared at the ceiling of our bedroom while Ash clung to me and breathed heavily in peaceful slumber.

Failure equaled weakness in my mind, but I looked forward to taking the next step where Ash would remain mine—and only mine as he'd always been.

My chest tightened over the excitement and yet I frowned, wondering how Ash would suffer if the surrogate mother didn't fulfill his hopes to stay in our child's life after birth.

A fuckton of emotion rolled through me, none of which I could handle or make disappear.

No way in hell would I allow my Ash to feel pain or disappointment if I could help it. He wanted a woman involved as a mother in the day-to-day living of his children, which wouldn't happen with surrogacy.

Said woman would need to live with us. There was no other option. Knowing Ash, he would adore her for fulfilling his dreams, and as affectionate as he was, I had no doubt their relationship wouldn't remain platonic. Eventually, a bond would solidify, and she would end up in our bed because I wouldn't be able to say no if gifted the opportunity to sink into a warm, wet pussy.

Unconditional love demanded a change, another chance, different from what I had done in taking the reins to keep on *my* course like a selfish asshole.

Fuck.

I exhaled firmly to settle a veering direction in my head and pulled away from Ash's heavy leg draped over mine. Sliding from bed, I created a new plan, one that would give Ash exactly what he dreamed of.

As children, I'd wanted to be his other half, promised to always be there for him to lean on—but he had ended up being the same for me. I longed to lay the world at his feet even if it meant the foundation of mine shifted.

I had the strength to endure—even if I wouldn't enjoy doing so.

Enough light shone from the sliver of moon outside the window to ease my way across the bedroom and down the stairs into the open concept area of our house's first floor.

We'd left New England behind after graduation, both of us needing a new start.

Him away from pain and constant memories of his grief, and me from my disconnected parents who had since retired to Florida. As an only child, I should have been their entire world, their focus, but that hadn't been the case. An emotionally repressed household hadn't offered much in the way of love, so having Ash's was a gift I wasn't about to disregard or let down out of goddamn selfishness.

I grabbed a bottle of cold water from our fridge and sat on the couch, my iPad in hand.

My chest swelled at the sight of the rainbow-colored, intertwined hearts of Missing Link's logo. It was Ash's design for the app we'd built together, the start of what had brought about our software development company that allowed us to purchase a home overlooking the Pacific Ocean.

He was the code wiz, and I'd never met a puzzle I couldn't figure out from beginning to end once I'd set a plan in place to do so. Add in both our work ethics, his easy ability to connect and communicate with others, and we made a hell of a team.

A lucrative partnership that offered a comfortable life, one I'd been perfectly content to live in relative quiet, without drama, until we breathed our last.

My chest ached from the slew of feelings inside me, but I put it from my mind by closing a mental door with ease. Fuck knew I'd had plenty of practice doing so as a kid.

I went into our shared profile that didn't mention we were the app's creators. Sifting through the information and personality testing we'd done for finding our perfect match revealed my wants rather than Ash's.

The MM looking for F part, I left alone.

Exhaling slow and steady as though releasing tension and selfishness from my core, I set about changing the answers we had originally input from my desires when he would have chosen differently.

College education, I clicked, wasn't a requirement as I'd answered previously. No longer were we seeking an accomplished woman who had her shit together career-wise.

"Easygoing," I mumbled. "Laid-back. A ray of sunshine

to brighten the day." I typed all the words he often spoke of while fighting off a cringe.

Ash needed someone with those traits in his life since I definitely couldn't give them to him.

The feeling of not being enough leaked through my conscience, but I slammed the door on that sense of frailty that left me floundering.

He would benefit from a woman who lived for the thrill of adventure, one who wouldn't balk at facing down daily living with a smile on her face while being a stay-at-home mom like his.

Always laughing, always seeing the bright side of things.

Such bubbly personalities clashed with my more stoic reservations, but I reminded myself there wasn't anything I wouldn't sacrifice for him.

Even if it made me feel...less than.

I hoped whoever ended up zinging with Ash would also be compatible enough with me that we might eventually find some sort of connection to create an enjoyable triad.

Fingers crossed, I clicked save to update our profile, hoping I wouldn't regret my decision to give his hopes yet another shot at fulfillment.

"What were you doing?" Ash murmured when I climbed back into bed a few moments later.

The scent of lavender from the dryer sheets he laundered with wafted past my nose, taking me back to the last time my mother had hugged me after I'd buried my one and only puppy. I remembered the comfort of her arms, the way she had soothed my back—and the flowery scent of her skin.

My one good emotional memory from childhood, and Ash made sure to remind me of it every night we slid between our sheets.

A lightness spread through my chest in the knowledge I'd done the right thing to bring fulfillment to his life.

"I changed our profile," I told him, finally relaxed and ready to sleep.

"Did you delete it?" He snuggled against me again, chest to chest, his skin warm from sleep.

"No," I replied, rubbing my hand down the bumps of his spine. "I changed our questionnaire answers to what they should have been from the beginning."

He lifted up onto an elbow, his face in shadows. "Rhett..."

"It's okay, baby." I cradled his face in my hands, my thumb caressing over his lower lip. "I know you want a mother for your children, not a faceless or dispassionate egg donor."

"But—"

"There's no buts, Ash." I pulled him down so our foreheads rested together. In my rare moments of vulnerability, I adored him so fucking much it made my chest ache—and I appreciated how he never invalidated whatever emotions I allowed to leak through in our quiet times together.

"Fuck, do I love you." He pressed a kiss to my mouth, and I groaned at the first swipe of his tongue along mine. Nothing compared to a happy Ash invested in physically showing his love.

Fucking nothing.

Heart rate kicking up, I rolled to my back beneath him, spreading my legs to make room for his hips. The heat, the intense need that had flared to unquenchable life between us in high school rose to full force, easing my mind and stilling my concerns.

Electrical currents ran over my skin, settling into my balls same as it always did whenever our mouths met.

"Rhett..." Ash groaned and kissed down my neck toward my chest. Knowing where he headed pulsed need through my aching length. "Let me take care of you—make you feel good," he whispered over my constricting lower abs and flicked his tongue over my skin. "Want to taste your delicious dick."

My cock bucked against his chin, anxious for the wet heat of his mouth. "Fuck yes."

A cell rang from my bedside table, halting Ash's hungry mouth hovering over my cock.

One a.m., our alarm clock read.

Brow furrowed, I reached for my phone and glanced at the screen. "It's my father."

And at such an hour with them being on the East Coast and our never catching up just for the hell of it, the reason for his call couldn't be good.

All thoughts of sex slipped from my mind as Ash rolled off me. I swiped to answer, my stomach clenched tight, my dick deflated.

"Dad?"

"Your mom had a stroke." His voice didn't waver. He showed zero emotion as always.

Considering the lack of attachment I felt for either of my parents, the sense of...*wrong* that pushed me upright in bed baffled me.

"They're taking her to the hospital," Dad stated in a nonchalant way, his usual since the man couldn't be moved.

"What happened?" I asked as Ash shuffled close and wound his arm across my lower back in his usual touchy-feely way of showing support.

He must have been able to make out Dad's words.

Mom had gotten up to use the bathroom and collapsed. Dad hadn't been able to rouse her and had called 911.

I found myself on my feet, striding across the bedroom, a plan settling into place in my head. Steps to focus on and follow.

"I'll catch the first available flight," I told him, and Ash flicked on the lamp beside him.

I blinked in the harsh glare, the brightness bringing clarity that things might go poorly for Mom. We'd never been close, so the unrest, the bothersome feelings wanting to wash over me furrowed my brow. I pushed them down exactly as my parents had taught me.

"There's no need—"

"I'm coming," I stated a bit harshly as reserved coolness slid into place, locking my emotions up tight from years of conditioning.

Dad told me which hospital they were taking Mom to, and I hung up seconds later, my mind as set as my jaw.

"What happened?" Ash asked as I placed my cell atop my bureau and pulled open the top drawer.

"Mom had a stroke. They're taking her to the hospital by ambulance." I tossed a few pairs of socks and briefs onto the bed.

"Oh no." Ash climbed from between our sheets and headed for me.

I knew he planned to drag me into his arms, but I moved toward the walk-in closet we shared to retrieve a carry-on bag, fully intending to refuse any comfort he thought I might need.

"Rhett." He stood in the closet's door when I turned around.

"I'm fine." I snipped the words.

He eyed me but didn't budge from my path. "Do you want me to go with you?"

My protective instincts over him roared to life. Hospitals

triggered Ash, and there was no way in hell I would allow him to set foot into one for someone who hadn't loved me like he did.

I moved closer and cupped his cheek, his scruff scratching my palm. "No."

His hands clasped at my waist, drawing me close, and giving in, I dropped the bag. Forcing my body to relax against him, I exhaled, closing my eyes for a few seconds, soaking in the warmth of his familiar embrace of the only love I trusted.

"If you need me..."

"I always will," I promised and pressed my lips to his, allowing myself a brief moment to share my sensitivities with the one person who deserved it.

4

SKYLAR

"You're late," my boss Julie snipped, her eyes like flint.

"I'm sorry," I hurried past her for the employee cubicles to unload my bag and water bottle. "I got caught up reorganizing the pantry—."

"Two days ago it was your sister's linen closet," Julie cut me off.

I bit back my annoyance at being talked over. God knew I experienced enough of that at home. "It won't happen again," I promised, my hands as shaky as my voice.

"I've heard that one before."

I cringed beneath her sarcastic tone and the truth of her words. Seeing as how my head was *in the clouds* as my sister often said, I couldn't help how easily distractions pulled me away from responsibilities.

A burst of giggles sounded from the toy store's show-room, a crash following on its heels.

"Now what?" Julie cursed and strode off, allowing me to breathe and try to get my bearings on my flighty thoughts and emotions.

Yes, my focus had turned over the mess Nora had made

of her pantry. Yes, I'd lost track of time while tidying up—and yes, I may have gone into autopilot while just rearranging all the groceries I'd bought for the two of us the day before.

Boundless energy had always kept my brain cells bouncing. I'd struggled since childhood to focus on anything that resembled schoolwork and had barely managed to graduate.

I didn't hold a PhD in astrophysics or work for NASA like my sister did, but I kept house for her like a pro in exchange for room and board.

Even though my parents had never outright said it, I knew they thought I would fail at city life when I'd moved in with Nora a few months earlier at Dad's prompting. There was too much distraction for someone easily led away from responsibility by all the shiny pretties.

I was like a dog, my attention snagged by every squirrel in the vicinity while Nora was the rigid, brainy owl, the valedictorian of her class. She'd graduated high school at sixteen and got her bachelor's then master's degree with ease. She studied physics and the stars thanks to the scholarships she'd landed due to her high honors and brilliance.

She also had a good head on her shoulders, while mine...well, sometimes my brain didn't exactly feel attached to the rest of my body.

A young child's laughter drew me back to reality that I was at *work*, and I scurried into the storefront and behind the counter.

The teenager I'd been scheduled to relieve glared at me.

"Sorry I'm—"

"Julie's gonna can your ass if you don't get your shit together, Skylar," she hissed, and I swallowed my apology and the irritation of being cut off a second time within a matter of minutes.

With a huff, my co-worker spun on her heel, leaving me alone with a line three customers deep.

I plastered on a smile that usually came easily and began ringing up the next sale, hating how people dismissed me or felt my words weren't worth their time just because I had difficulty focusing.

More giggles sounded, and I caught sight of a preschooler ripping across the store, clutching a teddy bear almost the same size as him. A harried woman hurried after him.

"Patrick James Ryan," she harshly whispered, "get your wiggly butt back over here this instant!"

Biting against a smirk and the memories of being that youngster myself twenty years earlier, I accepted the cash from the older, woman in front of me who pressed her lips in a tight line.

Thirty-seven dollars and fifty-two cents had been her total—

"Spoiled brat," the customer in front of me grumbled, erasing my smile and my ability to count out change. "Parents these days don't know how to manage their kids."

Perhaps the boy is ADHD and can't keep a handle on himself no matter how hard he tries.

I bit my tongue while pulling coins from the drawer.

My brain trailed after the little boy and his adventure—a tumble of the cowboy hat display followed in his wake.

"Bad, Patrick!" His mom didn't bother lowering her voice. "Bad!"

A cringe rippled over me at her admonition, a word I'd heard often enough as a child it churned my stomach.

He's not a dog...

I expected I would be setting the rack back up once he and his mom left.

A glance at the computer screen reminded me of the pennies I needed to count out for the board games purchases, but I couldn't focus. The rambunctious Patrick continued romping around the toy shop and laughing as though high from sugar, escaping his mother's grasping hands at every turn.

The next customer thankfully paid with a card.

A shattering of glass pulled my attention toward the front display. Little Patrick stood with tears filling his wide eyes, clutching that teddy bear with all he had left in him.

A pile of Precious Moments figurines lay in pieces at his feet.

His mother knelt and whisper-screamed at him, causing tears to slide down his cheeks. Those big blue orbs of his latched onto mine over his mom's shoulder, and my heart ached for the sweet boy with restless feet.

Perhaps he had misbehaved, but the inability to stand still and listen didn't come easily for some children.

My throat grew thick the longer we shared a moment as the world buzzed around us.

I longed to wrap him up in my arms and tell him he was a good boy, that he would grow up to be a lovely young man, one full of life and laughter.

That someday, someone would appreciate who he was. I clung to that hope myself, wanting my own happily ever after.

My boss Julie sent both mother and son out the door moments later without the stuffed animal, and I fought to keep my mind on my job.

The older woman who'd bought the board games

walked back through the front door and spoke to Julie while I struggled to center myself on bagging up a sale.

Julie and the board game customer headed toward the front counter, and my stomach dropped out. One stern mouth and the other with down-turned lips, they promised yet another uncomfortable moment.

"I gave you a hundred dollar bill," the woman snipped before Julie could speak. She looked down her nose at me, even though my five-foot-seven gave me a good two inches over her height.

"Go clean that up," Julie said to me while unlocking the cash drawer, dismissing me.

Usually, taking care of messes got assigned to me, tasks that didn't require too much thinking. But awareness of short-changing a customer after being late to work had me gnawing the inside of my lip while sweeping up the little boy's mess.

Couldn't I do anything right?

Simple math.

Count out the change showing on a damn computer screen I didn't need glasses to see.

My feet itched to move, my legs wanting to drag me back and forth until Julie finished with the upset woman. Unfortunately, I had to clean up ceramics broken by a child I'd wanted to assure he had worth. That he was loved regardless of the ants in his pants.

But I wouldn't ever get that chance.

"Three strikes and you're out" was the excuse Julie used to fire my scattered brain long before my shift was supposed to end.

I didn't argue, and wallowing in the sense of worthlessness I knew too damn well, I headed back home to my sister's house, wondering if I would succeed at anything.

I sulked at the dinner table, pushing grains of rice I'd cooked for Nora and me around my plate.

"What's your problem, Skylar?" Nora asked and wiped her mouth with her napkin. Of course, her fork sat upside down with her knife along the edge of her plate while my unused one lay haphazardly on my left.

How was it possible identical twins could be so different?

I'd already told her I'd lost the job she'd helped me find—and had gotten an earful about how I needed to start paying better attention to real life outside the books I devoured.

After the lecture, I'd locked myself in my room and did that very thing—picked up Annie Kelly's newest MMF romance novel. The story had only caused restlessness in my blood. I'd itched to do *something,* but needing to make dinner had kept me indoors.

I stood to clear the table, having to force my smile. "Nothing's wrong."

"You're a terrible liar."

Huffing an annoyed exhale, I set our dirty dishes in the sink and turned, leaning back against the counter.

Green eyes framed with auburn lashes exactly like mine studied me.

I felt like a science experiment beneath her gaze, same as always. "I'm horny and bored." Honesty came naturally for me, something Nora didn't understand. I used "too many words much too often."

Her cheeks flushed, and I rolled my eyes, returning to the dishes. Like our parents, Nora didn't discuss sex. She'd never even talked about boys. Or girls. I assumed she was asexual but wouldn't cross a line by asking.

"Find a hookup and get out of my hair for a while," she muttered.

I spun, my eyes blinking wide, sure some sort of living virus had taken over my sister's brain. She never said stuff like that. Ever. "*What* did you say?"

Nora's face still showed a deeper shade of pink beneath the overhead lights as she shrugged. "It's what my co-workers were discussing at break yesterday. That and dating apps." Her nose crinkled as though the idea sickened her.

But she'd repeated their words, giving me *ideas*.

Nibbling the inside of my lip, I wondered what could possibly have happened to make my straitlaced sister suggest such a thing. Maybe that stick up her ass had somehow jiggled loose.

The desire to veer and sprint with my usual reckless abandon down a path I knew nothing about sprang to life inside me. "Want to go to a bar or club with me?" I blurted the idea as soon as it shot through my brain.

She shook her head before I even finished my question. "Absolutely not! Both are a waste of time."

I should have known better than ask. Nora didn't do crowds. Or people. Period. Seeing as how I didn't have any friends in the entire state of California, that left me to the second option.

"Which apps did they say are the best?" I asked, already onto thought two.

She blinked. Frowned as though processing some great mathematical calculation in her perfect brain. "I don't—actually, forget I mentioned it. I have no idea what made me bring their conversation up. I've been too stressed out and need more sleep." Nora shook her head, tucking frizzy strands of red hair behind her elf-like ear, the only physical trait we didn't share.

Thank God I hadn't inherited the slightly pointed tips of our mother's like she had. It was bad enough having a river of red hair, pale lashes, and big green eyes like a Disney character.

"Well can you at least tell me what ones they were talking about?" I pushed, expecting guidance in this thing would be better than my usual traipsing along without direction.

"I will not." She pursed her lips again as though disgusted by the whole conversation *she* had started. "And it would be best if you didn't bother with such nonsense, Skylar. God knows you have enough problems as it is. We don't need your foolhardiness bringing stalkers and rapists to my front door."

Heat flushed through me even as I held in a snort. Arguing with someone as intelligent as my brainiac twin, even if she had zero people skills or street smarts, would be a waste of my time.

I'd never won an argument against her.

We washed and dried our dishes like we'd done since childhood on our parent's farm in South Dakota, side by side, silent in our personal musings. She probably daydreamed about stars and supernovas or whatever they were called while I thought about hookups. Dating apps. Bursting from the inside out between two men.

Give me all the happily ever afters had always been my motto when browsing for new books at the library back home in the middle of nowhere, but their romance collection paled in comparison to the one in the big city.

The move hadn't just opened my senses to nonstop noise, light in the night sky no matter the hour, and smells I hadn't even known existed, but it had also introduced Annie Kelly's words upon words of smut that made my nipples ache and panties damp.

Two men loving on their woman at the same time, kissing each other while she came undone between them had become my new favorite bedtime story. The female character watching her two men love on one other, a close second.

I struggled to stand still while waiting for Nora to methodically rinse each dish before handing it to me.

"Spare time isn't good for you," she said while unplugging the drain when she finally finished with the washing. "You need to find a job."

"I'm trying," I muttered, hanging up the damp tea towel on the stove handle and remembering how the Google search I'd done after getting fired had given me a headache.

"Well try harder. Use up your ridiculous energy tomorrow going store to store until someone hires you. I agreed to Mom and Dad's suggestion of letting you live with me, but you've got to find something that makes you money and gets you out of my house."

"If you don't want me here, just say so," I snipped, hands on my hips.

Lips pursed, she shook her head and glanced out the window overlooking her small backyard. "Some days, I just need space."

Nora had always been a recluse who enjoyed silence. Of course my noise and constant fumbling around the house drove her nuts like it always had when we'd been kids.

Worked up and my mind too occupied with dating apps to start yet another book, I headed to my room and stripped out of the jean shorts I'd made from an old pair of second-hand dungarees for the comfort of cotton sleep shorts.

The seed Nora had planted in my head sat ready to burst into a full-blown, squirrel-covered oak tree.

Why not attempt going out on a limb to find what I craved? What did I stand to lose besides a bit more worth in my sister's eyes?

If I even have any left...

A quiet question to Siri about dating apps slipped past my frowning lips as I sank onto the edge of my bed.

Dozens of search results filled the screen, overwhelming my ability to process words.

I asked Siri about menage dating apps instead.

Missing Link was listed first, the brief writeup by the search engine fluttering desire inside me. That was what I wanted to be. A link between two men. Either a bridge or the piece of a puzzle a loving bisexual couple wanted to complete their life.

My heart sped up as I clicked the hyperlink, the logo on the download page brightening my smile. Three intertwined rainbow-colored hearts.

This is it.

Giddy, I collapsed onto my back in the middle of my bed with more dramatic flair than any cartoon princess and clicked on the download button. My grin felt wide as a dork, and I hoped the cell wouldn't give face recognition any shit.

A tiny squeal left me as the download process began.

"Open," I whispered the breathless word while tapping the phone's screen.

I scrolled and clicked through the app, riveted by testimonials from people who had found the love they'd craved or had fantasized about. Dozens of variations rolled past. Three men. Three women. Two women and a man. A husband and wife finding their submissive. Two Doms sharing a twink—whatever that was.

Every positive, glowing review tickled my insides until I squirmed. Wiggling my way against the headboard, I pursed my lips and exhaled loudly.

"Okay." Lower lip between my teeth, I clicked on the ten-day free trial button that beckoned to my soul like a steaming cup of coffee. I input my name, which the app allowed people to keep private before stalling out on a username to identify me.

@AntsyFeet?

@ScatterBrain?

@FocusingFailure?

"Ugh." I slumped, my thumbs hovering over the screen's keyboard. Red Robin, the nickname Dad had given me because I sang way too often as a kid regardless of my inability to carry a tune flitted through my head. That sounded negative in my head though.

I wouldn't catch flies with vinegar, but honey...that was a different draw.

@RedHeadedRayofSunshine.

The positive description burst into my mind, and my grin returned. Perhaps the description tended toward too much, but my favorite English teacher from middle school had called me a burst of sunshine once, and the nickname had brightened my day.

So, yes. I named myself a ray of sunshine with red hair, stating I sought two men. I clicked on relationships rather than hookups and dove into the rest.

As with any test, I agonized over every question as I went through the profile creation. Having compared myself to my twin's type A personality my entire life, I knew exactly where I sat in that alphabet. A solid B with nothing else sprinkled in for extra flavoring.

A half hour had passed, and my brain had exhausted

itself. I was left with the final task—writing a brief summary of who and what I was to go along with a profile picture.

I basically needed to create an ad for myself.

"Oh shit." I giggled since marketing was definitely beyond my mental skills. "Let's start with a picture."

I scrolled through the few selfies I'd taken in the previous couple of months since Nora had purchased the cell for me, but nothing about my makeup-less face screamed "hottie you'll want for life."

Grimacing, I scrolled until I reached the beginning of my phone's images.

Nothing.

Huffing, I lifted my cell, tucked some wild hair behind my thankfully rounded ear, and kept my smile to a minimum. I blinked in the flash and burst into giggles at the awful half-lidded image on the screen.

I tried again and snorted a chuckle.

A third time.

Fourth.

By the fifth, I growled beneath my breath while clicking. I'd managed to keep my eyes open, but I looked constipated. Another burst of laughter escaped me, and I clicked another photo just for the hell of it before my giggles stopped.

"Well." My grin widened as I studied the candid shot. "Not too bad!"

I saved my laughing profile pic, the only one I'd managed that looked like the real me, then proceeded to agonize once more over writing an ad about myself that would lure the men I hoped to find.

My brain hurt to the point I couldn't think, same as with anytime I'd neared the end of a test in school. But since I couldn't just shade in alphabetized circles to guess at answers, I jotted down brief, unconnected tidbits about who I was.

A poor farm girl wishing to be barefoot and pregnant in a kitchen. One, five, or ten kids—I just wanted some of my own to love unconditionally. I dreamed about two men thanks to my newest favorite MMF author. They must love coffee. I promised organized closets and silly happiness and laughter.

Without rereading or second-guessing my brief bio, I saved my profile and sagged against my pillows propped against my headboard.

I'd never been one to pursue when it came to men, but I'd managed to lose my virginity fresh out of high school. I'd also dated an asshole farmer back home for six months before he grew weary of me and found someone quieter, more subdued.

While I didn't have extensive experience, I'd read and had daydreams aplenty.

A yawn attempted to split my face in half, so I exited the app before I got caught up in searching. Too many of the profile's identifying terms had boggled my mind. I would trust Missing Link to match me with what I hoped to find, same as it had done for thousands before me.

I stripped down to my panties and climbed under my blankets, thoughts of dark-haired princes riding in on white stallions pulling me into sleep. Not only did they promise multiple orgasms, fantasies fulfilled, and incandescent delight, but they loved everything about me—quirks and all.

5

ASHTON

I woke on the worst day of the year without my lover beside me for the first time since we had moved in together. Heaviness sat on my chest like it always did, and I rolled to escape its weight, grabbing my cell phone from the bedside table.

Rhett had texted me. **Thinking about you this morning. I love you more than life.**

My eyes welled, but I smiled while typing out a good morning and assurance of my love for him as well. **How's your mom?** I asked.

Rhett: **No change. Any luck on ML?**

My smile faded at his answer and his just as depressing question. I texted back a simple **No.**

Missing Link had matched us with a couple of women since Rhett had flown to Florida, but none of them had pinged my interest. Stubbornly, I held onto hope.

While Rhett would have made a plan to search through profiles, he was focused on his parents. His mother still lay in a coma, but other than facts about her health and his father's refusal to discuss the situation, I couldn't get a feel on Rhett. Even with FaceTime, I hadn't been able to read how he fared.

Any inquiry I made about his emotions had him answering with his usual "I'm fine."

I hated that I couldn't break him out of his shell beyond his showing of affection for me. It had been enough in the past, but I found myself craving more from him. I might understand how he dealt with situations, but I longed to know the emotions behind them he never voiced or owned. The thoughts that helped make his decisions. I wanted the stirrings of his innermost being expressed so I could share in them too.

But he wasn't there, and I couldn't poke him to distract me from my grief.

I could feel the desire for sunshine for both of us in the deepest parts of my soul like a tangible well of need. Mine had been present since Archer had passed.

I spent a reflective morning walking on the beach behind our home, recalling the best memories of his and my childhood before leukemia took him from us not long after we had turned nine.

He'd been so happy all the time, smiling in the face of illness and even death. Laughter and bright grins regardless of his pain. Sunbeams of light to the darkness that had begun to overshadow me when I learned at too young of an age that my other half wouldn't grow old with me.

I'd lived twenty-six years without Archer but only three truly alone.

Rhett had partially filled the chasm left by Archer's death, and I couldn't imagine living without him. We had accomplished so much together. Moved across the country, tossed our dating app into cyberspace with our fingers crossed—and greatly reaped the benefits when our baby took off and began fulfilling others' dreams.

Overlooking the ocean and filling my lungs with the scent of saltwater, I reminded myself how good we had it, how grateful I ought to be.

But that need for more weighed heavily on my mind.

Hunger pangs turned my feet through warm sand, back toward our quiet, empty house. Silence rang in my ears, a reminder of loneliness, and the stinging eyes upon waking returned to haunt me.

Although I wasn't hungry, I forced myself to eat a piece of toast. Travel mug refilled with sweetened black coffee, I curled up on the couch with my iPad, ready to FaceTime with Rhett.

My insides tightened over his appearance when he answered. His gorgeous face looked as haggard as I felt, eyes tired with dark shading beneath.

"You aren't sleeping," I stated instead of a hello, noting his AirPods and the fact he moved through a hospital corridor, his button-down shirt a bit rumpled compared to normal.

"Because you aren't here," he answered while entering what appeared to be a small waiting room. He settled into a chair and released a heavy sigh, his shoulders sagging.

"I told you I'll come to you if that's what you need."

"No." Lips pursed, Rhett shook his head.

I knew why he preferred I stay at home rather than be by his side in a hushed, sterile environment that smelled like bleach and sickness, and I loved him all the more for it.

The thought of any hospital or doctor's office stirred nausea to life in my stomach. Even going to my yearly physical proved beyond painful, and pre-visit stress always had me hugging the toilet for a few days prior.

"How is she?" I asked, pushing against the worst memories that weaseled into my head with the anniversary of my twin's death.

"No change." Rhett's tone and the same short answer he'd been giving me since arriving in Florida didn't reveal his feelings over learning his mother was brain-dead and breathing only because of life support.

His father sat by her side every hour allowed by the hospital, withdrawn and refusing to discuss the next steps that needed to be taken. Mr. Stirling showed no emotion either, Rhett had told me, silent and seemingly unaffected by his wife's demise.

"How are you?" Rhett asked, and I allowed him the turn of conversation, filling him in on my surprisingly peaceful morning and how I'd managed to keep my own sadness to a minimum for a change. While the beach walk hadn't brought about happiness, it had kept depression at bay.

"When we hang up," he said, "I want you to get on the app and search—"

"I prefer for ML to find her for us, Rhett," I said, cutting him off mid-sentence. He knew how I felt about forcing something that wasn't meant to be. I'd tried for three years and had failed every single time with women I thought might be a good match for us. "It's what we created the app for—let her do her work."

Lips tight, Rhett nodded. The hand rubbing over his scruffy jaw indicated his annoyance, but he didn't argue.

My cell pinged from the cushion beside me, and I glanced down to find the Missing Link logo staring up at me. The slight, lingering heaviness over my heart dissipated as though swept away by a strong wind.

"What?" Rhett asked, and I realized I smiled.

"We have a match." I propped my iPad on my drawn-up knees and grabbed my cell.

Rhett stayed silent while I opened the phone's app.

"Red Headed Ray of Sunshine." I read the woman's profile name, an actual chuckle rumbling through my chest. The small avatar didn't offer much at first glance, so I clicked on her image and swiped my fingers open across the screen to zoom in.

"Well?" Rhett prompted while I studied the woman.

"She's a redhead. Green eyes caught twinkling with laughter." A zap of excitement raced through me. "No makeup. Freckles. She's stunning, Rhett. Absolutely beautiful."

"What does her write-up say?"

A twinge of guilt twisted through me from having focused on her appearance. I tended toward shallow at times, looking for physical attraction first while Rhett would have preferred to see their retirement plan.

"She's twenty-four," I noted—perfect age to bear children if she was able and willing.

"Too young." Rhett grunted over the eleven-year age difference between her and us.

I ignored him.

The short summary she'd written about herself spilled from my lips as I rushed through the words, my grin stretching with every fragmented sentence she'd typed out.

"She's perfect," I whispered, flipping back to her profile picture and imagining her barefoot, belly swollen with my child, her laughter in our ears and Rhett's happiness evident on his face.

"No woman is perfect," Rhett stated, but I brushed off

his warning, too caught up in the fantasy of her sunshine filling us both up to overflowing.

Of all the days to find the woman to brighten our lives...

"It's fate, Rhett," I whispered. "I know it—I can *feel* it."

Rhett grunted, and I shot him a frown. "It's possible," I insisted.

"You need to guard your heart and not let your emotions override your better sense."

"I'm going to poke her," I stated, not heeding the advice I'd heard countless times.

"I would prefer to run a background check on her first, Ash."

He had done so with every single type A woman Missing Link had matched us with, going behind the scenes to retrieve their personal information. I had felt all kinds of wrong doing so, like it was an act of invading privacy, but Rhett's plans for finding us the right woman wouldn't be swayed off course.

"No," I stated firmly, determined to allow things to evolve organically for a change. "No more manipulating the outcomes. You made the decision to give this a shot one last time, so we're going to do it my way. No sneakiness. No vetting before poking. No digging into a woman's past to make sure they measure up to your high standards."

"Ash..."

"You gave me this opportunity by changing our match preference." I held his gaze, hating that cyberspace hung between us rather than shared air. "Please allow the rest to unfold in the manner we meant for this app to work. Yes, I'll guard my heart, but you ought to let go of your need for control. Trust me to know what is best for *us*."

Rhett exhaled slowly, seeming to slouch in his chair. "I do trust you. Wholeheartedly."

"Then let go."

His mouth once more set in a grim line, he nodded.

Heart racing, I poked the woman our creation had chosen to fulfill my desires.

6

SKYLAR

Less than forty-eight hours after I signed up for Missing Link, I had a dozen matches and seven pokes. I didn't dare return a poke to open lines of communication. Instead, I browsed through the profiles of those reaching out to me, quickly deleting a few partners and husbands whose write-ups sounded more like they hoped to find a live-in maid rather than an equal, shared lover.

Yes, I wanted to be a stay-at-home mom who cooked and cleaned, but I refused to bend the knee and submit like a woman from the fifties would.

I had a life of my own to live—I just wanted to share it with two sexy someones and spoil them rotten in return for loving me.

A rare occurrence had Nora and I both sitting on the couch, her with her nose in a physics book, me on my phone, enjoying the quiet of a Sunday afternoon. I'd yet to find a job although I'd landed interviews at two retail stores in the mall the following afternoon.

I pulled up the final profile the app decided would be a

good match, zooming in to get a better look at the two men who hadn't yet poked me. Partners for fifteen years, they were hoping to find a woman open to sharing their lives and carrying their children. They wanted a love match, not just an egg donor.

My heart thrummed at the possibility.

Their picture didn't reveal their faces as they stood barefoot in the sand with their backs to the camera, watching the sun set over the ocean. They clasped hands between them, both broad-shouldered and dark haired, one a few inches taller than the other.

Something about the way the shorter of the two leaned into his partner tugged at my empathy—like he needed the solidity of his lover's steady stance.

A smile curved my lips as I studied the men, imagining myself included in their peaceful moment by the salt water. Daydreams filled my mind of walking hand in hand along sandy shores, sitting together for meals I'd cooked for them, my belly swelled as they snuggled me between their hard bodies in bed.

Longing so intense and deep broke open inside me, stinging my eyes yet dampening my panties.

A red heart notification pinged in the app's top corner, and I tore my focus off the two men to see what Missing Link wished to share with me.

The very profile I studied had poked me—

A tiny squeal burst from me.

"Hmm?" Nora asked, lowering her book, but I couldn't be bothered to glance up and take in her sure scowl over my interruption.

"Finally, a promising match," I breathed the words as my pulse raced.

"What are you talking about?"

Oh shit. I'd spoken my thoughts out loud.

Nora's stare seared me like a laser beam, seeking every wrong thing about me.

Stomach churning over the conflict to come, I lifted my chin. "The other night you suggested I get on a dating app, so I *did.*"

"What a foolish—"

"It was *your* idea, so don't go all self-righteous on me!"

Nora exhaled as though exasperated with me, which wasn't anything new. "I suggested a hookup in a moment of exhaustion and retracted the unwise advice almost immediately."

She knew better than to toss a bone and think I wouldn't chase it like an unmanageable puppy.

My chin once more jutted outward. "I got matched up with these two men who are looking for a woman to share their life and carry their babies."

"You have *got* to be kidding me, Skylar Anne Larsen." Nora's disapproval sounded so much like our mother that I winced. "Are you out of your mind?"

My scatterbrained one that didn't compare to her intellectual one, she meant. It wasn't the first time she'd asked me that question.

Stomach hardening, I glanced back at my cell's screen and the picture I wanted to be a part of. "My life, my choice," I murmured.

I could sense her critical stare and felt like a speck of dirt on a glass slide beneath a microscope. "Yes, but our parents entrusted you to my care."

"I'm not a child!"

"Then for God's sake, Skylar, grow up and make better

choices for once! This path will lead to nothing but trouble —debauchery, diseases, pregnancy out of wedlock…I won't have that in this house!"

My shoulders curled inward on instinct. "Their profile is professional. They seem sincere—"

"Two men?" She cut me off. "What are they…lovers? Friends?"

"Partners since high school," I whispered, wishing, not for the first time, I'd kept a better watch over my mouth before spilling thoughts out loud.

"Even if they are sincere, you would actually subject yourself to becoming a third wheel where insecurities would arise from their relationship already having a solid foundation?"

Oh.

She had a point even though her voice lacked concern for my emotional well-being.

"I didn't think about that," I murmured, glancing once more at the profile picture of what could bring more than I'd dreamed of—and not in a good way.

"Why am I not surprised?" Nora muttered and returned to her book as though I wasn't worthy of her attention. "Harebrained decisions will lead to nothing but trouble in life. I think you would have learned that lesson by now."

Her dismissive tone flushed angry heat from my toes clear through to the roots of my hair. "At least I choose to live, *Nora Jane Larsen*." I emphasized her full name like she'd done with mine, proud that my voice didn't tremble. "At least I'm willing to try new stuff. Meet new people. Attempt friendships and find love—"

"Not everyone is looking for love," Nora snapped, her green eyes glinting. "Some of us are perfectly content without the mess of other people being all up in their space. And some of us can't afford to make rash decisions that could affect everything we've striven for."

My initial emotional reaction as a child would have had me yanking on her hair, but I studied my sister in silence, imagining smoke rolling from my ears. We hadn't ever desired the same things, never had a single goal in common.

But that didn't make her way or thoughts right and mine wrong. Or vice-versa. We were identical but two very different individuals—and both worthy of happiness.

"You wanted to study the stars your whole life," I said, my tone leveling out in hopes to stop the conflict I hated, "and you made that dream come true. All I've always dreamed about was to be loved and have a family of my own. Yes, two men isn't the norm, but it's what I hope to find. You don't have to understand or agree—and I *don't* need your approval same as you didn't need mine in order to move to the West Coast and work for NASA."

"What do you think Mom and Dad will have to say about this latest absurd idea of yours?" she asked, ignoring everything I'd said.

My anger returned at her flippant question. It had been *hers*.

I stood, ready to escape negativity I'd hoped to leave behind at the farm. "Quite frankly, I don't give a shit if they think a polyamorous relationship is strange or wrong. One man or three, love is love—and for once, I don't *care* if I don't measure up to your perfection!"

I stalked on shaking legs back the hallway toward my bedroom and slammed my door shut behind me, despising the fact that I *did* care.

My insides quivered, my eyes welling, but not from happy feels. I hated that I still compared myself to my twin, that her words stung even though we had both moved out from beneath our parents' wings.

I'd tried for too many years to live up to the standard Nora had set, and I was so done with trying to gain others' approval. Being like my sister was unattainable for a simpleton like me.

Owning my best self, creating ripples in the ocean of life, had become my goal since seeking out my own way and leaving my past behind.

That meant finding two men to appease my newly-found greedy nature, regardless of how silly others might see that type of relationship. Obviously, thousands of people had those same desires—plenty of raving reviews on Missing Link assured me I wasn't alone in my want of *more.*

Shut away in the privacy of my bedroom, I poked @desiringanangel back to open the lines of communication and curled up around a pillow wishing something, or rather some*one,* other than fabric-covered-fluff enjoyed my hugs and affection.

It took ten jittery minutes of agonizing forced patience before a message came through.

Desiringanangel: **Hi.**

Hi back, I wrote, clutching my cell in shaking hands. I grinned like a dork, my insides like a jumping bean.

Desiringanangel: **Finding out ML matched us was a much needed ray of sunshine today.**

My heart fluttered. "Aw!"

I'm glad to hear it, I hurried to reply, wishing I could reach through cyberspace and squeeze his hand.

Desiringanangel: **Thank you for poking back. We have been searching for our angel for over three years, and your profile seems too good to be true.**

"Too good to be true?" I echoed and snorted a laugh. No one in my life had ever thought that about me.

Ever.

Was he a pervert like Nora assumed, bullshitting me to get me into their bed?

I'm hopeful, but Rhett tends toward caution, he messaged before I came up with a response.

Or maybe he and his partner are *a perfect match.*

I bit the inside of my lip and typed out another message. **I'm hopeful too, but your partner sounds like a smart man.**

Desiringanangel: **He is.**

I hated the knocking of insecurity on my heart's door. My life already had enough intelligent people in it. But perhaps Rhett wouldn't be the type who cut people off or looked down their noses at those who didn't measure up to their standards.

Can I ask your name? I was ready for my thoughts to be back in positivity land.

Desiringanangel: **Ashton.**

"Ashton..." I smiled.

I'm Skylar, I typed. **And it's a pleasure to meet you.**

Desiringanangel: **Would you mind exchanging numbers? I'm not a fan of messaging since so much more can be accomplished through speaking over the phone.**

Me: **Yes, please! I feel the same.**

He offered his cell number, and I slowly inhaled, held my breath, and released the air from my lungs to the count of ten before I added him as a contact.

My fingers trembled as I hit the send button.

"Hi," he answered, and I swallowed a giggle at his same, singular greeting.

"Hi back," I echoed my own texted words from a few moments earlier.

We both laughed, mine from an attack of nerves. I felt like I was still in high school, crushing on the football's quarterback who'd glanced my way once—even if he'd only been scanning the cafeteria.

"Thank you for agreeing to talk," Ashton said, his soothing tone like a warm blanket I wanted to snuggle beneath.

"Thank you for suggesting it. I'm not good at typing on a cell screen, and speech to text hates me." My voice escaped squeaky as a mouse, and I grimaced, biting on the inside of my lower lip. "Sorry. I'm really nervous."

"Me too," he replied, sounding like he smiled.

"I've never been on a dating app before," I told him, closing my eyes so I could focus on his voice.

Smooth like whiskey was the simile that came to mind, but I'd never tasted the liquor...

"When did you upload your profile to Missing Link?" he asked.

Tingles swept through my core as I imagined hearing his whispers against my ear in the early morning light, the heat of his body pressed against my back.

I had to clear my throat. "Earlier this week," I answered. "You're my twelfth match, the eighth to poke me."

"Oh." Ashton's tone hinted at disappointment. "And have you connected with any of the others?"

"None of the matches looked like what I'm hoping to find. Yes, I want to be a stay-at-home mom and loved on by two men, but I will not be a maid or servant like some seem to be searching for." My eyelids popped open, and I found my chin lifted again, readying myself for the type of negative response that would ruin my good feels about Ashton and his partner.

"Rhett and I have a cleaning service, and we enjoy cooking together, so points for us!" Ashton sounded...giddy.

We shared another laugh that settled my defensiveness back to rest. "What was that you said about too good to be true?" I asked but continued since I didn't expect an answer. "I'm seriously glad I decided to poke you back, Ashton."

He let out a heavy exhale I clearly heard over the line, and again, I imagined his breath on my ear. Tickling. Tingling.

"So Rhett is in Florida dealing with some family things, but I would like to meet you to see if there's enough of a connection and chemistry between us to pursue something." Ashton's voice brought back my focus. "We have no desire to play games or waste anyone's time."

"This is my first go-round with a dating app, but skipping out on all that sounds awesome to me," I rushed my words. "Better than good, really. I'm sure I'll be nervous, but I want to try. Definitely. It's a yes for me."

"So. Dinner?" Ashton suggested when I paused for breath.

"Can I cook for you tomorrow night?" I blurted out and bit my lip, thinking I'd sounded too eager to please, even if I was. "I-I mean, it's Monday—a work day—but my sister will be late coming home, so we'll have the house to ourselves at least. And it's cheaper than going out somewhere." I bit my lip to keep from attempting to manipulate him further.

"I would *love* that." His semi-groaned reply pulsed arousal between my thighs.

Heart fluttering, I swallowed a rush of saliva. At least I hadn't squealed and made him think I was some giggling schoolgirl who didn't have a brain to speak of.

"It's a date, Ashton," I stated, my tone as breathless as my lungs.

Hopefully the first of many. Good ones. Full of easy conversation.

And lots of earthquaking orgasms and fantasies fulfilled.

I knew I needed to be cautious, but my imagination scampered forward, heedless as always.

7

RHETT

I hadn't seen my lover light up in months like he'd done while studying his phone. Our continued failures in finding the type of woman he wanted had dragged him down until I worried over depression escalating to the point he might need medication.

His soft smile while he'd studied the woman he'd deemed "perfect" had lanced a sweet ache through my chest, similar and yet different from the hurt I often rubbed at while watching my dad stare at Mom.

Her lungs continued to expand, her heart beat, but only due to man's intervention. Zero indication of brain activity suggested she might open her eyes and speak ever again.

The small chapel I'd hidden in to talk to my love pressed in on me long after we'd ended our video call, the dimmed light stifling.

Like a plastic bag settled over my head and cinched, I struggled to breathe from the tightening space, same as I'd done that first night all those years ago in the new home my parents had bought.

I strode from the room, intent on the cafeteria where I

had been spending meal times. At least they had a decent barista and good coffee—and having a destination gave me steps to allow and focus on.

When I'd gotten to the hospital a couple days earlier, I'd been exhausted, but numbness encased my heart and mind when I opened Mom's door. She lay exactly as I'd imagined: unmoving except for her chest, pale as a corpse, tubes and monitors stuck to her body.

Even though a machine kept her lungs inflating, I had the sense of something missing, as though her soul had already fled for the unknown.

An image had flashed in my mind like lightning in that moment of breathless silence.

Ash still as death on the bed.

Me sitting rigid by his side.

Air had rushed from my lungs, and my throat swelled—and I'd slammed the door on those fucking feels along with the horrible image in my mind.

Safely encased in my shell, I had strode into the room to greet my father who had barely acknowledged my presence.

Half-opening Mom's door once more, I poked my head in to find both my parents unmoved. At least my imagination stayed firmly locked up.

"Dad," I whispered, "I'm going down to get a coffee. Do you want anything?"

He shook his head. Didn't turn around. Just sat and stared at mom's pale face.

I couldn't keep my brow from furrowing.

Had I been asked to guess why he refused to pull the plug, I would have said love, but I'd never once seen them be affectionate with each other. Not one word of appreciation had been shared between them within hearing distance of their only son in the eighteen years I'd spent under their roof.

As I'd grown older, I figured theirs had been a marriage of convenience. Nothing had ever indicated otherwise.

So why would he sit there? How long would he keep her hooked up to machines when he could have simply unplugged them and gone on to live his life?

I had no fucking answers and felt like we sat in limbo. I needed a distraction, and the coffee wouldn't cut it.

Settling into a corner of the massive, cafeteria bright from dozens of windows, I pulled my cell from my pocket and scrolled through my short list of contacts.

Ash and I tended to keep to ourselves, and although we had a few friends outside work, I wasn't in the mood to talk to any of them.

Colton Payne.

I smirked over his name, wondering when I'd spoken to him last. It had to have been close to a year. Colton was a friend from back east. He'd gone to high school with us and had played football with me until that fantasy got stripped away.

Catching up and bullshitting would waste some minutes.

I hit the send button, and thankfully he picked up.

"Rhett! The fuck, man!" he answered. "I thought maybe California finally earthquaked its ass from the rest of us and you drowned or some shit."

I actually chuckled. "Sorry we haven't kept in touch lately."

"No problem. I'm guilty too."

"Are you working right now?" I asked.

"Yeah, but I can take a quick break. What's up? How's your better half? Wait...is this call to tell me you've found the woman the two of you have been looking for forever? Did Ash knock her up yet?"

"He's doing well," I semi-lied, "and no we haven't, so no he hasn't."

"Shit. That app you guys built has worked for a lot of people. Doesn't seem right it hasn't helped out its creators yet."

"It will," I said even though I wasn't so sure I would be too thrilled with whoever she ended up being. No higher education, someone who would probably bring a mess of feelings I would have to deal with...she'd doubtless get on my last nerve.

Thank fuck I had ones of steel.

I wondered over the redheaded ray of sunshine he planned to poke and chat with but pushed aside thoughts of him falling hard and fast, same as he'd done with me once we'd crossed the friendship line in eleventh grade.

If she proved to clash with my personality, maybe I'd get lucky and the sex would be so fucking spectacular I'd be willing to deal with the annoyances.

A man could hope.

"So what's going on in Boston these days?" I asked, needing to focus on something other than the own shit of my life. "Still working for Harper's Construction?"

"Yeah, Blake's a kickass boss. Easygoing and laid-back."

I remembered the kid from high school, a couple years behind us. He'd been loaded and gorgeous. Last I'd heard, he'd been named one of Boston's hottest bachelors who refused to ever settle down.

"Are you staying busy and out of trouble?" I asked.

"Work is crazy as fuck right now. We're starting a huge apartment building project down along the Merrimac River in the next couple of weeks. And as for the rest, that Missing

Link app of yours definitely keeps me busy in other ways but not out of trouble."

Ash and I had never focused on the hookup aspect of our app beyond its build, but fuck knew we had plenty of people happy for its use in fulfilling fantasies even if their end goal wasn't a committed polyamorous relationship.

"Maybe it's time to think about giving up your man whore ways," I suggested as I'd done once or twice before.

Colton had grown up in the system, jumping from one foster home to another because he'd been an antsy kid. And once he lost his virginity, there wasn't anything keeping him from hopping into a bed with willing girls and guys.

"I like variety," Colton stated. "Makes for a life void of boredom."

"Also void of real love, something steady and certain. Someone to go home to every night."

"Never had it, never will." He sounded so sure—beyond resigned.

While I was no romantic, I had such a person. "It's possible," I argued. "You just haven't found him or her yet."

"If I did believe in happily ever afters outside you and Ash, it would be me between both sexes. A soft, curvy woman to hold me and a hardened older man to slap my ass."

A barked laugh ripped from my lungs drew attention from other diners, and I coughed, smothering the noises coming from me with my palm over my mouth.

"Don't yuck on my yum," Colton muttered. "Have Ash redden your backside sometime. Then you'll know what I'm talking about."

"I don't need or want a daddy, thank you very much."

"Shit—I don't want a daddy-type either. Doesn't mean I can't enjoy a heavy hand now and then. Done right, a good spanking can take you outside your shitty head and make everything fuzzy and fucking fantastic for a while."

"Fuzzy and fantastic does sound perfect," I said, all jollity gone from my voice. I wondered what it would be like to give control to someone besides Ash—

"What's going on, Rhett? You sound like a dog shit in your shoe."

I exhaled heavily and told Colton about my mom and that I'd flown to Florida on my own. He knew why I wouldn't allow Ashton to come with me—he'd spent quite a few of those anniversaries alongside the two of us, keeping my boyfriend from getting too down.

"There's nothing that can be done?" he asked, his voice as serious as I'd ever heard it.

"No."

"Damn, man. I'm sorry. Anything you need me to do?"

"I appreciate the offer, but my hands are tied. It's just a waiting game at this point. Hopefully, my dad comes to terms with the future he has no power to change and allows the doctors to pull the plug." As usual, my statement came out matter-of-fact. Unmoved.

It is what it is.

How many times had that saying whispered through my head, the very thing my mom had said whenever I'd faced turmoil as a kid and had gone to her for comfort?

I remembered that day I'd shed a final tear in front of my mom, hoping for a hug or words to lessen my sadness.

And now, she lays on a hospital bed, a machine supplying the oxygen her body requires to fill her lungs.

Brain-dead.

Already gone.

Shouldn't I have sensed something other than cold

numbness? I wasn't completely void of emotion. Ash drew them out of me without difficulty when we were intimate.

Perhaps it was the pain of my being ignored as a child, my feelings taking a back seat to whatever it was my parents thought.

Dad deserved my sympathy—if he even cared about losing his wife, but I couldn't even rouse that little bit of humanity inside my soul.

I hung up with a promise to keep Colton in the know, and lips in a thin line, I tossed out my half-empty coffee and headed for my mom's room. It was time to have...not a heart-to-heart with my dad but definitely speaking some harsh truths.

It was time to accept what was and make a plan so we could both get back to living our lives and facing whatever fate had in store for us.

8

ASHTON

"It's a date." Skylar's breathless voice hit me low and hard.

I imagined her gorgeous red hair spread across my chest, her hot exhales panting over my chest as Rhett and I made love to her.

"Hopefully, the first of many," I added, grinning like a fool, my entire body buzzing with arousal and...sunshiny excitement.

"I was just thinking the exact same thing!" She laughed, the bell-like tinkle pleasant enough that even Rhett wouldn't be aggravated by its tone.

"So, did you want to wait to meet in person tomorrow to see if we feel a connection, or do you prefer to get to know one another better over the phone?"

"Now, please. I like listening to your voice," she rushed to say and squeaked as though she'd embarrassed herself by words not thought out.

My grin widened, my ego and mood buoyed. "I like yours too."

"Aw! Thank you."

Sprawling back onto the couch, I got comfortable, settled in for a nice long chat. "Tell me all about yourself, Skylar. Where you were born, your family, your hobbies, your aspirations. I want to hear everything."

She filled her lungs audibly before exhaling just as loudly—then launched into a rushed tale about growing up on the plains of South Dakota with her smart-as-a-whip twin sister and two parents.

Twin.

My eyes stung when she stated the first connection between us, one that whispered *perfect* yet again in my head. She would understand...but I kept my lips closed, soaking in the words pouring from her lips.

Skylar held nothing back, and I found myself shaking my head often at her candid attitude.

"But let me tell you," she continued on without pausing for breath, "growing up under Nora's shadow sucked because she got all Mom and Dad's attention. I haven't been actually diagnosed, but I'm sure I'm ADHD. I have restless feet—seriously bad, and my mind is even worse. I can't focus on much, but when I do, it's wholeheartedly until I either figure it out or complete the task.

"I tend to chase squirrels—not literal ones," she hastened to add with a soft giggle. "But I get easily distracted. I'll be drinking my morning coffee—can't live without it—see the mess of Nora's pantry, and next thing you know, I'm pulling everything out and making an even bigger disaster before getting the items properly rearranged."

"You like to organize." I chose to focus on the positive rather than asking about the unspoken words about her doubtless being compared to her sister.

"*Yes,*" Skylar emphasized her answer, drawing it out into

a hiss, and I found myself chuckling. "It's like a serious illness when you live with slobs. Nora might have the IQ of a genius, but she...she's the worst housekeeper in the world, I *swear.*"

"She's lucky she has you, then."

"Yeah, but...well, she doesn't appreciate my good qualities. She thinks I'm foolish, but I can't help who I am. Sorry. Enough about the mess of my mind. Tell me about you, Ashton."

"You don't have to apologize for your feelings," I said, wishing I could wrap her up in my arms. "They're valid. They're a part of who you are—and you deserve to be loved regardless of what others see as shortcomings."

Skylar exhaled loudly, muttering something about *too good to be true.*

"We all have issues," I continued. "Childhood trauma. Things we wish we could change about ourselves. But I'll be honest," I said, hoping she heard what I said and took it to heart. "I enjoy your randomness. I loved your fragmented bio that was short and to the point. Hearing your laughter between words brings a smile to my face."

"You're going to make me cry."

"None of that!" I grinned, her emotional openness a breath of fresh air.

"Tell me about you, Ashton," she repeated, her tone wobbly.

My smile faded as I decided to be just as candid since I longed for a connection with her.

"Today is the anniversary of my twin brother's death." What a way to start my story, but the loss of Archer had been what shaped me into the man Skylar listened to.

"A twin...oh, I'm so, so sorry," she whispered, sounding as though her heart ached along with mine.

"He was only two minutes older than me, and he never let me forget that."

"Nora has me beat by a few minutes too, and yes, *soooo* yes, I feel that."

I spilled my shit, leaving nothing out and tearing up a few times while discussing Archer's leukemia, his rapid decline, and inevitable death. Even though she and Nora didn't have the bond like Archer and I had, she understood my sense of loss regardless of my having four older sisters. There had been no one to even attempt to fill that void until Rhett had dropped from a tree and into my life.

Her empathetic sniffles on the other end allowed me freedom to express emotion knowing she empathized on a deep level—and that comforted me in ways Rhett hadn't ever been able to.

"I wish I'd been there to wrap my arms around you too that night in the cemetery," she said, and in that moment, I wanted nothing more.

"Same."

Hope buoyed inside me as our conversation turned toward our longings and dreams, the real reason we'd uploaded a profile onto Missing Link. I chose to keep the fact Rhett and I were the apps owners to myself for the time being, since I wanted Skylar to like me for the man I was and not because I had the kind of money she'd never experienced in her life growing up on a farm in the plains.

Family came first for both us, even though neither of us had the best relationships with all our blood relatives. Loyalty to loved ones and friends were a shared close second.

Our desired futures lined up, and had I created a list to check off, we would have had glowing results.

Skylar dreamed of a home filled with love and children

like my family of eight—then seven—had been. She hoped for two men already in a sturdy relationship to adore her, and she in return would spoil the hell out of them.

"I want to share in the love too, but..."

Immediately, I wondered if she wasn't interested in sex outside attempts to procreate—and that idea soured my stomach.

"But?" I pushed when she didn't continue, my fingers crossed I'd read her hesitation wrong.

"Um...well. Howbluntistooblunt?" she rushed the question like one quick, entangled word, and I bit back a chuckle.

Rhett was forthright with serious matters, but I had a feeling I would enjoy the hell out of whatever Skylar wished to share.

"You can be as open and honest as you want," I told her. "In fact, I prefer candid discussions. They're healthier than keeping everything inside."

"Yes!" She exhaled loudly—but didn't continue.

"So you want to share in the love, but..." I prompted and held my breath.

"I fantasize about seeing it play out in front of me too," she rushed the sentence.

A jolt of lust hit my groin, veering my mind off the usual getting-to-know-you topics.

I cleared my throat, hoping for clarity and assurance of sexual compatibility since bringing a woman into our lives didn't mean his and my relationship would be set aside. "So you're a voyeur?"

"A what?"

Oh, the innocence of this woman. My dick thickened. "You would enjoy watching me and Rhett fuck?"

"Oh God," she whispered and gulped.

I shifted to ease the tightness in my pants. "I'll take that as a yes."

She giggled, the sound more nervous than actual laughter. "Yes, *please*. Anything like that. Everything. I'm...not super experienced, but I've read enough spicy romance books that I don't think my thirst for smut will ever be truly satisfied. Because let's get real here. Even though I'm dying for a couple, there's no such thing as book boyfriends in real life."

"You read romance novels," I said, grinning like a dork.

"Yesss," she dragged the word out on a groan.

"Me too."

"No way!"

"Have you read any of Annie Kelly's books?"

"Sweet Joseph, Mary, and Jesus," she murmured as though to herself before perking up with, "She's my new favorite!"

"Mine too," I agreed. "But back to that statement of yours about there not being any such thing as book boyfriends in real life—I beg to differ. You haven't met Rhett. He's the epitome of the most mouthwatering male protagonist in any romance novel *ever*."

"Oh god. Is he hot?" she asked, and I laughed for the fiftieth time at least since first texting her.

"He's beyond gorgeous. He's six-two, so a couple inches taller than me. Eyes dark as chocolate and just as luscious-looking. I could go on and on."

"Yes, please."

I burst into laughter. "How blunt is too blunt?" I echoed her question, loving the flow of our conversation.

"There's no such thing when it comes to the fact that my imaginary man might really exist," she declared.

"He has broad shoulders I cling to whenever he's on top of me—"

"Oh, God," Skylar whispered.

"—pecs and abs worth exploring, thick thighs... Even his feet are beautiful to me. They're big, same as his delicious dick."

"Oh. My. God." It sounded like Skylar choked.

"Too much?" I asked, my grin attempting to split my face in half.

"No—never," she breathed. "Tell me more."

"All the smutty details?" I couldn't help but tease the obviously love and—I assumed—intimacy-starved woman.

"Yesss," she hissed/groaned the word again before abruptly cutting off. "That is, I mean, I don't want to make you uncomfortable, but no one...well, I've never talked like this with anyone about sex before. That's weird. It *is* weird, isn't it?"

Poor, poor girl. Skylar seemed like a coiled ball of excitement and sexual energy just waiting for someone to light her fuse. I imagined she'd be a firecracker between me and Rhett.

"I like that you haven't, Skylar," I told her, my voice leveling out and serious even though the thought of getting our hands on her spiked lust through my blood. "Can I ask about your experience?"

"I'm not a virgin, but—well, other than reading Annie's books, I know nothing about threesomes. I'm a polyvirgin." She giggled. "Is that even a word?"

"It is now," I assured her, my smile fixed back in place. What a ray of sunshine she was.

"You were saying?" she prodded.

"Are you chewing your fingernail?" I had to ask what she'd mentioned doing earlier when nervous.

"Damnit."

I chuckled. "There's no need to be anxious. I only ever want honesty between us, so feel free to ask questions you want answered."

"Are you versatile?" she blurted, and I laughed out loud. "Sorry—"

"Don't be!" I hurried to reply. "I love how uninhibited you are—and yes, we're vers even though I mostly bottom for Rhett."

"Because he's all alpha-growly and it's what he wants?"

"Well, that too, but there's nothing I wouldn't give the man, and he knows how to use his dick."

Skylar swore at my candid answer.

"Too much?" I asked again.

"Absolutely not, but I'm a little turned on right now. That's not weird to say is it, since we're being so honest?"

That truth rushed more need through my body, settling into my groin. I'd never had such an open conversation about sex before, not even with the women Rhett and I had hooked up with over the years.

Any acts of sex had transpired as though contracted. Thoroughly read and neatly signed with precise strokes of a pen—or rather, dicks.

Skylar was eye-opening. Refreshing.

A potent distraction from the day's grief.

"Not at all," I assured her. "So, are we still on for dinner?" I asked, ready to see if Skylar was as beautiful on the outside as she seemed on the inside.

She gave me her address, two hours north of where Rhett and I lived, and when we finally hung up with the promise to see each other the following evening, I couldn't contain the hope soaring me through the clouds she'd claimed to live in more often than not.

But I liked her that way.

Being among the billowing white fluff balls, as she'd called them, allowed her inner rays of sunshine to beam down on those in need of smiles and laughter.

I just knew the woman Missing Link had matched us with would be the perfect angel both Rhett and I needed in our lives.

9

RHETT

She *is* perfect.

I sat on the hard plastic chair in my mom's room and stared at Ash's text, my insides going tighter than they had while trying to talk to my father about pulling the plug on the machine keeping his wife's lungs inflating. Stoically reserved as always, he refused to budge past a stern "No."

He hadn't listened or responded to a goddamn word I'd spoken after that.

My stomach rotted from acid and too much coffee.

Add in that it seemed like my lover had found the woman of his dreams, and I struggled to keep *feelings* from rising to choke me out.

If my father knew half of the shit tearing me in opposing directions, he would ridicule me like always, even though I'd done nothing but try to be supportive for whatever he might be going through.

I refused to be overrun by internal reactions, and needing to expend some energy, I left the hospital for the evening, thinking an hour or so of working out in the hotel's gym would help quiet my mind and calm my stomach.

Since I hadn't responded to Ash's text and I couldn't put off a conversation any longer, I called him on speaker while driving the rental car toward my hotel.

"Hey," Ash answered, his voice full of concern. "Everything okay? You didn't text back, and I was starting to worry."

"I'm fine," I answered on autopilot while assuring myself the same damn thing.

"Your mom?"

"Nothing has changed, and my father is refusing to let her go."

"Are you sure you don't want me to fly over there—"

"No." I cut off what he'd asked me every conversation we'd had since I left. Of course I *wanted* him there—longed for him—but I would protect him from his childhood PTSD no matter the cost to me personally.

"I appreciate your willingness to be here for me, but I'll be fine," I repeated. "Tell me about your redheaded ray of sunshine." I veered the topic off sickness and death, thankful as fuck I managed to keep my request nonchalant.

"She's everything I've dreamed of, exactly what we both need," he started, his voice winding up as though ready to sing her praises.

I bit my tongue to keep from reminding him that while I enjoyed the hell out of pussy, *I* didn't need anyone but him.

A farm girl, just like her profile brief bio had stated, he went on to tell me. Well-versed in caring for a household and all sorts of animals—which I considered children to be: instinctual wildness that would give me a headache at the first cry.

"She graduated from high school but has ADHD and knew she wouldn't be able to handle college."

"What aspirations does she have?" I asked, hoping the

woman had some sort of plans outside wanting to birth and raise children.

She had none.

But, oh, her giggle was infectious...her candid, uninhibited spirit had struck Ash silly. I could imagine the hearts in his eyes already. He laughed like I hadn't heard him do in years, and a groan rose up my throat as he assured me she was the exact woman he'd been hoping for.

I rubbed my hands over my face as heaviness settled deep into my bones.

"She sounds amazing," I muttered, holding back on the *for you* I would have preferred tacking on, "but we have to be careful moving forward."

"She invited me for dinner tomorrow night," Ash blurted, ignoring my concern. "Her sister's house is a couple hours north—I figured I could just get a hotel room and stay there rather than driving home afterward if it gets too late."

My mind blanked for a few seconds as I pulled into the parking garage. Ash had made plans without checking in with me...not that he needed my permission, but the fact he'd taken that risky of a step without consulting me doubled the acid burning my stomach.

With it being the anniversary of Archer's death, I kept my true thoughts stifled.

Car in park and engine off, I sat staring at my cell in its holder, watching the seconds tick by in silence. I wasn't sure what to say—

"Rhett? Are you still there?"

"Yeah," I choked out and cleared my throat. "I'm here."

And I always will be for you...

"So what do you think?"

Fuck, he had to ask that question.

Filtering through the words in my head, I attempted to

choose them with care. "Getting to know her a bit better is the smart thing to do. Right now, you're riding a high of finding a match that seems perfect, and if you rush a face-to-face meeting, your desires might blind you to any red flags we need to be aware of. Maybe talk a bit more over the phone or FaceTime with her like we usually do with potential matches. We need to make sure she isn't some immature girl hoping to find a couple of sugar daddies."

It wouldn't have been the first time we'd brought a woman home only to have dollar signs light up in her eyes upon seeing the neighborhood where we lived and how our backyard overlooked the Pacific.

"This is fate, Rhett," Ash pushed, using the same word he swore led the two of us together. "I'm sure of it, and I'm not getting any younger."

I exhaled slowly, closed my eyes, and gave my face that palm-scrub I'd been wanting to do since reading his text. I could tell him to wait until I got home to meet with her—and he would listen to me since he said I always knew best.

But what if he didn't?

I'd never attempted to control Ash per se...would he do his own thing?

The thought of him acting without thinking shit through sent a shudder ratcheting down my spine. The man was too beautiful, too sweet and kind for any woman to not desire him.

And if he did go to meet her without me, would she end up being that puzzle piece to his life he felt he'd been missing, the one part of him I couldn't fulfill?

Regardless of whatever action he took and how it would stir my insides, how the fuck could I deny him what he wanted most?

"Just be careful," I managed to speak the words past the thickness in my throat.

"I will. I promise."

I swallowed hard before voicing my one request. "If she's everything you've been dreaming of, could you at least wait for me to get home before fucking her?"

"What the hell, Rhett?" Indignation radiated over the cell's speaker. "I would never touch another woman outside your presence—no matter how hot she is."

My insides settled in one way but twisted in another.

"I'm sorry," I muttered, scowling at the cement wall I faced. "I'm just..." I trailed off, refusing to break down like an undisciplined weakling.

Ash let out an audible exhale. "I love you more than anything on this earth."

"I love you too," I murmured, tipping my head back and closing my eyes. "And if she's what you've been searching for, then allow things to progress organically like you said you wanted. If that means kissing her good night, then do it."

Fuck, it made my chest ache to give him my blessing.

"You wouldn't mind?"

Yes.

"No."

"I'm not going to rush into anything." He attempted to soothe me again when I thought I'd successfully hidden my feelings from him.

I trusted Ash thoroughly, in every aspect of our relationship and in business, but I also knew how deeply the loss of his brother, survivor's guilt, and the pressure put on him by his father to carry on the Blackwood name drove him.

Ridiculous in my opinion, but it mattered to him, and I accepted it without argument.

He struggled with self-worth, wanting to prove he was good enough to provide an heir even though I assured him almost daily he was perfect in every way.

But uncertainty and my need for control battled with my love for him.

He already rushed forward, blinders without a doubt keeping him from seeing any warning signs.

"Please be careful, baby," I said, every word bleeding from my heart.

"I will be, but if anything changes with your mom and dad, please call me so I can be there for you."

"I will," I promised, somewhat soothed by his insistence even though I wouldn't ever allow him to face what I did. "Love you, baby."

"Love you too, Rhett. So damn much." The softness in his voice swept over me like a soft caress, one I wanted to sink into and take comfort in.

We hung up a few seconds later, and I sat in silence once more, the line between us severed.

He was going to meet a potential mother for his children in less than twenty-four hours, and I wouldn't be by his side. I feared his inability to make a smart decision faced with a woman who seemed too good to be true—his words, not mine.

"Shit."

What if she was? What if the fact she could give him the one thing I couldn't turned his focus fully on her? Would I be left behind? Alone and heartbroken because I was no longer enough for him?

My guts clenched up tight, twisting into a tight knot.

Sweat beads broke across my forehead as my mouth went dry.

"Fuck that." Lips set in a grim line, I pulled my ass from the car and headed to my hotel room to change.

Since Ash wasn't around to help relieve my stress, the gym would offer my muscles the burn and exhaustion I needed in order to pass out and forget the shit of my current life.

And in the morning, I would once more attempt to talk my father into letting his wife go so I could hop a plane and get back to Ash before he went and gave part of his heart away.

10

ASHTON

I couldn't help but feel guilty while heading to Skylar and her sister's house for dinner.

Rhett sat in a hospital room with his father, and I couldn't begin to imagine the lack of emotion between the two men at a time when grief ought to be allowed to flow freely. Accepted and shared, same as my family had done when Archer had passed. We'd been there to hold one another and offer comfort.

Rhett had no one outside of me, and while I appreciated his looking out for my mental health, he had to know I would face anxiety and nausea for him every day for the rest of my life if that was what he needed.

But he stubbornly insisted I stay put since my presence wouldn't change the outcome of his mother's demise.

Even though excitement raced my blood at the thought of meeting Skylar, I hurt for him, for his hardened exterior, the riotous mess he must be inside, and the fact he didn't know how or want to outwardly release his feelings.

He didn't have any type of relationship with his mother,

but for me, losing my mom would equate cutting off one of my hands or feet.

I wanted that same kind of bond for my own children, healing light for both Rhett and my souls.

Skylar would be the one. I knew it deep inside my marrow. Even having only seen her profile picture and hearing her voice for a few hours over the phone the day before, something beyond the natural assured my soul of that truth.

The three of us were meant to be.

Siri told me to turn left into a residential neighborhood, and I quickly scanned over the houses sitting proudly beneath the bright sun.

Skylar had told me Nora worked for NASA and had no student loans to speak of, so the place she'd chosen to purchase a home made sense. Upper-class but not ostentatious like our neighbors down south near Hollywood's hills.

Heart in my throat, I pulled up beside her sister's house for our early dinner. My palms sweated. Pulse raced. Both hands shook as I parked and turned off the engine.

The front door swung inward as though yanked by the Hulk—but a flow of red hair hung over pale shoulders instead of bulky green. Skylar stood tall. Thin. Ethereal.

Gorgeous.

My breath caught at her smile, and that sense of rightness I'd hoped for slammed into place.

I'd dealt with instant lust a time or two but never to the point where my fingers ached to touch, my ears to hear her voice, my eyes to soak in her beauty.

I sat and stared, enraptured, until her smile wobbled and shoulders slouched slightly. The edge of her thumbnail slid between her teeth...she must have thought my first eyeful of her had caused me disappointment—

"Oh no, no, no..." I hopped from the car at the signs of insecurity, slammed the door, and scurried up the walkway, my pulse racing along with my feet.

Her luminous green eyes widened as I neared, her hand dropped to her side.

"Hi," I burst out, jerking to a stop a few feet away from where she stood on the stoop—a solid three feet above me.

Her smile returned, radiant and addictive. What I wouldn't do to see that every morning upon opening my eyes, Rhett's sleepy gorgeousness snuggled up against her other side. "Hi back."

The same words from our phone conversation, the same chipper voice.

We both laughed, and I held out my arms. "I'm a hugger, so if that's not your thing—"

She leapt. Literally threw herself off the porch and landed against my chest before I could finish my sentence, causing me to stumble back two steps.

Rhett's favorite scent of coconuts filled my lungs. Soft breasts pressed against my chest. Silken hair caressed over my face. Slender hands grasped at my back.

There was no better word for Skylar Larsen than perfection.

My nervousness didn't stop my dick from thickening, and I quickly stepped away before my arousal made itself known. "Let me see you," I whispered, grabbing hold of both of her hands.

Our fingers laced as though they knew they belonged together, sending a staggering rush of need through me.

Pink flushed her cheeks beneath a spattering of freckles, and her eyes danced with the sparkle of a million emeralds beneath the sun as she looked me over. Auburn eyebrows matched the color of her cascading hair brushing the swells of her breasts. She wore a simple summer dress that fell to her knees, billowy like a flower child.

She went barefoot, and the sight of her pretty pink toes, clear of polish, caused butterflies to burst through my stomach.

"You're beautiful," we both spoke at the same time.

Warmth flooded my face as our gazes once more met, and I shifted on my feet.

"Thanks," we echoed—and grinned like a couple of dorks.

"Here...hold on." I dropped her hand and hurried back to my car to retrieve the bottle of white wine and rose I'd brought for her. "I wasn't sure if you liked either of these," I said, breathless when I'd reached her side once more, "but here."

I shoved both gifts her way like an awkward teenager faced with his crush on prom night.

"I love both," she claimed, clutching the presents to her chest. "Roses are my favorite—and lavender? Did you know that color rose stands for enchantment?"

I did, but she didn't allow me a chance to answer.

"And that a single rose given as a gift means you've fallen at first sight? I-I'm not suggesting that's what happened—that's what kept you in your car for too long...I'm just...um... Oh my." She bit her lip, wetness welling in her eyes.

I loved how expressive she was. "No crying. Please," I whispered, my own throat going tight, my hands itching to touch her again.

"They're happy tears," she insisted, her chin tilting upward slightly.

"That's good."

A pregnant moment expanded around us, one filled with hope and yearning. I wanted to sit and hold her. Talk until both our voices went hoarse. Kiss her soft lips and dip my tongue into her mouth to taste her sweetness.

Beeping from behind her jolted us both back to reality.

"The rolls!" Skylar whispered and spun, leaving me outside, alone, the scent of coconuts lingering in my nose.

The front door stood open, and even though Skylar hadn't invited me to follow her, I stepped into the house. Savory scents hit my face with delicious warmth, flooding my mouth with drool.

The clang of metal sounded from the back of the house, so I shut the door and ambled forward, taking note of the clean hardwood floors and living room on my right. Not a single speck of dust lay on the stair railing to my left or the framed pictures of space lining the hallway. Rhett would love that fact.

My throat tightened again at the thought of him alone, and I wondered if perhaps I shouldn't have listened to him when he insisted I stay in California. Heart torn, I moved into the brightly lit kitchen sprawling across the back of the house, vibrant white cabinets with black handles accented by bursts of blues throughout the backsplash and decor.

"I'm so nervous I don't think I'll be able to eat a damn thing," Skylar stated, breathless, her face flushed as she tipped a muffin pan to release the dinner rolls she'd taken from the oven.

Steam rose from the golden tops, and my stomach growled at the scent of freshly baked bread.

"I was too anxious earlier today to eat anything," I told her, "so I'm starved."

"Oh, thank goodness. Do you like pot roast?" She scampered toward a crockpot, pulling off her oven mitts to toss them onto the counter, but once more didn't give me time to respond. "I prefer mashed potatoes, but I was afraid I would be too scatterbrained to get them right, so I quartered some smaller ones, tossed in a bag of carrots—"

Her voice cut out, and she paused in front of the crockpot to draw a deep breath. She turned to face me. "I tend to ramble a bit sometimes."

"I like your rambling."

Her shoulders sagged, her eyes once more welling.

I stepped closer, itching to soothe her. Touch her. "What did I say about the crying?"

"But they're *happy* tears!" she exclaimed, grabbing hold of my hands again like she didn't want to go a minute without physical touch either.

That same sense of rightness eased through my blood, and I clasped her fingers tighter wishing like hell Rhett was there to enjoy the moment with us.

Her smile wobbled, her lower lip sucking between her teeth when my gaze dropped to her mouth.

Rhett had given his blessing—

I leaned forward without further thought, pressing my lips against hers.

She sucked in a quick breath, but I shifted away before she could kiss me back. "Oh...*zing*," she whispered.

"Zing?" I repeated, wondering if it meant the same to her as it did to me and Rhett.

"Yeah." She rubbed her lips together as though hoping to still sense mine. "Zing...like yes, please. More, please. 'Felt that all the way in my toes' type of kiss."

Same...definitely same.

"So, not too soon?" I murmured while reaching up to tuck wayward hair behind her cute, rounded ear, my insides a torturous, delicious mess.

"No." She swallowed hard as a tremor rippled through her. "I—I like kisses. Hugs. Affection is definitely my love language but also gifts like that beautiful rose. I soak up words of edification too. They say that what you need is what you give, but that's not true. I love acts of servitude..."

Her sweet rambling faded, and the sense of rightness rained down over me, comforting me in ways only Rhett had ever been able to do. Deep yearning for him to be there with us slammed into me, and I stepped back, clearing my throat.

"What's wrong?" Skylar asked, reaching to grasp my elbow before I could pull farther away. "Was it something I said?" Her hand slid down my forearm and held tight as though she was afraid I would walk off without a backward glance.

"I wish Rhett was here." I went with honesty. I'd told her all about my partner, the years we'd been together, how he was my rock, the love of my life.

"I do too," she agreed, "but I'm kind of happy to have you all to myself for this first meeting. Being faced with one gorgeous man is nerve-wracking enough. Just look—" she stuck out her foot, checking it over "—even my feet are shaking! I couldn't imagine having you both at once."

I bit back my smirk but couldn't keep an eyebrow from rising.

"Oh!" She squeaked, her face flushing again as she put her foot down and met my gaze. "You're bad."

A barked laugh burst from my lips.

"Stop it!" She pulled her fingers from mine and set her hands on her hips even though her green eyes sparkled with mischief and delight. "I'm semi-innocent but not that naive. I know exactly where I'll end up if things go in my favor."

"In our bed." I'd decided to continue with honesty—no games. She swallowed audibly, her smile fading, and I grabbed her hand once more. "Are you more nervous about making a polyamorous relationship work or the physical aspects of a threesome?"

"Um...both?" She bit her lower lip again, her focus flitting to the crockpot behind her.

"Why don't we sit down and enjoy dinner. We can chat about expectations—if you're still interested in seeing where this goes."

"I am. Yes. Let's." Skylar burst into action again, flitting about the kitchen like a hummingbird, retrieving glasses and a corkscrew. I took both and poured us some wine while she dished up the meal.

For a moment, comfortable silence kept us company while we worked alongside one another in the kitchen. Grinning with how much the feeling reminded me of cooking with Rhett, I allowed my hope to grow, sure that nothing would hinder forward progress.

11

———

SKYLAR

Ashton Blackwood was sex on a stick.

At least that was my initial thought seeing as how I'd read that very metaphor for the first time earlier in the morning about my latest book boyfriend.

Tall, sun-kissed brown locks and handsome as anything...wide shoulders and a trim waist...he wore his green button-down and black slacks better than any mannequin I'd ever seen.

And his eyes.

Oh, those beautiful, hazel-green orbs that appeared deep as an ocean yet clear as the summer sky. His had a kind face, and how he leaned in while listening as though fully intent on my every word fluttered silliness in my belly.

He'd pulled in front of Nora's house with his fancy car, his shiny dress shoes and flashy watch suggesting he lived better than where I'd grown up on the farm.

Clean-shaven, wavy hair artfully styled, straight white teeth...

And a dimple in his left cheek.

A dimple.

I sighed as it once more flashed my way as we settled into our chairs at the dining room table. Set for two since Nora had told me she would be working late every night that week—the only reason I'd invited Ashton to the house. A lone candle flickered between us, as well as a slender vase and the rose Ashton had given me.

The meaning behind the lavender color, the fact he'd only brought me one, spoke volumes and made my romantic heart giddy. Our initial thoughts toward each another aligned after a single phone conversation, and I couldn't wait to learn more about Ashton and his partner.

"How are Rhett and his mother doing?" I asked rather than spewing out nonsense about my nerves and crazy attraction I felt for him.

He stared a moment as though surprised by my question.

Discussing an imminent death wasn't exactly pleasant dinner conversation, but I cared about the other half of the partnership I hoped to become a part of. Even if I hadn't spoken to or met Rhett, he was Ashton's other half and just as important as the man staring at me.

"I have an abundance of empathy," I explained with a rushed voice when he didn't respond, shifting on my chair over thoughts that I'd disappointed him in some way. "And it's not always a good thing."

"It's a lovely character trait," he murmured, a soft smile curving his lips back up. No dimple popped, but his assurance settled my antsy backside. "And there's been no change, nor will there be until his father acknowledges she's already gone."

"How is Rhett holding up? I can imagine he probably wishes you were there with him. If I faced that sort of grief, I would want the person I love by my side."

Ashton served himself some of the roast from the platter before handing it to me. "Rhett is..." He pursed his lips and stared at the candle's flame while I put a little food on my plate. "Well, I want you to understand him so he doesn't scare you away when you meet him. He grew up in a very emotionally repressed household. Neither parent gave him very much of their time, and he learned from an early age that acting out didn't award him the positive attention he craved."

My heart squeezed in my chest. I knew all about that.

"He was taught to keep his emotions in check, that allowing his feelings free reign was a sign of weakness."

"Oh, no," I whispered, my heart breaking for the little boy he'd been.

"He doesn't share much and always states that he's fine even when he's not. We've been together long enough that I can oftentimes read him, and even though right now I know he would appreciate having me with him during what must be a difficult time, he doesn't want me there because hospitals trigger me."

"I can imagine," I said, my soul aching for both of them.

"He's very careful in everything he does. A true type A personality."

Like Nora—who clashed with my opposite nature.

Unease slithered into my mind like a garter snake, unwanted and scary. Rhett would find me annoying, I had no doubt.

"Tell me more about him?" I forced myself to take a bite of my dinner, but it coated my tongue like dust. Focusing on Ashton's stories about how he'd been drawn to the quiet, gangly boy with the mop of dark hair who never got upset or appeared happy in middle school proved almost impossible.

Perhaps meeting with Ashton first hadn't been such a good idea. It would be easy peasy to fall for a man like him, but he was only half of a whole.

I'd attempted to jump plenty of hurdles in my life, but Rhett Stirling intimidated the hell out of me—and I'd never even shared a single word with him.

The front door opened and closed, cutting Ashton off mid-sentence and pulling his gaze toward the hallway.

My stomach twisted and heart seized.

Oh no...no, no!

"It's my sister," I barely managed a whisper, my stomach tying up in knots.

Her footsteps brought her closer, and seconds later, she halted abruptly in the dining room's entryway. She took in the table and the smiling man pushing back his chair to stand before flicking her gaze at me.

"You're obviously Nora," Ashton said to my mirror image, moving forward and offering his hand like the true gentleman. "I'm Ashton Blackwood. It's a pleasure to meet you."

She eyed his outstretched hand but ignored it to once more glare at me. "Skylar, can I speak with you in the kitchen?" she snipped. "*Alone?*"

I slammed my eyelids shut and breathed deeply, wishing I could sink into the floor and disappear.

Her footsteps—heavier than before—took her toward the back of the house.

"Should I go," Ashton asked quietly, and I jerked my eyelids back open. He still stood, his gaze full of concern.

"No!" I hopped up and squeezed his forearm, needing a physical connection like all the previous ones that had helped ease my nervousness. "I didn't...please don't. I'm sure she...um just had a bad day at work or something? I'm sorry. She's not normally this rude."

At least, not to others.

"Just...wait here. Please. I'll be right back." My legs weakened with every shuffling step toward the kitchen and my sister.

"What the hell were you thinking inviting a man you *don't even know* into my home?" Nora shot at me, hands firmly planted on her hips, her eyes as hard as Dad's whenever I'd landed myself in trouble. "He could be some sick stalker—a rapist! And you're sitting down to eat food *I* paid for—at *my* dining room table!"

I cringed at her rising tone, terrified Ashton would hear her ranting. "I'm sorry, Nora—"

"You're always sorry because all you ever do is make *inappropriate* decisions that land you in trouble!"

Anger and embarrassment swept through me as her voice ratcheted up yet another notch.

"Why can't you think before acting and opening your mouth?" Nora continued her rant as I struggled to sputter any words to defend myself. "You dive into whatever grabs your attention, regardless of the lack of water to slow your fall. I told you I won't allow hookups in this house. No strange men. None. My God, Skylar. It's bad enough you lost that job I got for you. You need to start using your *brain!*" She pressed her lips tight and shook her head.

My brain.

I wanted to snort and cry at the same time. She knew my mind didn't work like hers and never would.

"You didn't have to be so rude," I whispered harshly, leaning toward her to keep our tones low, which she didn't seem to care about. "Ashton is a sweet man—"

"It's a front to sneak his way up under your dress," she hissed.

"It is not! He's one of the most genuine people I've ever met."

"You've known him all of what? Twenty-four hours?" she exclaimed with a sarcastic laugh, throwing her hands up into the air like she always did when she got fed up with my "ridiculousness."

My chest ached, and the sting in my eyes promised tears. I shifted my stance, wanting to rush back to the dining room but to also slap my sister silly.

Ashton must have heard every word...our voices had gone way beyond conversational.

"Why couldn't you just shake his hand and be kind for a change?" I whispered past the tightness closing off my throat.

Nora snorted. "Why be welcoming to someone I didn't invite into my home, my safe place that I keep *private* for a reason?" She bit out her words like she wanted to physically hurt me with them.

"Because I live here too, and *I* asked him over to dinner! And you...you made me look like a fool!" I cried out, tears erupting to stream down my cheeks.

"Because you *are* a fool, Skylar!" Nora let loose with a shriek that forced my feet to shy away from her. "You have no idea how easy you have it! Never having to feel the pressure to do better even when you've tried your best—"

Nora cut off abruptly, lips tight for all of two seconds, but she opened her mouth before I could process her words. "I refuse to be responsible for your *stupidity* any longer," she spat and pointed toward the front hall. "You need to leave. Go home to the farm."

I reared back as though she'd slapped me. Over the

years, she'd put me down plenty of times but not once had she called me stupid. And while I knew I drove her nuts sometimes, I made up for it by all the work I did around the house to keep her comfortable and well-fed.

Swallowing hard, I brushed my palms over my eyes. "You're really kicking me out?"

"I just can't deal with you anymore! You're just...too much. Always have been and always will be. I'm done babysitting you, Skylar. *Done.* Clean up your mess, then take your skirt-chasing man friend and get the hell out of my house!" Nora spun and headed for the stairs.

I didn't bother asking if she wanted any dinner. My time of servitude to my sister had come to an end, and if she thought I would make anything easier for her before leaving, she could go suck a duck egg and choke.

Inhaling a shaky breath, I forced my feet toward the dining room, my stomach threatening to heave up the small amount of food I'd eaten.

Ashton sat at the table, hands on his lap, his brow furrowed.

"Sorry," I whispered and wrung my hands, tears hazing my vision, "but I think it's best if you leave."

"Are you okay?"

I nodded, unable to speak.

"Come here." Ashton stood and pulled me into his arms.

I collapsed against his strong chest, breathing in his expensive cologne that smelled like spice and warmth. Tears slid down my cheeks as I clung to him, his arms wrapping me up tightly against him.

"Did you hear?" I gasped out between hitched breaths while fighting off sobs.

"Every word. What are you going to do?" he asked.

"Go back home," I said even though the idea made me

want to vomit. "I got fired last week because I kept messing up, so I have no money of my own to get an apartment. No savings. No car. I took the bus to work, and now…"

"Do you *want* to return to the farm?"

"Hell no," I muttered, and shuddered with a heavy sigh, getting a steadier hold on myself. "There's no life for me there anymore—and sometimes my parents can be just as cruel as Nora."

Ashton grasped my upper arms and pulled away, dipping his head slightly to meet my eyes. "You have nowhere else to go? No friends you can stay with for a little while?"

I shook my head, the wavering image of him through my tears even more beautiful because of the concern he showed me.

"I don't want you to leave California—we just met," he continued, the words tumbling over each other. "What if… Rhett and I have a guest room. You're welcome to it until you can figure something else out."

His suggestion floored me—my jaw dropped. "Y-you hardly know me," I sputtered.

"That doesn't matter," he stated firmly. "I heard enough to recognize verbal abuse, and you can't stay here even if your sister changes her mind. She's toxic to your sunshine, and I refuse to see you fade beneath her shadow."

The ache in my chest lessened, a sense sweet as honey replacing the feeling. I went all warm and gooey inside like a cinnamon bun fresh out of the oven.

"That's the nicest thing anyone has ever said to me," I whispered through my tears.

Ashton cradled my face in his hands as I laid my hands on his hard chest. His heart beat heavy and a little fast beneath my palms. "Will you come home with me?"

"What? Now?"

"She made it quite obvious she wants you gone," he stated matter-of-factly, those beautiful eyes of his studying mine, hints of gold around his pupils. "I'm here with an empty trunk. If we pack up what you need just for now, I'm sure we could put the rest in storage until you have things figured out."

"I don't have much to my name." I hated admitting how poor I was, considering his nice clothes and that fancy car.

"Then take me to your room, and I'll help you pack your things."

I searched his kind eyes for any hint of lying or manipulation. Not that I had ever been the best judge of character, but Ashton seemed real. Genuine. Too good to be true. "You're serious, aren't you?"

His shy smile flipped my belly upside down. "I've always wanted to be a knight in shining armor. I'll call Rhett once we get home to let him know what's going on, but in the meantime, let's get out of here before she comes back in and starts tearing you down again."

Oh, Nora and my parents would have a fit if I went along with him, but as with any metaphorical squirrel, my attention scampered toward the nut he'd tossed and latched on, my better sense heedless of the path ahead of me.

"Okay," I whispered and took his hand without another thought on the matter.

12

———

ASHTON

Hearing how Nora treated Skylar had shifted something inside me, a sense of protectiveness I'd only felt for my siblings and Rhett. I'd wanted to tear into that kitchen and set the bitch straight on how awesome her sister was, how her sunny disposition outshone any brain smarts.

The fallout had been worse than I'd expected, but I hadn't known Skylar that long. She'd been overcome with emotions and had melted against me, clinging, seeming to soak up my arms—as if no one had ever offered her comfort before.

Anger still simmered in my gut long after we bagged up Skylar's things and filled my trunk before heading south.

Nora hadn't left her room, thank God. Hadn't said goodbye—but neither had Skylar.

Using trash bags, we had quickly packed up her meager belongings, which consisted mainly of clothing and books.

Skylar left her house key on the kitchen counter beside our dinner's dirty dishes she'd refused to wash even though her sister had demanded she do so. Nora, she'd claimed while closing the front door behind us, could clean up someone else's mess for a change.

Chin held high, Skylar had marched to my car and sat rigidly on the passenger seat. She'd softened again when I reached for her hand and promised everything would work out in the way it was meant to.

Emotional exhaustion drooped her eyelids, and she slept propped up against the window before the first hour of travel passed.

I let her sleep, considering the next couple of days ahead of us.

A conversation with Rhett awaited, one I expected wouldn't be enjoyable atop the stress he already found himself under. But as much as he pretended to be, he wasn't a completely coldhearted bastard. He would understand why I'd offered the room to Skylar once I explained what had happened. I felt sure of it.

Once I knew Skylar's employment history and skills, we would help her find a job, but I secretly hoped she might come to work for me and Rhett. But if things didn't progress between the three of us in the way I yearned for, that might prove awkward.

I didn't have any other ideas until we arrived home, and I hated to wake Skylar, but the smile she gifted me as she blinked to alertness while we sat in the garage made my pulse race.

"Okay?" I asked, trailing the backs of my fingers over her cheek.

"Yes. I had a good nap, and even though I could sleep for another ten hours without interruption, I'm feeling relieved. I can't thank you enough."

I grinned when I would have rather leaned in for a quick kiss. "Come on, then. Let's get you settled in the guest room, then I'll call Rhett to tell him what happened. Knowing him, he'll have a plan to help you out and set in place within minutes."

"Are you sure he's going to be okay with this?" she asked, her voice quiet.

"As much as he pretends to be unmoved, he hates to see people suffering. Trust me on that one." My own heart squeezed at the memory of his words that night in the cemetery when he'd given me a shoulder to lean on.

He would be drawn to Skylar same as he'd been to me. I knew it in the deepest marrow of my bones.

Skylar exhaled loudly and nodded. "Okay."

I squeezed her hand quickly before hopping from the car.

She hadn't gotten a look at the front of the house, but her eyes widened when we entered the kitchen through the garage and I flicked on the lights. While I'd grown accustomed to our chef's kitchen with its stainless steel appliances, massive gas stove, and marble countertops, she stumbled to a stop to take it all in.

"Holy shit!"

I smirked at her squeak.

"Oh my God, this kitchen is...spectacular! Will you let me cook breakfast tomorrow?" she asked, her voice pitched high with wonder and delight while trailing her fingertips over the cool marble.

"You can cook any meal you want—whenever you want. But for now—" I bumped her backside with a clothing-stuffed trash bag "—let's head upstairs."

We lugged her belongings to the second floor, and I showed her to the guest room.

She gasped at the sight of the sunset glinting off the

ocean beyond the windows. Her shoulders sagged as she dropped her bags to the floor.

"Oh wow," she whispered, moving quickly across the bedroom to place her palms on the glass. "It's breathtaking."

I set the bags I held onto the floor and watched her.

Skylar now knew Rhett and I weren't exactly scraping the bottom of the barrel to survive, but I felt she and I had already made enough of a connection that our money wouldn't be a drawing factor. A bonus, sure, but—

She spun, her smile gone and eyes wide. "This...it's too much, Ashton. I-I'm not...well, look at me." Her hand fluttered over her billowy dress. "I wear secondhand clothing. Worn shoes from discount stores. I cut off dungarees to make my own shorts. I can't afford haircuts every six weeks, and I refuse to paint my face with caking makeup like all your female friends must do. Oh! And I hate high heels with a *passion*."

"None of that matters to me," I stated quietly, moving quickly to cup her cheeks in my hands. "You're beautiful just the way you are. I wouldn't change one thing about you."

"I'm a scatterbrain."

"You're *refreshing*," I argued, rubbing my thumbs over her pointed chin that trembled.

"I'm forgetful."

"That's what reminder notes are for."

Wetness coated her eyes. "I grew up on a *farm*."

"I love that you learned how to be a hard worker at a young age."

"You're stubborn, aren't you?" she asked with a soft, unsteady chuckle.

I grinned. "I can be, yes."

Her gaze dropped to my mouth, and the hunger in her eyes dissolved my smile. "I like that you hardly know me and yet you argue in my defense when I point out my flaws," she said, her voice thick.

I slid my thumb over her lower lip, the soft flesh parting from the upper. Her breath caught, and my groin tightened.

"I really want to kiss you," I murmured, stepping closer, leaving a mere inch between our bodies.

Her gaze lifted to my eyes. Black pupils swelled, revealing mutual desire. "What about Rhett?" she whispered.

My smile returned, and I brushed my nose over hers, loving how she thought of him and how he might feel about us kissing without him being present.

"He gave me his blessing to kiss you good night if things went well," I said, still cradling her cheeks in my hands.

"And do you think it did?" Her warm, sweet breath caressed my mouth. "Go well?"

I rubbed my nose along hers again, drawing out the moment. Teasing. Driving me insane with intense longing. "Yes."

One step brought our bodies into contact from knees to chest—and she felt better against my front than any woman ever had.

"Sky..." I whispered her name and kissed her.

Softly. Gently. A mere brush of lips.

"Oh God," she whispered against my mouth—and wound her arms around my neck, holding on tight, a harsh tremble causing her to shudder.

I licked into her mouth, and she let me in, meeting me stroke for stroke, igniting the sparks between us into combustible flames. My dick hardened in seconds, throbbing, begging me to grind against her.

But Rhett had given his blessing on kissing, not full-on making out.

At the thought of him, my arousal kicked in times two, and I groaned into Skylar's mouth, wishing he stood behind her, his lips on her neck, his hands reaching around to grab my ass to bracket her warmth between us.

My cell buzzed in my back pocket, and I tore myself away from her, easing back. Both of us breathed hard. The black of her pupils dominated her green eyes, and her mouth appeared swollen and red from mine. She licked her lower lip, shooting another bolt of lust through my groin.

Hungry girl.

I smirked and gave her a quick peck on the tip of her nose while fishing out my cell.

Rhett: **Dad finally pulled the plug. I'll call you in the morning.**

My breath left in a rush, arousal leaking away as my throat tightened over his blunt words and their crystal clear meaning.

"What's wrong?" Sky asked, touching my forearm.

"Rhett's father finally made the choice to take his wife off life support." I wanted to call Rhett, but his stating he would get in contact with me in the morning was typical Rhett, shutting down whatever emotions he felt rising up inside him. He indirectly asked for space, and while I would give him silence to process overnight, I refused to allow him to be alone.

Skylar threw her arms around me, hugging me tight. "You need to go to him."

"Yes," I didn't hesitate to answer, tears stinging my eyes.

"I-I can catch an Uber or something back to Nora's," she said, pulling away to wrap her arms around herself.

"No." I swallowed hard. "You're staying here."

"But..." She bit her lip.

"No buts. You're going to soak in the bathtub, jets on full

blast, then crawl into that nice big bed and sleep. And in the morning, you're going to explore your new home and make that kitchen your own. It'll be the perfect job for now—house-sitting until we return."

"When will you be back?" she whispered.

"As soon as his parent's affairs are put in order. It could be two days or it could be a week. Rhett will help his dad to plan the details of the wake and funeral, and I'll be there for them both whether they think they need me or not."

She grabbed hold of my hand, lacing our fingers together. "You're a good man, Ashton Blackwood. Let's go pack your bag."

13

———

RHETT

Dad finally pulled the plug. I'll call you in the morning.

I had kept the texted news short since exhaustion tempted to drag me under. Turning off and tossing aside my cell, I scrubbed a weary hand over my face, grimacing at the thick scruff I usually kept neatly trimmed. I needed a long, hot shower and a good night's sleep on the hotel's mattress where my phone rested.

Dad had ignored my pleas earlier in the day to let her go and once again hadn't said a word beyond a muttered "No."

Eventually, I had retired to my hard, plastic chair beside the window in my mom's hospital room and gave Dad the silence he wanted. Without another plan to move forward, I'd grown more agitated with every passing hour, a sense of helplessness I couldn't stand looming over my head.

Time had wasted away while I sat powerless to make shit happen.

I'd concluded there was no use in my sticking around in Florida, and as I'd opened my mouth to announce I was leaving, Dad had released a harsh sob.

My jaw had snapped shut, and I'd stared at his bowed head and heaving shoulders.

Why the man had broken down—I didn't understand. He'd never shown an ounce of emotion, not even anger, when I'd been a child. But the grief he'd portrayed in that moment...he was a fucking mess.

He'd clung to her fingers, kissing and stroking the back of her hand over his cheek.

An ache had slidden over my chest, and I'd rubbed at it, trying to align the man I'd known to the one I'd stared at.

Nothing made sense—until he had straightened, dried his tears, and stood, a heavy exhale relaxing the tension in his shoulders. His spine set, he'd pressed the nurse's button.

"It's time," he'd told the nurse, his voice unmoved as always.

There, I'd thought, *there's the strong backbone.*

I'd stayed out of the way when Dad spoke with the doctors, and arrangements were made to let Mom go. He hadn't glanced my way, nor had he acknowledged my presence in the room.

Mom's chest had stopped rising, and Dad had once more sat silent and stoic as though the death of his wife hadn't affected him.

I had barreled forward toward the next step we had to take, needing to finish so I could return home.

"Tomorrow," Dad had snipped when I'd attempted to discuss Mom's burial.

I forced myself to shower before collapsing on the hotel bed, ready to pass the fuck out so I would be rested for the following day of details and attempting to work with my father to create a plan.

Blackness offered release from thought, and I welcomed it with open arms.

Details could wait for the sunrise.

A knock stirred me from deep sleep in the middle of the night.

Cursing at my first good rest since arriving in Florida being interrupted, I crawled from the bed and peered out the peephole.

Ash.

I swallowed hard, agitated and yet thankful as fuck to see him standing before me when I opened the door. He wore my favorite olive-green shirt...

"Rhett," he whispered my name, but I stepped back to let him enter rather than falling into him like my entire body desired to do.

He set his bag aside while I flipped the locks, and he pulled me against him before I'd fully turned.

Any fight, all thoughts of self-preservation fled, and I gave over to my need for him. The warm solidity of him settled the deepest reaches of me I hadn't realized still ached. He claimed I was his rock, but Ash was my escape, the only safe place I could trust with my feelings.

"Love you," I murmured, my cheek on his shoulder and eyes stinging.

Pulling back, he held my face in his hands, searching as he always did for words I most times couldn't give.

"I'm fine," I claimed through the tightness wanting to close off my throat.

His soft smile stated he knew I lied—and I didn't argue. "Crawl back into bed. I'll join you in a minute."

I did as told and managed to stay awake until he slid beneath the sheets, pressing up against my chest.

Winding my arms around him, I rested my forehead to his and closed my eyes. "I felt...lost without you. Needed you, baby," I whispered my truth.

He brushed his lips over mine in a tender kiss. "You'll always have me."

"Don't leave me," I murmured, already half asleep and uncaring of the thoughts slipping free.

"Never," he promised.

———

I was the little spoon when I woke, something that rarely happened, and I lay still, savoring the closeness of Ash's body, his heavy exhales heating my scalp.

Our fingers twined over my heart, and for the first time since leaving him back at home in order to be with my dad, peacefulness settled into my bones. I'd slept like the dead, unlike the previous couple of nights without my lover beside me.

While allowing my body to slowly wake, I enjoyed the warmth of his embrace and the silence surrounding us. My mind always perked before the rest of me, so I focused on what needed to be done while Ash continued to sleep.

Dad had refused to speak about a service, hadn't made any arrangements as far as I was aware. Those would be the top priority. I didn't know what Mom's last wishes had been —if she'd even had any. Hell, I wasn't even sure my parents had burial plots or if they preferred cremation.

Both Mom and Dad had dozens of friends, hundreds of acquaintances...it would be best to have donations to a worthy cause rather than flowers.

Brain firing on all cylinders, I sped through possibilities and different plans concerning wakes and funerals to help Dad make decisions.

"Your thoughts are loud," Ash muttered, his hot breath wafting the hair on the back of my head.

"Sorry." I lifted our twined fingers to my lips and brushed them over his knuckles.

"It's okay." He kissed my neck. "There's a lot to do in the next couple of days."

"Mmm," I hummed and rolled to face him. Gorgeous, sleepy hazel eyes peered at me, trying to read into the deepest reaches of my soul same as always, but I still felt contentment, a lack of grief even though I faced burying my mom.

He released a heavy sigh, seemingly relieved at my peace. "You're okay."

"I am." I kissed him, just a caress of lips. "But only because you came. You didn't have to."

"Of course I did. It was only a red-eye with one quick layover. I wish I could have made it sooner, but there weren't any direct flights. You seemed surprised to see me—didn't you get my texts?"

"I shut my phone off after I sent you the message about my mom. I just wanted to sleep uninterrupted."

"I'm not sorry for waking you up."

"Neither am I." Our foreheads tipped together, and I closed my eyes. "Thank you."

We lay in silence for a few moments, my mind once more on the day ahead.

"How's your dad?"

"Fine." A lie, I was sure after his emotional outburst, but he revealed about as many feelings as I did.

"What do we have to do today?" Ash asked, knowing I wouldn't desire to discuss sorrow of any type—or my lack thereof.

"A lot, but first..." I rolled him onto his back and slid down his body, hoping to lose myself in him for a while.

"Rhett—you don't have to—"

"I want to," I told him and nipped at his pec while heading southward. "You flew across the country for me." I nosed over his abs, my heart fluttering over his actions even when I'd told him to stay home. "The least I can do is give you a reason to smile this morning."

"You always make me smile—"

I closed my mouth over his morning wood and sucked hard, focusing fully on him.

"—oh *fuck*." Ash grabbed hold of my head as his cock swelled against my tongue. "Just like that. Christ, your mouth is so hot."

"Mmm," I hummed my agreement and swallowed him down, smiling around the girth stretching my lips.

Nothing on earth tasted as good as Ash. No words uttered or sang lit me up inside like his groans. And the way he whispered my name while throbbing on my tongue and coming down my throat...

Too many feels—goddamn emotions ached my chest, but I wouldn't have things any other way with Ash. Bringing him happiness, giving him everything he desired, was the only way I could repay him for his selfless love.

14

———

SKYLAR

Seagulls cried nearby, pulling me from a delicious dream of warm skin and sleepy kisses...

Or maybe I didn't dream.

I jerked my eyes open—and found myself alone in Ashton and Rhett's guest bed.

"Damn," I muttered, stretching life into my muscles and joints.

Indirect sunbeams flooded the west-facing bedroom with light, the beach-themed bedding and walls muted blues and greens. The sand-colored rug I'd dug my toes into the night before greeted my bare feet as I slid from the satiny sheets.

Massive windows overlooked the Pacific directly in front of me, the cry of another seabird begging me to join him outdoors.

A whole day to myself, and while I'd rather have had Ashton and Rhett there with me, excitement for the hours ahead made my feet itch to move.

Ashton had told me to explore—so I did.

Flitting from room to room, I grinned like a little kid. I

squealed over the library packed full of shelves lined with books and trailed my fingertips over spines, wondering if Rhett too enjoyed romance books as his guilty pleasure like Ashton and me.

My focus paused on a spine I recognized. "No. Way." I pulled the book from its place and squealed again.

Annie Kelly. Ashton had claimed to have read her latest release, but to see he'd ordered a paperback?

Clutching the book to my chest, I gave the rest of the room heart eyes, that too-good-to-be-true thought fluttering through my head on repeat.

"They can't be perfect." I slid the book home and hurried back into the hallway, finding an office next.

Dark, heavy furniture—two desks as though the men shared the space. A picture of Ashton and Rhett sat on the closest table, and a quick glance at the other revealed a second one. I grabbed both photographs and stared, swooning at the sweetness of the partners.

Rhett didn't smile in the first but had his arms wrapped around Ashton, his nose against his cheek and eyes closed while Ashton grinned at the camera. Definitely a selfie and achingly precious.

How Rhett leaned into Ashton, clutched him close spoke volumes. He adored the man.

The second image showed them both laughing, and the sparkle in Rhett's dark eyes swooped through me, taking my heart to my toes. Ashton had stated Rhett was gorgeous, but Jiminy Cricket on a cracker.

I swallowed a rush of saliva and pinched myself to make sure I wasn't still dreaming.

Pain radiated from the skin I abused.

"This is real," I muttered to myself, hoping to see that carefree smile in real life. That sort of happiness he portrayed in the picture meant he wasn't a complete grump like my sister. "This is happening."

Jitters skittered through me, and I quickly replaced the pictures, traipsing around the office to see what else I could find.

College degrees for business hung on the walls.

Leather chairs hugged the desks.

The air smelled of cologne, coffee, and something rich and earthy. I filled my lungs over and over, sucking the scent in until I memorized its deliciousness.

Coffee...

My gaze flitted over the desk...files. Papers on one along with strewn pencils. The other sat cleared except for a closed laptop of sorts.

A sticky notepad lay beside it, I noted while moving closer.

Three rainbow-colored intertwined hearts printed along the top of the first piece of paper.

The Missing Link logo.

Grinning, I picked it up and ran my fingers over the edge like the pad was a deck of cards, the soft flicking of papers loud in the silence around me. The app had possibly given me the one thing I dreamed about, and I bit my lip, trailing my fingertips over the edges again.

I wanted to tuck the treasure away...

Ashton would tell me where they'd gotten it, and I would find a way to land some notepads of my own.

But I had no job. No money. And I still had my sister's cell phone.

I should have left that behind, I thought while leaving the office and heading toward the kitchen, realizing I'd yet to have a sip of caffeine. With the state-of-the-art-space I'd taken in the night before, I expected some newfangled coffee machine with gadgets and gizmos galore.

They had a Keurig.

I squealed and started looking in cabinets and drawers until I found a mug, sugar, and spoon. "Hurry up," I poked at the machine as it gurgled slowly into my cup. "I need you in my belly."

Snickering at myself, I threw open the double doors of the huge fridge, and my jaw dropped. It was packed full of heathy food—cuts of meat, fresh veggies, and fruit. Organic milk and creamer, eggs, and yogurt. Non-nitrate bacon, sprouted grain bread, and orange juice.

The same type of items Nora had always put on her grocery list for me to buy.

I pushed aside thoughts of my sister, determined to move forward on the path I'd chosen, chasing squirrels and nuts for as long as I could.

Still grinning like a dork, I loaded up my arms, ready to fill my stomach. For the following half hour, I enjoyed having the house to myself so I could sing at the top of my lungs and not make faces cringe.

A songbird I was not, but that didn't keep me from twittering my happiness to the stainless steel six-burner stove and wine fridge that held more bottles than I could count.

I moaned at the first sip of coffee. Rolled my eyes at the crunch of bacon between my teeth. Bit into the toast with its slather of pure Irish butter and whimpered.

A girl could get used to this...

My cell jangled from the pocket of my sleep shorts I'd pulled on before exploring, my pulse picking up. Ashton had already left a good morning text I'd found after rolling from bed but hadn't replied to my response.

The grin on my face faded at the name on the screen.

Mom.

"Ugh." I grimaced, the toast turning to a rock in my stomach. Not answering wasn't an option. She would ring relentlessly until I picked up. Turning off the phone...nope. I needed to be available for when Ashton finally called me back to tell me about his flight and how Rhett was doing like I'd asked him to do.

I swiped to answer. "Hi, Mom."

"*Skylar Anne Larsen.*"

My eyelids slammed shut, and I braced myself.

"What have you done!" She didn't ask a question, so I didn't bother with answering. Not that she gave me time for one anyway. "I just got off the phone with Nora..."

I started to clean up the breakfast mess I'd made even though I hadn't finished while Mom ranted at me about my impulsiveness and poor, inappropriate choices just like Nora had told her.

"Where is your mind at?" Mom finally ran out of steam, and I realized she waited for a response.

In the clouds, I wanted to snark, but that would only lead to more lectures.

"Ashton is a good man. He's sweet and kind."

"Nora told me you've known him less than a day!"

I rolled my eyes. "A bit longer than that, Mom, but he's genuine. Doesn't play games or try to manipulate me—"

"Did you sleep in his bed last night?"

"Mom," I groaned, slumping back onto the kitchen chair I'd vacated to pretty up the room.

"Did you allow that stranger to put his hands on you? Take what doesn't belong to him like you did with that last boy you dated?"

My stomach knotted, raising the reckless side of my nature I hadn't dealt with for months.

"What if I want to belong to him, Mom?" I shot back, my voice hard.

"Nora said he's married!"

"They're partners—not married," I explained, not that it would make a difference. My parents tended toward the straitlaced way of life and wouldn't ever understand.

"Bad enough they're gay, but to pull you into this type of relationship—"

"They're bisexual," I muttered, but she didn't stop.

Slumping, I thumped my forehead onto the table as she went off again on how unnatural poly relationships were.

I held in a snort on that one. Mom obviously hadn't read Annie Kelly's latest. What an eye-opener that would be! Giggles rose up my throat, and I swallowed them down, choking.

"I'm serious, young lady," Mom chided, having heard me fight the snickering wanting to bubble from me. "I knew sending you off to California was a mistake, but your father insisted you needed to spread your wings a bit and learn how to fly on your own. Make something of yourself like Nora has done."

My eyes rolled so damn hard back into my head that I sat fully upright. "I'll never *make something of myself*," I quoted and emphasized my words, the snark taking the lead, "because Nora set the bar too damn high. I'll never measure up—ever. What's the point of trying?"

"Making decisions after thinking them through would be a good start!"

Again with the lecture.

Mom and Dad hadn't ever outright put me down, called me less than or too much—that shit all came from Nora— but reality was, I was nothing like her and never would be.

I tuned Mom out. Put her on speaker and got back up to

clean the kitchen, muttering agreement noises here and there so she knew I semi-listened.

If Mom saw the house I would call home until I got my feet beneath me, she'd shut up real quick. Ashton and Rhett were loaded, no doubt about it. They made a lot more than Nora, and in my parents' minds, she was a millionaire who'd reached the top.

But I kept my thoughts to myself, not wanting to share the good state—the lucky place—I'd landed in all thanks to one little app.

My cell pinged, alerting me that the battery ran low.

"Mom," I interrupted, picking up the phone, "my cell is about to die. I have to go."

"I expect you to head back to Nora's immediately. Your father and I will find a way to fly you home."

Yeah, no thanks.

"I love you, Mom, but Dad told me to spread my wings— and I plan on it. I gotta go," I repeated and hung up without another word.

I breathed in a deep breath, glorying in the freedom even though I had almost nothing to my name.

A chance lay at the end of my path, one that could bring the type of love and happiness I craved. Children. Affection. Appreciation.

If my nature didn't curl Rhett's nose like it did most people.

Sudden tears stung my eyes, and I went in search of a phone charger I could borrow since I hadn't brought mine.

Hopefully, Ashton texted soon, letting me know how Rhett fared and when they would be home.

Home.

I stood in their bedroom doorway, eyeing the massive bed with its navy coverlet and countless pillows. Longing to be in its center, surrounded by hard muscle and warm skin rushed through me like a prairie-swept storm.

I leapt into action, my feet taking me across the room before the thought made sense in my head.

"Oomph!" My breath left in a rush as I landed face-first on a pile of fluff, feathers, and comfort.

Oh yes, I could definitely get used to this.

As long as two men bookended me like I was the most precious book in their library.

Like me, I whispered in my head, recalling the image of Rhett's smiling face in that picture on the desk. *Please.*

15

ASHTON

Rhett's father had already set plans in place prior to our arrival at their home midmorning.

A cremation had already been ordered—no services would be held.

Nothing public for friends to show their respects and offer condolences. While that choice hurt my heart, Rhett breathed easier. No wake or funeral meant a lack of people in his face, looking to soothe his grief. It meant no vulnerability, no need for indifference that I wondered about.

But Rhett didn't appear or seem broken over the death of his mother. They hadn't ever been close like me and my mom, and not for the first time, I wanted to pull him into my arms and give him all the love and affection he'd missed out on as a child.

The same I felt sure Skylar would offer ours. While she hadn't been super handsy with me, those fingers of hers had twitched enough I wondered if she'd kept from reaching out for simple touches more often than she'd given during our short hours together.

I wondered how she fared back at our house—and I

hadn't yet told Rhett about the choice I'd made without him. He had enough to deal with.

We planned to fly home the next day, and I shot off a quick text to Skylar to expect our arrival. We ate an early dinner at the hotel's restaurant, and I downed two glasses of wine, which soured my stomach, or perhaps it was my nerves over the impeding conversation I'd procrastinated in starting.

We both collapsed onto the hotel bed, our bodies finding each other as natural as breathing. Dark circles still clung beneath Rhett's closed eyes, but half the lines he'd had on his face the night before had smoothed away.

I expected him to pass the fuck out—

"Tell me about your date," he murmured, his quiet words fluttering anxiety through my chest and churning my stomach even more.

"It was perfect." *Until it wasn't—then it was again.* I closed my eyes while remembering the light in Sky's expressive eyes, the softness of her touch. How she'd insisted on helping me quickly pack for my red-eye flight across the country.

The softest of kisses we shared before I'd left for the airport.

Obsession seemed the right word for what I felt. I definitely hadn't done a good job of guarding my heart like Rhett had insisted upon.

"She's even more beautiful in person," I said, needing him to want her in the same way I did. "There's an innocence about her, and it's sexy as hell."

Rhett tensed slightly, which tightened my own stomach again. "Did you kiss her?"

"Yes."

"And?"

"Zing."

He snorted at the word Skylar had used—the same I'd told him after the first time our lips had met all those years ago. His eyelids lifted, allowing his dark orbs to peer into mine. "You like her."

Rhett hadn't asked a question, but I nodded.

"She's truly amazing—but her twin doesn't understand that fact."

"Skylar has a twin?"

"Yes." The truth of the statement made me smile, but the memory of the snob who'd shared the womb with Sky caused the happiness to fade from my face.

"What?" Rhett pushed, reading me as easily as he always did.

"Her sister is a bitch. She came home while we were eating dinner and lit into Sky over inviting a stranger into her house, accusing me of being a sick stalker and rapist and calling Sky stupid..."

I clenched my jaw shut, my still-churning stomach hardening at the memory of Nora's hurtful words. "She kicked Sky out of the house right then and there."

Rhett's brow furrowed, and I could hear his mind working. "What did you do, Ash?"

I inhaled deeply and glanced at his chin since I couldn't hold his gaze. "I told her she could stay in our guest room until we helped her figure something else out."

Rhett tensed against me. "I really wish you had discussed it with me first," he stated, annoyance more than leaking from his words.

"I know I should have, but I had to make a decision on the spot and didn't want to burden you with another person's issues when you have enough going on. With how hurtful Sky's sister had been, I couldn't allow her to stay there another minute. I was going to call you to explain the situation after I got Sky settled but then I got your text and could only think about getting here to be with you."

"You don't know this woman—"

"I do!" I insisted, lifting my gaze back to his. His dark eyes had closed off completely. "We have a connection I can't explain any more than I can mine with you."

"You have one with me because of the twenty-three years we've spent attached at the hip," he snipped.

"What we have is more than being close for so long, and you know it. It's *always* been more. Fate intended us to be together, same as she did for Skylar to complete us."

A hint of vulnerability flitted across his face and disappeared just as quickly. "I never felt we lacked in any way."

"Neither did I," I assured him, cupping his scruffy cheek, "until I met her. Trust me, Rhett. She's going to change our lives for the better. We'll be happier than we've ever been."

"I'm already happy."

I searched his face, wishing I could sift through the emotions he kept buried deep inside. "She's delicious, Rhett. Smells like coconuts."

A frown furrowed his brow, but I settled in against him and pushed on, desperate to change his mind toward a woman he'd yet to meet and had already judged.

"Sweet and addictive—but you don't have to be afraid I'll leave you—"

"I fear no such thing," Rhett muttered, but his scowl remained.

"Then keep an open mind," I urged, running my hands over his back. "Please."

The displeasure in Rhett's gaze faded the longer the silence stretched between us. I'd have given a million dollars to know his feelings.

"She is sunshine," I promised, believing he just had to meet her and his mind would be set at rest. "Bright and energizing."

"How flighty is she, Ash?" Rhett asked, his tone stern.

A smile broke over my face as I imagined her in my mind, flitting around Nora's kitchen and chattering like a tweety bird.

"Shit," Rhett muttered and exhaled loudly, finally relaxing against me. "You're already half in love, aren't you?"

"She's a kind, generous creature." I grinned, recognizing the signs of his relenting. "And you're going to love her too."

"You mentioned coconuts."

Leave it to Rhett to latch onto the one redeeming quality he'd heard and would approve of.

"She claims to make a mean coconut cream pie too," I told him, my smile fixed firmly in place as excitement replaced the concern I'd felt moments earlier.

Rhett groaned and tugged me closer, his nose finding my neck. "If she's half as tasty as you, I promise to keep an open mind."

I slung my leg over Rhett's hip and pressed our groins together, my heart lighter than it had been in...years even though my stomach continued with its unhappiness from the dry wine.

"I'm sorry I didn't talk to you first before offering to be her knight in shining armor, but she's going to fit perfectly between us in every way. I'm just sure of it."

"And if I want you all to myself some days?" he asked, the question telling me he trusted me and had resigned himself to the possibility of a future with Sky.

"She fantasizes about watching."

"Fuck." Life stirred in Rhett's dick. "How kinky is this woman?"

"That remains to be seen, but I can't wait to find out." The thought of Sky in our bed in any way, shape, or form swelled my dick.

"I want your ass," Rhett said and grazed his teeth over my neck.

Flipping over without another word, I offered my body to him, knowing he would take me along with him. Thoughts of Skylar being there with us in the flesh played out in my head, but everything beyond Rhett faded away once he sank deep into my body, stretching me with stinging, delicious pain/pleasure.

His loving strokes quickly led to jolting thrusts until three days' worth of cum began to coat the sheet beneath me.

"Love. You." Two deep plunges and Rhett groaned against my shoulder blade, releasing inside me as my hole spasmed around his cock.

"Love you too," I gasped with one last shudder.

We both panted for breath, his chest sticky with sweat against my back.

Lax and grinning, I could help but think of Skylar. "You're going to love me even more when you see how perfect she is."

Rhett brushed his lips over my neck and pulled out, leaving me empty and chilled. "We'll see."

His words didn't hold an ounce of hope, but I clung to it, sure she was meant to be in our lives.

I just prayed she would help him see the light and that her happiness wouldn't make him retreat further into himself.

16

RHETT

Ash had always been a romantic, and I'll admit he'd rubbed off on me enough I actually appreciated a few of the books he kept in our small library. He tended toward gay romance while I preferred where a woman joined in the fun. But I'd always enjoyed women more than Ash ever had.

We had been together from such an early age that neither of us had dated a woman alone before, and the only pussy we'd come into contact with had been as a threesome.

Fucking one without me, I expected, wouldn't appeal to Ash at all, but the idea definitely intrigued me. While the thoughts of attempting to connect emotionally with a woman churned unease in my guts, the fantasy of losing myself in her soft clutches stirred my blood.

It always had.

Ash sat silent in the passenger seat as I drove us home from the airport, but I could feel his nervous energy. I'd been unable to hide my disappointment from my voice the night before after learning he'd brought a woman into our house without discussing it with me.

We rarely made decisions without consulting the other, and the step he'd taken hadn't been as light as choosing what we would have for dinner that night.

A stranger had taken up residence in my house, a woman Ash had mentioned within seconds of groaning while coming undone beneath me the night before.

A muscle ticked in my jaw at the memory, and I forced myself to relax, determined to keep an open mind—to trust Ash regardless of how I felt sure his excitement might have driven him past red flags.

I cursed the timing of Mom's stroke and death. Hated the sense of unburied shit building inside me.

We'd said goodbye to my dad earlier that morning, a mere handshake that was as uncomfortable as fuck. Like strangers without a care for one another, we separated without promises to keep in touch.

Even though a slew of emotion ought to have roiled deep inside me, hollowness haunted me. Emptiness toward all feelings attempted to occupy my mind.

But I had other shit to contemplate.

I thought about our arrival at home, imagined every scenario possible concerning the supposed redheaded beauty who waited for us and what steps or things I might say to quietly test her personality.

Had I more time and not promised Ash to allow organic progression with Skylar, I'd have done that background check I always did before agreeing to meet up with women Missing Link had matched us with.

I hated not having my ducks in a row.

Loathed the unknown—and the fact I couldn't plan for situations in advance without some sort of assurance of truth to back up those decisions.

Turning onto our street, I noted Lionel's Landscaping's truck pulling away from the front of our house.

I slowed, and Wyatt did the same with his work truck and rolled down the window as we drew abreast of one another.

"Rhett. Ash." He greeted us both with a grin while turning down his radio. "What's going on?"

"Just getting back from Florida," I told him.

"Vacation?" he asked.

"My mom passed."

His grin faded. "Shit. Sorry to hear it."

"Thanks. How are Garrett and Haley?" I asked, having no wish to linger on any condolences.

Wyatt had been in charge of our lawn care for years, and we'd shared more than a couple beers on our back patio. He and his two partners had even exchanged vows on the beach behind our home a few weeks earlier.

It'd been a lovely, small wedding but depressing as fuck for Ash.

"Never been happier," Wyatt stated, a huge grin on his face.

"Did you happen to meet Skylar?" Ash asked, leaning forward to better see Wyatt.

"Skylar?"

"Our houseguest."

I could hear the joy in Ash's voice, his excitement to put those last few feet behind us so *I* could meet her.

"Nope." Wyatt glanced between us as though waiting for us to fill him in.

Of course, Ash couldn't contain himself. "We matched through the app, and long story short, I invited her to stay with us for a while. She watched the house while we were in Florida."

"I didn't see her—but I'm always pretty focused on my work."

Maybe she came to her senses and left.

Considering Ash had told me she'd grown up poor and on a farm, I expected the woman had firmly embedded herself in our house that most would consider a mansion and had done no such thing.

Keeping my inner scowl masked didn't come easy.

We said our goodbyes to Wyatt, and he once more offered his condolences before driving off.

I hit the button for the garage door and slowly pulled in.

Ash squirmed on his seat like a little kid, and even though I wanted to snicker at his excitement, I didn't. Too much unease raked through my guts. We both grabbed our bags off the back seat, but he was the first through the kitchen door.

The scent of roasting chicken and coconuts set my mouth to watering—a pie cooled atop the stove. Two loaves of freshly baked bread sat on the counter.

My scowl eased.

"Sky!" Ash called, and the fast pattering of feet sounded from the other side of the house near the library.

The appearance of Skylar hit my solar plexus like a punch, ripping the air from my lungs.

Gorgeous, he'd said, but there was no single word to describe her beauty.

Her wide smile sparkled clear through her big green eyes as her gaze landed on my lover, and she let out a tiny squeal, her quick steps drawing her closer.

A river of auburn hair rippled behind her, the white tank top clutching to her perfectly-sized breasts and making my mouth water. Cutoff shorts fringed along pale thighs. Slender calves gave way to bare feet void of polish.

Grinning like a fool, Ash dropped his bag, took three steps, and they came together like two long-lost lovers denied each other's presence for far too long. He swept her into his arms, twirling her around, both of them giggling.

I stood and stared, turned on by the gorgeous sight of the two of them intertwined—and yet hating how she fit so goddamn perfectly against him. How she seemed to light him up from the inside out.

Something I'd never been able to do.

Tension rose to my shoulders as an uncomfortable dryness owned my throat.

I stamped whatever the fuck those feelings were down, determined to see things through to their end, good or bad.

Ash set Skylar back on her feet and laced their fingers together, turning to bring her toward me since I hadn't made a move to approach them.

I gave Skylar my attention, and that punch hit again as our gazes connected.

"Oh wow," she whispered and blinked, swallowing hard as she and Ash came to a stop less than two feet from my personal space.

"Rhett, this is Sky. Sky, Rhett."

I tried and failed to smile at the woman who stared at me as though starstruck. "Hi," I said without offering my hand like I should have done.

"Hi *back*." Her face lit up like my simple greeting had made her day while Ash chuckled over our brief exchange.

"Ashton said you were gorgeous, but seriously...just *wow*," Skylar spewed thoughts like a scampering chipmunk, the words all flowing together fast enough I had to really focus to catch what she said. "Your eyes *are* dark chocolate —I bet your dick is even more delicious than he claims too." Her eyes shot wide, her smile gone in a flash as red flushed her face. She slapped a palm over her mouth, still clutching to Ash's with the other.

"Oh! I'm sorry!" She hastened to add around her hand that couldn't keep the shit from spilling from her vocal cords. "Stuff just flies from my lips when I'm super nervous. Ignore me. Wait!" She uncovered her mouth and grabbed my shirt as though thinking I was about to turn away. "No. Don't do that—I *hate* being ignored. Well, cut off and dismissed too. Maybe just pretend I'm not word vomiting all over you?" She legit cringed and blew out a breath. "Okay... um...it's nice to finally meet you? And oh, shit—I'm sorry about your mom. Should have said that first..."

She finally shut up, firmly biting on her lower lip.

More than anything, I wanted to fulfill Ash's hopes and dreams, but the flighty magpie making a fool of herself in front of me wasn't the winged angel I'd envisioned—even if embarrassment looked good on her.

I tore my focus off her expressive, beautiful face to find Ash gazing at her with fucking hearts in his eyes—exactly as I'd dreaded.

Clearing my throat drew his attention toward me.

Pink stained his cheeks, and he grinned and shrugged as though unsure whether he should apologize or state again how perfect Skylar was.

No smile curved my lips in response to his.

17

SKYLAR

I diot...moron!

Never had my nerves gotten the best of me in such a way. Telling him I bet his dick was delicious? Seriously?

I wanted to sink into the floor and disappear as all the bad feels flushed through me. Heat had ignited inside me when Ashton had called out my name, and the sight of Rhett had intensified the overwhelming sense of wow-ness to the point I'd lost what little brains I had.

Rhett stared at Ashton, his face void of emotion as silence settled thickly between us.

A robot—that was what he reminded me of from his carefully styled hair to his ironed button-down, perfectly knotted tie—who wore a tie for a plane ride across the country?—and slacks that didn't appear to have a single, rumpled crease. Shiny shoes like Ashton, a fancy watch like Ashton...too...picture-perfect.

I released Ashton's fingers without thought and reached for Rhett's hair. A quick run of both of my hands through his thick locks to ruin his perfection brought back my grin.

"There. Now you look human," I murmured my thoughts out loud.

He held still beneath my unplanned attack on his hair but didn't glance away from Ashton. "You *can't* be serious," Rhett muttered, and I slunk back a step at the cold words.

Being ignored hadn't ever hurt so bad.

My heart felt like a jagged knife attempted to plunge in its depths, and I blinked against sudden tears.

Ashton snickered—laughed—shaking his head at Rhett and grabbed my hand to tug me against his side fast enough that I squeaked.

The welling anxiety and sadness inside me eased at his physical show of affection. He brushed his lips over my cheek, further settling my roller-coaster emotions, as did the happiness in his eyes as he gave me his attention.

I'd messed up our first meeting with Rhett, but I would win him over in order to keep Ashton's dimple and those beautiful hazel eyes in my life.

Chin lifting, I inhaled a deep, shaky breath and turned toward Rhett once more. I held out my hand and clamped my mouth shut even though nerves still demanded I fill the tense silence.

He slowly pulled his focus off Ashton's face and studied my calloused hand.

His presence dominated the cavernous kitchen, the scent of pine needles mingling with Ash's cologne headier than pheromones to my sex-starved imagination.

He was intimidating as hell.

Composed and breathtaking, Rhett Stirling made me feel small. Worthless.

His cold stare created the need to cave in on myself.

Perhaps Rhett was jealous of me. God knew I was of him

and the twenty-some years he'd gotten to enjoy having Ashton in his life.

I needed to find a way to show Rhett that I wanted him too, that he was just as important to me as his partner—or that he could be if only he'd let me in.

The longer he ignored my hand, the more my anxiety rose. But I told myself I needed to give Rhett time due to his recent loss. I imagined the sadness he didn't allow to show on his face, combined with having a strange woman in his home when he probably just wanted to be alone with Ashton in his grief. Ashton had said Rhett was stoic, but the man's face didn't twitch when I'd offered my condolences. He couldn't be completely unmoved.

Perhaps he needed a hug, my strong sense of empathy suggested.

Chasing after that falling acorn of a thought, I released my hold on Ashton's hand and threw my arms around Rhett regardless of his coolness toward me. I closed my eyes at the delicious scent of man and pine, the warmth of his hard chest against my cheek. His heart thumped beneath my ear in a steady cadence.

I wished to caress his soul, to ease whatever pain he felt that kept him so tightly bottled up inside.

Rhett didn't hug me in return—but he didn't push me away either.

"I-I made dinner," I stated quietly, stepping back and giving Rhett space since he obviously wasn't the touchy-feely type like Ashton and me. My gaze flitted from the floor to Ashton who watched us with a soft smile on his face. If he wasn't worried about Rhett's reaction to my silly, unintended words, then maybe there was hope.

"I'm starved," Ashton said, grabbing his bag off the floor from where he'd dropped it to spin me around in his arms.

What a moment that had been—

I glanced once more at Rhett to find his eyes less harsh than moments before. Perhaps my hug had comforted him in some way. "Rhett?" I asked even though I wasn't sure what I needed answered, so many questions flitting about in my brain.

Do you like me even the slightest?

Think I'm pretty—or a stupid idiot?

Are you ready for me to leave without giving me a chance?

"I could eat," he murmured an answer I hadn't expected, and I smiled in the slight relief his words offered.

"Why don't you two take your things to your room and get...more comfortable." I found myself loosening Rhett's tie —and he humored me. "I'll set the table and pour some wine to go with our roasted chicken." I retreated from his personal space once more, my hands dropping to my sides. "I was thinking a light-bodied red like—"

"Pinot noir," Rhett suggested at the same time I did.

My chest lightened as I smiled, feeling calm for the first time since he'd walked in the door.

A flash of something moved through his eyes, so damn quickly I didn't catch it—but it hadn't been disgust or annoyance.

He nodded and followed Ashton toward their bedroom.

I released my breath until it felt like my lungs caved in before turning to pull the chicken from the oven to let it rest. I'd already slaved over creamy mashed potatoes made with sour cream and butter, and the fresh broccoli I'd roasted with garlic, salt, and pepper just need a quick reheat.

The table sat ready, wine poured, and the two men still hadn't come downstairs. Did I call out that dinner was ready? Wait while the food grew cold? Or go look for them?

I couldn't imagine raising my voice would impress Rhett any...

My feet took me up the stairs, on course without much thought beyond finding them unpacking, wasting time until I let them know it was time to eat.

Their bedroom door stood open.

Rhett and Ashton had changed into lounge-type pants and T-shirts, and they stood wrapped up in each other's arms, foreheads pressed together in a beautiful picture of unconditional love.

My chest ached even as warmth blossomed between my thighs.

A sigh escaped me, drawing their focus off one another.

Ashton's face lit in a grin.

Rhett frowned, his soft eyes hardening at the sight of me.

"Dinner's ready," I whispered. "Sorry..."

I scurried away, wringing my hands.

Somehow, someway, I needed to show that man I was no threat, that I was worthy of his time and attention.

I'd already fallen in too deep with Ashton for things to go anywhere but how I'd been dreaming about since first laying eyes on one half of @desiringanangel.

I might not be exactly what Rhett had envisioned—he'd made that crystal clear without a single word—but I would find a way to bring sunshine into his life or I would find myself jobless *and* homeless.

18

ASHTON

The whole flight then car ride home from the airport, I'd dealt with lingering nausea from the wine the night before. Or perhaps underlying anxiety had continued to sneak its way through my excitement to see Skylar again.

God knew I was exhausted from all the traveling in such a short time.

I had felt pale, and Rhett had even questioned if I was all right, but I'd waved off his concern, assuring him I was fine.

A tummy bug, probably.

Or indigestion since slight abdominal pain had come with that latest upset stomach after eating a quick breakfast.

The sight of Skylar, having her in my arms had made me forget my discomfort, but the second Rhett and I left her in the kitchen to finish preparing dinner, my insides heaved.

I hugged our toilet, retching and coughing even though I hadn't eaten much all day.

"Ash."

"I'm fine." I spit bile into the toilet bowl and flushed. Pushing to my feet left me a little weak.

Rhett lay his hand on the back of my neck and squeezed, but I turned away to brush my teeth.

"It's just an upset stomach. I haven't been right since drinking that second glass of wine last night."

"Are you feverish? Need a couple Tylenol or something?"

"No."

"Sure you're okay, baby?"

"Yep." I brushed my teeth, and Rhett retreated to our bedroom, leaving me alone.

I peered at myself in the mirror above the sink, noting my paler than usual skin and smudges beneath my eyes. The violent heaves felt like they'd pulled a muscle in my sternum too—similar to what I'd experienced before but definite muscle soreness.

I probably just needed to curl up in our bed and sleep to set myself straight.

Emptied, my stomach seemed better, and that sense of hunger for the dinner Skylar had prepared for us returned.

Rhett pulled me into his arms before I crossed our room for the open door. "Sorry for how I reacted to her, but she's young and immature...she's...a *lot*."

I grinned. "Refreshing, I think you mean."

Rhett grunted, but it wasn't an agreement sound. "She messed up my hair."

"Gave you my favorite look—like you'd been thoroughly fucked," I joked, hoping to keep things light.

"She untied my tie like she had the right to touch me."

"Don't tell me you weren't dying to rip it off on your own. Why the hell you wear those damn things while flying, I'll never understand."

"It makes me feel put together."

Because his insides weren't, he didn't tack on, but I knew his tics.

"Loosen up a bit, Rhett. That's all she was impulsively hoping to help you do. It's been a rough couple of days, but we're home now. This is a safe place for you to relax."

"Doesn't feel too safe right now," he muttered, and I bit back a smirk.

Skylar threatened him in oh so many good ways.

"Give her a chance."

"I'll try, baby, but I'm so damn tired."

I squeezed him tighter, my heart overflowing with the vulnerability he'd been showing lately.

A soft sigh drew our attention to the doorway.

Skylar stood there staring. She mumbled something about dinner and hurried off.

Rhett scowled at the spot she'd vacated.

"You scared her away—and don't tell me your frown was an involuntary reaction."

"It was."

I rolled my eyes and messed up his hair again before moving toward the hallway. "Let's go eat, and for the love of fucking my sweet ass, please be kind. Skylar has heard enough negativity and judgment for her personality."

"You mean immaturity," Rhett muttered from behind me.

"Her sunshiny attitude," I corrected him while glancing over my shoulder to find him fixing his hair again. "Give her a chance, Rhett," I repeated. "*Please.*"

Lips pressed into a tight line, he nodded and followed me from our bedroom.

Skylar had set the table with precision, flatware aligned on their proper sides, glasses of wine off to the right and closer to the center than the water glass. She even had the dessert fork laying above the plates and cloth napkins folded atop to look like fans.

Surely Rhett would approve.

I lifted an eyebrow his way, but he ignored my unspoken nudge and moved to the head of the table.

Skylar came in from the kitchen, a cut-up chicken on the platter in her shaking hands.

I hurried to take it from her before she dropped it.

"Thanks," she whispered and eyed the spread as I set the dish down. "That's everything…"

I pulled out her chair to the left of Rhett and helped settle her before rounding around my lover to sit across from her. My grin stretched my lips even though neither of the people sitting down to dinner with me appeared happy to be there.

My mouth watered regardless of the tense silence, and I picked up the chicken platter, ready to fill my plate.

"So what did you do all day yesterday and today?" I asked Skylar and handed her the chicken.

"Um…walked on the beach? Searched online for job openings?" She made the statements more like questions as though asking if we approved of her actions, and my smile threatened to dissolve.

Talk about fucking baggage. I wanted to pull her into my arms and help her find her fiery confidence I'd caught sight of a few times with how she tilted her chin in small acts of defiance.

"Did you find anything that sounds promising?"

"There's a grocery store a few miles away hiring baggers."

I piled some mashed potatoes on my plate while glancing over at Rhett.

He frowned—big surprise.

At least the boy ate his veggies. Half his plate was filled with the roasted broccoli, his favorite.

"What does your resume look like?" Rhett asked, but his tone didn't sound interested in the least.

"I don't have one?"

Again with the question.

"That's alright." I smiled across the table. "We can make one together tomorrow and then we'll drive around and fill out applications at wherever you think might be a good fit for you."

"I used to work in a toy store."

"Used to?" Rhett asked, and even though I appreciated his trying to converse, I didn't like his tone or his questions.

"I was late one too many times, and my boss let me go."

The sounds of clinking silverware on plates sounded loud as I reminded myself Rhett was exhausted and probably internally grieving the loss of his mom even if he wouldn't acknowledge that truth.

"I saw you made pie," Rhett surprised me by saying.

Pink flushed Skylar's cheeks as she glanced at him. "Ashton said coconut cream was your favorite, so..." She shrugged as though what she'd done was no big deal, but her act portrayed how much she wanted to please him.

Warmth filled my chest at the way she gazed shyly at Rhett, and her obvious attraction to him enticed blood to my groin.

Rhett studied her face, and had I not known the man better, I would have thought him unmoved.

He appreciated her beauty as I'd expected he would. The lure of her innocence and lack of pretenses and games like those we surrounded ourselves with intrigued him even if he wouldn't admit to it.

My dick swelled with optimism.

Perhaps Rhett needed to get out of his head and allow

his body to respond to her draw like I expected his instincts suggested.

"Dinner is delicious, a perfect pairing for the pinot noir." Rhett finally broke their stare off, his voice full of warmth. "Thank you."

Skylar visibly shivered at his lowered tone, licking over her lip as Rhett's focus shifted to his plate. She glanced across the table at me, and I winked, deepening her blush.

Hope was a heady thing.

19

RHETT

There was no denying Skylar called out to me like a sexy siren, but she'd entered my line of sight like a wrecking ball, creating havoc in my brain with every word and action.

Delicious dick—why the hell would Ash discuss our sex life with a complete stranger? Sure, how he'd describe my cock made my chest want to puff up in pride, but still.

The rest of her going-ons about how gorgeous she found me swelled my ego too, but the messing my hair? Loosening my tie?

The woman didn't understand personal space.

You'd like to be all up in hers and bury your face between her thighs.

My jaw ticked, but I wouldn't refute its truth. Imagining her writhing beneath me, panting against Ash's neck made me hard.

Add in she'd baked me my favorite pie, and I wanted to cave regardless of her many shortcomings.

Impulsive.

Silly.

Unpolished as they came.

Skylar annoyed and intrigued the hell out of me in equal measure, and I felt like a rope being pulled in two directions.

She'd stirred up a neediness inside me that went beyond desiring her physically—I had a deep urge to hear assurance of Ash's love. Pulling him against me in our bedroom before dinner had been a reaction of the sense of our foundation rocking.

I hated that she made me sense weakness inside—but it was the way Ash stared at her with longing in his eyes that twisted me up tight.

He wanted her in our bed for more reasons than my body did, and I fought the need to say no and the equally strong desire to give him everything he dreamed about.

I shoved against the barrage of thoughts clamoring for attention in my head and focused on eating the surprisingly good meal Skylar had made. Having grown up on a farm, I expected simple meat and potatoes, but she'd somehow honed her skills.

A hint of rosemary flavored the chicken, and I'd never tasted such creamy, decadent mashed potatoes. The broccoli? To fucking die for with the perfect amount of garlic that hadn't burned while roasting, the black pepper just spicy enough to hit the tongue in all the right places.

Having promised to try at giving the ridiculous woman a chance, I asked Skylar about her background, hoping Ash didn't think I did so merely to examine with my usual critical mind.

She eventually relaxed enough that her smile returned as the three of us talked like any other threesome date Ash and I had gone on. Their connection was as obvious as the air I filled my lungs with, as potent as the rich wine cleaning my palate.

It went beyond both of them having twin siblings, like their souls had already somehow intertwined through intimacy I knew they hadn't yet shared. He was already besotted with the woman, that much was clear with how he stared at her and gave her his full attention.

I almost walked out a few times as they got caught up speaking to one another, leaving me on what felt like the outskirts of their own little world. My usual self-control had me biting my tongue on more than one occasion to one-up the whirlwind of a girl who'd shaken my life's footing. I wanted to snarl at her that Ash belonged to me, but being vocally possessive would reveal my weakness.

I couldn't have that.

The way her fork slid past her lips, the flick of her tongue over the lower...how her mouth lightly touched her wine glass's rim drew my focus over and over, dissolving my tightened guts time and again.

It would be easy to allow the lust I experienced for her to overrule my better sense.

She didn't appear or sound manipulative. Like Ash had stated, Skylar seemed genuine and sweet, uninterested in games like some of the money-hungry women we'd interacted with over the previous couple of years.

She also leaned forward and listened intently to every word Ash spoke, validating whatever emotions he so willingly shared.

But I didn't smile or allowed myself to admit she was a breath of fresh air.

The first bite of the pie she'd made for me wrecked me —enticed a moan from my lungs and brought silence to the table.

I glanced over to find Skylar staring, pupils swelling and pink flushing her unpainted cheeks.

Well fuck.

Clearing my throat, I shifted to ease the sudden ache in my groin. "Best coconut cream pie I've ever tasted."

Her face beamed like a burst of sunlight through the clouds, and I swallowed back another groan attempting to rise from my chest. It physically hurt to pull my focus off her beauty, but pie made it easier.

I stuffed myself until I didn't want to move.

The three of us cleaned up together, and I refused to admit how easily Skylar fit in our space, flitting around the kitchen while tidying up and putting everything away exactly where she'd found it without fail.

Ash had warned me she had difficulty focusing, but she seemed to have no issues once she set her mind on a task.

I could appreciate that in a woman...

"It's still early," Ash said when we finished up. "Want to have another glass of wine and cool off in the pool?"

While I'd have preferred to pass the fuck out, Skylar's smile lit the goddamn room. She glanced at me, pink once more flushing her cheeks. "Um...sure? If you're up for it, Rhett? I can imagine you must be exhausted."

"I'm fine." A lie, but what else was new?

"Another bottle of pinot noir?" Ash asked, bending to open the wine fridge.

"Riesling," Skylar and I both replied as one.

My lips twitched, but I fought off the smile, same as the first time we'd agreed on the choice of wine to go with our dinner.

Heat still clung to the air and the pavers of our patio when Ash and I let ourselves outside. We had both changed into swimming trunks even though I had no intention of getting in the water.

I settled into a lounger facing the pool and ocean beyond, enjoying the slight breeze that came with the crashing of waves along the beach while I popped the cork on the riesling.

Three glasses in hand, Ash leaned down, and I tipped back my head, offering my mouth. He kissed me gently, a lingering of lips without intent to take things further.

"Thank you."

I knew what he meant and simply nodded while pouring into the glasses he held. Not bothering with being skimpy, I filled all three to the brim, emptying the bottle.

"Would you mind if I invited her into our bed tonight?" Ash asked quietly.

"I'm too tired to fuck," I stated the honest truth even though thoughts of the three of us definitely interested my body.

"How about pleasuring her?"

"I'll probably pass out the second my head hits the pillow, but if not..." I shrugged, knowing very damn well my bed and his presence would give me the sleep I craved after almost a week of living in a damn hotel room.

Ash hesitated, glancing at the house.

"As long as you're in the middle," I said, "I don't mind what goes down tonight. Just...keep your dick to yourself unless I'm awake and involved."

Ash leaned over and kissed me again. "Love you."

"You too." I sipped my wine, the tangy sweetness slid down my throat, and I sat back, stretching my legs out in front of me.

The French door opened behind us, and Ash grinned at the sight of our houseguest. Heat flushed through me, but it wasn't arousal—it accompanied that fucking dry throat shit I'd had going on since we got home.

What the fuck?

Frowning, I took a large gulp of my wine.

We needed to have a serious discussion about moving forward outside the sexual draw which I couldn't deny. Not having a plan set into place for a future relationship or even knowing Skylar's thoughts on how to get her feet under her didn't encourage relaxation in my muscles.

She entered my periphery, stealing my breath.

Rather than the itty-bitty bikini I'd expected she would tempt us with, a modest one-piece covered her pale skin. But the moonlight kissed along her curves, making her glow with a radiance that caused me to hunger for a taste.

"Come on." Ash gave her one glass and laced their free hands together. "We can sit on the seat cut into the pool's side."

Skylar glanced at me as though questioning if I wanted to join.

I'd had a long as fuck day and wasn't in the mood to entertain or flirt even if my dick could easily be persuaded. "Go on."

I brooded as they settled onto the water-covered seat, giggling quietly about something. They clinked their glasses together and sipped, and I bit back a moan as Ash held Skylar's wine so she could twist up her hair and reveal her long, slender neck.

My mouth drooled to latch on and mark her delicate skin.

Dick once more swelling, I took a good swallow of my wine, staring as the two angled closer, getting cozy as fuck.

Underwater lights illuminated their bodies, giving me a

clear view of Ash's hand on her thigh and how her nipples hardened at his touch.

I sipped again, turned on as fuck yet thoroughly exhausted.

Skylar Larsen wasn't exactly the type of woman I wanted in our lives, a seemingly live wire of emotion who unsettled...and I'll admit scared the hell out of me.

Ash leaned in and whispered in her ear.

Skylar's gaze shot to me. That luscious shade of pink rose across her cheekbones again before she once more faced Ash.

He looked at me, and I could all but hear his question.

Do you mind if I kiss her?

I nodded, bracing myself for whatever negative feelings attempted to tear me apart from the inside out.

20

SKYLAR

Ashton touched my cheek and leaned in, erasing all thoughts of anything but the softness of his lips, the sweetness of his exhaled sigh.

I could feel the potency of Rhett's stare as powerfully as I did Ashton's tongue when he licked into my mouth. Arousal swept through my blood, thoroughly heating my core, and I whimpered, trying to shift closer when we already touched thigh to thigh.

My pussy contracted at the gentle nip of Ashton's teeth over my lower lip, and I realized my wine glass tipped.

"Oh shit!" I pulled back, righting the glass even though a healthy swallow or two had added to the pool water. "Sorry. You kind of made me forget I was holding this."

Ashton chuckled like he didn't care I'd spilled wine in their pool I'd lazed around in the day before. "I'm not sorry."

I smiled from the radiant joy washing through me, knowing too many feelings shone in my eyes. "Then I'm not either."

We laughed again, and the silence from the other side of the patio drew my focus.

Rhett held my gaze while finishing off his wine, and I swallowed hard, my upturned lips losing their ability to stay that way.

He hadn't been nearly as mean or cutting at dinner as I'd expected for someone with his personality type—especially considering all the stupid shit I'd said when we first met. I appreciated he seemed to be giving me the opportunity to prove myself to him, but that only intensified my itchy feet and jittery insides.

"I'm heading in to bed," he announced, standing to his feet. Ashton shifted away as though to follow him, but Rhett held up his hand. "I don't mind if you stay up later," he told Ashton, "and even though the sight of the two of you kissing is hot as fuck, I just can't keep my eyes open any longer."

He turned and strode into the house.

Ashton sat on the seat's edge, poised to move, yet he stayed put as Rhett had suggested.

"You can go," I said even though I wanted to beg him to remain with me.

He hesitated another moment but shook his head and slid back into place, his thigh against mine. Ashton retrieved his glass from where he'd set it on the pool's ledge. "It *is* still early, I've got a gorgeous woman beside me, and the weather couldn't be better."

"It's California—the weather is always perfect," I stated, shivering over the thoughts of winter winds across the plains.

No way in hell I would ever go back there.

"Were you serious about helping me make a resume tomorrow? I'm not sure there's much to brag about with my work history, but I guess I should have one anyway."

"We'll find you something, Sky. But in the meantime, I

hope you'll treat our home as your own. You definitely acquainted yourself with the kitchen."

"And the rest of both floors," I declared before thinking I ought to keep my explorations to myself even though he had suggested I do so.

"Did you open every drawer and cupboard you found?" he asked, his eyes telling me he joked.

"Spent too much time rifling through your underwear drawers and bedside tables," I shot back, giggling.

"So, you found our stash of sex toys."

I choked on the wine I'd sipped, coughing while Ash laughed. "N-No," I sputtered since I hadn't gone *that* crazy in my nosiness.

"Sometime soon you'll get to play with us." Ash held my gaze while swallowing some wine.

"Tease," I whispered.

He took my wine and set both our glasses aside. "Come here." Warm hands clasped my waist and easily pulled me through the water so I sat atop his lap, straddling his strong, thick thighs. He slid his hands around my waist, drawing me closer.

"Oh!" I touched his chest with both my palms as his hard length brushed against my aching clit. A few gyrations would easily get me off—

"I have a good feeling about this, Sky," he murmured, the nickname he'd gifted me causing tears to spring to my eyes.

"So do I," I whispered, sliding my hands over his shoulders and settling my breasts against his chest.

He brushed his nose over mine, teasing as he'd done before the first time our lips had become acquainted. "We've only just met, but it's like we were destined to come into each other's lives at the perfect time. I know that's weird—"

"It's not weird. I feel the same way."

Ashton pulled his head back enough he could see my face. "Falling would be so easy, and even though I should guard my heart...I don't want to."

"Neither do I."

He banded one arm around my waist, his other hand sliding up my back to tangle in my messy bun. "The timing isn't perfect for Rhett with his mom and all—he doesn't know how to handle grief, but your being here will help."

"Distraction," I added what he didn't say.

"No—you're an emotional creature who can't help but draw others out of their shells. Rhett needs you in his life just as much as I do."

A sweet ache swelled inside my chest.

Was it possible to fall in love so quickly? To experience a connection so deep you feared living if the other disappeared from existence?

Overwhelmed and having no words to explain the feels Ash had woken up inside me, I leaned in and brushed his soft lips with mine.

"Sky," he murmured, tightening his hold on me before deepening our kiss.

There was no rush of lust, no frantic clothes-ripping to sate our bodies, but he quickly took me to the edge of reason.

Had Ashton pulled out his dick, pushed my bathing suit off to the side to reveal my aching pussy, I'd have gladly let him thrust up into me. Spill in me. Make a baby inside me.

I hovered on the edge of ecstasy, whimpering over the fact two layers of clothing separated our skin where I needed his touch the most—but he eased me back, slowing the rising urgency in our kiss.

We both breathed heavy when our lips separated, the

moonlight and the underwater lights of the pool illuminating the desire etched on his face. Black pupils dominated the hazel-green of his eyes, a flush on his cheeks.

"Rhett," he whispered, and I knew that's why he'd stopped us from taking things too far.

I nodded because I agreed, even though I'd have given anything to tip over the edge and come undone in Ashton's arms. "It's probably best if we both went to bed too," I suggested, sliding from his lap.

He let out a sigh that sounded as frustrated as I felt and followed me out of the pool and back into the kitchen once we'd dried off.

"Leave them," Ashton said when I reached to turn on the water to wash our wine glasses and the one Rhett had left in the sink. He entwined our fingers and pulled me against his warm body, nosing along my jawline to my ear. "Stay in our bed tonight?"

A shiver slid down my spine, raising the hairs on every inch of my body. "T-To sleep?"

"Yes." He kissed my cheekbone, my nose, then my lips. "I'm tired, but I'm not ready to let go of you just yet."

I hesitated from answering, thinking of Rhett and what he might want, but the desire to give Ashton what he asked for attempted to sway my mind.

Strong people, *intelligent* people knew what choices to make. They had knowledge of what to do and when, then did it—exactly like Nora had done since our childhood.

Thoughts of inadequacy slammed into me, and I tightened my hold on Ashton's hand.

"Will Rhett be upset to wake up and find me sharing a bed with the two of you?" I decided to ask, not wanting to step on any toes.

"I already talked to him about it, and he gave his consent."

My breath rushed from me as my heart fluttered. "Then yes."

A rash decision, but I didn't care.

His smile in response to my answer sent tingles throughout my body.

Ash led me from the kitchen, flicking off the lights behind us. My pulse thundered as we crept up the stairs, but the warmth of his grasp on my hand gave me courage to continue forward.

I left him in the hallway beside my bedroom door, promising him I would go to him and Rhett as soon as I changed out of my wet suit.

"Don't make me wait too long," he whispered and quickly kissed me.

Hands shaking, I stripped off the wet bathing suit and hung it in my bathroom to dry. I brushed the taste of wine off my teeth and tongue and pulled on a thin tank top and sleep shorts.

Just to sleep, I reminded myself, but I couldn't keep arousal from flushing my chest and heating my core. All four limbs shaky, I hurried down the hallway for the other side of the house and their bedroom.

The door stood open, the large windows spilling in moonlight across their king-sized bed.

Rhett breathed deeply from one side—light still shone beneath their bathroom door.

I stood unmoving, inhales shallow while waiting for Ashton to finish readying for bed. No way in hell would I climb onto that mattress without him even though I felt sure Rhett slept.

Ash exited a minute or so later, wearing boxer briefs that

hugged his half-hard length and ass. The rest of his muscular body wove in and out of moonlight and shadow as he approached the bed.

Ash held out his hand.

Swallowing a rush of drool, I moved toward him.

"Okay?" he whispered as our hands clasped.

"Yeah." I sure as hell didn't sound it, and the jitters quaking me in my skin didn't back up that answer, but nothing in that moment raised any sort of discomfort or thoughts that I ought to leave.

Ashton tugged me, leading me to their bed. He crawled in first, his back to Rhett. As though his slumbering lover knew he'd arrived, Rhett wrapped his arms around Ash, sighing heavily.

My chest squeezed tight, but Ash held out his hand again, and I couldn't deny the offering. Like a ninja squirrel, I scampered carefully onto the bed, making him chuckle with how I couldn't seem to join him quickly enough.

"Hi," he whispered, pulling me fully against his front.

"Hi back," I whispered my reply, arousal once more pulsing through me at the warmth of his skin, the hardness of muscle along my front.

Rhett's arm lay trapped between our chests, and he shifted, letting out another soft exhaled sigh.

Ash smiled and kissed me gently. "Sleep, Sky."

I doubted that would happen anytime soon, but I closed my eyes anyway, attempting to ignore the more than semi hardened dick pressed against my thigh and the heat of Rhett's arm against my beaded nipples.

Torture of the sweetest kind...

21

ASHTON

Roiling nausea pulled me from sleep, and I swallowed a few times, determined to will away the sudden need to vomit.

My body didn't listen.

It was the middle of the night, and both Rhett and Skylar slept like the dead as I maneuvered from the heaven between them to hurry for the guest room's bathroom so my retching wouldn't wake them.

Violent heaves emptied my stomach, and still I hugged the toilet, my insides attempting to exit up my raw throat.

I ached a little, but I wasn't feverish, didn't feel sick beyond the stomach.

Not food poisoning, otherwise I wouldn't be alone in my misery since we'd all eaten the same dinner.

Definitely a tummy bug...

Memories flooded my brain of my pale twin weak and vomiting with the same kind of force I did.

I retched again, coughing on nothing.

"Fuck." I spit the acidic taste from my mouth, eyes clenched tight thinking about Archer and the signs no one in our family had considered to be serious until it was too late for a cure.

My heart sped up, and I went lightheaded. I lay on the cool marble floor, focusing on counting to keep a panic attack from taking over.

Or were my dizziness and shortness of breath two more symptoms...

I turned off my morbid thoughts, focusing on the picture in my head of Skylar in our bed. Her soft, satiny skin beneath my fingertips, the way she fit against me as perfectly as Rhett did.

He had been out of sorts since learning about our houseguest, but I hadn't expected any different. He did, however, surprise me by conversing like a normal human being over dinner, same as he did whenever we'd met up with potential women.

That hope I'd had remained throughout the evening, overshadowing the slight nausea and indigestion that had returned after eating.

He'd watched us in the pool after giving me the okay to invite Sky into our bed, but his gaze remained closed off as usual. He wasn't averse to her—I recognized the flashes of heat in his gaze a few times during dinner.

When he reached out of his own accord to touch and taste would be the day I knew his interest went beyond the physical. He'd never agreed to sex with a woman since we'd begun searching for our angel unless he approved of her character.

If something happened to me...

The air rushed from my lungs as though I'd been punched.

No, no, no...

I opened my eyes and blinked against the harsh light I'd flicked on overhead before falling to my knees.

Rhett would be torn apart if I got sick and cancer ate at my blood and bones like it had to Archer. He would need someone to hold, a rock to cling to, someone else to love him and help him deal with his emotions.

"You're overthinking this shit," I muttered to myself and pushed up to lean against the wall. "Stop focusing on it…"

The lightheaded feeling had faded, the nausea gone.

"It's acid reflux or a virus that needs to work its course, nothing more."

I used one of the packaged toothbrushes we kept beneath the sink for guests, scrubbing away the taste of bile and acid from my mouth.

When I returned to our bedroom, Rhett hadn't moved, but Skylar had rolled over to face the wall. Her hand lay beneath her face, without doubt leaving finger lines indented in her cheek. Lips parted, she breathed quietly, as peaceful as a sweet little lamb.

A perfectly-sized Ashton space lay empty between the two of them.

I couldn't help my smile or the sense of contentment as I crawled into the spot I'd vacated. Rhett gravitated to my back, same as he always did in his sleep, his arm once more wrapping tight around my chest to hold me close.

I reached out for Skylar's waist, tugging until she stirred and shifted toward me. Nosing over her mass of lush hair, I breathed in the scent of coconuts, my fingers splayed over her soft belly.

Blood trickled southward into my groin regardless of the previous half-hour of heaving and talking myself out of a panic attack.

My pinkie moved on its own, caressing back and forth

along the bottom hem of Skylar's tank top, easing beneath to rub over soft skin.

She sighed and snuggled closer, the round globes of her ass pressing right up against my dick.

Fucking hell.

I closed my eyes, my pinkie still caressing, my heartbeat picking up pace.

Skylar shifted against me, a blatant rub against my hard cock.

"Sky?" I whispered, and she pushed my hand down over her belly, cupping my palm over her pussy. Damp heat radiated from her core through her shorts, and I bit back a groan.

She moved against me as though seeking release. Asleep or not, she'd given me the green light at the question in my voice when I'd said her name.

Rhett had said I could pleasure her...

My dick bucked against her ass, wanting in on the fun too, but fucking would wait until Rhett was fully on board.

I shifted my hold back up to her belly—and slid my entire hand beneath her sleep shorts.

No. Fucking. Panties.

"Fuck," I whispered, my eyes clenched tight as my fingers slid over slippery, smooth folds.

She'd shaved herself bare, and the nub of her clit swelled, thicker than I'd ever felt on a woman. While I'd never gone down on a woman before, my tongue salivated to suckle and lick, draw her hardened flesh as deep into my mouth as possible.

Skylar lifted her hips toward my fingertips trailing over her clit, and I slid them down, giving her what she wanted.

Wet heat clasped at my middle finger as it pressed deep into her pussy.

A whimper assured me she was awake.

I ground against her ass, moving in time with my finger as I fucked in and out of her soaked core.

Precum smeared inside my briefs, but I pushed against the desire to rut and focused on making her feel good. "Take these off," I whispered, pulling from her slick heat to tug on her shorts.

She shimmied quietly, gently, as though having no wish to pop the bubble around us, and I snaked my free arm beneath her torso, up under her shirt. She lifted her thigh, offering free access. I gently squeezed her hardened nipple and slid two fingers into her tight sheath.

"Ash," she whispered, arching as I ground the heel of my palm against her clit and fucked her with slow strokes.

"Come on my fingers," I whispered over her ear, needing her release more than I wanted to find my own.

Either Skylar had gone too long without an orgasm or our kissing earlier had edged her to the point of combustion even though she'd slept.

She came quickly with a quiet gasp, her pussy clamping down on my fingers, her cum coating them. A shudder rippled over her, and the second she went lax, I lifted my fingers from between her thighs and sucked them clean.

Sweet yet musky, her taste throbbed lust through my groin. She rolled to face me, grasping my face and kissing me deeply as though wanting to suck her flavor from my tongue.

She reached down between us, but I grabbed hold of her wrist to keep her from my dick.

"Please," she whispered, but I pulled our clasped hands back up between our chests.

"Go back to sleep, sunshine," I murmured even though I

knew I wouldn't be doing so any time soon if at all the rest of the night.

She huffed but settled in, nestling me tightly between her soft body and Rhett's much harder frame.

I should have felt trapped in a hell of frustration, but I'd found heaven. Balls aching, dick throbbing, I closed my eyes and smiled.

Someday, it would be my dick her pussy tried to suck in deeper, attempting to coax every last drop of cum from my balls to coat her womb.

22

RHETT

Reality leaked into my brain, pulling me from sleep, but I ignored my mind's desire to fire on all cylinders and start planning for the day.

Ash's back plastered to my chest and groin made grinding my morning wood against his ass a necessity as it always did when I woke up hard and horny for him.

I splayed my fingers over his abs—and realized soft skin pressed against the back of my hand.

The scent of coconuts registered in my mind at the same time, jolting my length against Ash's backside.

A simple lift of my head, a few blinks to clear my sleep-hazed vision, and my suspicions confirmed as truth.

Skylar snuggled into Ash's front, her hair a wild mane of red over our pillows.

Images from the night before flashed through my brain —Ash's hand on her thigh beneath the water, their lips tasting each other's. I'd lusted to join in but hadn't been in good headspace to get caught up in the physical, hookup or more.

Cracks had ruptured in my wall, which had sent me

hurrying to bed. Even though I wondered what they did in my absence, I knew Ash wouldn't put his dick in her, and she'd chipped away at my resolve throughout our evening, lessening my dislike over the thought of the two of them touching outside my presence.

I'd passed out into darkness, gladly giving my thoughts over to sleep.

That vulnerability that had me escaping them the night before returned in full force as I stared at her in our bed, a longing for something deeper than I'd ever felt leaving me off balance.

Uncomfortable.

I shoved against the foreign feeling attempting to take control over my mind and body.

My grip on Ash's hip tightened, and he reached down, sliding his fingers through mine.

He was awake.

As though of the same mind, we moved our hands across his flesh to Skylar's thigh. My skin burned at the contact of her smoothness, and we skimmed higher, straight to her bare fucking ass cheek that fit in my hand like she'd been created just for me.

"Fuck," I grunted the word, lust jerking my dick against Ash.

"I touched her last night," Ash whispered. "Got her off with my fingers—but that was all."

His ass felt so fucking good against my hard dick, and her sweet globe filling my palm showed me exactly why he hadn't been able to keep his hands to himself.

"This ass," I hissed, rubbing hers and thrusting against his.

"Mmm," he hummed in agreement, leaving my palm on her backside to skate his down along her thigh again.

Skylar stirred, her long auburn lashes blinking as her eyelids fluttered upward.

Her pale green eyes gaze flitted from Ash to me where I'd propped on an elbow behind him.

She didn't speak, but her swelling pupils, hardened nipples beneath her tank, and the parting of her lips stated what she wanted.

And I was too goddamn horny to overthink denying the gorgeous minx.

I rolled away, yanked open the bedside table's drawer, and fished for what I needed. A quick tear of the foil wrapper by my teeth, and I huddled over Ash once more, reaching between him and Skylar to roll the condom onto his hard length. Intentional brushes of the backs of my knuckles against her pussy assured me she was wet and ready for him.

Holding her gaze, I bit his earlobe. "Give Skylar your dick, baby."

I grabbed the back of her knee, lifting her leg over his hip—she didn't fight my granting him access to her body. Skylar scooted in closer and held my gaze as Ash shifted.

She blinked rapidly, her mouth falling open as his ass flexed, and he sank his length into her pussy.

"Oh fuck," he groaned, his grasp on her thigh tightening.

"She feel good?" I whispered over his ear, flicking my tongue out to make him shiver.

"So good. Yes. Fuck."

Lust hazed Skylar's eyes, but she still stared at me with unwavering focus, all trace of silly girl gone to the woman gazing at me like I'd made her dreams come true.

"I think she wants you to move, baby," I told Ash.

He pulled out and pushed back into her body, both of them moaning, Skylar's eyelids fluttering closed.

I wasn't the only one with a delicious dick.

But mine dripped like a mother fucker, and Ash's ass felt *so—damn—good*—rubbing over my sensitive cock head.

I rolled once more, my stomach tight with the need to shove home, and a quick lubing allowed me to smear up through his crack as he slowly fucked in and out of Skylar.

Getting off in that position would be easy, but I wanted —needed—more, to be connected to the two of them.

My fingers replaced my cock, a few slides between his cheeks coating them in lube. I rubbed over his hole.

"Rhett..." He groaned, bearing down on his outward stroke. "Yes."

I slid one finger deep into his ass without resistance, moving my hand forward with him as he sank back into Skylar with a deep, guttural moan.

Two fingers earned me a curse and a mystified glance from Skylar whose face flushed a gorgeous shade of pink.

"I'm fucking his ass with my fingers," I murmured the answer to her unspoken question.

"Oh..." She swallowed hard and reached over Ash to grab hold of my wrist.

Kinky little thing...

I couldn't help a lust-filled grin while twisting my hand to gain control of hers and wrap it around my dick. "Help me out, Skylar," I murmured, moving my hips forward and touching the tip of my dick against his hole.

"Fuck yes, Rhett..." Ash pushed against me, and I slid into his body.

Skylar's hand moved away, and I pressed in fully until his body moved against hers.

"You just... oh wow. Just...*wow*." She gulped and clutched at my hip as I pulled out and shoved back into Ash's ass, fucking his dick deeper into her body.

I didn't even have time to set a rhythm before she came with a soft cry, shuddering in Ash's arms.

"Oh fuck." Ash choked on the words. "So fucking close. Rhett," he begged through clenched teeth, and I grasped both of his hips, angling to peg his prostate.

"I'll always take care of you, baby." Three harsh strokes, and he shot off, his ass clenching at my girth, dragging me along with him for one of the shortest rides of our lives.

"Holy shit...Christ." I erupted with a deep groan, each spurt contracting my abs and jerking my dick deep in his silken ass. "*Fuuuck*," I moaned at the last twitch that left me rasping for breath and damn near boneless in contented bliss.

Skylar released a shuddered sigh but surprisingly didn't say a word. Guess we'd fucked her senseless.

Still buried deep, I moved to wrap Ash in my arms—but reached beyond, my fingers finding softer flesh to help better bracket him in a cocoon of spent, satiated warmth.

I'd orchestrated the event, allowing Ash to have a taste of Skylar, but fuck if I could keep that unease from earlier creeping back in and leaving me questioning the decision I'd made.

Skylar and I had connected over a silly thing like wine the night before, and my damn reservations crack a little more as she trailed her fingertips over Ash's face and sighed again.

Giving into lust and my desire to please Ash had taken us past the point of safe exploration where hearts wouldn't get involved.

Both of theirs already had, but until I figured her out...

I slammed my walls back into place since I didn't know the woman. Couldn't fucking trust her with Ash's heart let alone mine until she proved herself.

She kissed his forehead, his nose. His mouth, their lips lingering together.

Her eyes lifted to my face—and I rolled away before her impulsiveness landed her mouth on mine.

That would be a line I couldn't cross with any hope of remaining untangled in what both seemed to have set their minds on.

I slipped into the bathroom and put on the shower's harshest setting.

For the first time since working together with Ash to help a woman find release, I was the one to leave our bed.

My stomach twisted up as tight as my jaw. I needed to focus on some sort of plan to redirect the path I'd opened up into the unknown. A new beginning...or an ending.

I wasn't sure which I wished for.

23

SKYLAR

I dreamed...surely I did.

A pinch to my arm revealed I didn't.

"Did you...just pinch yourself?" Ashton asked with a chuckle while smoothing my hair away from my face.

"Um...yes?"

The shower turned on in the bathroom, and Ashton crushed my chest to his, fingers running through my hair until I wanted to purr like a kitten against his hard pecs. "You're cute," he murmured.

"And your dick is delicious," I spewed the first compliment that came to mind, very aware of his softening length still lodged inside me.

He chuckled again. "Wait until you have Rhett deep in your body."

"You think he'd want that?" I asked, remembering the wariness in his eyes when I'd considered kissing his lips too.

"He loves pussy as much as he loves a woman's ass, so that's a definite yes."

"How much is too much?" I bit my lower lip.

"Dick or information?"

I giggled and shoved at his chest, but the steel trap of his arms didn't budge from his place firmly locked around me.

"There's no such thing for the second, but as for the first, I wouldn't know. I've only had Rhett's, and he fits me perfectly."

Heat rushed through me again at the thought that Rhett had buried himself in Ashton while he'd been fucking me. "What's it like?"

"Anal sex?"

"Yeah."

"Uncomfortable at first, but once I adjust, my body craves more. Harder. Deeper. I can't get enough of him—never have, never will."

"And what's it like being inside me at the same time he's fucking you?"

Ashton moaned as his dick slid from my body. "Absolute perfection—heaven."

He shifted onto his back, removed the condom, and I soaked in the sight of his naked body since the morning light flooded through the windows unhindered by blinds or curtains.

Light brown hair covered his legs up over powerful-looking thighs, but he trimmed the patch around his groin area. A spattering of hair lined his lower abs that contracted as he tossed the tied-off condom aside, but his chest was smooth as a baby's butt.

I reached out to slide my hand over his pecs, and they flexed beneath my fingertips. "You have a gorgeous body," I murmured, my tone having a dream-like quality that made me sound like a lovesick fool.

"Did you catch sight of Rhett when he hightailed it out of bed?"

"A glimpse—not nearly enough. Why'd he leave us?" I

let out a huffed sigh and snuggled back against Ashton's pillow. I'd never cuddled after sex, never had someone who wanted to just lay there and chat about whatever popped into my mind.

"Don't take his escaping as a bad thing. It's not. I promise." Ashton grinned as though he held the secrets of the world while gathering me up in his arms again.

He didn't care about morning breath, so I didn't either, offering him my tongue when he licked over my mouth. The man's soft lips and the way he moved them over mine spiraled fresh arousal through my core. I was ready for round two, but I expected that wouldn't be happening anytime soon until Rhett figured out...whatever had sent him off in a rush to the bathroom.

I'd definitely made him uncomfortable, and it was more than just my personality that clashed with his.

"Do you think...I threaten him in some way?" I asked as Ashton's lips slid along my jawbone.

He pulled back enough to focus on my eyes. "Yes—and it's what he needs, so don't go getting all insecure, okay? Outside of bed, I haven't been able to help him release all the emotions he keeps clammed up inside, but I have hope that you can."

The Rhett Whisperer...

I giggled, but another idea popped in my head. "So you think I really am a good match for the two of you?" I wondered out loud then cringed. "I'm not fishing for compliments! That was my usual flighty thoughts spilling before they're fully processed."

Ashton's smile eased the sudden antsy feeling in my feet that made me want to pull away before he did. He held me tighter and nibbled on my chin. "You, my dear, are the sweetest ray of sunshine ever."

I met Ashton in the kitchen a half hour later, both of us freshly showered and dressed. Rhett wasn't with him. The thought he'd taken off to escape whatever he was feeling made my stomach twist.

"Where's Rhett?" I asked, heading toward the coffee pot where Ashton waited for the machine to finish gurgling him a cup.

"Office."

Needing to touch Ashton, I laid my hand on his lower back. The heat of his body reached through his T-shirt to warm my palm. "Is he okay?"

"Yeah." He offered me a smile, but I took in the paleness of his face and frowned.

"Are you alright? Don't take this the wrong way, but you don't look so good."

He huffed a laugh and turned away to retrieve his coffee. "I'm fine. Just need some caffeine."

I didn't know Ashton enough to tell if he was lying or not, but his assurance didn't ring true.

Perhaps he and Rhett had words in the bathroom after I'd left their room for my own shower. Perhaps Rhett had regretted what we'd done or how much his partner had seemed to enjoy being with me.

But Ashton had told me they'd shared women before. Had our hooking up somehow hit Rhett in a different way? Was he second-guessing what had happened? Did he want me to leave?

All the questions made me realize the three of us moved forward a lightning speed, but I wouldn't go back and do things differently if given that option. Ashton and I had something real, and maybe Rhett and I had too earlier that morning, but what had sent him scurrying off like he was the one with antsy feet—

"Sky."

I realized I stared at the cabinet, unmoving for who knew how long. Forcing a smile, I turned to find Ashton peering at me. Concern furrowed his brow as his gaze flitted over my face. "Hmm?" I asked.

"Where'd you go just now?"

"Oh, just in the clouds." I waved my hand as though brushing aside my weirdness and set my sights on making my own coffee. "Two scoops of sugar and one unhealthy dollop of cream," I half-sang to myself, flitting toward the refrigerator.

I pulled open the door, and thoughts of coffee fled.

"Ooo, bacon!" I grabbed the rest of the pack I'd cooked from my first morning in Ash and Rhett's house, but my stomach screamed *French toast!*, so I retrieved the eggs and milk too. "Cinnamon…" I placed my supplies on the countertop and searched the spice drawer for what I wanted. "Powdered sugar?" I asked Ashton without turning.

"No—sorry."

"Not a problem!" I sing-songed. "Griddle?"

"Cabinet at your knees." His voice held a hint of a smile.

"Maple syrup or berries?" I tossed out my next thought as the image of a carton of blueberries I'd seen seconds before in the fridge registered in my brain.

"Syrup."

I hurried on itchy feet to gather a mixing bowl, a whisk, plates and forks.

Loaf of bread—check.

Butter—check.

Frying pan for the bacon…that should have been done first since it would take the longest.

I lit the stove's flame, focusing on peeling off strips of bacon from the pack and lying them in the heating pan.

Perfect.

Now...bread.

Already got that—

"Sky."

I jerked around, having forgotten I wasn't alone in the kitchen.

Ashton grinned at me, holding out a mug of coffee.

"How did I...never mind." Face flaming over my absent-mindedness, I took his offering and sipped the blonde, steaming liquid. Perfectly sweet. "Thank you."

"You're welcome." His eyes glowed in a way that tingled arousal through my entire body, and my mind went back to the feel of his thickness pushing into my body and how I'd stretched to accommodate his girth.

An achingly sweet shiver rolled over me.

"Bacon," Ash murmured, pulling my focus back to the present—and his smile.

"Oh shit." I spun, the sizzle of fat and scent of bacon registering to my senses.

I used a pair of tongs to flip the bacon and ignored the eyes I could feel on my back in order to get the rest of our breakfast started.

"You said you've never been medically diagnosed with ADHD?" Ash asked, and I shook my head.

"My parents focused their attention on Nora, the gifted twin, since I just drove them nuts. She got all the brains, leaving me with close to none."

"I think you're incredibly intelligent," Ash argued, and I huffed my disagreement. "Perhaps not book smarts, but you're intuitive. Sensitive to other souls. Your empathy and the natural desire to soothe others is more important to me than straight A's or any college degree."

"I'll bet Rhett doesn't feel the same though, does he?" I asked with a slight frown, my wrist flying as I whisked the eggs into a froth of yellow.

Ash didn't answer right away, confirming my suspicions.

"How did Missing Link match us when Rhett and I are total opposites?" I asked, insecurity brewing in my stomach alongside the coffee.

"Because our profile showed what I desired—an angel to give us what we both need."

Children and emotional release.

But what about love—was that on the table? And if not, would I be content to have a piece of Ashton's heart and not Rhett's? Was my first adventure in a menage a one and done? What if Rhett wasn't interested in any part of me, simply wanted a physical relationship?

My shoulders tensed as I shook cinnamon into the egg mixture, remembering what Nora had told me about being a third wheel. "Is there even room in your relationship for another person, Ashton? Or am I wasting my time dreaming about dark-haired knights on white horses and happily ever afters?"

Ashton wrapped his arms around my waist, his chin on my shoulder.

The anxiety fled at his comforting touch, my body sagging against him.

"I desire more than your womb—so much more, Sky. I want your smiles, your laughter, and tears. All the good moments *and* the bad."

I ignored the voices in my head that sounded like Mom and Dad saying it was way too soon to be declaring such things.

"And what if that isn't what Rhett wants?"

"Then we have to change his mind." Ash pressed his lips to my neck and squeezed me tight. "There's no rush and no need to worry. With you all up in our space, he'll have no choice but to admit how perfect you are in every way."

I held in my snort, knowing Rhett would never see me as anything more than annoying.

But perhaps I could attempt to tone down a bit. Maybe I would grow on him if I made enough pies and created a happier home than the one he and Ashton had already built.

Chin lifting, I decided to do that very thing.

"There's the fire I needed to see." Ashton kissed my neck again and released me. "Should I let Rhett know breakfast will be ready soon?"

"The best one he's ever tasted," I sassed over my shoulder and winked.

Ashton snickered and left me to finish preparing their meal.

If only attempting to win someone over came as easily for me as cooking.

24

ASHTON

Rhett was the type who needed time to process, so I hadn't pushed a conversation that would set him on edge when I'd joined him in the shower. He'd already finished washing, so we shared a quick kiss while changing places.

Slight body aches had hounded me on and off since the day before, but the hot water soothed them away.

Rhett had been gone from the bathroom when I finished.

The kitchen had been empty—until it no longer was.

Sky's arrival had brought warmth to my blood and a smile to my lips. A simple sundress covered her gorgeous body, and the memory of being inside her for too damn short of a time had me wanting another taste.

I'd bid her a good morning, and her smile dazzled and enlivened every cell in my body with an addictive warmth. Pink had stained her cheeks when I'd asked if she'd slept all right. Her murmured affirmation had made my insides smile.

She'd zipped around the kitchen like a ball in a pinball

machine, every little murmur and quirk lighting me up with buzzing energy. Rather than helping her, I'd stood back and enjoyed the sight of her making herself right at home in our kitchen.

I'd imagined her belly swollen, her hand on the baby bump in loving caresses while she flipped the French toast.

Longing to see that reality weakened my knees and caused my throat to tighten. I used the excuse of telling Rhett that breakfast was ready to keep from crying.

I got hold of my emotions before I reached the office.

Rhett stood at the window with his back to the door. "You're helping her with her resume and headed out to fill applications today?"

He was in plan mode—all business as usual.

"I was thinking she could maybe come work for us."

Rhett turned toward me, face unreadable. His defenses were up— "No."

"It would give you the right to run a background check," I tossed out what might sway him.

"It's not a good idea, Ash. You fucked her, I know you want to do it again—and being involved with employees is a hard limit."

He had a point, but I wanted her near us all the damn time.

"Look." Rhett came closer, grasping the back of my neck. "She's got you wrapped up around her little finger, but we have to think with our brains, not our dicks. Instigating sex this morning wasn't one of my smartest ideas—"

"It's the most I've ever connected with a woman," I said, grabbing hold of his hips and pulling him against me.

He studied me in silence, his dark eyes assessing as always. "I'll admit she's beautiful, but she's...too much."

Her sister had stated the same.

My stomach tightened.

"What's wrong?"

I smoothed away the involuntary grimace on my face. "Keep an open mind, Rhett. Look beyond the quirks for the inner beauty, the sweet-natured woman who desires to give love and be loved. She has so much to offer..."

"Bacon," he murmured at the same time the scent drifted past my nose.

"And French toast." I grinned, grabbed his hand, and tugged him toward the office door. "Let her spoil you rotten and show her appreciation in one of the ways she claims to do best."

I imagined being a recipient of her love in our bed but squashed the idea so my dick didn't lead the way into the kitchen.

Sky had settings on the breakfast nook table. A flush still painted her cheeks, and she'd wound her hair up atop her head in a messy bun.

Regardless of what Rhett decided he wanted, he couldn't take his eyes off her as she ordered us to sit.

"How do you like your coffee, Rhett?" she asked while pulling another mug from the cabinet.

"Black."

She huffed a quiet snicker. "Not surprised," she murmured but loud enough we both heard.

I choked back a laugh at Rhett's raised eyebrow.

"She has you pegged," I whispered, elbowing him.

A flash of heat went through Rhett's eyes and disappeared just as quickly as he shut down whatever thought—

Oh fuck.

Lust kicked me in the groin, and I glanced between him and Sky a few times. He'd never given his ass to anyone but me...did he have a secret kink I wasn't aware of? We had dildos aplenty but hadn't ever played with one attached to a female.

"What are you thinking about?" I asked while leaning into his space and sliding my palm over his groin.

He'd gone half-hard.

Snickering, I squeezed until he shifted beneath my hold. "Maybe Sky and I will stop by our favorite toy store—"

"Ash." Rhett's tone didn't recommend an argument, so I gave him space, having every intention of sitting back and enjoying the hell out of that show some day.

Sky set a steaming mug of coffee in front of Rhett, and his low, murmured "Thank you" tightened her nipples.

"You're welcome. I hope you like French toast. Bacon too. Oh, and cinnamon," she chatted while turning away. "I used the rest of the canned coconut cream leftover from the pie in the egg mixture—it smells divine—I think it'll taste good? I'm sure it will. Maybe."

Rhett's eyes tracked her as she retrieved a platter of French toast.

Her nervousness didn't dampen the sexual tension between them I'd noted from the moment they'd met.

My lover fought a losing battle, I assured myself when he closed his eyes and moaned around his first bite of breakfast.

The coconut twist wouldn't have been my first choice, but Sky's attention to pleasing him clicked all my buttons. I would gladly gorge on coconut everything if it meant she eventually won his heart.

Rhett went into the office downtown but told me to take the day and help Skylar find a job. He spoke as though he wanted her gone as soon as possible, but with the many limits she had—no car and no savings—I knew it would be a long time before she could afford to live on her own.

Sure, I could have easily have offered a loan to get her set, but that wouldn't allow her time to be all up in Rhett's space and break him down.

Considering her short work history, even I wondered over the skimpy resume we pieced together. No matter the exaggerated wording about customer service skills on paper, Skylar had no chance of landing anything other than a basic, entry-level job like high schoolers managed.

"Would you be open to seeing a doctor about your ADHD?" I asked as we headed to a small restaurant for lunch after filling out applications at most of the mall's stores.

"I don't have insurance, and I don't need a label beyond idiot."

I yanked my focus off the road to find her frowning. "It's a neurodevelopmental disorder, Sky."

"I'm well aware—I've read everything I could get my hands on. Struggling to focus on definitions, symptoms, and diagnosis has been proof enough I have issues."

"If you've read all that, then you know it's possible to manage."

"This is who I am!" she burst out, angling toward me and waving a hand around herself. "I-I thought you liked me—now you're talking like you want me to change to better fit the image of that angel yyou want. Well, I'm no angel. I'm a damn mess." Tears clogged her throat, and I cursed myself for causing her outburst.

"I *don't* want to change you," I assured her. "But you said you hate how antsy your feet get, how you wish you could focus beyond mundane tasks that you enjoy. There's medication that can help—and it won't alter *who you are*, Sky. No drug is going to take away your sparkle, the light and joy you bring into people's lives."

"Not all persons," she muttered, turning to stare out the passenger window.

"Their loss," I hastened to correct her negative thought. "And if people can't appreciate your sunshine, then you're better off without them."

"Rhett doesn't enjoy my type of sunshine."

A slow exhale sagged me into the driver seat as I pulled into a diner's parking lot. "Because he's never had it. Delightful happiness is something he doesn't understand or know how to process. His emotions are so damn repressed..." I shook my head, my heart aching over the inner wounds he hadn't yet learned to overcome.

The one time I'd suggested speaking with a therapist, he'd revealed his annoyance easily—and vocally. Not one for confrontation, I'd accepted the line he set in front of me and hadn't spoken of it again.

But his outburst had been proof those emotions he kept bottled up needed exorcised—by someone exactly like the woman sitting beside me. I felt sure Sky was the perfect chisel to breach his heart—or perhaps the flame to ignite the keg waiting to explode.

He had shown me his love, his unbridled passion, countless times in bed, but I rarely caught glimpses outside sex.

Bed.

The one place Rhett allowed vulnerability.

He hadn't been pleased with himself initiating sex that morning, but he'd been caught up in desire. We just needed to get him there and often, show him how lowering his walls would lend to breaking down his stoic life.

I parked, and Sky grabbed my forearm before I could climb from the car.

"I'm sorry for my outburst."

"There's no need to apologize for your emotions," I reminded her. "I understand your sensitivity—but I promise you, you're not alone, and the last name I would ever call you is an idiot." I cupped her cheek, and she leaned into my touch, her eyes closing. "You're beautiful just the way you are, Sky. I wouldn't change a thing—but I want you to be comfortable with yourself, to be happier. I think seeing a doctor and getting recommendations on how to regulate some of the tics you dislike about yourself will only add to your life. Not take away from."

She nodded. "You're right. I...I've just been called so many names—"

"Wouldn't you rather have a medical diagnosis than ignorant people's labels?"

"Yes." She opened her eyes, wetness causing the green of her orbs to intensify.

"You're so very beautiful—inside and out. I'll never stop saying it until you believe it."

Sky opened her mouth but slammed it shut in a rare display of self-control.

I grinned. "Don't you dare start regulating yourself now."

"I could fall in love with you so damn easily—I...I kind of am already—and that's weird, right? Too quick. I hardly know you. You're way outside my league but everything I've ever dreamed about. I want to carry your babies—"

I leaned in and claimed her mouth, my hand on her nape in a possessive hold like Rhett always did to me. She gave me hope so damn addicting I couldn't let her go.

"See?" she croaked out when I allowed her to breathe. "I'm so damn annoying you had to kiss me to shut me up."

"I kissed you because I'm falling for you too—easily. Happily. You're everything I desire and need in my life, Skylar Anne Larsen—and don't you ever forget it."

She sighed but didn't smile. "But Rhett..."

"He'll get there. You just keep being yourself. Spoil him rotten how I can see you'd like to do. Shower him with attention and affection."

"He doesn't seem to want it."

"You don't see the way he looks at you."

Her eyebrows shot up. "How's that?"

"Like he's dreaming of devouring you like a decadent meal and gorging on seconds."

"Oh!" Her pupils swelled.

"Yeah." Grinning, I pushed open my door. "Now let's go grab some lunch and plan how we can get him to fall too." My eyebrow waggle caused the car to fill with her laughter.

I wanted to hear her happiness until death parted us.

Hopefully later rather than sooner.

25

RHETT

A day away from the house and the whirlwind of erratic behavior sounded like what I needed, but with every passing hour buried under work at the office, I found myself restless...

To return home.

Unease kept me from focusing on details, but I managed to ignore the strangeness inside me and stayed through the regular hour when Ash and I usually headed back to the house.

He hadn't come into the office, taking a personal day to spend with Skylar, helping her find a job.

I hadn't said anything, but I wasn't fooled into thinking she would be out on her own, leaving my safe place in peaceful silence anytime soon. According to Ash, Skylar had no money for a deposit or first month's rent. She didn't have a car to get her to and from work. The cell phone she had belonged to her sister, and I was surprised her twin hadn't already turned the number off considering how Ash had said they'd left things when Skylar had driven away with him.

She had parents on the farm in South Dakota where she refused to return even if they paid for her ticket. Sounded like she didn't have a good relationship with them, something I knew all too well.

I didn't want to feel a pull toward her for that reason and squashed it as quickly as it had begun, giving my attention to the next thought.

I'd seen my fair share of manipulative women, but Skylar didn't give off that vibe. Either she was one hell of an actress, or she was simply a girl with issues and in desperate need of assistance.

While I didn't know much about ADHD, it was obvious she had problems focusing, and like a little kid, she had energy to spare. Both would be a hindrance in getting and keeping *any* job.

Finding a position for her in our corporation wouldn't work for the exact reasons I'd explained to Ash, not that she had the ability to complete tasks on time and in an organized manner like we required of our employees.

But that didn't mean we couldn't help her out.

Rather than give my secretary something to gossip over, I browsed local listings for apartments on my own. Ash and I could easily afford to get her a place that didn't include being in our space, but I feared he was already in too deep to let her go.

I'd consented to his inviting her into our bed and hadn't been surprised to find her there when I woke. But telling him to fuck her? Taking his ass while he did what I knew he'd woken up thinking about?

Impulsive.

Not like me at all.

I didn't step forward without plotting first, but something in that moment had felt too right, too enticing to consider fully. Rushing forward in my horniness without thoughts of consequence had left us sated, but what sort of emotional connection had I inadvertently allowed to settle into place between the two of them?

Skylar had watched Ash like she was half in love with him already while we had eaten breakfast, and he did the same with her. I caught her gaze flitting my way dozens of times, and I recognized her longing for what it was, but she just...didn't fit into the plans I'd laid for our lives.

Stubborn was my middle name, but I clutched to my damn self-preservation same as I did to the coldness instilled in me from childhood to keep emotion under wraps.

Fortitude.

Endurance.

Being unmoved in the face of danger—emotional or otherwise.

"Damn control freak." I rubbed over my scruffy jawline, knowing I had to let go, but how? Stoicism had been ingrained in my bone marrow.

I wasn't aware of any other way, and giving into *feelings* would be nothing but weakness.

Being unable to set a course or figure out the puzzle of myself brought on a goddamn headache. I made it through the rest of the work day, barely able to withhold a scowl from etching into my facial muscles.

I needed the silence of my home, the comfort of Ash's body, but I expected I wouldn't have either because of our houseguest.

Pop music blared from the house's sound system when I let myself into the kitchen.

Savory scents flooded my nose, but it was the noise level

and the sight on the far side of the kitchen that pulled me to a halt at the threshold.

Ash and Skylar danced around as if they were a couple of teenagers drunk on Boon's.

The running man.

The sprinkler.

Ash attempted a...was that a twerk? The man had one fine as fuck ass, but he sure couldn't shimmy it around.

I burst out laughing—and both jolted to a stop, gazes flying my way. Skylar's face went red, but Ash's grin widened.

"Come dance!" he called while spinning around and beckoning with his fingers.

I shook my head, willed my smile away, and put my bag on the countertop.

"Oh shit! Dinner!" Skylar hurried to the oven and pulled it open.

The scent of beef swarmed over me, turning my saliva glands the fuck on.

"Is that—"

"Beef Wellington, yes." She set the roasting pan atop the oven, and I crept closer for another sniff as the music shut off around us. "Ash said it was your favorite. And potatoes dauphinoise made with Gruyere and roasted brussels."

My mouth fucking *watered*. I swallowed. "Wine?"

"Bordeaux, of course."

She gently cupped my cheek, her smile dazzling— drawing me in like a siren and coiling tension in my muscles—

A soft giggle, and she moved off before I could crush my mouth to hers.

Goddamn. I stared in silence as Skylar did her thing, flitting around the kitchen like a beautiful fairy, all swaying hips and unbound breasts beneath her sundress causing my blood to race.

Ash elbowed me, pulling my focus. He smirked and loosened my tie before kissing me, his soft mouth lingering long enough that blood seeped into my dick, making my slacks feel too damn tight. "Welcome home."

"Mmm."

He tugged me by my tie toward the dining room.

"Are you attempting to seduce me?" I murmured, not hating the idea in the least.

"Do you *want* to be seduced?" he shot over his shoulder with a sexy smirk I hadn't seen in...far too fucking long.

"I'm not averse to the idea." Neither was my dick. I'd gone rock hard from that look in his eyes.

Three place settings sat atop the table, same as the night before. Two candles flickering, wine already poured and waiting. Ash pulled out my seat like a true gentleman and reached over my shoulder after I sat to shake open the fanned napkin and spread it on my lap.

His hot breath coasted over my ear as his knuckles brushed over my hard length. "Hungry?"

"You have no fucking idea," I muttered, knowing he spoke about more than food.

"We aim to please." His lips pressed against my neck, and I bit back a groan as my dick bucked beneath his touch.

Deciding there was nothing wrong with letting loose after the shitty week I didn't wish to think about, I set my focus on enjoying the evening ahead. Good food and a gorgeous, willing woman between us. Details could wait...I was feeling too damn gluttonous for all things delicious food and sex.

"Yes," I stated as firmly as I shifted to relieve the ache in my groin.

"Yes?" Ash echoed, stroking over my bulge.

"To whatever scheme you two plotted out."

His laughter drew a smile to my lips. "Drink your wine. I'll help Skylar bring in dinner."

My focus stayed on his fine-as-fuck ass until he disappeared from sight.

"Jesus fucking Christ," I muttered, pressing down on my dick that behaved like I hadn't unloaded in Ash's silken heat earlier that morning.

My body was insatiable when it came to him, but thoughts of having the gorgeous redhead between us heightened my lust until my pulse raced and my hand shook as I cut into my beef Wellington a short time later.

"Have you ever considered opening a restaurant?" I asked Skylar after the melt-in-your-mouth first bite landed on my tongue.

Skylar snorted, but the unladylike sound didn't curl my nose like it would have a mere week earlier. "That's a joke and a half."

I imagined running such an establishment would be beyond her ability. "You're an incredible cook." I found myself offering a compliment rather than saying anything else that might feed her insecurities.

"Thank you." That pink flush kissed her cheeks, and she glanced away when I held her gaze a second too long.

Hell, not long enough.

I got why Ash stared at her as often as he did. My own gaze trailed her way too. Everything from dining with her the night before hit me again. The fork between her lips. Peek of tongue. Lips on the wine glass.

The need throbbing through my dick didn't relent one goddamn bit.

"So how did the job hunt go today?" I asked, needing

something other than sex to occupy my mind—and I wanted to know when we might be rid of our houseguest, even though she'd grown on me...just a little.

"Twelve applications total," Skylar said, "and the grocery store Ash told me the two of you go to every week offered me a job on the spot—the last stop of the afternoon."

"Did you accept?"

"Yes. I start tomorrow." Her smile quickly faded. "I suck at counting change, so it's a good thing I'll be bagging the groceries rather than ringing them up. I'm so easily distracted. Hopefully, I'll last longer there than I did at the toy shop."

"Her shift starts a half hour after we head into work," Ash said, "so I can give her a ride and just come into the office a bit later."

I nodded, forking up my last bite of potatoes.

"And I'll catch an Uber home since it's not that far," Skylar tacked on.

Home—she made it sound as though she'd moved in permanently with Ash's blessing.

Unease brewed inside my guts along with that strange sense of rightness, and I didn't know what the fuck to think about either feeling.

"I'm going to clean up," Ash said as though hearing my thoughts and not wanting me to expand on them. "You two can take your wine into the living room."

Ash was giving me time alone with the woman who'd already captured his attention—and possibly a part of his heart. But how far was I willing to go before she got on my last nerve and I told him she wasn't going to work out?

I stood at the living room's edge, eyeing the couch and two chairs, my dick suggesting I sit on the first, my brain pushing for the second.

A gentle touch cradled my hip just like Ash always did, but soft breasts replaced hard pecs as Skylar leaned against my back. "Couch," she suggested in a near whisper that rippled awareness over my skin and had me biting back a groan.

I did *not* want to like her...or want her. But that latter part? Too fucking late.

26

SKYLAR

We sat on the couch, both of us half-facing one another, and he sipped his wine in my periphery while I studied my drink.

Ashton and I had planned for me to spend a little time alone with Rhett, and even though I thought I'd hit the jackpot as far as pleasing him with the dinner Ashton had suggested I make, I still felt highly inadequate to hold a conversation with Rhett.

Like Ashton, Rhett was polished, but he also held an air of reserved sternness that seemed more like superiority to me. My backside squirmed beneath his stare.

"Tell me your plans for the future, Skylar. Aspirations, goals...where do you see yourself in five years?"

The question turned my focus inward as a gazillion ideas leapt to life in answer to his question, but I managed to hold my tongue.

Barely.

I couldn't get my head on straight though.

"Don't overthink, Skylar. I want to know your thoughts, no matter how messy or fragmented. Just be honest."

Rhett's kind words eased the twisting in my stomach, and I chanced a glance at his face. Like that morning, he peered at me with something other than cool reserve.

A little heat, perhaps? That was probably just my fanciful mind dreaming.

My knee bounced as my feet grew itchy. I clutched my wine glass tighter, unable to hold his gaze. One last swallow, and I forced myself to set my empty glass on the coffee table in front of us.

"I desire to be loved for who I am," I spewed out my number wish while sitting back again. "Quirks and all—unconditionally. But, um...who doesn't?" I huffed a little laugh and rubbed my palms on my dress, more nerves than anything.

"What else?"

"A house of my own. Children." I shrugged, expecting the things I wished to pursue wouldn't have been his choice in a second partner. "I know I'm not smart enough for the corporate world. I barely squeaked by for my high school diploma, and even then only got it because a few of my teachers nudged me toward passing grades when I didn't deserve them."

"Did you have ADHD symptoms as a child? That's when most people with the disorder are diagnosed."

"I've always been absent-minded. *Head in the clouds,*" I added the sing-song tone to my voice on that last bit. "Hyperactive—but my parents thought I was just looking for attention. I got it, just not the good kind."

"Now that, I understand entirely."

I dared another peek. Rhett's eyes had shuttered down, his emotions behind a bland façade.

"Were you a wild child?" I asked.

"Until I learned at an early age that pushing for

acknowledgment and love got me negativity and punishment instead."

My hand reached over to grasp his forearm without thought as empathy swelled inside me. "I'm sorry."

Rhett seemed to stop breathing, so I quickly removed my light touch.

"Nora received most of our parent's attention," I started to spill to fill the tense silence between us. "I'm her mirror twin except for our ears—hers are pointed like an elf while mine are rounded. I actually got the good gene there. Yay me!" I giggled, my knee bouncing again. "But I felt like soggy leftovers my entire life since she got all the brains when that cell split inside Mom's womb. She's brilliant. An astrophysicist, or at least I think that's what she's called. Anyway, she's got her doctorate and works for NASA while I'm the babysitting queen—or at least, I had been back in South Dakota. I don't know anyone here well enough to offer to watch their kids."

"It takes all kinds of people to make the world go round," Rhett murmured.

"I suppose," I agreed even though I didn't have nearly the worth Nora did in society's eyes.

"If your sister ever decides to have a family of her own and continue working, she's going to need a nanny. So—" he twirled the stem of his glass before polishing his wine off with one swallow "—you could say that someone like you is imperative to her job—thus her happiness."

I stared, my restlessness shut down at his words as I processed what he'd said.

He set aside his own glass. "I've left you speechless," he said with a small smirk, one eyebrow raised in a provocative, sexy arch as he settled into the couch's corner, arms stretched along the arm and across the back. His fingertips brushed over my bare shoulder. "I feel I ought to get a reward."

I didn't think—just acted—crawling into his lap so damn fast he didn't have time to keep me from invading his personal space.

His large hands found my backside as our lips met, and he yanked me right up against him without hesitation, causing a flash of fireworks to explode in my ears.

I captured his scruffy jaw in my hands, whimpering when his tongue slid into my mouth, so many *zings* fluttering through me my heart thrummed. The tartness of the wine, undertones of spice and man overrode my tastebuds, but it was the feel of his fingertips grasping at my ass, kneading and pulling me against his hard length over and over that dampened my panties.

If he didn't stop, I would soak through since my dress rucked up to my waist.

"Rhett," I gasped when he bit my lower lip. "I-I'm so turned on." I swallowed hard as he slid his lips down my neck, my head tipping to offer him better access.

"Mmm," he moaned his approval and took my mouth with more passion than I'd expected from how he held himself in check.

Rhett Stirling bottled up more feels than he let on—and he unleashed in the perfect way.

I clutched at his hair, grinding against him, as he ate at my mouth like a man who'd gone too long without sustenance. Like he thirsted for something only I could give him.

Panting, I pulled away, still holding his face in my hands as he ground us together. I moved with him, glancing down between our bodies. "I soaked through my panties," I whispered, breathless from the arousal rushing through me with the force of a blizzard at the sight of the wet spot on his slacks.

Rhett released a throaty growl that shivered my skin and made the hairs on my nape stand on end. "Want to taste your pussy."

"Yes—oh, yes, yes, yes," I rushed on a single breath.

He lifted me like I weighed nothing, twisting on the couch cushion to lay me on my back. Up went my dress with no finesse whatsoever, and he ripped my satiny bikini panties from my hips with one yank.

I gasped at the sting from his actions, but he shoved up my legs and dove in—

"Oh!" I cried out, back arching as he latched onto my clit and suckled to the point of pain. "Love it—more—don't stop..." I continued to spew words, senseless or not I had no clue.

The warmth of his mouth on my tender flesh, the nips of his teeth erased reality as I soared upward toward the clouds.

Rhett tongued up through my slit. "Christ, you're so fucking sweet," he all but growled, a damn book boyfriend come to life just like Ashton had said.

Thick fingers slid into my pussy, pushing me closer upward with every thrust into my soaked core.

"Fuck, Sky...so tight. Wet." His tongue fluttered over my clit, and my climax tingled low in my belly faster than seemed possible.

"Suck on me—make it hurt...oh yes!" I gasped, thrusting my hips up toward his face as he gave me what I needed. "I'm going to come...oh my *God*, I'm going to come! Rhett!"

He groaned, his face buried between my thighs, and I erupted.

I may have shrieked his name—and I definitely detonated from deep inside where I ached to be filled with more than fingers, squirming with every spasm through my core.

"Fuck, yes." Rhett groaned, lapping and fucking me with his fingers until I collapsed backward, every inch of my body tingling.

My ears rang.

Tongue felt dry and thick in my mouth as I panted for breath.

And my mind...blessed Mary, Joseph, and Jesus—or whatever—sat quiet. Utterly wrecked.

Rhett licked through my lower lips, placed a sweet kiss on my sensitive clit, and nosed up my belly until his face came into contact with my dress bunched around my breasts.

"I've left you speechless for a second time." The rasp of his low voice sent a shiver across my skin.

"I...Best. Way. Ever." A grin attempted to split my face in half as I sprawled, weak and completely relaxed.

He chuckled and moved even higher until he planked over me, his face hovering mere inches above mine. Warmth filled his eyes, a softness I'd never seen, more like milk chocolate than bitter dark.

I captured his face in my hands, studying the gorgeous man who allowed me a moment to glimpse inside his soul. Happiness welled up in my chest, filling me with jitters. Sudden energy made me want to move.

"Ash said you have a delicious dick," I spewed the words. "Can I taste you too? I really would like to—I'm not very experienced with blow jobs, and I'll probably suck at it—" I burst into laughter but couldn't stop the words from pouring from me, especially since he smirked rather than rolled his eyes.

Ashton and I had hoped for a breakthrough with Rhett that night—and evidence of our having succeeded stared down at me with actual happiness lining his face.

27

ASHTON

The damn indigestion had attacked again after we finished eating, but I focused on their murmurs from the kitchen where I cleaned up. Even uncomfortable, I grinned nonstop over the fact that Rhett's walls had thinned out since his arrival home. A burst of laughter at our dancing? Rarer than a unicorn in real life. No frowns or curls of his nose happened over Sky's silly chatter, and he'd offered her a compliment rather than dismissal when she admitted to her inability to run a business.

Hope seemed to keep my spirit buoyed, and I felt like my feet hovered over the floor while washing the dishes.

Rhett had told me he wasn't against being seduced, exactly as Sky and I had planned, but what if he'd only meant by *me*?

Sky mentioned earlier in the day that Rhett had seen her intention that morning to kiss him, and she figured that's why he had left us alone in the bed as quickly as he had.

Kissing crossed barriers for Rhett.

That lightness in my body slowly dissipated as their

voices continued. They were talking—but what if Rhett wasn't even attracted to her in a sexual way? He'd definitely checked her out with lust in his eyes, but what if the idea of having her between us didn't appeal to him?

My new non-friend nausea weaseled its way in atop the slight pain in my upper abdomen, churning my stomach.

"Shit."

Sweat broke out on my brow, and I hurried to rinse the last dish, knowing my dinner wasn't going to stay down. No amount of denying that fact would change the sure eruption.

A quick sprint to the upstairs bathroom where I wouldn't be overheard retching and disturb their conversation landed me on my knees, already out of breath and exhausted.

Goodbye dinner, hello weakness and the lightheadedness that made me feel like my soul wanted to drift toward the heavens.

Finished with emptying my stomach, I gasped for breath, my head hanging between my knees where I propped against the bathroom wall. A few steady breaths calmed my racing heart as I counted like I'd been taught to help panic attacks subside.

I needed to see a doctor.

No. Absolutely not. No fucking way.

The thought of sterility and bleach heaved my stomach again, and I moaned a whimper.

Rhett *had* to fall in love with Sky just in case ...

"Fuck." I pushed to my feet and rinsed out my mouth, fear twisting my insides up tight and keeping me on edge. A splash of water rid my face of the cold sweat I'd broken into, and a pinch to my cheeks gave my pale face some color.

"No," I whispered, refusing to dwell on my morbid thoughts hammering at my brain.

But what if—

"Goddamnit," I whispered harshly, eyes closing and breathing heavily. "Go downstairs. Continue on as though you're fine—it's nothing but a stomach bug."

One steadying inhale, and I nodded to myself, determined to be as stoic as Rhett in my denial of illness.

The voices had faded, I noted as I crept back down the stairs on still-weak knees.

Sky's whimper hit my ears, making my heart race again. A few quick steps brought the living room into sight, and arousal slammed into me—

Rhett's face buried between her thighs.

Head tipped and back arched, Sky writhed against his mouth, her hands grasping at his dark hair. She whisper-moaned something about coming.

Then shrieked his name.

Her climax on Rhett's tongue jolted lust through my groin, drying out my mouth.

He kissed up her lax body until he planked over her. "I've left you speechless for a second time."

"I...Best. Way. Ever." Her smile left me breathless as her voice. She cupped his face like he was the most precious gift on earth—the affectionate touch being one I knew he loved.

"Ash said you have a delicious dick."

I bit my tongue over the sudden chuckle wanting to burst from me as quickly as the words did from Sky.

"Can I taste you too? I really would like to—I'm not very experienced with blow jobs, I'll probably suck at it—" Sky erupted into laughter, something no woman had ever done in our bed.

I expected Rhett to move off her, tidy her dress, and send her on her way.

He smirked instead.

Legit smiled when he normally would have been turned off by a woman's silliness.

I stepped into the room, my recent hugging of the toilet and what it might mean for my future deciding my next move. Rhett needed to connect emotionally with Sky as he'd done with me that first time he'd looked into my eyes while sinking into my body.

Both became aware of my presence at the same time, their heads turning my way as I approached. Pulling the condoms I'd tucked into my back pocket earlier in the day in the event things went according to plan, I closed the distance.

My hand held steady as I offered a foil packet to Rhett. "I want to watch you fuck her."

"Yes," Sky agreed without hesitation. "I mean, if that's what you...please, Rhett? I-I just need to make you feel good, give you something in exchange for allowing me to stay here."

The plea rushed from her mouth, and Rhett frowned, took the condom, and gazed back down at her. "This is no transaction."

His stern voice, the choice of words sent that light hope racing through my chest again. Sex with women had *always* been that exact thing with emotions safely locked away.

Legs once more going weak, I sat my ass down in the other chair, shifting my hard length around for some breathing room between my spread thighs.

Sky gulped and peered up at Rhett as he backed onto his knees to kneel between her splayed thighs.

The clinking of his belt as he loosened it heightened my

pulse. The rustle of clothing as he shifted to pull out his dick, how his pants lowered beneath his firm ass, tightened my balls. The bead of pre-cum on the head of his straining cock made my mouth water for a taste.

But he belonged to Sky in that moment, and I wouldn't dare impose or draw his attention off her until they finished.

Rhett rolled the rubber down and once more planked over her, and goddamnit, the angle didn't afford me a good view of—

"Oh!" Sky gasped as Rhett's ass flexed, her hands grasping at his dress shirt. "Oh, *yes*." She hissed and wrapped her heels around his ass, lithe muscles flexing until their groins pressed tight.

Their gazes didn't waver from each other's faces.

I blinked back tears at the flood of joy rising up inside my chest.

Rhett hadn't ever looked at anyone but me with his shields down. Fucking had always been a cold, emotionless hookup with others, even when we'd agreed they had the potential to be the angel we'd been searching for.

The passion he unleashed with me alone showered down onto Sky with every gyration of his hips, every deep moan that rumbled from his lips as she lifted hers to meet his slow thrusts.

"Rhett," she whispered, cupping his cheek—he gave her his mouth and stole my breath.

He never kissed women.

Ever.

They moved in a sensual dance, both still half-clothed but their souls left bared.

My chest ached with the sweetest pain I had ever experienced as I watched my two lovers offer themselves to each other. The scent of sex permeated the air, and gasps and moans created a symphony of love and ecstatic hope in my mind that promised incandescent happiness in my future.

For however long fate allowed breath to fill my lungs.

Rhett wouldn't be alone if my fear over what caused my recent illness proved true. He would have someone to hold him, love him, stand by his side when he struggled to allow himself to *feel*.

Sky had done that—our sweet, sexy angel.

I wanted to worship at her feet, to show her how very special she was regardless of what her family or even *she* thought about herself.

She'd been sent from heaven to fulfill my dreams, and I owed her the world.

28

———

RHETT

S o lush. Warm and tight.

And those eyes holding me captive...crystalline emeralds, full of need I felt along with her, the same vulnerability I experienced in my chest whenever making love to Ash.

Desire to not just burrow deeper into her body but into her soul rose inside me.

Wrong, one part of me whispered.

Right, the other side insisted.

Goddamn dichotomous mind, warring thoughts, didn't keep my hips from moving of their own accord, my dick from dragging through her sweet clasp. I pushed against the disagreeing voices and focused on pleasing the woman beneath me.

Igniting another climax in her body to milk my aching balls dry.

Chasing orgasms that promised mutual satisfaction.

"Sky..." Ash whispered her name, drawing my attention. His eyes remained on her face, his hands shaking as he shoved down his pants to palm his rock-hard dick. "So beautiful...my sunshine," he moaned, working his length in time with my thrusts—but I faltered. "I'm so damn close," he rasped. "Need you to come."

Skylar's pussy clamped down on my length, let out a heady moan, and at the wet heat dripping down my balls, my climax erupted.

Teeth clenched to keep from cursing and praising how she pulsed around me, I fucked every last drop of cum into the condom before going still. Planked on my elbows, I hung my head and sucked wind.

The sweetness of release ripped away as Ash's presence slid over me like a hair-raising sixth sense, bringing his words back to my mind. He'd been completely focused on her...

I shifted my eyes to find he'd moved across the living room to stand beside us, his still-hard dick in hand.

"Open for me," he whispered, and I did as told—but he slid over Sky's tongue rather than mine.

Tipping back my head, I found he only had eyes for her once again. He fed her his cum with a soft grunt, a tremor rippling over him as he finished.

In her.

Not me.

I ought to have been thrilled by the knowledge Ash had chosen the woman to fulfill his dreams, the ones I wanted for him more than anything, so why did my stomach clench? Why did pain lash at my chest like a knife? Why did I frown when I should have been smiling?

My backing out of Skylar's body didn't draw either of their attention.

The feelings coursing through me—I'd never dealt with them before. My inner strength flagged. I was fucking *weak*.

I stumbled from the living room, intent on the half-bath around the corner.

Shutting down the shit stirring inside me didn't come as easily as usual. For the first time, I struggled to grasp my strong identity, the usual fortitude whenever my heart threatened overwhelming emotion.

I couldn't be vulnerable.

I wouldn't.

Mind set on a course of action and jaw clenched, I cleaned up and wet a hand towel for Skylar.

Dick tucked away, shirt tucked in, and belt firmly clasped, I returned to the living room and put back together a form of armor I desperately needed against the unsettled roiling inside me.

Ash sat on the edge of the couch, gently running his fingertips over Sky's face. Both smiled with the light of a thousand suns while I cast shadows like the moon in a solar eclipse.

I might be a coldhearted bastard, but I wasn't an asshole. Continuing with my approach, I held out the towel. Ash took it with a flashed grin of thanks, and I watched him attend to her how I normally would have done with our hookups while he escaped to the shower.

Skylar kept her eyes on me as he wiped gently between her thighs, murmuring something about how perfect she was, how much she pleased him...

Angel.

Sunshine.

I gritted my teeth against the choking need to rip him away from her regardless of the hearts in her eyes peering up at me—

"That was lovely, Rhett," Skylar whispered, her emerald

orbs luminous and gorgeously sated. Fucking stunning. Breath stealing.

I held steady against the desire to loosen the rigidity I'd wrapped myself in and soak in the warmth she offered.

"Your dick did feel absolutely delicious inside me," she said and giggled, glancing once more at Ash. "You were *so* right. No wonder you've held onto him for so long. I will too —or, um, I *would* if given the chance." She focused on me once more, the question she surprisingly didn't spew without doubt on the tip of her loose tongue.

My guts twisting, I ignored the obvious request and faced Ash who had finally turned his focus on me. "I'm tired." My words came out abrupt as I spun and walked away, clamping down whatever shit emotions stirred to life inside me.

"Rhett..." Ash called after me.

"I'm going to bed." I prided myself in not muttering or sounding like a petulant child who'd had his favorite toy taken away from him.

Because that's how it fucking felt—and I despised the churning in my stomach.

It is what it is.

Mom's voice echoed from the grave, tightening my jaw. I'd made my bed—but that didn't mean I had to lay in it and wallow.

Coolness eased over my mind as I stifled and locked up any thought but sliding between our sheets and closing my eyes.

I stripped down and put every article of clothing in its proper place. Brushed my teeth. Climbed into bed in my usual spot but faced the wall and waited. I wasn't surprised when their hushed whispers filled the room a few moments later.

Clothing rustled.

The bed dipped.

Ash's warm hand settled on my shoulder, but I remained unmoving, feigning sleep since I had zero capacity to communicate or even name what I wanted or how I felt about his actions in the living room.

The mattress shifted, and I listened as the two of them got all comfy for the night. Probably snuggling face to face and sharing breath.

Unable to help myself, I rolled and wrapped my arm around Ash's waist, pulling his back against me tight as though...desperate.

Other words to describe the shit coursing through me flitted through my mind, but I slammed the door shut.

I forced my muscles to relax—but I refused to reach out and touch Skylar too.

———

No discussion took place around Skylar's moving into our bed, but a week passed, and she slept there every night, Ash snuggled between us.

I hadn't touched her since that one time we fucked in the living room, but since I couldn't deny Ash fully, I told them I wanted to watch. I had his ass once while he was balls deep in Skylar, but his focus had been on her again.

No morning blow jobs from the mouth I missed on my body. No familiar hands washing me in the shower. No more passionate kisses that ended with us fucking over the couch or against a kitchen cabinet in our insatiable need for one another.

I was feeling left out, my insides pouting like a toddler on the verge of throwing a temper tantrum. Communicating my emotions didn't come easy for me, and I fought to find a way how to show Ash what went down inside me. I wouldn't act out like a child, but the ability to express what I endured eluded me.

But even if I'd found them, I wouldn't unveil my frailty.

"I'm fine," I stated firmly whenever he asked if I was okay or what was bothering me.

But I wasn't. Far fucking from it.

Exactly seven days after the night I fucked her, I had Ash to myself in the office for a meeting along with our secretary. We were supposed to be discussing our latest investment in a startup software company, but I couldn't focus.

"Rhett."

I glanced up from the pen in my hand I hadn't realized I stared at. "Hmm?"

"Did you hear a word I just said?"

My attention flitted to our secretary Louise. "Sorry. I'm a little...preoccupied."

His hand twitched like he wanted to reach over my desk and lace our fingers together.

My chest tightened—throat thickened—and I coughed slightly, bottling up my longing from his recognizable movement.

"Louise," Ash murmured, "would you give us a few?"

"Of course." She set her legal pad aside and left us alone.

The silence sat heavy in the air, and I couldn't bring myself to look at him.

"I know you think you're fine, but it's obvious you aren't. Do you need to talk about your mom?" Ash asked, empathy lacing his tone. "You weren't close, but loss is never easy."

I fought the desire to toss my pen down at his obvious blindness. "I'm not grieving her death."

"Then what's bothering you? You've been...closed off. I figured it was because of her passing."

A muscle ticked in my jaw. The fact he didn't see the problem, didn't discern how Skylar's imposing on our lives had changed the dynamic between us, hurt almost as bad as his ignoring me.

"You don't have to tell me how you're feeling," Ash said quietly. "Just state cold facts so I can at least help you put to rest whatever is going on."

"Skylar." I managed to say her name without a bite in my voice.

"What about her?"

"She's coming between us."

"She actually hasn't yet." Ash chuckled, and I shot him a glare. His grin faded, and I held his gaze, imploring him to understand like he used to seem so good at doing when I couldn't verbally express.

"I thought she clicked into place without any drama—"

"Because I'm unable to let people know how I feel," I snipped, my stomach roiling over facts from my childhood I couldn't change or seem to overcome.

Ash didn't respond for a few minutes—actually checked his phone and typed out a message.

Probably texting Skylar...

I turned back toward the file on my desk, ready for the uncomfortable discussion to be over.

He was falling in love with her and clueless about how I felt about that fact because I sucked at communicating.

Weak as fuck when I always thought I was so goddamn strong—

Ash stood and rounded my desk, rolling my chair back.

"Wha—"

He bent down and took my mouth while sliding onto my lap.

My hands found his ass and squeezed as our tongues met, going from sweet to hungry within a pounding heartbeat. Lust shot through my groin, stiffening me, and I dug my fingers into his round backside, rutting against him until he grew hard.

Every cell in my body vibrating, I spun him around, scattering shit from my desk with one swipe of my arm.

He fumbled with his belt and slacks while I did the same, urgent to release my dick.

The second his ass came into view, I pushed his upper body onto my desk and dropped to my knees.

I shoved my tongue into his hole without finesse, pushing in as deep as I could to taste what I'd been missing.

"Ah, fuck," he moaned, reaching back to grab his cheeks, pulling them apart, and giving me better access.

Hand on my dick, I ate at his ass, starved—fucking desperate for him. Licking and sucking, fucking with my tongue until he whimpered.

"Rhett. Please."

I left his hole a sloppy mess, spit on my hand, and stood, smearing saliva over my aching length. Trembling at the desire to thrust in and claim, I fought for my usual calm and came up empty.

"Sorry—" I gritted my teeth and pushed into his tight heat as far as I could without lube, driving Ash up onto his toes, his hips into my desk.

"F-fucking hell, Rhett—Jesus, fuck." He shuddered and moaned, his ring clenching around me.

"Christ." I gasped, buried halfway in his body, my fingers grasping his hips as I fought to stay still. "Want—fuck, Ash, I'm sorry. Gotta fuck you..."

Ash turned his head, his gorgeous hazel eyes glazed over with the same emotion coursing through me. "I'm yours—take what you need."

I backed off, spit on his hole, and snapped my hips forward, pulling a grunt from both of us as I bottomed out inside his silken heat.

As with every time we came together, my reservations slipped toward the back of my mind as Ash became my focus. Every moan, every curse I punched from his lungs soothed the tension inside my gut, easing my mind until all I saw was him.

Dress shirt rucked up his back, his hair a mess from where I grasped hold to keep him steady.

"Love you," I told him through panted breaths, the slapping of our skin loud in the cavernous office. "Missed this—missed *you.*"

"I've—been—caught—up," he gasped out with each thrust, his hands reaching for the front of my desk to steady himself. "So—sorry."

I grabbed his dick and leaned over his back, my face finding his neck. "Don't ever stop loving me," I gasped, my voice broken, bleeding the consuming need inside me.

"Never," he swore, reaching back to grasp the back of my head.

I sank my teeth into his skin, sucking hard, leaving my mark. "Want you to come in my hand, baby. Soak my fist while I spill deep inside your ass."

"Oh fuck...yes, Rhett..goddamn—"

Wet heat erupted over my fingers.

"Fuck, yes. Ash." My balls seized, and I grunted with every spurt through my length, coating him. Claiming him. I'd marked my love inside and out. Both filled me with such a sense of rightness and satisfaction that my throat tightened and my eyes stung.

We panted and stilled, Ash boneless on my desk, me wishing I could collapse atop him on our bed. The office afforded no such luxury.

Thank fuck for attached bathrooms.

I kissed where I'd bitten and ran my tongue over his neck, tasting remnants of his natural salt and soap.

So fucking delicious.

"Goddamn, baby," I groaned, slowly backing out of him, my dick sensitive as fuck as he clenched around me as though unwilling to let me go too.

Ash shuddered as I slipped free, and I spread his ass cheeks watching my cum drip from his asshole. I shoved some back in, reaching deep until he hissed.

"Fucking caveman."

"Mmm hmm," I agreed, then gave his thigh a quick slap.

Every cell in my body tingling, I cleaned us both up, tucked my spent dick away, and pulled him down onto my lap again.

Eyes closed, our foreheads rested together.

My muscles went lax, and I simply breathed him in, loving how we fit, how my mind and soul quieted while wrapped up in him.

"I'm sorry I haven't been giving you my attention lately," he whispered.

I knew why he hadn't been, how his drive to find a mother for his children and sunshine for our lives gave him tunnel vision. The fact he recognized what I'd been going through since Skylar's arrival stilled some of my deep-seated unrest over her barreling into our lives.

He kissed me softly, a mere press of lips. "How about we go out on a date tonight? Just you and me."

That was the best idea he'd had since flying to Florida to offer his shoulder for me to lean on.

I agreed and answered with a simple, "Yes," hopeful that things would somehow work out for all three of us to be happy—satisfied.

But I didn't hold my breath.

29

SKYLAR

Bagging groceries was easy. Mundane. Required no thought beyond *don't put bananas on top of lettuce or canned goods with bread.*

I seemed to have found a job that only required the skills I possessed. Organization.

Life was going well.

Sharing a bed with two men, one of which loved on me nonstop, the other just as standoffish as Ashton had warned me about Rhett's character. But I would wear him down eventually.

I'd done so once, so it was only a matter of time before he relented to the pull between us again.

Since I worked daytime hours, the three of us had ended up cooking dinner with each other, and I felt as though I fit in their dynamic pretty well.

Home goods...in one bag. Dryer sheets wrapped in a plastic bag first...

I'd hoped that Rhett would soften toward me after that night in the living room when we'd connected, but with every passing day, I wondered over his renewed coldness that had begun when Ashton had come in my mouth.

Rhett had closed down after retreating to the bathroom and hadn't touched me since.

Not wanting to cause waves, I kept my concern of his experiencing jealousy and insecurities to myself and tried to figure out what to do, refusing to acknowledge Nora might be right about that whole third wheel thing. It seemed I normally ended up on Ashton's left while Rhett had his right—in bed and out of it.

I counted myself lucky that Ashton invited me to join them every night and I hadn't yet been tossed out on my backside.

Another bagger came over to relieve me, and I couldn't believe how quickly the morning had flown by. I grabbed a premade salad with grilled chicken from the deli and went to the break room to eat my lunch and try not to stew over the unrest in the house I'd begun to see as my home.

A text waited for me from twenty minutes earlier, causing my heart to stutter and take to flight. I skimmed his message, my eyes flitting across the words as a whole.

Ashton: **Rhett and I are going out to dinner tonight.**

Grinning, I texted back, butterflies in my belly over dating in public as a triad for the first time. **Do you want me to just take an Uber and meet you there, or did you plan to go home and change before heading out?**

I popped the lid on my salad, poured two packets of ranch atop it, and dug in. The savory buttermilk and herb flavor burst on my tongue, and I moaned while chewing.

Picking up my phone, I saw he hadn't texted back yet—and I looked at the message I hadn't taken the time to read word for word the first time.

The two of *them* were going out. Not all of us.

My smile dissolved.

I'd made a fool out of myself by not slowing my brain down.

Idiot. Moron.

Other put-me-downs rushed through my head as another message came through.

Ashton: **We need some alone time.**

I swallowed hard and dropped my fork, my hands too shaky to text.

Tapping the speech-to-text button, I lifted my cell closer to my mouth and let loose with the thoughts zapping through my brain at the pace of a lightning bolt.

"Is this your way of putting distance between us? I'm a lot, but I really feel like we have something good going on, Ashton. Have you tired of me already?" My throat attempted to swell shut as tears stung my eyes, and I stumbled over my words in my haste to spew them. "If I did wrong, please tell me. I burned the toast this morning and spilled your coffee, but that was me just being clumsy. I—I can do better. I promise. Just let me know what to do and I'll do it."

Breathless, I hit send and chewed on the inside of my lip rather than my salad. No way in hell my stomach would handle food with how it had tightened up.

Ashton: **I'm not upset with you, and the last thing I want is to end this beautiful connection we've made.**

"Oh, thank *fuck.*" I rarely used the F word, but the situation of giddy to anxiety to relief, demanded more than an *oh crap*!

My fingers worked a bit better as I typed a response. **So if you aren't mad, can I ask why it's just the two of you going out to dinner?**

Ashton: **I've been so caught up in you that I think Rhett is a little jealous and missing me.**

Rhett jealous of little old me...exactly as I'd wondered even though it seemed impossible since I'd known Ashton all of two weeks and they'd had decades together.

Ashton: **We aren't used to sharing each other beyond one-night stands. It's something we're all going to have to work on. Being in a polyamorous relationship isn't going to be easy, but it'll be worth the effort of trying—I just know it.**

All I saw in that message was one-night stands.

He and Rhett had women between them before, something I'd known but hadn't really thought about that much.

My stomach refused to relax, and I put the top back on my salad and tossed it in the trash, my forehead dented with a frown.

I hated the fact I didn't have them all to myself, that I had to share them with memories of other women...

The thought trailed off.

I suddenly understood Rhett's jealousy.

A swell of empathy attempted to drown me in the need to smother him with the assurance and affection he'd seemed to thrive under that one night he'd allowed me a glimpse of his true self.

My fingers once more shook, but I texted Ashton back. **I hope you have a relaxing dinner together. I think it's best too if I stay in the guest room tonight. In fact, I'll probably be sleeping by the time you get home.**

Ashton: **Please don't feel bad about this. I really want things to work out between the three of us.**

"Such a sweetheart," I murmured to myself while smiling even though my heart ached for Rhett and the entire emotional situation he found himself in. I could do better to help him—maybe even heal whatever crack my arrival had caused in their relationship.

Me: **I understand how Rhett is feeling, and I know your love for him runs deep. Enjoy your date night. I'll have breakfast ready for you in the morning. Sleep well—and be as loud as you want before doing so. I won't complain.**

I included a wink emoji, a couple of kissing ones, and hopped up to get back to work.

My cell pinged again, and I dug it out of my back pocket, still smiling.

For the second time in twenty minutes, my lips flatlined.

Nora had texted.

Not Ashton.

I hadn't spoken to my sister since she'd kicked me out of the house. Her single line text took me from relaxed to anxious once more.

I'm taking your cell off my plan.

No, *how are you doing*? No, *I hope you're doing well*. Not even something sarcastic about bad choices and wondering over if I'd reaped the consequences yet of running off with a man I didn't even know.

The cell pinged again.

Mom told me you won't listen to reason, and even though Dad said you're free to fly, I hope you realize the bed you're making for yourself will end in nothing but heartache.

I didn't respond, simply shoved my cell back into my pocket and trudged back to work, my mind preoccupied with my own situation.

Finances.

Affording a cell phone plan of my own.

No credit.

Working long hours for minimum wage that was far from what a person could live off in sunny California where a loaf of bread cost three times as much as the middle of nowhere South Dakota.

I crushed a box of strawberries with a bag of apples.

Flattened two packages of hamburger rolls with boxes of their frozen counterparts.

The first customer to gripe at my inability to properly pack groceries got me an eye roll from the cashier I bagged for.

The second and third had me again muttering an apology, but I couldn't keep tears from welling in my eyes.

Paying attention became impossible, and before long, the manager came over to check on me.

More apologies, tears slipping down my cheeks, promises to do better...and she kindly suggested I take the rest of the afternoon off.

"A-Are you firing me?" I managed to squeak out, wanting to curl inward at the attention our conversation drew from customers and co-workers alike.

"Of course not." She lightly touched my shoulder, and I blew out a breath at her kind smile.

"I'm really sorry. Sometimes my brain goes all wonky, and I can't focus. It's even worse when my feet get antsy too," I blurted.

The manager steered me by my elbow toward the customer service station at the store's front. Once in relative privacy, she turned toward me, her lips still curled upward.

"My son has ADHD dend is a living jumping bean."

A huff of relieved laughter escaped me. "You understand."

"I do. Some days are better than others, that's for sure. What meds does your doctor have you on?"

"Um...none?" I shrugged. "I don't have insurance. I've

never even been properly diagnosed—but it's pretty obvious I have issues."

"You said you just moved to town," my manager said, pulling her cell from her pocket.

"Yeah." I rubbed my palms down my jeans, my toes tapping to move.

"I'm going to send you my mother-in-law's office number. She's a primary care physician and has studied ADHD extensively because of my son. I think she'd be able to help you."

Tears once more stung my eyes, and I gave her my number to text the contact info.

"Your health insurance benefits won't kick in for close to three months, but my mom will set up an easy payment plan of what you can afford, okay?"

I nodded, dashing my forearm across my cheek.

"Now head home and rearrange a closet or two," she suggested with a knowing smile.

Laughing, I promised that I would.

And I did.

I wanted to attack Rhett and Ashton's walk-ins to color-coordinate everything they owned, but I needed to give them space outside close proximity.

The linen closet got a thorough clean out, as did the fridge. A half-dozen or so different bottles of sauces, dressings, and condiments that had expired landed in the trash can.

Once finished, I cooked myself dinner for one, wondering how my men fared wherever they'd gone to dine.

My men...I felt I had a right to claim a piece of Ashton's heart, but Rhett needed some persuading once he settled his thoughts and heart into accepting our connection and how right the three of us could be as a triad.

Doubled down in my determination to win him over, I crawled into bed at too early of an hour with a couple of romance novels from the library.

Annie Kelly swept me from reality, reigniting my desire for a proper threesome, and although my body burned when I heard Ashton and Rhett return home, I stayed put.

Ears straining, I listened as they reset the alarm and went to their bedroom.

I imagined their door locked.

The shower turned on and washing away the work day.

They would crawl into their big bed and make love to one another, reassuring each other of their devotion.

I'd seen Rhett's passion for Ashton. Hopefully, Ashton would draw it out, and Rhett's emotions would settle.

Because I wanted more with him too.

And there was no way I could afford to move elsewhere anytime soon.

30

RHETT

Ingesting a half-glass of wine and our appetizer sent Ash rushing to the bathroom.

He returned a full ten minutes later, pale and shaky, unable to eat the dinner that had been delivered in his absence. We boxed the food up to take with us. Ashton's "I'm fine—just a bug or something" rang false in my ears, but he waved me off the two times I tried to question him.

We'd left his car at the office, and I told him we could head in together in the morning after dropping Skylar at work. Arriving a little later than my usual time would be fine.

I didn't want him driving alone.

Allowing him his mental space, I held his hand atop his thigh on the way home from the restaurant.

"Sure you're okay, baby?" I murmured when his head tipped back against the headrest.

"Everything will be fine. I just need to sleep."

Skylar has been wearing his ass out—

I cut the thought because they didn't fuck more than he

and I had before she'd entered our lives. But, I had taken him hard and rough over my desk earlier that day.

The memory twitched my groin with interest, but I set aside fantasies of doing anything more than cuddling chest to chest.

He'd told Skylar he and I were going on a date, and she offered to sleep in the guest room so we could have some alone time.

I didn't want to appreciate her selflessness, but I did.

Immensely.

Once home, I insisted we shower, taking my time to wash Ash from head to toe. He sank into my focused attention as though soaking every caress, every loving touch to his skin as gentle rain-like water from the shower heads above us filled the room with steam and soothing warmth.

Dried and naked, we crawled into our bed, both of us letting out sighs as we pressed in close together in a cocoon of heated bodies and soothing hands.

Ashton's paleness had lessened, but he seemed...frail. Fragile.

He slid a hand between us and pressed a fist to his sternum like he had indigestion.

"Sure you're okay?" I whispered and kissed his forehead, his damp hair tickling my nose.

"Just tired and achy." He snuggled in closer, and I trailed my fingertips down his spine.

"I'm sorry for taking you so hard today."

"Don't be. It was hot as fuck."

I chuckled, loving the smile in his voice.

"It reminded me of when we were teenagers and couldn't keep our hands off each other."

I still couldn't get enough of him, but we'd definitely lost some of the desperation we'd had as kids.

Kissing him again, I breathed in the scent of the body wash we shared, woodsy with hints of spice beneath. I could easily lick every inch of his skin, grow hard, and beg for his ass again, but he lay unmoving, exhausted.

"Want me to give you a blow job?" he asked, making me smile again.

"Sleep, baby," I murmured, loving how easily he read my mind so I wouldn't have to use words. "But you can wake me up that way if you want."

"I *do* want," he whispered, already half asleep.

Me too.

———

A few days passed with Ash giving me more attention while I did my best to ignore Skylar and her nonstop chatter. She tried so hard to win me over, but I wouldn't be moved in my stance against emotional involvement.

Just the thought of lowering my walls and allowing feelings to dictate my actions made me cringe.

Ash experienced indigestion after every meal, rubbing at his sternum, but told us both there was nothing to be concerned about. Those were the instances where I liked Skylar—she watched him closely, always put her hands on him with a soothing touch like he'd told me his mom had often done when he hadn't felt well.

The way she took care of him eased some of the tension inside me, but a part of me still remained...off toward her, and I couldn't figure out why.

Ash managed to sit through the whole meal without going to the bathroom on Thursday night and leaving Skylar and I alone but excused himself the second we finished.

With Skylar's attention focused on cleaning off the table with me, her usual chattiness flitting from one topic to another and giving me whiplash didn't occur.

For the first time since moving into our home, she appeared subdued, her smiles fake.

I hated that I considered her strange behavior, even more than I missed her happiness.

Ash hadn't seemed to be aware of the change in her all through dinner, but I'd picked up on the forced sound of her laughter, the lack of a twinkle in her eyes.

Keeping Ash happy meant trying to do the same for Skylar...

"Are you alright?" I asked, my tone lacking its usual bite.

Her head whipped toward me, her lips parted in a way that made me want to ravage her mouth, and she blinked. Stared as I dried one of the wine glasses she'd washed.

"Are *you* alright?" she echoed, emphasis on wondering the same about me.

"I'm fine."

"You—you've never asked me...um...well, it's been a shitty couple of days."

"Why?" I surprised myself by asking since I'd been enjoying the silence between us.

She blinked rapidly as though trying to clear her vision, or perhaps her mind, of confusion over my strange question.

I hadn't inquired about her day or her feelings since meeting her—not a single time.

Asshole, much?

I didn't have to get involved with my emotions, but common courtesy would be required if we decided as a whole to move forward in our relationship, the idea of which still made me want to dig in my heels and deny the possibility because...*noise.*

"I keep messing up at work," she admitted, returning to washing dishes. "My focus is there—honestly, bagging groceries is no different than organizing closets."

She definitely had a way with that. I enjoyed the hell out of the tidiness she left behind when she couldn't sit still. That part of our personalities clicked perfectly.

"But then a squirrel snatches my attention. A screaming kid. An old man bent over his cane trying to carry two bags of groceries. My cashier's body odor that makes me grimace and wonder why the hell he doesn't shower. Or maybe he can't afford deodorant. One manager twirls keys in his hand nonstop, and I can't help but think they're going to fly off his fingers someday, hit a woman's face, blood will be everywhere, and a lawsuit will end up bankrupting the store so I'll lose my job."

Words poured from her lips like normal, and I got what she was saying without growing too annoyed over her chatter.

She faced distractions left and right with the constant ebb and flow of customers.

"You need to see a doctor," I interjected, my stern words snapping her jaw shut.

Shoulder hunched, she continued washing and rinsing dishes before handing them to me.

"I—I won't have insurance for another three months or so, and that's only if I don't get fired. My one shift manager understands ADHD—she gave me her mother-in-law's number. She's a doctor. Her husband's mom, not my manager. She said the office would offer me a payment plan if I pay cash, but I can't afford it right now since Nora shut off my cell this morning."

She whipped her head up, her eyes wide as though she hadn't meant to share that bit of news.

"Don't tell Ash," she rushed to whisper. "He'll be worried. I don't want to upset him. But without a cell, I can't check online to find the cost of cell phones. I don't even have much cash to get an Uber to take me to a cell phone store when it'll probably be a waste of time because I don't have money for one anyway."

I stood silent, drying dishes as she blathered on about finances. My usual suspicions when it came to women attempting to get more from me and Ash than a hookup rose to life in my mind—not for the first time.

Or perhaps I grasped at straws to find reasons the triad wouldn't work.

Yes, Skylar seemed genuine most of the time, but I wondered how much of the attention she showed Ash and attempted to give me came from a heartfelt place.

Was she after handouts? Ash already spoiled her plenty by offering her a place to live and feeding her.

Did she truly care about Ash at all? It might appear so, but neither of us knew her well enough to trust her intentions. She'd been kicked out of her sister's house, desperate for someone to step in and rescue her.

My forehead dented at the possibility she put on a show, one we'd seen a couple of times before feelings got tangled up. Ash would be devastated to learn she'd lied. While I didn't mind being his rock to lean on when emotion overwhelmed him, my guts tightened over the thought of him having to face more grief and heartache.

Skylar continued to spew her woes since I'd asked for her mouth faucet to turn on, but I tuned her out.

She needed to take her manager's mother-in-law up on the payment plan and get herself sorted to ensure she kept her job and started saving money in order to find her footing financially.

Noise filled my ears, and the need to escape moved me to hang up the damp hand towel and walk away without excusing myself.

I'd been called a coldhearted bastard more than once in my lifetime, and I owned that shit since I seemed unable to empathize or take pity on people.

Skylar's words cut off mid-sentence as I left her alone in the kitchen, desperately needing the silence of my office.

I shut the door firmly behind me.

"Goddamm." Weariness took root in my ears and slid down my spine. I sat hard on my chair, releasing a heavily grunted exhale.

Blessed *fucking* silence I never got enough of anymore.

I couldn't imagine what our acquaintances were going to think of our houseguest and her constant whiplash-inducing chatter.

We would have a houseful in a couple of weeks to celebrate Ash's birthday. Since he enjoyed socializing, I always packed our home full of people to take his mind off the fact he celebrated every year without Archer. His birthday tended to be the second worst day of the year beyond the anniversary of his brother's death.

I'd already set that plan into motion from caterers to decorations and invitations—and I couldn't imagine what kind of ripples Skylar would make amongst our guests.

The usual cocktail-sipping, upper class, quiet conversationalists we'd come to know in the area would stare at Skylar as she prattled on and wonder what the fuck we were thinking bringing her into our lives.

Personally, I could do without the acquaintances we'd surrounded ourselves with, but Ash enjoyed having a social life. People to interact with and bring a little supposed happiness to our life.

I didn't need anyone but him.

My cell dinged, and I actually grinned at seeing Colton's name.

Too bad he didn't live closer—I'd have loved to hang with friends outside the uppity ones we would wine and dine at Ash's party.

Colton: **I need to vent, and since you'll give shit to me straight, I want your ear. Call me so I can annoy you.**

Snickering, I dialed his number.

"You know me too well," I said when he answered.

"Yeah, which is why I trust you to figure out a plan and tell me what the fuck to do."

"What's going on?" I settled back in my chair.

"Remember that variety I used to enjoy? Well, my dick has decided it's tired of being a playboy."

I barked an outright laugh.

"I'm serious! All of my buddies had the same pussy-hungry attitude I used to—hell, a few work for Elite Escorts, so they're getting plenty, but I'm *bored*, man. Seriously. The only thing that interests me is something real, you know? Like you and Ash have. Guy, girl, I don't really care either way."

"Elite Escorts?"

"You know...*escorts.*"

"Prostitution?" I asked for clarity—not that I would judge a person for how they earned a living.

"Lots of them get paid to use their dicks, but sometimes it's just to be eye candy for events and that sort of shit. Why? Do you think it's wrong?"

I snorted. "As long as someone works hard to pay their bills, what do I care?"

"Hard." Colton let out a chuckle, and I rolled my eyes.

"You're adventurous. Why don't you switch over to looking for relationships instead of hookups on Missing Link? See what you can find. There are thousands of profiles of people hoping for something real, just like you."

"You guys have any luck yet?"

I considered Skylar, my thoughts torn.

In some ways, Colton reminded me of her—impulsive, chatty, unable to focus on more than instant gratification... and I loved the guy.

So what was it about Skylar that thickened my walls and made me twice as stubborn as normal?

"That's some long-assed silence, Rhett. Daydreaming about someone?"

"I wouldn't call it daydreaming," I muttered.

"Hmm. Sounds like someone has your panties all twisted up."

I scowled, the sense of instability inside me a feeling that turned my thoughts dark. "Skylar falls terribly short of being the type of woman who could make me lose my head like Ash has done."

"Ooo!" He laughed evilly, and I could imagine him rubbing his hands together. "A woman has gotten under your skin—she's threatening the wall of granite you think you are."

"Fuck off," I muttered.

"She makes you feel, doesn't she?"

"She doesn't stop talking. And smiling. Her mind flits from one thing to the next like a hummingbird—she can't focus worth a shit, and it drives me nuts. She's always laughing with Ash, touching him like she can't keep her hands off his body."

"Some—one's jea—lous," he sang the words, deepening my frown.

I didn't deny his assumption because the term sounded appropriate for the feelings I had toward Skylar.

"What's she look like?" Colton asked.

"Gorgeous. Pale skin, auburn hair, and she has these big green eyes that are so damn expressive..." My thought trailed off as I recalled the way she'd looked at me when I'd been buried balls deep in her body.

Colton's chuckle pulled me back to the present. "Someone has it *bad*."

My scowl slammed into place once more. "I do not."

"She makes you feel *alllll* the damn feels, am I right? *That's* what you can't stand. Go ahead and deny it, Rhett Stirling, Mr. I-Hate-Vulnerability Asshole."

"This doesn't sound like you venting," I muttered since I *couldn't* deny the truth he spoke.

It wasn't Skylar's sunshiny nature that rubbed me the wrong way. A part of me secretly enjoyed the sense of life she'd brought inside the walls of our home.

Most of the time, at least. Earlier? Well, the silence I'd sought out in my office had been golden.

There was never a dull moment with her around—and fuck knew we'd had plenty of those the previous couple of years. While Ash's and my love and passion hadn't ever lagged, it sometimes felt as though we'd perhaps grown too comfortable. Content to let the time slip by without fully enjoying every minute, feeling excitement in day-to-day existence.

"Your life is more interesting," Colton stated with a chuckle.

I scrubbed a hand down over my face and stretched my

neck side to side, once again thinking the recent spark was due to Skylar's arrival.

No doubt she brought sunshine, warm and nurturing, enticing excitement in the mundane. Some of her qualities, I couldn't deny, added to Ash's and my life in ways I hadn't realized we needed.

"So. Missing Link." I took the conversation back onto Colton so I wouldn't have to further consider the shit he'd pointed out. "Change your profile to show you're looking for a relationship. Trust her to bring what you need."

"Like she did for you?"

"Fuck off," I muttered.

31

ASHTON

I stood in the shower, head tipped against the tiled wall, hot water raining down over me but not cleansing in the way I wished it would. Sickness riddled my body, I had no doubt. And fear owned my mind.

My symptoms were too similar to what I remember Archer dealing with to be anything else. Memories of my twin in the hospital haunted my mind, and I couldn't handle the thought of enduring what he had.

My desire to have children had always been a driving force in my decisions throughout life, but the urgency rising inside me took my tension levels to a different plane.

Yes, I ought to see a doctor—but the thought of going to a hospital clenched my insides up to the point of pain. I heaved. Fucking again.

"No, no, no…" I whispered my denial mantra, my eyes clenched shut as though I could will the truth away.

While I was no professional at smothering emotions, I tried my damned best in order to function, choosing to focus on what I could control.

Attempting to get Sky pregnant and make Rhett fall in love with her so he would have someone when...

Swallowing hard, I once more had to stifle rising panic while chanting that damn two-lettered word in my head over and over again.

Time...I just required a little more time—I needed to keep my eyes on what was important, not the cancer dragging me toward the grave.

Sky had burrowed slightly beneath Rhett's hardened exterior, but he still held back from allowing himself to fully enjoy her spirit, her heart in the same ways I did. He needed help breaking down those damn walls whenever the three of us fucked.

Determination settled like a rock in my churning stomach, and even though my aching body would enjoy staying beneath the hot water and steam, I got out of the shower and threw on some lounge pants, a plan settled firmly in my brain, giving me a focal point to obsess on.

It was time to push Rhett since he refused to lower his defenses.

Skylar and Rhett had finished the dishes, and neither were in the kitchen or living room.

Hope sent me back up to her bedroom since they hadn't been in ours.

The sound of her shower reached me through her door but no voices.

I went back downstairs and found Rhett in the office, staring out the window from where he leaned in his chair.

He turned even though I hadn't made much noise letting myself in.

"Feeling better?" he asked, getting up and approaching me where I stood just inside the door.

My hands fisted at my sides as I readied to tell him what

I needed, expecting he wouldn't ever deny a request from my lips.

"I want Skylar between us tonight—without condoms."

He studied me with his dark, closed-off eyes, knowing exactly what I asked for.

The next step in a plan he had helped create...commitment.

Our end goal.

Rhett hesitated long enough that I began to tremble, fearing rejection. His tension, his reservations assured me he had no wish to sink into her body again, but if only he'd open up and allow himself to *feel*, we would all benefit from how fate had brought us together.

I needed his consent to the point I trembled, on the verge of breaking down.

"Please, Rhett." My voice cracked, and I swallowed hard, fighting off the tremors.

I couldn't tell him the truth about why I pushed with desperation to move forward—it would ruin him, rip him apart from the inside out. Seeing him in that kind of pain would kill me faster than any cancer...

Yanking my focus back to the present, I stared at my lover, silently begging fate to allow me one—*two*—last requests.

Rhett exhaled heavily as though reading my mind and moved in close, reaching for me. "Okay."

I sank against his firm chest for a moment and filled my lungs with the scent of pine as some of the tension drained from my body.

I have this night and at least a few more...

That sense of urgency returned, and I grasped Rhett's hand, starting toward the stairs, hoping Skylar had finished in the bathroom.

"Take a quick shower, then get your ass in our bed," I told Rhett, my heart and mind focused on the end game.

He chuckled. "You *must* be feeling better. You hardly ever boss me around."

"Just do it." I pushed him toward our bedroom and knocked on Skylar's door.

Rhett disappeared from view, and Skylar's door swung inward. She stood wrapped in a towel, hair wet and a darker shade of red than her eyelashes.

I couldn't help the butterflies erupting around the stone in my stomach or the smile that her presence always brought to my face.

"Come." I grabbed her hand and tugged, but she hesitated.

A slight frown marred the smooth, pale skin of her brow.

"I-I'm not sure I should be in your bed tonight," she stated quietly—and having too many sisters, I understood.

My smile dissolved. "Is it that time of the month?"

Pink flushed her cheeks, and she shook her head.

"You aren't in the mood?" I asked when she didn't elaborate, every cell in my body vibrating with *need*.

She glanced at our bedroom door down the hall as though considering.

"What's wrong? You aren't usually this quiet."

"Maybe I should be," I whispered.

"What?" I couldn't keep the surprise from my voice. "Why would you say such a thing? I adore your quirkiness. You're my sunshine, Sky."

"I'm not so sure Rhett appreciates who I am as much as you do."

Her insecurity slammed me upside the head, and I took her face in my hands, placing a slow, gentle kiss to her soft lips. "I told him I wanted you between us tonight, and he agreed. Don't give up on him, Sky. You're the refreshing happiness his grumpy ass needs. Give him another taste—I'm sure he'll be unable to continue hiding behind those walls protecting his vulnerability."

I studied her troubled eyes while she nibbled on her lower lip.

Anxiety flared again, cramping my stomach. We didn't have time to dawdle...

"Please, Sky," I whispered, not above begging her too.

She must have read the desperation on my face, because hers relaxed, and she clasped her hand atop mine on her cheek. "Anything for you, Ashton."

Relief should have rushed through me, calmed my anxiety, but I hovered on the verge of a panic attack.

Taking measured breaths, I led Sky to our bedroom and stripped her of her towel as Rhett showered. Her pale, freckled skin called to my fingertips, but I encouraged her onto the bed before touching her.

"Are you okay?" she asked, her gorgeous green eyes wide and full of empathy as I pushed down my pants with shaking hands.

"I will be," I promised a lie while climbing in to lay beside her.

She sighed as I rubbed my nose over hers. She smelled of mint, coconuts, and dreams fulfilled. Her simple touch eased some of my nerves, bringing a sense of relaxation that would allow me to enjoy our evening together.

"I'm falling in love with you, Sky," I whispered, needing her to know one truth of my existence.

She hugged me tight, her eyes growing misty. "I feel the same."

"We just need to get Rhett in on this love fest," I said and kissed her.

"Mmm," she hummed her agreement against my mouth.

I rolled to my back, taking her along with me, settling her atop my aching body.

She straddled my waist, our mouths breaking apart as we stared at one another, both of us breathless.

"I'm all in, Sky," I murmured, smoothing her hair away from her face and cradling her cheeks in my hands. "I want this for a long as possible. Us."

"Me too," she whispered, her eyes welling.

"Can we have you tonight—nothing between us?" I asked, my heart thrumming. "I-I know it's a lot to ask, but we aren't promised tomorrow, and I really...well." I swallowed hard. "Rhett and I get tested regularly, and we always wear condoms when we invite someone into our bed."

"I haven't been with anyone except for the two of you in years—and my last doctor recommended testing too since my ex was a cheating asshole."

"So you're okay going bare?" I asked and held my breath.

"Yes. I know this has all happened really quickly, and my family would call me a fool for making decisions like this, but I want a future with you and Rhett. Children. Lots of them. And if that happens sooner than later, I won't complain."

"So you aren't on birth control?"

Lower lip catching between her teeth, she shook her head.

My throat clogged up, and I pulled her down for a tender kiss. The sense of rightness welled inside my soul, flooding me with the same emotions I felt for Rhett—and yet slightly different in its bonding strength.

The softness of her mouth, the sweetness of her breath, how she pressed her body against mine with a sigh rushed contentment through me. A longing so damn deep I couldn't fathom its depths welled up inside me, capturing my full focus.

Her tongue stirred my blood, and her fingers in my hair and small moans thickened my dick.

Fate had gifted us the perfect angel, and it was time for Rhett to open his heart and see the truth.

The shower's water turned off, and I forced myself to pull away from Sky regardless of my anxiousness to push inside her and fill her with my seed. I encouraged her to sit, her slick folds rubbing against the back of my hardened length.

"Let him see how gorgeous you are, sunshine." I palmed her breasts and rolled her tight nipples between my fingers until her head tipped back on a whimper.

I felt Rhett's presence before I saw him in my periphery.

He watched for a few moments as I drove Skylar to squirming on my lap, her hands restless on my abs.

So responsive and expressive...

Every slide of her soaked pussy over my cock shot an ache through my balls. They firmed up, and I hissed. "Rhett."

He finally approached, and I gave him my attention as he drew closer. Dark, wet hair mussed from a quick drying of the towel, he stood naked and gorgeous, his dick half-hard.

Our gazes met and held, and I hoped he could see my thankfulness for agreeing to share her in the way fate had intended.

His eyes weren't hard or closed off. I didn't get a sense of jealousy.

His attention flitted over Skylar, but she kept her focus on me, going still at his presence.

I ran my hands up her thighs, thumbs caressing her hip bones. "Okay?"

She nodded—but didn't speak.

Rhett pulled open the bedside table drawer and grabbed the bottle of lube. "You're alright with us not using condoms, Skylar?" he asked, his tone as tense as her body.

"Yes." Skylar turned toward him, fire in her eyes. "Whether you want it or not, I'm going to thoroughly bask in the love of this generous man who dreams of nothing but happiness for all three of us." Her voice shook, but she tilted her chin up slightly as though expecting Rhett would argue. "How about you let go of your goddamn stubbornness for once and simply choose to enjoy life outside your comfort zone?"

Her words hit me like a punch—but warmth rose inside me. Fuck, did I love her fire, how she called him out and pushed him to grow.

Sky shifted forward, tipped her hips, and took me into her body with one hot, clenching slide.

"Ah, fuck." I gritted my teeth and flexed my ass, gaining another inch inside her tight sheath as she settled fully atop me.

"You know you want my ass," Skylar told Rhett, the heat still in her voice. "How about you find the strength to stop denying we could be something beautiful?"

She didn't wait for an answer or for him to make a move. Sky grabbed hold of my hair and took my mouth in a possessive kiss full of longing and lust.

Her pussy walls squeezed around me, tight and wet, sending my eyes rolling into the back of my head. Fucking perfection. Every gyration of her hips glided hot silk over my length and caused tingles to race through my balls.

I grabbed her ass cheeks and kneaded, pulling them

apart, trying like fuck to get Rhett where he needed to be before I busted prematurely.

The bed dipped near my knees, and I straightened my legs fully for him to straddle my thighs.

"Anyone ever have your ass before, Skylar?" The rasp in his voice suggested arousal, but a hard thread of resolve lay beneath.

He was doing this for me—not her or because of the words she'd challenged him with.

"No," she whispered, her forehead tipping against mine as though some of the fight had left her.

Rhett clasped her hip and stilled her movements atop me.

She released a low moan, and I imagined him lubing her hole with a gentle circular motion.

"Relax," he murmured.

Sky gasped and tensed around me.

I soothed my hands along her spine, my balls still throbbing, dick wanting to plunder. "Bear down when he presses in—trust me, angel."

She exhaled slowly and nodded.

Rhett's finger moved along my length through the thin membrane of her inner flesh.

"Christ, Rhett." I gritted my teeth as he stroked deeper, caressing us both.

"Oh..." Sky grimaced.

I took her mouth, hoping to distract her from the stretching burn I knew all too well. She slowly relaxed against me, her fingers once more tightening in my hair.

Rhett added a second finger.

"Ow, ow, ow," Sky chanted, her forehead deeply dented in a frown as her back arched slightly.

"Shh." I attempted to soothe her since Rhett kept silent.

"Come here again," I whispered and tugged her face down to mine. I kissed her again, desperate to offer her something else to focus on while Rhett readied her body for him.

Thank fuck she held still or I would have blown my load before Rhett even breached her ring.

Coming was inevitable—and when I did, I laser focused on accomplishing at least one of my goals.

Surely fate had led us together. I could trust her for the rest.

Sky would give me a child, and even if I didn't live to see my son, she would be there to hold him.

And Rhett too.

32

SKYLAR

Initial double penetration was not what I'd expected.

Those smutty romance novels were lies wrapped up in rainbows and heart-shaped clouds of stark, painful reality.

It felt like Rhett had shoved his fist up my backside even though it was only three of his fingers. His dick, I knew, would stretch me beyond even those.

Ashton licked into my mouth, trying to distract me, but I couldn't take my focus off the man behind me—or the memory of his walking out on me mid-conversation in the kitchen as I'd poured my heart out to him.

Zero damn regard or sense of human decency lay inside his heart in that moment, and I felt like a waste of his time.

Had it not been for my connection with Ashton, for the bond that had settled into place between us, I'd have packed up my shit and left.

Lived on the streets.

Escaped Rhett's negativity, the way he made me feel worthless and unwanted, same as my sister always had...

No—I wouldn't have. Bitterness and self-preservation

had insisted on those courses of actions I'd ended up dismissing.

Rhett had feelings for me outside of annoyance—I'd seen it in his eyes that night he'd taken me on the couch. Regardless of what he might think, our coming together had been more than mere fucking.

We'd shared on an intimate level in that moment, something achingly sweet and precious.

It had to be fear that kept his emotions bottled up.

I'd finally found the strength to call him out, but he still seemed...distant even though his fingers pumped deep into my ass in the most intimate experience of my life.

I breathed easier, finally relaxing enough that the burn eased.

He pulled out and spread my cheeks, and I'd never felt so damn naked and vulnerable in my life. My pulse thrummed from more than arousal for the sweet man beneath me and the hope we might create something beautiful just like I'd told Rhett.

Ash peered up at me with his expressive hazel eyes, capturing yet another piece of my soul with the happiness shining in their depths.

His dimple popped, and I swooned, going full-on boneless atop him. "That's my sweet girl," he whispered.

Something much larger than fingers pressed against my hole, but I focused on the love in Ashton's gaze, the acceptance and adoration clearly written on his face.

Love you—

The thought ripped from my head as Rhett pushed against my barrier, and I hissed, fighting to keep myself relaxed.

"Bear down, Sky," Ash murmured, and I did as told, the sudden need to pant tensing my body.

Rhett invaded my body, and I automatically clenched around his girth, the flare of pain catching my breath.

Too big...t-too much...

"Fuck," he cursed with a low groan, his hands grasping my waist in a bruising grip.

Ashton moaned and shifted, his length throbbing inside me, giving me something to focus on other than the massive intrusion up my backside.

Rhett pushed in deeper, splitting my body in two.

"Oh...fuck." I swallowed hard, trembling at the feeling of being stuffed beyond healthy even though he couldn't have even been halfway inside my ass. "Too much—too fucking much," I whined, unable to keep from squirming.

Out—he needed to pull back and go away.

"Fuck," I muttered again, the desire to flee making me restless. Antsy. Desperate.

They both stilled inside me, but Ash began rubbing his hands over my skin. My back, my hair, my sides, my thighs clamped tightly around his waist, holding onto his grounding of my thoughts.

Shushing noises filled my ears, and I panted, eyes clenched tight, trying to just relax and let Rhett in.

Teeth gritted, I hardened my resolve to have this with both men. "Do it."

Rhett backed off, easing the ache in my ass but slid inside once more.

Less pain, I noted, but I still couldn't relax at the intrusion.

Ashton moved beneath me, pulling out—which allowed Rhett to sink deeper.

Zings of actual pleasure radiated through my entire core at the slick glide through my ass. "Oh...wow. Um...okay. It's not *too* bad. Not delicious though. Definitely not that."

Ashton chuckled and pushed in as Rhett retreated.

Jimmy Cricket. I groaned and went boneless again as every nerve ending inside my pussy and ass lit up regardless of the continuing stinging stretch.

"Yes," Ashton moaned as they synchronized another slow thrust in and out of my body.

I lay my cheek on his chest, giving over to the fantasy of a lifetime coming true as they took turns pumping into me. Two hard cocks, four grasping hands. Gasps and groans filling my ears as all three of us let go of walls and hurtful words and just *felt*.

I allowed myself to take pleasure in Rhett even if he didn't want me in the way I couldn't help from feeling for him. Yes, his dismissal had hurt and so did his thrusting length, but I still longed to break through the barriers he'd erected between us.

"I'm so close, Rhett." Ashton's rasped words brought me back to the fact no latex existed between us.

He was going to release inside me.

Maybe make our dreams come true about creating a child.

Rhett's hand reached between me and Ashton, his fingers finding my clit as he buried deep and held still.

My throat went tight as hope sprang to life in my chest.

He wanted to give me pleasure—

Ashton punched upward with his hips, the head of his dick bumping against my cervix. "Oh!" I gasped and bit my lip.

"Come around his cock, Sky," Rhett commanded, playing me like a fine-tuned fiddle with his fingertips over my throbbing nub.

My climax didn't well up and wash over me like usual.

Inner walls clamping around them both like a vise, I

shot toward the stratosphere like a rocket, shrieking and babbling nonsensical things. Words. Curses. Ashton's name—Rhett's—while arching toward the ceiling, shuddering with every pulse of euphoria zapping through my body.

I flew like Annie Kelly's characters did, but Ashton yanking me down to claim my mouth brought me back to earth.

Ashton erupted deep inside my pussy, and I squeezed his throbbing cock tight, trying to pull him in deeper, wanting to hold every drop he offered inside my body.

Rhett let out a harsh grunt and backed out of my ass so quickly, I cried out over the discomfort.

Hot cum shot over my back, spurts of sticky wetness marking me.

But I knew in the deepest parts of me that he didn't see his cum on my skin as a claiming. He might have given pleasure, but I would never measure up to the woman he'd envisioned for the two of them.

Someone as polished as him and Ashton, who would bring value to their lives. Perhaps rich, but definitely stable. Mature. Not so...flighty or foolish.

Tears slid over my cheeks, soaking Ashton's chest where I rested, wrung out, backside aching more than I'd expected and far from comfortable physically and emotionally.

Ash's hands glided up and down my back again, but the pain in my heart wouldn't be soothed.

Rhett left us for the bathroom, and I managed to draw an easier breath in his absence.

"Did we hurt you?" Ashton asked, his breath hot against my hair.

I took stock of my backside, squeezing enough that Ashton groaned. His dick still lodged inside me like a plug for his cum, and I was determined to hold him there as long as possible.

"I'm fine," I whispered the half-truth—even if my mind wasn't.

We had crossed serious boundaries, and I should have been drowning in a glorious river of sweet deliciousness.

But I felt as though I'd been dragged across jagged rocks.

Ashton tightened his hold on me, shifting his knees upward to plant his feet on the bed and keep his softening length from slipping free from my body.

A heavy sigh shuddered him beneath me.

"Are *you* okay?" I asked.

"Yeah," he murmured and kissed my hair. "I'm just dreaming about babies and happily ever afters."

His whispered words made me lift my head so I could see his face.

There was no more falling.

I was in love with Ashton Blackwood—fully and thoroughly. My eyes welled.

His responded in kind.

"Hi," I whispered, smiling as a fresh tear slid down my cheek.

"Hi back." His dimple popped, and I pressed my lips to his, hoping what I felt for him would be enough for the unclear future ahead of us.

33

RHETT

There was no denying Skylar had a sweet ass.

But she hated having my dick shoved up there. It had taken quite a bit of patient stretching, but she still resisted the hell out of my cock regardless of the bottle of lube I'd emptied in her and over my length.

Breaking in a virgin hole while another dick fucked her pussy hadn't been the smartest thing Ashton and I had done, but it was what he'd asked for.

And what my love hoped for I would move the world to make happen.

If only I could lower my defenses toward the woman he'd fallen in love with.

Yes, he'd addressed me while we'd fucked her senseless between us, but his eyes had stayed on her face.

That love, that passion, I soaked in when pleasuring him shone clearly in his eyes as he'd gazed at her.

The balance I'd thought we'd found once more shifted around us. Her words had shaken my resolve—made me feel weak as fuck, but I couldn't. Let. Go. The walls I'd hidden behind my entire life had grown too thick, too dominating to crumble beneath a woman simply calling me out on my bullshit.

Two weeks passed, and every goddamn night, Ashton stuck his dick inside her pussy without a condom, loving on her until he filled her full of his spunk.

I refused to do the same.

Yes, I took her ass when not requesting to just watch them and tear apart my insides, but it wasn't her hole I lusted for.

I wanted Ash. His kisses. His affection.

But like a light switched on, he'd become overly focused on his quest to impregnate Skylar. I'd never seen him so driven and unwavering. As though a ticking clock and desperation had taken control of his mind, he didn't talk about anything else. Refused to, shutting me down anytime I approached a conversation outside work or unimportant details of life.

Perhaps once he succeeded, his relentless pursuit of pussy would abate, and he would emotionally return to me.

That was my hope, the thing I clung to as every day passed and the distance between us grew.

If only I knew how to express what his actions did to me...

The ache in my chest while waiting for balance to return went beyond anything I'd experienced. The memory of begging him to never leave me in the early morning hours after my mother's death shredded my thoughts.

There was nothing strong or stoic about the storm inside me.

I refused to reach a breaking point as my father had done while losing his shit beside Mom's hospital bed.

No one would ever see how emotionally fragile I was in the deepest reaches of my soul. How weak I'd become.

Skylar got her period the morning of Ash's birthday party.

I shouldn't have been relieved—but I was—and I hated myself for it.

She cried, curled on her bed, and Ash wrapped himself around her, tears in his eyes as well.

So much for his having a happy birthday.

Unable to stand the sense of *asshole* I felt inside, I left them alone and went outside to sit by the pool with a cold beer since we had at least an hour before the party planner and caterers arrived.

Canceling the event would have been best for them, but I couldn't fathom the long hours ahead with no hope of distraction.

I should have been pleased Ash had something other than his own sadness at facing yet another birthday without Archer, but I couldn't get beyond the hurt that he clung to her rather than me in his grief.

The still pool directly in front of me invoked memories of Ash and Skylar kissing while half-submerged, so I moved my attention to the ocean beyond. Swells, waves, and breaks played over the water in soothing, rhythmic motions, never ceasing.

Restless depths lay below full of violence as creatures fought for survival.

But it was beautiful topside, hypnotic...luring.

I'd never been a fan of swimming in the ocean. Too many unknowns, the inability to see what lurked beneath, made me feel small...pathetically uncertain.

My heart began to race, and restlessness tugged at my senses urging my thoughts to flee from danger.

I turned my focus to the patio around the pool Lionel's Landscaping had replaced earlier in the spring. Every paver had been laid with precision, perfectly aligned. Set into place and unmoved by whatever storm might pass through.

I imagined myself as the same until my muscles once more relaxed, and I turned my mind to the party taking place that evening.

Ash would probably ask to cancel our plans, but I wouldn't allow it. He needed something to occupy his mind, to bring a smile to his face. A reminder that life continued on outside impregnating Skylar, that there would be another night, another moment, to fulfill his dreams.

We had nothing but time.

But how could I make him slow down the train barreling us forward down a path I couldn't see clearly?

———

Smooth jazz filtered throughout the house's sound system, a quiet backdrop for hushed conversations and the mingling of our party guests.

As always, I'd dressed in a button-down and tie, and while comfortable on the outside, my insides weren't so put together as my outward armor.

Ash stood beside me, gorgeous as ever although a little pale.

Skylar had yet to make an appearance.

Ash pressed his fist into his sternum like he always did after a meal, and I frowned. We hadn't yet eaten anything.

He'd been popping antacids the past couple of days, and I wondered if the stress of his obsessively trying to get Skylar pregnant had given him an ulcer.

The more I thought about it, the more I expected my assumption was spot on.

An ulcer had wrecked him years earlier when we'd been

nearing the finish line of the Missing Link app when we'd both been stressed out.

Same as then—fuck, as anytime I saw Ash in pain—longing to ease him drew me in like a magnet.

I slid my arm around his waist and tugged him against my side, wishing I could make him smile like Skylar did.

"Okay?" I whispered against his ear.

A shiver slid over him from my tender touch, and he sagged against me.

Relief rushed through my body, lust jolting straight to my dick.

I hadn't felt that in...

Fuck.

Since that rough taking over my desk, I hadn't reached out to my love to offer comfort or affection. Not one single fucking time.

Asshole.

"I'm fine." Ash's quiet answer did nothing to reassure me in the least or ease the unrest returning to tighten my guts.

"You look sexy as fuck in that color," I reminded him like I always did of the olive button-down that pulled out the green in his hazel eyes.

He smiled up at me, but the usual happiness a social party, regardless of its reserved guests, brought to his face didn't make an appearance.

"Sorry if I've been distant," I murmured, tracing a finger over his jawline, wishing I could lock us away from the world and love on him until he passed out in my arms.

Ash leaned into my touch, his eyelashes fluttering closed. A heavy sigh lifted then relaxed his shoulders. "Everything is going to be fine," he whispered, but it sounded like he assured himself rather than accepting my apology.

Introspection always hit Ash hardest during the anniversary of his brother's death or on their birthday, so rather than poke and stir up emotions, I squeezed him a little tighter and kissed his temple.

Tonight, I told myself. Once everyone left us in peace, I would get him alone and remind us both of the closeness we'd lost due to my being a selfish prick.

Skylar appeared at the bottom of the steps in a little black dress that accentuated her curves and set her hair on fire. The disappointment over getting her period that morning seemed to have faded completely. No makeup painted her face, but she seized my lungs for a second with how she smiled, her eyes flitting around our household full of designer clothes and jewels.

Ash didn't rush to her side as I'd expected. He lingered in my hold, even though I knew he'd caught sight of her with how his body tensed like mine did.

Without doubt, those muscle responses in each of us resulted from totally different feelings.

Him with longing, me with suspicion and that familiar sense of unease rocking my foundation.

Her gaze landed on us, and her smile lit the goddamn room, shining light through the storm clouds inside me.

My face dented with a scowl.

Our gazes clashed, and her happiness dimmed.

Ash pulled away from me, and I let him go, clutching my wine glass a little tighter as he moved through the crowd intent on her.

I prepared myself for noise and judging looks his introducing her to people would bring. Backlash and ridicule.

But I told myself I didn't care what others thought.

"Rhett!"

A familiar voice pulled my focus off Skylar, and I turned, my scowl dissolving at the threesome headed my way.

Wyatt stuck out his hand, and I clasped it firmly.

"Thanks for coming," I said, my voice warmer than it would have been with anyone else in the room except for Ash.

"Wouldn't have missed it." His free hand clutched at Haley's, and Garrett stood close behind her, his palm on her lower back.

Haley glanced around the room wide-eyed, just as out of place and starstruck among California's rich and famous as Skylar had appeared. At least Wyatt's woman knew how to keep her unfiltered mouth shut and not make a spectacle of herself when necessary.

"Garrett," I shook his hand, then smiled at Haley when she finally looked up at me. "Are these two treating you well?"

"Could be better," she sassed and squeaked a breath later, sidling away from Garrett as if he'd pinched her ass. "Jerk," she hissed at him.

"Later," he stated with a wink and grin.

Haley rolled her eyes.

"Is that your houseguest? The woman hanging on Ashton?" Wyatt asked, and I glanced toward where he'd tipped his chin.

Skylar clung to Ash's hand and upper arm, leaning into him. They were a gorgeous couple, dick-thickeningly so, their faces close together as they spoke.

I fought off another frown while sipping my wine. "She's the potential mother of Ash's children," I went with, my tone bland, considering the storm from that morning still roiling my insides.

"A match through the app?" Garrett asked.

I nodded, unable to tear my focus off my lovers as Ash drew her forward toward some of our guests.

We hadn't discussed how to introduce Skylar but should have.

Most of those in attendance knew why Ash and I had created Missing Link, so the fact a woman would one day share our lives in some capacity wouldn't come as a surprise to them.

"She's the perfect match," I answered Wyatt without adding *for Ash* like I did in my mind.

"Congratulations," he said, and I made myself nod in acceptance.

"She's stunning," Haley said.

"She's got nothing on you, cuddle bug," Garrett told Haley, pressing in close against her in my periphery.

Haley laughed lightly and leaned upward to whisper something in his ear.

He groaned. "Let's go get a drink." Clasping her hand, he pulled her away from Wyatt, tearing my focus off Ash and Skylar.

Wyatt stared after his lovers, so much goddamn contentment in his eyes a muscle ticked in my jaw.

"The honeymoon phase is still going strong, I see," I said, truly happy for them.

Same as during the ceremony binding them together, I forced a smile, determined to keep my own emotions from showing on my face.

"Better than ever." Wyatt turned toward me, grinning. "I hope you, Ash, and whoever she is find the same."

"Skylar," I offered her name, "and Ash is already there."

Anyone with eyes would note his possessive hand on her back while introducing her to others. The way he watched her face while she spoke with our guests outed him almost as much as if he'd dropped to one knee and proposed right there.

"What's holding you back?"

Lifting an eyebrow, I once more glanced at Wyatt.

"Don't give me that look," he said with a chuckle. "I've spilled my shit to you plenty of times."

He had me there, and maybe some perspective from someone else in a triad wouldn't hurt. "She has no aspirations beyond having babies and being a mom." I gave him one bit of truth.

"That sounds more like what Ash wanted than what I remember your profile stating."

"I changed our preferences a few weeks back."

"Enter the angel of your dreams."

Flighty laughter rose over the other voices around us, drawing the focus of half the room and keeping me from correcting Wyatt's assumption.

The volume of Skylar's giggles rose, and she clapped a hand over her mouth, but she'd already drawn the attention of the rest of the guests who hadn't noticed her arrive on the scene.

I studied the crowd, seeing gazes take her in from head to shifting feet, people speaking to those beside them while eyeing the beauty still clinging to Ash's hand.

Another bark of laughter tipped Skylar's head back, and I sipped my wine again, ready for the circus to begin.

"I've never seen you uptight like this."

I yanked my attention back toward Wyatt who studied me with a knowing look. "Is it jealousy or anxiety that has you tensed like you're on the verge of explosion?"

Rarely did a person call me out, labeling the feelings that seemed like a growing cancer inside my gut.

Jealousy sounded right for every harsh, negativity Skylar stirred up inside me whenever Ash put her first.

"You know some might judge," Wyatt said, "but don't let other's opinions keep you from happiness."

I didn't respond, and Wyatt eventually nodded as though accepting my disinterest in discussing the situation I'd created for myself.

"I'm always available if you need an ear, Rhett." He clasped my shoulder briefly and moved off, heading in the direction where Garrett and Haley had disappeared.

He'd found his place with his partners, and I'd named the emotion inside me for what it was at seeing the three of them together without any distance.

Envy.

34

ASHTON

Skylar's sunshine didn't light up too many faces like I had expected.

Our usual guests, even those I considered actual friends in attendance at my birthday party, seemed closed off to her bright personality.

And Rhett? He'd shut down the second she'd made an appearance.

I'd thought he and I had a sweet moment together, his affirmation and affection soothing parts of me I'd been ignoring in my attention to Skylar—but then she'd descended the stairs, ending what had filled me with warmth and a sense of hope I hadn't felt for weeks.

His silent intolerance for her nature continued throughout the next half hour and revealed itself countless times with disapproving glances and thinned lips.

We hadn't discussed how to introduce Skylar, so I took it upon myself to label her as our girlfriend. No one knew she lived with us outside her sister and parents—and the cleaning ladies who came in weekly, but the term for our angel fit.

Regardless of what words I used to explain her connection with us, Rhett wouldn't have been pleased, just as he hadn't been about anything the previous few weeks.

He hadn't said another word about our ditching condoms and poked nonstop about how I was feeling whenever a grimace lined my face, which was more often than not.

He worried—rightfully so, but I pushed aside his concern and focused on getting him to open up to the happiness Sky offered us.

Fucking her again, having her between us hadn't accomplished all I'd prayed for. And the exhaustion of fighting against my illness ate at my tunnel vision determination to find a way to make him love her for when I couldn't.

I smiled. Chatted as though nothing had changed. Clung to Sky's hand with a grip that bordered on manic desperation.

The caterers brought out a chocolate-frosted cake, the same as Rhett ordered every year, but before he could make his yearly toast toward good health and happiness, Skylar started singing "Happy Birthday" at the top of her lungs with a gorgeous smile on her face.

Skylar swung our clasped hands and continued until others joined in, most hesitant except for Haley, Wyatt, and Garrett who stood off to our right.

Usually, there were just a few quiet toasts and well-wishes.

No one had sung that jingle to me since I'd moved out of my parent's house, and the fact it was Skylar who had taken the lead warmed my chest.

I couldn't tear my gaze off her glowing face as she attempted to carry a tune, her luminous eyes like emeralds shining at me. Others might have looked on with disdain, but thankfulness for her realness, her ability to bounce back from that morning's heartache flooded through me, easing my own sadness over failing to plant a baby in her belly like we both hoped for.

Skylar was lovely inside and out, and if others couldn't see that, then their loss. I just prayed Rhett got his act together before it was too late.

The song ended to absolute hushed silence over those around us, and I squeezed her hand. "Thank you," I whispered, my throat tight even as I grinned like a kid.

"Blow them out!" She giggled and wiggled. "Make a wish —for *you know what!*"

Such hope, such joy...my eyesight hazed.

Internally begging fate to give us the desires of both our hearts, I attempted to do what she'd said to the thirty-six candles atop my cake.

Skylar laughed when I failed and leaned down to help me with the remaining flickering flames.

We prevailed as a team.

Straightening, she threw her arms around me. "Happy birthday, Ashton! I didn't buy you an actual present, but I'll make it up to you later! Well, um...maybe without that bow around my body like I'd planned, but my mouth will?" She laughed, her eyes sparkling as she pulled back—the happiness died on her face as she glanced behind me.

Rhett.

I looked over my shoulder to find him scowling, his shoulders rigid. Pink stained his cheeks like he was embarrassed by the silent people around us who'd heard Skylar's outburst and the lack of filter on her mouth.

"Inappropriate," he snipped, his eyes hard as granite.

I could feel Skylar shrivel up inside at his chiding, and my own heart squeezed in my chest at the memory of her sister using the exact same word with her that night we'd first met.

While emotional, I'd never experienced the type of anger that brought on red.

I did in that moment. Heat rushed through me, my hands and jaw clenched.

"Hi! I'm Haley." A sweet voice interrupted the tension.

She held out her hand to Skylar, her smile warm and accepting as conversation began filling back in around us.

Skylar attempted to portray happiness, but her face fell flat. "H-Hi." Her voice shook, and I cursed Rhett in my head.

Haley introduced Wyatt and Garrett, but I couldn't focus on their exchange as my mind lingered on Rhett's single-worded rebuke and the fallout of his disdain.

I could understand his jealousy, but he'd gone too fucking far. To see and actually *feel* the woman I loved wanting to wilt inside herself and hide away because she didn't measure up to his standards...his *perfection*, damn near choked the air from my lungs.

My stomach churned, and even though I hadn't yet eaten, I expected I wouldn't have long before emptying whatever liquids sloshed inside.

Squeezing Sky's hand, I turned toward Haley. "Watch over my angel?" I managed to rasp out. God knew Rhett would do no such thing.

"Of course!" Haley wound her arm through Sky's as though they were best friends, hanging onto her in a posses-sive hold that promised protection I could trust.

"I'll be back in a few." I kissed Skylar's temple.

Without a glance at Rhett, I headed for the stairs on shaking legs, needing the privacy of our bedroom.

Closing the door behind me released the control I'd held over myself.

"Fucking hell!" My entire body thrummed with the need to punch a wall, but I couldn't break my hand.

My churning stomach was more than enough to deal with. At least its contents stayed where they belonged while I paced, my pulse speeding and jaw aching from grinding my teeth.

I loved Rhett. Wholeheartedly, with every bit of my soul, but goddamn that man to hell and back again. Why couldn't he grow the fuck up and own his emotions? He thought he was so strong in hiding his true feelings from the world, but naming them, accepting them, learning to deal with that shit every other human on the planet did would have taken even greater toughness than he thought he possessed.

"Fuck!" Shaking my head, I spun around to pace the other way.

The door pushed inward, and Rhett crossed the threshold, concern etching his brow.

I didn't expect to hear an apology—but wouldn't have accepted it anyway. Sky was the one he ought to have gone to, dropped to his knees, and begged forgiveness for being an absolute fucking ass, not me.

He opened his mouth, and I held up my shaking hand before he could say a word.

"Don't." I bit the word out, spun, and walked away, gathering my thoughts to lambast him.

I seethed, face hot and heart thumping. For the first time in our lives, disgust for my partner's choices flamed through me.

"How could you?" I finally let loose, spinning to face him.

Rhett straightened, his gaze going cold.

"You had to realize how nervous Skylar was about meeting our friends tonight. You *know* her insecurities about her inability to control herself sometimes and yet you have the balls to criticize her in front of our guests?"

"She was making a spectacle of herself."

"Since when do you give a fuck about what other people think, huh?" I shouted. "How many times have you stated you could easily survive without the social circle we've surrounded ourselves with? Let's be honest here...unless you're balls deep in Skylar's ass, Rhett, you act like you can't stand her! Fuck...after that goddamn *fucking* word, she's damn well aware of it too!"

Rhett's jaw ticked, but he didn't argue.

"*You're* the one who changed our profile," I reminded him, my voice wavering, hands fisted at my sides, "so you have *no* right to climb aboard a high horse like the rest of those rich snobs downstairs. You have *no* excuse for your rude behavior to a woman who isn't the angel you'd have preferred."

I took a quick breath, but Rhett didn't bother trying to inject in my tirade.

"If you knew you weren't mature enough to deal with the petty feelings you would have for a woman of my choice, then you shouldn't have made that change!"

My stomach heaved—and I bolted toward the bathroom, barely falling onto my knees before emptying my stomach of wine and bile.

I gagged and coughed, the harsh heaves causing tears to spill down my cheeks.

"Ash—"

"Just *go*," I rasped, hanging onto the toilet bowl so I wouldn't slump over from weakness.

I was in no state to argue or listen to excuses.

"Ash, please—"

"Go away," I bit out and coughed again.

He didn't speak before his footfalls carried him from me, leaving the air cold as ice.

Frigid.

As vacant of life as the grave.

I heaved again, my stomach attempting to turn itself inside out as the pain I'd been dealing with for weeks intensified.

Failure.

The word rang in my ears, mocking me.

No baby...

And I felt as though I'd lost my first love, the immovable rock I'd always trusted with my heart.

35

SKYLAR

I sipped my coffee by the living room window, watching the ocean roll and dip. The sun had been up for a few hours, but Ashton still slept.

Rhett hadn't joined us in our bed the night before, and for once, I didn't care what the man did.

He'd embarrassed the hell out of me at Ashton's birthday party—after I'd done the very same thing to myself without realizing it until the words about my gift for him had thoughtlessly tumbled from my mouth.

I knew I'd been judged left and right before that moment Rhett muttered something that knifed my heart like a killing blow.

Inappropriate.

I didn't fit in with Rhett's crowd—because that was what those guests had been—just as reserved and noses-in-the-air as him. They weren't Ashton's people.

Well, except for the other triad in attendance.

Haley had latched onto my side when Ashton had gone upstairs, and she'd even given me her number before they left so I could reach out whenever I was in the mood for a girl's night out with her and her cousin Lily—who also had two lovers.

I'd watched how Wyatt and Garrett interacted with Haley and each other after the party had returned to normal around us. Coveting what the three of them had found, the fact no jealousy mingled among them, just pure acceptance and a complete sharing of love, worsened the hurt in my chest.

My heart ached almost as much as the cramps over my lower abdomen. The arrival of my period the morning before had saddened me more than I'd expected, but it was the devastation on Ashton's face that had sunk my spirits low to the point of tears.

He'd grown consumed with getting me pregnant, and while I'd been enjoying all the sex we'd been having, I felt as though Ash become...too *focused*. As if single-mindedness had taken over his brain, he rarely spoke about anything else but the child we would have and how perfect of a mother I would be.

I knew about Ashton's father, but I didn't understand his desperation that bordered on lunacy. I also didn't have access to his mind and the thoughts he wouldn't share concerning the matter whenever I found the gall to ask him.

But I loved him and desired a future with him regardless of whatever turmoil drove him.

Rhett's involvement in Ashton's and my future would be up to him, but I no longer pined for the man to want me in the same way Ashton did.

I would never ask Ashton to choose, nor did I expect him to. Somehow, someway, the three of us would have to find a peaceful path and make things work regardless of the boulders Rhett placed before us, because I wasn't going anywhere.

He and I both loved Ashton too much for any other option.

I had considered trying to sit and talk to Rhett, but after his treatment of me during the party, I had no wish to discuss anything with him. From the minute he saw me at the bottom of the steps and his frown appeared to the second he'd uttered a word I hated, he'd pretty much been a jerk who needed to grow the hell up.

But I wasn't one to talk.

I hadn't taken his advice to seek medical help. I hadn't made further attempts to seduce him. And I sure as hell had given up just trying to be kind and maybe win him over.

Emotionally exhausted, I felt as though I was failing left and right, that I wouldn't ever be good enough for what both men might need.

Could I continue on with a big fat elephant sitting in the room whenever the three of us were together? Would feigning ignorance of Rhett's true colors, his disgust over my personality, even work?

Just the memory, the muttered echo, of his chiding me the night before curled my shoulders forward and stung my eyes.

Something had to give before one of us broke down.

The doorbell sounded, pulling my attention back to the window in front of me and the ocean beyond.

I wasn't aware that Rhett or Ashton expected anyone, but I wasn't about to hesitate in the event they rang again and woke Ashton up.

The office door had stood open when I'd come downstairs, so I knew Rhett wasn't at the house to answer.

I scurried toward the entryway, its windows alongside the front door allowing me to see the visitor.

Nora.

My feet stumbled to a stop, my heart rate racing forward and ripping the air from my lungs.

She peered into the window, catching sight of me—I couldn't slip away and pretend I hadn't heard the doorbell.

"Shit," I muttered and swallowed hard, my entire body going cold.

Three steps, and I threw open the door, clutching my coffee in the other hand. "What do you want?" I snapped.

She took her time glancing down over my silk camisole and sleep shorts Ashton had bought for me the week before.

"Mom and Dad sent me to check on you since you won't answer their calls." She sounded bored.

"How did you find me?"

"Your...boyfriend introduced himself to me that night at my house, and Google did the rest," she said with a shrug. "I'll admit you've done well for yourself. He and his partner are quite the catch."

Because they had money? Prestige?

"I would have left you and stayed with them even if they lived in a trailer," I stated, my chin lifting though my pulse still thundered. Hell, if that had been their circumstances, I doubted their so-called friends from the night before would be in the picture. Rhett wouldn't care about reputation or putting on a good show for them.

Never before had I desired poverty or wished pennilessness on a person, but in that moment, I yearned for that exact thing.

"How many other women have those two taken advantage of?" Nora asked, glancing over my shoulder as though seeking out all of Ashton and Rhett's flaws.

"You don't know what you're talking about," I huffed, annoyed she would judge them without taking the time to see their characters.

"Ashton Blackwood and Rhett Stirling are Missing Link's creators, Skylar. Don't be so naive. They made that app for a reason: Find women willing to engage in unnatural sexual acts."

My brain took a few seconds to process what she claimed, and a riot of thoughts and feelings rushed through me, swamping my mind.

I'd seen the notepad on Rhett's desk that first morning of exploration but hadn't even guessed they might be the owners of the app that had matched us together.

But why hadn't they told me?

They'd claimed to own a software company but had to know I wouldn't understand what that vague term meant. Was it possible Nora spoke the truth?

And what did she care about my engaging in supposed unnatural sexual acts? We hadn't actually been raised by religious, homophobic parents, but with how Nora focused on science and the means of populating the earth...

Still.

My forehead dented with a frown. "There's nothing wrong with loving two people," I finally spouted off one of the things flitting around in my brain like a sparrow.

"Love, is it?" she asked, an eyebrow rising while her lips continued to frown. "It's a little soon for that, I'm afraid. It's more an obsession with their lifestyle, their money. But I'll admit this unwise decision landed you in a pretty cushy place for a change. It won't last though, same as when you chose to date what's-his-name back home." She shrugged and glanced over me a second time as I fought to stay still beneath her scrutiny. "But this time, you won't just get cheated on. You'll end up pregnant, tossed out on your backside, and begging to return to the farm."

I clutched my mug of coffee, even though I burned to

toss the cooling liquid in her face. "Never in a million years," I hissed.

"When all this freedom lands you in a heap of trouble, don't bother calling me for help. I'll let Mom and Dad know to expect you." Nora spun on her heel and strode away with all the confidence in the world, same as always.

Damn stick up her ass too with how straight her back stayed.

My shoulders rounded, but I couldn't help having the last word. "I'll never ask you for anything ever again!" I slammed the door and shook with the adrenaline coursing through my system. "Bitch!" I hollered—and burst into tears.

Damn hormones.

Damn sister.

Damn insecurity!

I scurried up the stairs, threw open my bedroom door, landed on my bed, and screamed into my pillow.

Warm arms wrapped around me, tugging me against a hard body. I didn't need to open my eyes to know it was Ashton. I clung to him and sobbed, wishing I could burrow into his chest and live in his heart forever.

He accepted me. He loved me.

And fuck everyone else—I would do anything within my power to keep him.

"What is it, Sky?" he murmured against my hair when I finally quieted.

"Nora showed up."

He stiffened, his hands on my back stilling in their soothing motion of rubbing my spine. "What did she want?"

"My parents sent her to check on me," I replied, sounding as miserable as I felt. "She said some awful things."

Ashton tightened his hold on me.

"She told me that you and Rhett made Missing Link and that you use it to sleep with women all the time." I held my breath, praying he would deny her words.

"Well, we did create the app, and yes, we've met women because of it, but our intentions were pure. Like I told you during our first conversation, neither of us are interested in playing games. If a match didn't gel, we sent them on their way."

"I don't gel," I muttered, my eyelids clenched shut as I pressed my face against his tear-dampened chest.

"I beg to differ."

I snorted.

"Maybe not with Rhett," Ashton agreed, "but I haven't given up hope."

I pulled back to peer into his sleepy eyes. "Even after how he treated me last night? Look, I don't want to push you one way or another—" I hastened to spew some thoughts as they raced through my head "—but I don't know how long I can put up with his negativity. He hurt me last night. Bad. And I wasn't one bit sad he left and didn't share our bed."

"He's not downstairs?" Ashton asked, and I shook my head. "Shit." He rolled onto his back, rubbing a hand over his face.

I hated that I cared—and more words spilled out. "Where would he have gone last night after the party?"

"Maybe a hotel, or our office—the one downtown."

Ashton climbed off my bed.

"Are you going to go find him?" I asked, my voice small. "Because it's okay if you do—you love him. That won't ever change, but I'm just scared." My hands wrung as I considered the thought Ashton might not come back to me willing to share his heart. "A-and I don't hate him. Not really. I want to though—I'll be honest about that too."

Ashton turned to face me but didn't approach the bed where I huddled in on myself. "I'll always love Rhett, yes, but I've also fallen in love with you too, sunshine. There's no choosing, no one winning over the other. Your words have renewed my hope that I can find a way to make this work. I promise."

Biting my inner lip, I nodded, giving him my trust.

I just prayed he didn't break that along with my heart.

36

ASHTON

Rhett must have gone to the office since we didn't have any friends close enough he could have called up and asked to spend the night.

Or perhaps he'd gotten a hotel room.

I sent him a text asking him where he was and quickly dressed before brushing my teeth. I'd told him to go away the night before, but it was time to clear the air. To tell him about the cancer I could feel eating away at my blood no matter how much I tried to ignore it. He needed to hear how my time would be short like Archer's. How he should let Skylar past his walls so he would have someone to love him when I was gone, because I knew she would. They'd connected on a deeper level than either of them had seemed to realize.

It was ridiculous that hidden feelings and a lack of communication had brought us to the point of breaking, but perhaps that was what the three of us needed.

Honesty. Openness. Owning our actions, emotions, and the choices we'd made without thought for the others.

I'd never been a leader, but I could be brave when necessary.

I would take that first step. I would bring the change we needed to move forward before it was too late.

"Are you okay?" Sky asked when I dragged myself into the kitchen. Eyes still red-rimmed from tears, she held out a travel mug of coffee to me.

There was no way my stomach would handle its bitterness, so I shook my head. Throat clogged, I tried to smile. "I will be—but Rhett hasn't texted back, and I'm really feeling..."

"Antsy?" Sky suggested as my feet shifted.

I blew out a breath. She and I would have to talk too—all my truth needed to come out, but Rhett ought to hear about the illness I'd been denying first.

"Drive careful, okay?" Sky said as I made for the door leading into the garage.

"Mmm hmm." Too preoccupied with the words I fought to find for Rhett, I left Sky behind without a goodbye kiss.

With a shaking hand, I checked my cell one last time.

Rhett still hadn't responded.

"Office," I mumbled to myself and backed out of our driveway, hoping like hell he was there because I honestly didn't know where else to look.

The entire night before ran through my head as I headed downtown, from Sky's walking down the stairs to how she sang happy birthday to me, off-tune and completely unconscious of her beauty and the raised brows she'd probably gotten.

Nausea and anger had sent me upstairs, and it had taken every ounce of strength I'd had to force my feet to carry me back downstairs after telling Rhett to go. I hadn't wanted to mingle with guests, and I'd have preferred pushing everyone out the door on their merry way. If they didn't like Skylar, I had no wish for them to occupy space in my home or life.

Rhett had already been gone by the time I'd plastered a smile on my face and joined the party once more.

He'd made no excuses, Wyatt had told me, simply walked out the door without a word to anyone.

His car had been missing from the garage, so I'd known he'd left the property, but I'd still been too hurt for my angel to reach out to him.

Skylar and I had both put on smiles for the next two hours, but exhaustion wilted both our shoulders before the last guest, party planner, and caterers finally left.

All of which would never be invited to step into our home again save Wyatt, Garrett, and Haley. At least the three of them had welcomed Sky and acted...normal. Real. I'd never appreciated three people so much in my entire life.

Sky and I had collapsed on our bed, clutching at each other in silence. Both too worn out to discuss the events of the night, we'd agreed to rest and talk in the morning.

Bad enough we'd had a horrible evening...to have Nora show up on our front step uninvited, being judgmental and mean before I'd gotten out of bed...my hackles had raised, and the acid from anxiety and anger made for one unhappy stomach.

My disappointment in Rhett's behavior still lay fresh in my mind while driving, my insides raw from what seemed like a million emotions. Too many to count, too many for peace of mind.

Exhaustion.

Sorrow.

Annoyance.

Anger.

The thought of having to confront Rhett with the truth tensed my body to the point of pain as I made my way downtown. He would be pissed. Heartbroken—at least I hoped he still cared after I'd told him to leave the night before.

Pain lanced through my abdomen.

"Shit." I clutched the steering wheel tighter, swallowing rapidly.

My stomach turned upside down, and vomit spewed from my lips all over my lap and dashboard. I jerked the wheel to get off the road, the force of my heaving hazing my vision.

Tires squealed.

A massive crash of metal registered half a heartbeat before something smashed into my head and stole consciousness from my mind.

———

Someone hollered.

I could barely blink. Blinding...beams of sunshine.

Skylar—I tried to smile at the light filling my chest.

Darkness swooped down and dragged me under.

Muffled words whispered nearby. Searching hands prodded at my body.

Rhett...

Sirens sounded in the distance, coming to clarity in my ears as though I rose to the surface of a pool.

Pain lanced through my head, and I gasped, reaching—

"Shh." Someone grasped my arm. "You're alright. We're on the way to the hospital."

"H-happened?" I asked, the agony squeezing my brain unbearable. Couldn't keep my eyes open. Too bright.

"You were in a car accident and hit your head."

"Not dead," I whispered, not even able to handle my own voice echoing inside my skull.

"You're not dead," someone agreed with a chuckle.

"H-hurts."

A needle shoved into my arm, and I hissed at the sting.

"You're going to be okay…"

The voice faded as numbness crept in.

I thought I remained somewhat alert. Hands kept touching me. Voices nudged me to stay awake when all I wanted to do was slip back into darkness where nothing hurt.

"Need Rhett. My angel." I kept repeating the words—in my mind or out loud, I couldn't tell.

Floating in the clouds…I understood the saying, but no jumbled thoughts flitted around my head like Sky's.

Did I smile?

Her green eyes made me want to.

"Ashton?"

"Hmm?" I hummed in agreement.

The voice repeated my home address.

I hummed, realizing it wasn't anyone I knew talking to me.

"Is there anyone we should call?"

"Rhett. My angel," I murmured again—or perhaps for the first time.

My eyelids peeled back, bright light causing me to whimper at the resulting stab of pain through my head.

"Can you tell me your name?"

"Ashton Blackwood." I couldn't blink reality into focus.

"Do you know what happened?"

Vomit. Car accident. Not dead.

"Who is Rhett?"

"Partner—Stirling," I remembered to add, closing my eyes, too tired to care about anything but rest.

No more pain seized my breath, but I could *not* stay awake.

A loud clanking noise echoed through the darkness while I floated. Hours...days.

Sudden silence filled my ears, the peaceful sort that brought a smile to an exhausted person's mind.

Death isn't so bad...

No more aches riddled my body—but I became conscious of an insistent beep slowly growing in volume nearby.

I attempted to blink, but my eyelashes behaved as though they'd been glued together, refusing to peel upward.

Rest.

The next time clarity moved through my mind, I rose fully to awareness.

A white ceiling hung above me. White walls closed in on me. An IV bag hung on my left...a line went into my hand.

"Huh." I lifted my arm, inspecting the clear bandage over the needle nestled into my skin.

I couldn't feel it.

"Mr. Blackwood?" a kind, feminine voice stated, and I turned to find a smiling face I didn't recognize.

"Hmm?"

"It's good to finally see you lucid," she said, moving closer to my bed. "How are you feeling?"

She checked the drip while my mind slowly processed.

Hospital.

Nurse.

Accident.

Bleach.

I grimaced as my stomach churned. Pain radiated

through my temple. "I hit my head." I sounded like I'd downed a whole bottle of vodka by myself.

The nurse smiled, poking around on a bandage over my left ear. "You did—and pretty badly. I haven't had a chance to clean up the dried blood that well, but now that you're awake, we'll get to it, okay?"

Fuzzy—that's how my thoughts felt. Not...all there. "Where's Rhett?"

"Was someone in the car with you?" she asked, backing up enough to look me in the face.

I recalled driving. Vomiting.

"No. Did you call him?" I slurred the words.

"I can get in touch with whoever you need me to, sweetie."

I recited his cell number without difficulty, but exhaustion once more weighed heavy on my eyelids.

"He's my partner," I murmured. "I'm tired."

"You go ahead and rest. I'll call him and let him know you're here and that you're going to be just fine."

I didn't *feel* fine...and there was something else wrong with me, but I couldn't remember what it was.

Eyes closing, I did as the kind nurse said and stopped thinking before the fact I lay in a hospital freaked me the fuck out.

37

RHETT

I laid on the couch in my office long after I should have gotten up, but I had no energy.

Weak-willed, I'd allowed the storm inside me to wipe my ass out.

The ceiling above me had a slight water stain in the shape of a tearing heart, almost shorn in half right down the middle.

Fitting.

Ash had told me to leave because I'd crossed a line and hurt his angel. Never mind how some of his actions since her arrival had been stabbing my chest with lethal force.

Should have opened your goddamn mouth and told him so, you idiot.

I hated the voice in my head that spoke the truth. There was no one to blame for our circumstances other than myself. If I'd explained to him from the start how his actions had made me feel, shit wouldn't have gotten out of control.

Yes, he'd done wrong, but I'd only made things worse by ignoring the red flags.

It had taken me a night of no sleep on the uncomfortable couch while staring through the darkness with gritty eyes to realize *not* communicating feelings wasn't smart or a sign of strength.

It was stupid, an almost unforgivable weakness.

Stifling emotions equaled withholding the truth, thus a lie. And I'd been dishonest in that regard almost my entire life.

Casting blame on my parents would be easy, but that would be feebleness as well...and I could *prove* myself strong in other ways.

By owning my shortcomings.

Claiming the title of selfish asshole aloud for both Ash and Skylar to hear.

Begging forgiveness without excuses for my dickhead behavior.

I rolled off the cushions that had refused to cradle my back all night and sat on the edge of the couch, face in my hands. Scruff scratched my palms as I groaned.

I had amends to make, but coffee first.

Then a slow drive home while figuring out what the fuck to say to make things right.

Would Ash even give me the chance to explain and apologize for the shit I'd been bottling up inside?

Would Skylar?

My cell rang, my mouth drying at the thought of having a conversation I hadn't yet planned out.

I didn't recognize the number but answered anyway.

Processing the words of the female voice took me a few seconds, but when their meaning slammed into place in my exhausted brain, my breath seized, tightening my chest.

Ash had been in a bad car accident and was in the ER.

Exhaustion fled as a rush of adrenaline took over my

system. Heart rate jacked, I shot off the couch, grabbed my keys, and sprinted out of the office.

Head trauma, she continued—no coma thank fucking Christ, but the doctors were running further tests.

What the fuck for, I didn't wait to find out.

I hung up, tossed my cell onto my car's passenger seat, and screamed at every asshole on the road with me. Slow drivers got in my way. Twice, no turn signals almost caused accidents. Fuckers cut me off—then went into goddamn granny-mode while putting ahead of me and wasting precious moments.

My insides twisted like a coiling snake, a python determined to steal the air in my lungs and swallow me whole.

He's going to be fine. Just fine.

But that word had been a lie my entire life, and I couldn't trust its meaning anymore.

Head trauma—what sort? And would there be permanent damage? Was it amnesia? Would he know who I was? Remember all we had, all the shit I'd done in my desperation to not lose his heart?

I made it to the hospital without smashing up my own car, my hands and knees shaking as I rushed through the sliding doors.

"Ashton Blackwood," I rasped to the woman at the ER's front desk. "He was in a car accident and brought in about an hour ago."

I swallowed hard at the words, determined to stay strong.

Whatever the fuck *that* looked like.

I felt like a first-class mess inside. Without doubt, I appeared the same with my dress shirt unbuttoned halfway and wrinkled by attempted sleep on a couch, my hair probably mussed from trying to rip it out by its roots thanks to every asshole driver on the goddamn planet.

He's going to be fine...

I clung to the hope he really was, that he had no plans to toss twenty-some years of love down the drain over my poor choices leading up to the admonishment I'd spewed out at Skylar the night before.

A nurse took me through double doors into a hallway. "So you're his angel," she said, smiling as though everything was peachy in the world.

"What?" I asked, too brain too fucking fragile, too wound up, to focus on her words.

"He kept asking for Rhett, his angel."

It took a few seconds for me to put together the simple misplacing of a comma rather than a period.

Angel wasn't a definition but a second person.

Skylar.

If they didn't know that bit of information, it meant she hadn't shown up yet, probably hadn't been notified—

The nurse pushed aside a privacy curtain, and I shuffled to a stop, my heart stuttering at seeing my love laid out on a hospital bed.

Just like Mom.

Pale and eyes closed, my love didn't move—but his chest rose.

I quickly scanned over his body, the lack of anything but an IV attached to him.

No machines pushed air into his lungs.

My breath left in a rush, relief flooding through me, and I forced myself to take a slower look over Ash while my feet took me closer.

A bandage covered part of his head, but there was a distinct lack of blood like I'd expected. His hair stuck out in all directions, slightly damp, as though a nurse had sponged him down.

Stinging lit in my eyes, and I blinked back tears while swallowing hard against the thickness in my throat.

Someone touched my elbow, and I tore my focus off my love.

"Are you Rhett Stirling?" A man too young to be a doctor introduced himself as such after I nodded, his voice hushed.

"Can you tell me anything about Ashton's symptoms over the past couple of weeks?" he asked.

"Symptoms?" I croaked, once more turning my focus on Ash to watch the steady rise and fall of his chest.

"He was going on and on about cancer eating away at his insides—symptoms like Archer's?"

My knees went weak, and I sank into the lone chair of Ash's cubicle. "Oh fuck."

The doctor kept silent while I stared at Ash, so many goddamn things clicking to place in my head. My stomach went hard as a rock, my palms suddenly sweaty.

Beeps and voices I hadn't noticed before seemed to crescendo in my ears, making me wince.

"H-His twin brother died from leukemia when they were young." I barely managed the words.

"He said he'd been having body aches—stomach pain especially. Exhaustion and light-headedness. What's his physician's name and has he been seen?"

I rattled off our PCP's name but knew without asking Ash hadn't gone to get checked out. Chances were, he'd self-diagnosed himself rather than stepping foot in a doctor's office.

"He claimed he vomited while driving to his office and that's what caused the accident," the doctor stated quietly.

He'd been coming to find me.

"Christ." I scrubbed a trembling hand down over my face. If I'd stayed home, faced what I'd done rather than escaping to lick my wounds, he wouldn't be there. Wouldn't be—

"We're running some tests, but—"

Ash's eyelids fluttered, and I hopped up, rushing to crowd his bed, ignoring whatever else the doctor had to say.

"Hey, baby." I tried to keep my voice light while gently threading our hands together and cupping his cheek.

"Rhett." He worked moisture to his lips and forced his eyelids open with slow blinks.

"We had to give him something to calm him down," the doctor explained. "He was pretty upset about his symptoms and wanting you here."

Ash finally gazed up at me, taking a bit to focus on me.

I forced a wobbly smile, my damn eyes stinging again.

A shuddering sigh shivered through him, a slow smile curling his lips. "Am I dead?" The words slurred from his mouth like he was drunk off his ass.

"Far from it," I stated firmly, fighting the tears that yearned to drip down my face.

"Oh good." He closed his eyes again, his smile widening. "I don't want you to be alone when I'm gone. Love her. She's what you need Rhett. You just have to lower your defenses. Needed...to let you know that first."

"You aren't going to die," I bit the words out, sure the swell of emotions inside me was about to burst through the iron dam I'd kept it behind for too fucking long.

"Okay," he murmured, his eyes closing.

"I'm sorry I've been an absolute ass the past couple of weeks." I spilled the words, needing them off my fucking chest before he passed out again. "There's no excuse for my behavior, and I'm going to fix things. I promise."

"Forgive you..." He went silent, lips parting again.

"Ash?"

"Love *you*, Rhett," he slurred as though half-asleep. "Stoic man...my rock. No one...will ever change that." He let out a sigh and went silent as my chest squeezed tight.

"Ash?" I whispered again, but he didn't stir. "What's going on—the tests being run, the plan moving forward," I demanded of the doctor, not taking my focus off Ash's slack face.

There was some swelling where he'd hit his head, the doctor told me, but other than a concussion, he would be fine. It had been his ranting about symptoms and dying of cancer that had them running some bloodwork and putting through orders for scans. He assured me he'd get in touch with our PCP immediately and left us alone.

Ash had withheld information from me, no different than my keeping my feelings from him—we'd both been in the wrong, and shit needed to change.

I *ached* over the fact he'd been dealing with that fear alone. It fucking killed me he hadn't allowed me to be his rock like he'd claimed I was, that he hadn't leaned on me for doctor visits and diagnosis—if he'd even gone, which I highly doubted.

His obsession, his desperation to get Skylar pregnant suddenly made sense as shit clicked together in my brain.

"Fuck," I muttered, running my hand through my hair, my insides growing restless.

Without sure answers about his health, I floundered, *too much* swirling around inside me I couldn't breathe...

I untangled my fingers from Ash's limp ones and strode from his little cubicle, moving aimlessly down the hallway.

Attempting to put shit into perspective and lay groundwork for some sort of foundation to base the next step on, I paced back and forth. The inability to organize my thoughts left me with a sense of helplessness I didn't know how to safely contain inside as I'd always done.

Couldn't take control.

Couldn't plan.

Couldn't fucking *deal*.

My stomach churned with every stride and turn, like a bottle of soda being shaken, pressure building until every muscle in my body trembled, ready to explode.

A hushed whimper rose in my throat regardless of how it swelled shut.

I was going to lose my shit, my goddamn mind—

"Rhett?"

I spun on my heel.

She appeared like sweet sunshine with a messy bun and widened bloodshot eyes.

"Skylar," I croaked out.

A tear slid down her cheek in unchecked release.

She would never ridicule me for being weak like my parents had done. I could trust Skylar with my vulnerabilities, same as I did Ash.

Sobs ripped from my lungs, a keening noise I didn't recognize as the shit I'd kept locked up inside me let loose.

"Oh, Rhett." She sprinted toward me, tears pouring down her cheeks, and I grabbed her up in my arms.

I buried my face in her neck and clung to her softness, the scent of coconuts filling my nose with every gasped inhale. Although my mind reeled with all the words I needed to say to her, I couldn't stop the anguish from stealing my voice, the tears from soaking her skin.

No questions poured from her lips, no blabbering with worry. Skylar kept silent and clutched at my back. Fucking held me tight like a promise she would never let go.

The familiarity, the sense of comfort her forgiving arms offered, made me feel...safe. Accepted. Regardless of the shit I'd caused between us, she *gave* in my moment of heartache.

I'd been a fool to withhold myself from her, and Ash had been right.

I needed her sunshine to light up all the dark corners I'd shoved my emotions into.

And I would find a way to keep our Ash on the earth because the three of us had a future to look forward to.

38

SKYLAR

The hospital had put in a call to the landline at home —I'd been the one to give the operator Rhett's cell number since I didn't have the guts to contact him myself.

I'd shed more tears than I had in my entire life while waiting for the Uber to pick me up and take me to the ER. Still tired from the weekend, cramps riddling my core, and miserable from that time of the month, I'd left my hair in a messy bun. I'd hopped in the car in old sweats and a T-shirt of Ashton's when my ride showed up.

I hadn't even bothered with a bra.

My mind had flitted from one possible tragedy to the next, and I almost forgot the house key before leaving.

Until I got to the hospital, I hadn't been able to think straight, couldn't stop the jitters itching my legs—or how I'd freaked on the receptionist.

"I-I'm here to see Ashton Blackwood," I croaked, my entire body twitchy with anxiety.

"Are you family?"

"Um...no? I mean, not really?"

"Then I'm sorry, but I can't let you in to see him."

My breath left like she'd hauled off and punched me in the gut. All the bad feels erupted at once, my face going hot. "What do you mean I can't go in there!" I shrieked, arms flailing like a madwoman. "I-I'm pregnant with his child! And I'm an emotional wreck—hormones, you know! If...if you don't let me back there right now to see my baby daddy, there will be hell to pay!"

The receptionist stared. Blinked. Glanced down over my clothes—and I quickly pushed my stomach out to make myself look a little less thin.

"I understand," she stated quietly. "I'm sorry...would you please just fill this out?"

Since the woman asked so damn kindly, I did as told with my shaking hand, listing my name and who I was there to visit.

"You can go straight through those doors," she said, pointing to the double ones to my right.

I'd found Rhett beyond, pacing away from me, his broad shoulders slumped.

The second his gaze had landed on me, my heart had broken all over again at the raw vulnerability in his eyes. My tears had started as he allowed his emotions free, and I'd hurried to throw my arms around him.

We stood in the hallway for countless minutes, crying, noses running, holding on like we were each other's life vests in a stormy ocean. And in that moment, every word he'd said and hadn't said since we'd met, every curl of his lip, every dismissal...I put my hurt aside, wanting to give him comfort.

Eventually, we would need to talk, but bigger matters lay in front of us—

"I'm sorry for crying like a baby," he muttered, traces of tears still in his shaky voice as he kept his face tucked in my neck. "There's no need for this kind of emotional outburst."

Anger kindled inside me, an ache in my chest forming for the broken man. How fucking dare his childhood trauma rise up to make him feel guilty at such a time?

"Releasing emotions is nothing to be ashamed of, Rhett," I stated sternly, still holding him since he allowed it. "Every single person's feelings are valid. Worthy of being heard—and I'll listen and try to understand with an open heart if you'll let me."

Rhett released a sigh that shuddered him in my arms.

"Mr. Stirling?" someone called before he could respond.

Rhett and I both eased away from each other at the nurse's voice, but our fingers threaded together and held tight without effort on either of our part. It was like our souls recognized the need for one another, and I'd never felt such contentment in the face of potential tragedy.

"Yes?" he asked, his tone as haggard as his face. Exhaustion lined his skin, dark circles beneath his eyes. Still gorgeous. Sexy as hell.

"We have a room ready."

Rhett nodded, and I clutched to his hand as we stood back, watching a volunteer ready Ash's bed.

He lay unmoving except for his chest, pale and bandaged. I'd expected him to appear—more broken having heard head trauma. I'd feared a disfigured face. Smashed nose. Sterile strips of white hiding his beautiful eyes from sight.

A mere bandage covered the side of his head, and other than pale, he appeared as unblemished and gorgeous as ever.

I breathed easier and fell into step beside Rhett as the volunteer rolled Ashton's bed down a hallway.

Rhett filled me in on what the doctor had told him earlier as an elevator carried us up a few floors—no debilitating injuries, but Ashton would have to be in the hospital for observation for a day or two.

It was the mention of cancer and other testing that caused my eyes to well again as we moved down another hallway toward our destination.

Rhett's voice broke at that bit of shared information.

"Did he see a doctor?"

"I doubt it," Rhett said, rubbing a hand over his face. "Knowing Ash, he got caught up in his emotions over indigestion and thinks he's dying. It would be like him to deny it too. If he didn't talk about it, it wasn't real."

"What do you think?" I asked and started to chew on my thumbnail.

Rhett shrugged, his focus on the volunteer ahead of us. "I don't know. I-I'm struggling right now to just breathe."

I squeezed his hand tighter, thrilled that he shared his feelings with me.

If Ashton feared he had cancer, it was no wonder his sole focus in the previous couple of weeks had been to get me pregnant. His fixation on sex and releasing inside me hadn't just been the closeness, the claiming, and enjoyment of a honeymoon-type phase I'd thought it had been.

The idea he didn't see me as more than a womb flitted through my head, and I fought to push it away. We had shared too much closeness, connected on too deep of a level for that to be true.

At least, I hoped.

Two chairs waited in the private room, and both Rhett and I sat on opposite sides of Ashton once they had him settled.

So many thoughts swirled through my head, but the hush over the room felt...sacred in some way.

I refused to fill it with chatter, with fragmented thoughts

I'd built up since first moving into their home. My desires hadn't changed toward either man, but the timing definitely wasn't right to discuss forward progress until we had answers.

But...

Insecurity hounded my mind over Ashton's desire—obsession, perhaps—to find a woman who was willing to carry his children. The timing...that would answer at least one question hounding my brain.

"Was Ashton showing any signs of sickness before he met me?" I asked quietly, hating to even hear my voice in the room but too disturbed by the idea to stay silent.

Rhett didn't answer right away as he studied Ashton's still face, and I grew agitated, antsy, for an answer.

"I—I keep thinking that maybe he doesn't really love me, that he just wanted to have a child as quickly as possible—and I know I shouldn't be worried about *myself* right now, but there's so much going on inside my mind..."

Rhett's dark eyes roamed my way, the pain in their depths once more hitting me like a truck and causing my eyes to well with more tears. "He met you first, Skylar."

My breath escaped in a rush, and eyesight hazing, I nodded. "He—he has to be okay, right? I mean, his symptoms could be dozens of things," I blurted. "Stress. Ulcers. A stomach virus. Maybe he's developed a food allergy or something."

I chewed on my thumbnail again to shut up even though Rhett didn't tense like he usually would over my chattering. Nervousness made it so damn hard to keep quiet.

Someone from imaging came moments later and wheeled Ashton away.

Rhett stood. "I'm going to go get some coffee," he said, his gaze on the floor.

Since he hadn't invited me, I didn't ask if he wanted company.

"I'll wait here for them to bring Ashton back," I whispered.

He nodded and left me alone with my full mind.

I had assurance Ashton truly liked me for me, not just the fact I had a womb.

But my biggest worry, the possibility of cancer, tangled my thoughts until tears of frustration and worry once more dripped onto my lap.

———

Ashton was awake when they brought him back to his room.

"Hi," I said, smiling through a fresh round of welling eyes as they locked his bed's wheels into place.

"Hi back." He grinned and blinked slowly, reaching for me.

I scooted my chair close and wound our fingers together before kissing his hand.

"My sunshine," he murmured, sounding drunk.

"How are you feeling?"

His eyelids fluttered closed as the nurse moved his IV stand. "Fine."

"Ashton."

"Hmm?" He opened his eyes and struggled to focus on me.

"What happened?"

"I got sick and wrecked the car. Hit my head. I have cancer like Archer."

I glanced toward the nurse, hoping for some sort of sign or at least words for me to not worry.

She gave me nothing but frowned at Ashton. "We haven't gotten any test results back, Mr. Blackwood."

"What makes you think you have cancer?" I asked Ashton while smoothing down his wayward hair.

"Same symptoms as Archer." Ashton blinked a few times, seeming to better see my face. "You need to love him, Sky. And let him hold you too when I'm gone."

I knew he was talking about Rhett, but I was *not* going to listen to that shit. It stirred back up too many fears and emotions inside my heart I'd managed to get a grasp on.

"You aren't going anywhere!" I chided, swiping at the tears sliding down my cheeks. "I just found you. We have babies to make!"

"It was my desire for children that began Missing Link."

I didn't say anything, just let him slur his way through whatever he felt the need to tell me.

"I...I forced this whole situation on Rhett—it's no wonder he shut down even though he wants you just as much as I do."

A huffed snort—*yeah right*—ripped from my nose. Sure, Rhett had enjoyed my body quite a few times, but there was no way in hell his feelings for me ran anywhere close to Ashton's.

"I was selfish, and things didn't go according to my plan. But it's okay because you'll be here for him. And you'll have him and won't ever have to go back to Nora or the farm."

I wrapped Ashton's hand around my cheek and leaned into him.

His dimple popped, and I laughed through my tears. "I love you, Ashton."

"Love you too, sunshine. My angel."

Angling my body over the bed, I kissed his dry lips.

The sure feelings inside me for the sweetheart of a man wouldn't ever fade.

Neither would the similar ones I'd experienced with Rhett. While he'd come undone in my arms, I realized falling in love with him would be easy as singing—even if I did it off-tune and at the most inappropriate time.

I wanted to soothe them both, love them emotionally and physically until we all grew old and gray. Even more, I hoped to bring sunshine to not just Ashton's but Rhett's life as well.

If he would let me.

39

ASHTON

Words kept spilling from my mouth like I'd gone to confession, and I didn't care. I felt like I'd had one glass of champagne too many. There was no pain, no worry.

Just my sweet angel and me.

"Rhett," I stated his name abruptly, cutting off whatever I was blathering on about.

"He went to get some coffee." Skylar leaned in close to the bed, holding my hand with both of hers.

"He always puts me first. I've been so selfish. Self-centered." I rolled my head, my attention lifting to the white ceiling.

"You don't have a selfish bone in your body, Ashton."

I didn't argue because my Sky wore rose-colored glasses.

But it was time to put *him* first.

"Go get coffee with him," I said, still sounding three sheets to the wind even though I didn't feel drunk.

"It didn't seem like he wanted company." Her voice seemed guarded.

"You can lead him through his emotions," I told her, clarity slipping in a little better with every passing second.

"You're the perfect woman for that job. I knew it the second we met."

"I don't want to leave you."

My head rolled over the pillow again, bringing her beautiful bright eyes into view.

I smiled, my heart overflowing with love for her. "I'm not going anywhere...at least right now. Please find him?"

She released a heavy sigh. "Okay."

"Tell him I said he needs to apologize and beg your forgiveness for being an ass."

Her soft giggle lightened the hovering sense of doom over my head. "He doesn't listen to anyone."

"He does with me when he's vulnerable. And trust me." I shifted on the bed, easing a sudden ache in my hip. "He definitely needs someone to help him deal with this...shit." I waved my IV hand around.

Sky kissed my forehead. "I'll go—if you promise to rest."

"Gotta call my parents first. Is my cell around here?"

"The nurse put your belongings in the closet," Sky told me and got up to move across the room for a narrow cabinet. She rifled through a large plastic bag that held my clothes. "My God, these stink like puke. I'm going to throw them in the bathroom and rinse them out when I get back. Here you go," she murmured, handing me my phone.

Numbness tingled my fingers as I swiped the screen to life. "Twenty-two percent," I muttered to myself, trying to blink myself to a full-capacity brain. "Good enough."

"I'll be back soon." Another kiss to my forehead and Sky left my room for Rhett.

My mind was still a bit fuzzy for the upcoming conversation, but I didn't want to wait to talk to my mom. She would be pissed that I'd allowed my circumstances to progress to such a state without informing her.

Mom answered—and hollered for my dad that I was on the phone before I could greet her.

"How are you, honey?" she asked.

"I crashed my car, hit my head, and I'm sick like Archer." Silence.

I rubbed at one of my eyes and blinked the white ceiling a little better into view. Had I enunciated my words enough? "Mom?"

"Ashton, what is going on?" she asked, her voice trembling.

"I crashed my car, hit my head, and I'm sick like Archer," I repeated, slower, figuring she hadn't made out my mumbled words the first time.

"I-I heard—is Rhett close by that I can talk to him?"

"He's getting coffee."

"I'm putting you on speaker so your father can hear. Where are you?"

"At the hospital—I don't know which one. I wasn't awake when they brought me in." I closed my eyes against the dull ache beginning to throb in my head.

It was probably time for more pain meds. Fuzzy clouds sounded good. Comforting.

"What happened?"

"I got sick and threw up while driving. Guess I hit something. Not sure," I murmured, wanting to sleep but forcing my eyelids to remain open.

"You're alright though?"

"Headache. Concussion. No major injuries."

"And what do you mean you're sick like Archer?" Mom asked.

I blinked hard, bringing the white ceiling into focus against sweet darkness on the edges of my vision. "I have the same symptoms he did, but I've been living in denial—what else is new?" I snorted a laugh that sounded too sad to be happy. "I've been focused on getting Skylar pregnant to keep my mind occupied."

"Who is Skylar—"

"She's the angel Rhett and I have been searching for, and they're going to live happily ever after." I found myself smiling at the image in my head of them holding each other.

But I wouldn't be there.

Pain ripped through my chest, stealing my breath and flatlining my lips.

"Ashton, is there a doctor or nurse we can talk to?" Dad asked, his voice clear as though right beside me while I fought off sobs.

"Hey, Dad," I choked out, glancing around the too-brightly lit room, expecting to see him. "No doctors or nurse —just like there's no you. But I'll have Rhett call you when all the test results come back."

"Are you okay, honey?" Mom asked, concern evident in her tone.

The darkness crept inward again. "No, but Rhett will have Skylar when I'm gone. I'm just really sad I wasn't able to give you a grandson, Dad."

"What? Why?" Dad asked.

I shifted to wake myself fully, wincing as various aches made their way up my nerve endings. Why did dying have to hurt so damn much? And how had Ashton smiled through to the very end?

My throat tightened, but Dad had asked me a question.

"I heard how upset you were when I fell in love with Rhett instead of a girl, but I couldn't help it," I explained, my voice sounding...wobbly. "I've been searching for years for the right woman to fulfill your legacy, Dad, and I found her —but it's too late. She's not pregnant, and I'm dying." I swallowed a sob because if I started to cry, so would Mom. Then I would really be upset.

"You don't know that for sure, son," Dad stated sternly while Mom sniffled. "And I'm sorry for putting my hopes and desires onto you. Sometimes we get overcome with grief and emotions and say things we don't really mean. Whatever I did to make you think I disliked Rhett or your relationship, I'm sorry. I love him like a second son."

"You were just so devastated," I insisted, my childhood memories ingrained, written in my blood and replaying through my mind. "Like the golden boy had perished, leaving behind the sullen twin who couldn't make anyone happy." Words poured from me, things I'd shared with my therapist but hadn't ever confronted my father with. "Add in I liked boys, and boom! I'm a failure."

"No you're not, Ashton," Dad said, his tone firm, same as every time I'd been disciplined as a kid. "Yes, I was wrecked by Archer's death, but I've never wanted anything but for you to live a full life and enjoy every minute you have on this earth. My father put pressure on me to have sons, and I'm so damn sorry I made you feel the same. That was never my intention, son. Ever."

"My head wants to pop," I muttered as pain radiated through my temple again, stealing my concentration. "Sorry —I forgive you, Dad. Every anniversary hurts, every birthday...oh, I got your message, Mom." I spoke like Sky, flitting like a tweety bird from subject to subject, but my brain was just so damn fuzzy. Tired. "Sorry I never called back on Saturday. Rhett threw a birthday party for me, and well...it was a long night."

"It's fine, sweetheart," Mom said, her voice soothing in my ear even though it sounded like she had tears in her eyes.

"I love you both. I'll have Rhett call you once we have answers since I'm feeling a little...strange. Maybe drunk? But that's probably the meds."

"Do you want us to come out there?" Mom asked. "We can catch a flight tonight and be there tomorrow morning."

While I would love to have her arms around me when I got the bad news about cancer, I didn't want her and Dad to have to watch their only remaining son waste away.

They'd done it once. I refused to let them suffer seeing it again.

"I have Rhett and Skylar for now, but when we get answers, I'll be in touch. Maybe you could spend a couple of weeks here...depending on how long I have."

"What did the doctors have to say about your symptoms?" Dad asked.

"That it sounds like indigestion, maybe pancreatitis." I struggled to keep my eyes from closing. "But I remember Archer feeling like this, and by the time his doctors figured it out, it was too late."

"Because we brushed off his ailments," Mom whispered.

"What?" I blinked my eyes open again.

"Of the two of you, he was the one who complained about everything—bath water too hot, nightlight too bright."

"Didn't he say that his water was too dry one time?" I asked, the memory floating through my brain even though I didn't remember any of the things Mom had said.

"He did." It sounded like Mom smiled again. "He made every little boo-boo seem like an amputated limb. When he didn't like dinner, he said he had a bellyache so he wouldn't have to finish."

How had I forgotten what a whiny brat he'd been? Sure, he'd been happy-go-lucky, always positive with me, making me laugh, but I guess I'd only remembered the one side of him.

"When he started moaning about not feeling well, we didn't take him seriously—and we've dealt with guilt ever since learning we'd waited too long."

My throat squeezed shut, but I forced words through. "You and Dad did an amazing job raising all us kids—don't ever think otherwise. Sometimes shit happens that we can't control, and life is what it is. I can't complain about the childhood I had. With you. My four annoying sisters. Rhett. And lastly, Sky. She's my sunshine, and you're going to love her."

"I always wanted another daughter," Mom said with a teary laugh while Dad grumbled something about being even more outnumbered by all the women in our family.

"I'll call you as soon as I know something," I promised.

We said our goodbyes, and I hung up, finally ready for relaxation to creep in.

There was nothing more to do but wait. I closed my eyes and told myself to sleep. Enough drugs still filtered through my system that the lack of visitors allowed me to slip away.

40

RHETT

I sat and stared at the cup of coffee I hadn't sipped from. Without doubt, it would taste like shit, same as the stuff in the hospital Mom had died at.

Fucking hospitals—I'd gained firsthand knowledge of why Ash hated them so much.

While thankful for them and the people showing up daily to help those in need, I wanted to blow up the building closing in on me. After sobbing like a baby in Skylar's arms, I felt drained. Emotionless, just plain old bone-weary tired from my outburst in the hallway.

Skylar's simple bit of logic about every emotion having validity lingered in my mind—with potency. I recognized how my parents had failed in teaching me that, and fuck, did I want to do better.

A spring of feelings began to once more well up inside me as the minutes passed, and I focused on them rather than forcing them away as I'd been taught to in order to escape ridicule.

It was time to label the shit. Own it.

The churning stomach? The fucker causing that was *fear*. Raw and visceral in its attack.

My clenched jaw tightened from *anger* over the fact I was the one responsible for Ash's driving. Had I not taken off the night before, he never would have gone looking for me. He never would have vomited in his car and gotten into the accident.

Itchiness in my limbs, the strain of tensed muscles grew from *impatience* at having to wait for goddamn answers when all I wanted to do was drive forward in creating a plan for our future regardless of how it might look.

Once I relented the hold I'd kept on myself since childhood, a slew of words rushed through my head, and I called them all by name.

Guilt.

Desperation.

Regret.

Longing.

Fucking *helplessness* that made me feel unsteady on my feet, trembling in my soul without anything to hold, no rock, no life jacket.

Eyes closed, I attempted to slow my breathing, my heart rate, that thumped inside my chest like it wanted to escape while still allowing the emotions their place.

It wasn't weakness to feel—and giving them space to live inside me took *strength*.

My parents had been wrong. *I* had been wrong to let their bullshit dictate the man I'd become.

But it wasn't too late to change.

"Ashton said you have to apologize for being an asshole—"

Skylar's voice cut off with a squeak as I jerked my head toward her. She shook like a leaf standing beside me, but how she rubbed her palms over her too-large sweats suggested nervousness rather than her usual inability to stay still.

"You spoke with him." No jealousy rose to coat my words —I didn't even experience that sentiment surprisingly.

"He was awake when they brought him back from the scan," she said with rushed, exhaled words as though she'd been holding her breath.

I started to stand, but she put her hand on my shoulder, stopping me.

"He's fine for now and told me to come be with you. Can I sit?" She motioned toward the empty chair opposite me.

I settled back in mine, nodding, actually thankful for the interruption of my introspection. "No results yet?"

"No."

"How did he seem to you?"

A soft smile curved her lips. "A little drunk."

"Yeah, that's the meds." I held her gaze, the clatter of the cafeteria around us quieting in my mind. "I'm sorry for being an asshole," I murmured, meaning every goddamn word.

I'd have apologized even without Ash's demand I make amends with her.

Pink flushed her cheeks, and she opened her mouth, but I wasn't done yet. It was well past time for me to spew all the thoughts inside me as she so often did.

"I've been overwhelmed with jealousy since we came back from Florida. I've never had to share Ash with anyone outside of physical interactions, and I took that shit out on you instead of being truthful about my feelings."

"I forgive you," she stated simply.

"Easy as that?" I asked, raising an eyebrow.

She shrugged a shoulder and smiled, and a hint of

sunshine in her eyes seemed to trickle over my soul like warm water.

"You're so goddamn beautiful, Skylar. I'm sorry I haven't been telling you that every day. You make Ash happy, which truthfully, brought me contentment from day one even if I refused to acknowledge it out of sheer stubbornness and self-preservation.

"But there have been so many other emotions I've never named," I continued, "haven't allowed myself to be aware of. I grew up in a very repressed household."

"Ash told me," she stated quietly, her eyes without pity or judgment.

"My upbringing isn't an excuse for the way I've chosen to behave my entire adulthood, but I've caused others to suffer for fear of ridicule. I'm not saying I'll be able to change overnight, that I had a single aha moment that will turn my life around with one decision, but I'm determined to be more self-aware."

"You're amazing, Rhett." Skylar reached over the table and snagged one of my hands still wrapped around my coffee cup.

My throat tightened for the fifty-thousandth time in less than twenty-four hours as I wound my fingers through hers. That warmth expanded through my center like a life-giving force, and I studied her face, drinking her in.

Dark circles lay beneath her eyes, those long auburn lashes naturally curling in an enticing way. The bloodshot red through the whites of her eyes only heightened the green.

There were no pretenses with Skylar, no fake smiles in that moment attempting to put me at ease. She simply held my hand and let me just *be*.

"What are you feeling right now?" she whispered when

the silence between us grew and her backside shifted on the seat.

A smile curved my lips at her usual ants-in-the-pants inability to sit still. I rubbed my thumb over the back of hers, causing her lips to part.

Fuck, did I love how she wanted my thoughts and was interested in my inner workings. She'd proven in that hallway that she wouldn't invalidate them as my parents had always done either.

I didn't deserve a tenth chance, but I sure as fuck was going to take it.

"I'm scared as fuck for Ash's test results," I admitted, releasing some tension in my chest, "but strangely at peace too."

I didn't tell her that Ash wanted me to love her, cling to her when he was gone, because his death wasn't going to happen for many years down the road.

"I'm scared too." Skylar swallowed audibly and glanced around the cafeteria, wetness welling in her eyes. "I've only just met him—you—and I'm terrified that it'll be too late to make his dreams come true. I failed in getting pregnant—"

"It's not your fault, Skylar," I stated quietly.

"I—I *know* that, but I can't help how I feel." She smiled as a tear slid down her cheek.

"And I won't attempt to negate those feelings," I assured her, my eyes stinging at making a right choice in saying that —hopefully the first good decision of many when it came to her. "But you must know Ash would never lay blame on you. He's a firm believer in fate. We'll take things one day at a time. Hell, one hour at a time. We'll have answers soon, then we can plan a course of action. Ash will have the best care no matter the diagnosis. Money isn't an issue, and I can work remotely for as long as necessary to help make sure he's comfortable."

"I'll do whatever you need me to," Skylar said. "Quit my job and be his full-time nurse. I can drive him to every appointment. I'm going to be there for you too." Her hold on my hand tightened. "We've gotten off to a rough start, but I haven't given up on you yet, Rhett Stirling. It'll take a lot more than negativity and poor choices to make me turn my back on you."

I noted the flash of pain in her eyes. "You had a lot of that in your childhood, didn't you?"

She blew out a heavy exhale. "You have no idea."

"Book smarts aren't everything," I stated quietly, leaning forward to emphasize my words. "I'd rather listen to your ramblings that keep my brain on my toes than suffer through most of our acquaintances going on and on about their latest accomplishments.

"You're a breath of fresh air," I added, "and I'm sorry for not allowing myself to like you or tell you that before today."

"Sometimes it takes tragedy to open our eyes to what's truly important in life," she said. "Do I want Ashton to be sick or face death?" Her voice broke, but she lifted her chin and barreled forward. "Absolutely not, but I think all things happen for a reason. Fate has led us here to this moment in time, and I'm going to accept the outcome and grow from it regardless of whatever our emotions drag us through."

"You're very brave," I murmured, loving the fire in her eyes.

"I'm a *dreamer*," Skylar attempted to correct me, but I shook my head.

"It takes courage to face the future without a plan—and that's something I don't have." I untangled my fingers from hers and re-laced them once more in a different pattern, squeezing tight. "Will you let me hold your hand when I need to?"

"I'll always be here for you," she whispered and smiled.

Her promise flooded me with hope, not just for Ash's diagnosis but for the future ahead of us.

41

———

SKYLAR

R hett's smile trembled, and I yearned to leap over the table and hug him tight, to soothe all his worries away.

"I'm getting a little antsy to head back upstairs," Rhett said, glancing toward the cafeteria's exit.

I couldn't help my grin since I understood that statement all too well. Ashton had sent me to Rhett to offer comfort, and I felt we'd accomplished more in our short minutes together than we'd done since he'd first faced me in the kitchen.

Even then, I'd thought him gorgeous, all stoic and untouchable, a man who didn't want to be tampered with. But the one with the unshuttered gaze full of helplessness and vulnerability gazing at me across the table?

Heart-wrenchingly beautiful in a way that hurt my chest and stole my breath.

He'd been broken down completely, any walls he'd built to keep me at arm's length demolished by the situation we found ourselves in with our shared lover.

No, I didn't want to see Ash hurt. I hated he feared facing death like his brother had.

But...

Oh, that sometimes glorious word allowed for greater meaning in circumstances, greater reward, greater end results from potential devastation.

I clung to hope same as I did to Rhett's hand as we made our way back toward Ashton's room. If I'd been able to, I'd have wrapped Rhett up in my arms like he'd done with me in the hallway, exactly as I had for Ashton on Saturday morning when I'd gotten my period.

Even if Ashton did have cancer, we would have a little bit of time to try again. There was always test-tube baby type stuff...I wasn't positive how all that worked, but surely the doctors could get his sperm while he was still somewhat healthy and somehow impregnate me.

At least, I'd heard about that sort of thing on the news, and I thought my cousin had tried something like that. They'd spent thousands, going through their savings.

They never got their baby though, just an empty bank account.

Lips tight, I refused to think about the negative. Ashton had told me they owned Missing Link, and to see their house, their cars, and fancy watches...there would be no shortage of money in getting a baby inside me if it could be afforded.

But how did it work?

I imagined needles, syringes, and stirrups...and a grimace lined my face. Would any part of the process be enjoyable—or only painful? Embarrassing? Unpleasant?

If it could be done with cows on the farm, I could trust doctors and science, right?

A scene flashed through my ridiculous mind of me bent

over and mooing, and I bit back a snort of laughter.

Shaking my head, I put aside rambling thoughts about eggs, sperm, and cows. We had more important things to face first—together as a triad.

Three would be stronger than two when hearing Ashton's diagnosis, and I wanted nothing more than to be available to him and Rhett both in whatever way they needed me.

If it meant eventual sponge baths and bedpans for Ashton, then I would serve with a willing, loving heart. If that included holding Rhett again while he allowed himself to feel everything he'd been stifling since childhood, then I would gladly offer my shoulder for him to soak no matter the time of day.

My arms would be available.

My hands theirs to cling to.

My ears to hear while I bit my tongue to keep quiet and just listen.

But most importantly, my heart to accept and love unconditionally regardless of the outcome.

Rhett and I had connected intimately just the one time, but I'd felt potential, potently so, in those brief moments he had allowed me to touch his soul. And after managing to hold my silence as he'd unloaded and named each and every emotion he'd been repressing since meeting me?

I'd never seen anything so damn sexy as a man recognizing his feelings and deciding how to deal with them.

But that was Rhett. He always had a plan, and his confidence even in the face of the unknown turned me on and made me feel safer than I'd ever been.

Had we been anywhere but a hospital facing possible life-changing news, I'd have thrown myself at him, begged him to kiss me, to share his soul with mine again.

To fill up that part of me that craved his presence along with Ashton's.

A heavy sigh flatted my lungs as we approached our lover's door. Our feet slowed.

Rhett hesitated, tightening his clutch on my hand rather than reaching for the doorknob.

"It's okay," I murmured, peering up at him while soothing my thumb over the back of his hand.

"What if it's not?" he asked, turning to meet my gaze, his dark eyes intense and filled with rare insecurity. Even his shoulders slumped as though a heavy weight pressed him toward the grave.

My heart ached for the man broken down by instability, from his feelings finally having free rein.

I cupped his cheek, loving how he leaned into my touch as though absorbing strength from me. "I meant it's okay to be *afraid*."

Wetness glazed his eyes, and his Adam's apple bobbed as he swallowed. He pulled me into his arms, burying his face in my hair and neck.

I'd never felt such a sense of rightness, as though fate whispered in my ear she intended this all to happen for Rhett's healing. In that moment, hope rose inside me, and I gladly accepted the circumstances of what we faced.

"We're going in there together," I murmured, squeezing him tight, "hopefully forward as three, and if not, I'll be here for you."

"Thank you," he whispered, and while I wasn't sure for what exactly, I rubbed his back until he took a fortifying breath and straightened. "Ready?"

"No," I stated the honest truth. "But if you hold my hand, I will be."

Rhett didn't outright smile, but his eyes lightened. He

leaned down and gently pressed his lips to mine. Chaste and fleeting but far from unmoving.

Coils of desire rose inside me at the softness of his lips, the slight scrape of his scruff.

Potent, sexy man...he knew how to distract me in the sweetest way possible.

I refrained from grabbing him and wrapping a leg around his thigh.

Barely.

Happiness bubbled inside me, prepared to war with the darkness waiting for us beyond the door, the possibility of tragedy and heartache.

"I'm *really* ready now," I whispered as he backed away.

Lips thinning, his shoulders straightening, Rhett seemed to pull back on the armor I'd seen him wear dozens of times before. But I was sure it was for strength to face the other side—not to push against the emotions he felt on a deep level due to the unknown.

He opened the door in front of us.

Ashton's bed had been angled upward, allowing him to semi-sit. Eyes closed...tears streamed down his cheeks.

My heart stuttered along with Rhett's second step as though he'd noted the same thing I had.

Bad news.

Eyes welling and throat squeezing, I tugged on Rhett's hand and led him into Ashton's room.

There would be no distance between us in our lover's greatest time of need. We would all hold hands in an unbroken circle as our hearts shattered.

But Rhett would make a plan like always. He would set things in motion toward an end goal—Ashton being comfortable, living out his final days in whatever happiness we could find.

42

ASHTON

I couldn't stop the tears from slipping beneath my clenched eyelids or the pain in my chest no amount of pain meds could touch. Never had I ever felt such intense *need*—far beyond longing and desire. My soul, every cell inside my body ached for Rhett, for Skylar.

At the sound of shuffling footsteps, I opened my eyes, fighting to focus through the tears and lingering haze of drugs.

A sob erupted from my throat at the sight of them.

Hands clenched tight, they approached my bed, and the way they leaned into each other as though needing support from one another filled me to the breaking point.

I held out both my shaking hands, and Rhett and Sky separated long enough to flank my bed. Their fingers met atop my lap as mine laced with their free ones.

Attempting to breathe steadily and slow my racing heart, I placed both of our clasped hands over theirs on my stomach. Knotted fingers clung in a tight embrace. A beautiful sight of unity.

They leaned down as though of the same mind, Rhett's

forehead to mine, Skylar's against my cheek, bringing the sweet scent of coconuts.

Another sob made me shudder beneath their gentle touch.

Three words had wrecked me, but I couldn't wait to share them with my love and sunshine.

"It's not cancer," I croaked the doctor's assurance from minutes earlier, and relief once more rushed through me like a swelling wave, bringing on choking whines.

"Thank fucking Christ." Rhett's voice broke, and he buried his face in my neck, his tears smearing over my skin.

Skylar simply let out a soft sigh, snuggling against my other shoulder.

"I'm going to be okay," I whispered through my tears what I'd been repeating in my head since the doctor had left me alone.

Skylar pulled away first, her eyes shining with so much happiness my chest felt like it was going to explode. "We're going to make dozens of babies and live happily ever after!" Laughter bubbled from her.

Rhett groaned and straightened, pulling away from our hold to scrub his palms over his face. "No."

"What do you mean no!" Skylar shot at him, her brow furrowing and chin rising.

"Three, max. Otherwise, I'll go insane," he muttered, his eyes still wet as he gave her his attention, his own head tilted back in stubbornness.

She opened her mouth, probably to argue, but Rhett simply raised an eyebrow, a look I knew well that invited an argument and the promise he would end it.

"Pancreatitis," I blurted, pulling both of their gazes to me. "The abdominal tenderness and aching was similar to what I remember Archer complaining about. I never handled pain well, so add in the stress of thinking I was dying, a slew of emotions, and voila—puking."

I shrugged, hating that I had allowed myself to get so focused on death and failure that I hadn't properly taken care of my body or the situation I'd thought I was in.

A simple discussion with the doctor, bloodwork, and imaging had cleared my mind of all anxiety. Never again would I allow my brain to grab hold of worry and run away without proper management. Nor would I live in denial when facing the truth might not be as bad as I'd expected.

"No more hiding what you're feeling," Skylar stated with a stern, mother-like voice while glancing between the two of us. "Emotionally or physically, *both* of you, because I swear to all things holy—*if* there are such things like angels and demons—wait. Demons can't be holy...can they? No, definitely not. But anyway." She shook her head while getting back on track. "We need to talk all the words, share everything we have going on inside our hearts and minds. Got it?"

"Speak," Rhett murmured, the twitch of his lips causing mine to curl upward.

"What?" Skylar asked.

"We need to speak all the words."

Skylar reached over my bed and backhanded his chest. "Don't be an asshole."

Rhett grabbed her hand and lifted her knuckles to his lips, their gazes locking.

Weakness slid through my legs, and I wondered how Skylar held hers upright beneath Rhett's potent stare. Fuck knew I couldn't.

Her lips parted.

He grinned.

A heavy exhale left me depleted and completely at rest. Pleasantly buzzed from pain meds. Smiling like an idiot.

"I have some words," Rhett murmured, his low tone a sexy rumble that fluttered my heart even though he wasn't addressing me.

"Oh?" Skylar asked, the simple word breathless with desire.

He lay their clasped hands atop mine and Skylar's once more, topping the stack with his free one in a protective hold.

"We've been offered a second chance, and I have every intention of taking advantage of that gift. If that means opening myself to the rawness of emotions, I'll do so every minute of the day. Life is too short." His voice broke, and he swallowed hard. "We aren't promised today, so I'm going to love you both with all I have like it's the last sunrise, the last night beneath the stars."

Tears slid down Skylar's cheeks again, but her face shone with an angelic light that pierced through my heart. "Every day to the fullest," she whispered.

"Why don't you two get started," I said, grinning like a loon even though mental weariness readied to knock my ass out again.

"Not without you," Skylar said, turning toward me.

I glanced at Rhett. "I have to stay here a couple nights, so how about you take our angel home, shower together, crawl into bed naked, make love like it's your first time, then get some rest."

Skylar blinked, and I could imagine the explosion of thoughts going off in her head.

"You don't want us to wait for you?" she asked with a hushed tone instead, reminding me of how she'd always mentioned Rhett when we'd touched after first meeting.

I grinned, but my blink seemed to take forever as my limbs grew heavier. "Show him what it's like to have your undivided attention while I rest up for when I'm home and it's my turn to love on you again."

She giggled and pressed her mouth to mine in a kiss but quickly straightened, her lips flatlining.

"What?" Rhett asked, and a beautiful pink hue bloomed on her cheeks.

"I...um...well, it's not a good time? For that?" She shifted on her feet, her face flushing a deeper shade of red. "It would be really awkward. Um...gross."

Rhett's steady gaze on her heated to the point even I shifted on the hospital bed. "Nothing about you is gross, Skylar," he spoke quietly, not inviting argument. "And it will only be awkward if I allow you to think too much."

"Oh God," she whispered, tearing her focus off his face for mine. "He's so..."

I chuckled over her lack of words, my eyelids sliding closed. "I know. Don't bother resisting. It's futile."

Soft lips landed on my cheek then lips. Firmer ones brushed my forehead then my mouth.

"Love you," I murmured, smiling even as darkness tugged on my mind.

"Love you too, baby," Rhett murmured, his voice close.

"Love *her*," I added, feeling myself drifting into content peace.

"I plan on it."

The best thing about Rhett Stirling? When he decided a course of action, he stuck to it. I didn't doubt Skylar had one hell of a night ahead of her.

My smile still held in place as sleep claimed me.

43

RHETT

The prognosis couldn't be better.

We spoke with the doctor after Ash had fallen asleep. No damage had occurred to his pancreas, and no surgery would be necessary.

However, he would be in the hospital for a few days, on antibiotics and an IV for extra fluids. Rest, a bland diet for the foreseeable future, and they expected Ash to be okay.

No more alcohol would be the biggest lifestyle change but more for me than him. I enjoyed wine with dinner but would give it up to do away with the temptation for him altogether.

Whatever Ash needed, he would have.

That included me loving on our angel, giving her the attentiveness she craved and should have had from me all along.

She clung to my hand the entire ride home, surprisingly silent and still. I expected extreme tiredness similar to mine subdued her usual liveliness.

Or perhaps nervousness clammed her up seeing as how she chewed on a fingernail.

"What are you thinking?" I asked.

She turned to face me. "You want my racing thoughts?"

"I wouldn't ask if I didn't."

"Okay. Well...I'm so damn tired but happy. I could sing at the top of my lungs even though it would suck and yet I want to burrow under some blankets and snore for hours on end."

"You don't snore."

That shut her mouth for a few seconds. "I don't?"

"Nope."

"Do you hate that I'm in your bed?" she blurted and bit her lip.

"It's *our* bed," I corrected her, flipping the turn signal to take a right. "Ash's, yours, and mine."

Silence settled again, and I glanced over. "What?"

"You're sure about this—really sure? Like there are no reservations lingering somewhere deep inside you that are waiting to leap up and strangle my hope? Because I'm nervous as hell right now. I'm afraid you'll have another taste of me and shut down again."

"I'm sorry for what happened that night." I recalled the feelings that had knocked me on my ass when Ash had been all about her, ignoring the fact I'd been buried balls deep inside her body and offered him my mouth. "I was jealous, plain and simple. I wanted his attention in that moment, and he gave it to you."

"And what will you do if something similar happens again? Because it might. Sometimes I focus on Ashton being inside me, and sometimes your presence is so overwhelming that I can't think of anything but how deeply you're buried in my ass. The pain. The pleasure of you... it's...often too much."

"You don't like anal, do you?"

"I think…I think I might enjoy it more knowing that you aren't just shoving your dick into me because it's what Ashton wants. Perhaps if the emotional connection is there, I would be able to relax more. We can try tonight—because of the other situation down there." Her voice went all squeaky, likely from embarrassment.

I pulled into our garage. "I never just took your ass for him," I corrected her while turning off the car, "but because it's gorgeous, tempting as fuck, and so goddamn tight my eyes cross whenever I sink into your body."

"Oh." Pink flushed her face. "Well, then."

"And while we're being honest, I'm not afraid of a little blood either, Skylar, nor should you be ashamed of that part of womanhood."

She rubbed her lips together and nodded. "I-I'll try, but…"

"We don't have to do anything but curl up in bed and sleep if that's what you want."

"What do *you* want, Rhett?"

I glanced over the oversized T-shirt doing nothing to hide her pebbled nipples and the sweatpants masking her curves. "To wash you from head to toe, lavish you with affection, and satisfy whatever desires you have."

"A shower sounds good." She barely breathed the words, and the lust darkening her eyes roused life in my groin.

"Then that's where we'll start." A plan automatically began forming in my head for all I wouldn't mind following in a thorough wash down's wake.

No warring thoughts crowded my mind as I led Skylar into the quiet house. Our footfalls filled the hushed silence as we climbed the stairs. No feelings of wrongness fought with the one of *right* coursing through my center as I turned on the shower.

She nibbled her lower lip as I pulled the T-shirt off over her head, revealing pale skin I wouldn't mind marking with my mouth.

She grabbed hold of my hands as I went to push down the sweats.

"C-Can I have a minute?" she whispered, her face red.

"You need privacy?"

She bit her lip and nodded.

I wanted to argue that being in our lives meant sharing every single piece of her—inside and out. One day, I hoped she to see her carry Ash's child, and we would both be there while she labored, and no amount of blood would change my thoughts toward her.

I kissed her forehead and left her alone, stripping to my skin in the bedroom as she flushed the toilet.

"Okay?" Skylar called out with more of a question in her voice than beckoning—but I went back into the bathroom anyway.

She'd climbed into the shower, the fog on the glass enclosure hiding her from me.

"I'm coming in," I warned and opened the shower door before she could deny me.

A flush covered her chest, neck, and face, and she studied her feet.

I shut myself in with her, but rather than pulling her into my arms and devouring her mouth, I kept a few inches between us and tipped her head back into the spray.

Her eyes closed, a soft smile on her lips as I lathered her hair, massaging her scalp until she relaxed.

The scent of coconuts surrounded us, every lungful and soft sigh from her parted lips thickening my dick.

I used my hands to wash her from neck to hips, but she

once more grasped my wrist to stop me from going any further.

"I..."

"It's okay." I kissed her shoulder and turned her toward the spray, focusing on her back. Her pale ass cheeks bumped out from the bottom of her spine, calling to my hands.

She prohibited me from sudsing her backside too, so I dropped to my knees and took care of every inch from her thighs to her toes. Standing once more, I crowded in close, running my hands over her hip bones, my hard dick nestled along her crack she hadn't allowed me to touch.

Her nipples furled tight, her pulse thrumming in her neck beneath my lips as she sagged against me. She once more held my wrists as I slid my hands forward, my fingertips teasing over her pubis.

"Rhett..."

"I want to wash all of you," I whispered against her ear, my index finger gliding over her protruding clit.

She swallowed hard, tension once more returning to her body.

"Let me."

A shudder rippled through her at my near-groan, and she loosened her grasp.

Arms wrapped around her, I reached for a bit more of her body wash, lathering up my hands. "Spread your legs for me."

"Oh my God this is so embarrassing," she whined but did as told.

I palmed one of her breasts, giving her something else to focus on as I slid my other fingers through her folds.

Her head tipped back onto my shoulder, and I took

advantage of her giving in, thoroughly cleaning her from clit to asshole.

My dick throbbed against her lower back, the water washing away the soap I'd rubbed over her chest until I thumbed over her nipple without slickness.

She moaned and shifted in my hold, her hips rocking as I teased over her lower lips, my fingertip rimming her front hole. "Rhett."

"Hmm?" I hummed against her ear and nipped at her lobe, probing slightly up into her tight heat.

"C-Can we do it? In here?"

I bit back a grin and nipped her lobe, cupping her warm pussy. "Do what?"

"It's just...I really want you right now, and if we make a mess, it'll be easier to clean up, you know?" She rubbed against my palm, her legs widening.

I eyed the lube Ash and I kept in the shower. Still holding her firmly in one hand, I reached between us. "Where do you want me?" I slid the head of my dick between my fingers where I gripped her, brushing over her pussy. "Here?"

"Yes," she gasped out before I could ask about her ass.

I angled and pushed in with one slow thrust that took Skylar up onto her toes.

"Oh fuck," she moaned and shuddered, reaching back to grab my neck. "Mary, Jesus, and Joseph."

I chuckled and plastered against her back, my length in a stranglehold from her tight sheath. "I've never been bare inside a woman like this...you're so wet and warm, Sky." I pulled out and sank back in, making both of us groan. "Fuck, you feel so damn good. It's no wonder Ash can't get enough of you."

My lips found her neck, and I latched on, sucking and pulling while fucking in and out of her tight clasp with slow, persistent thrusts.

I imagined releasing inside her but knew sperm could live long enough to possibly impregnate her, even though she had her period. The only seed I wanted finding her womb was Ash's, and as my balls drew up tight, I took measures to finish.

Rolling her left nipple with one thumb, I slid my other hand down her belly to her thickened clit. "Need you to come for me, angel. Want this pussy to make a filthy mess all over my cock."

"Oh my God." Skylar gulped and grabbed at my hair. "Why is that so damn hot? Like...seriously...oh fuck, don't stop." She writhed against me, whimpering and uttering nonsense as I flicked my fingertips over her clit.

I gritted my teeth to keep from busting a nut. She needed to fucking let go so I could do the same. I pinched both bits of flesh beneath my fingers—and she shot off like a goddamn firecracker.

She shrieked, bucking against me, her pussy like a vise around my dick, pulsing and so goddamn wet.

"Fuck." I thrust once more and backed out, shoving my dick up along her crack twice before cum erupted from my balls. "*Fuuuck...*" I held her tight against my chest, nudging and emptying every last drop over her lower back.

We both finally stilled, our pants louder than the shower raining down over us.

A tinge of red swirled through the water draining in front of us, but it didn't gross me out, and it sure as hell wasn't anything to be embarrassed about.

Skylar belonged to me. To Ash. Every delicious inch of her.

And I couldn't wait until my lover returned home so we could both love on her thoroughly in the way she deserved.

44

SKYLAR

Rhett wrecked me in the best way possible, once more allowing intimacy like we'd shared on the couch all those weeks ago. He kept nothing from me. He also wouldn't allow me to hide my feelings.

Everything about him felt good because it wasn't just fucking. It was a sharing of emotion, of souls.

I didn't argue when he once more washed me between my tender thighs. Didn't shy away when he hopped from the shower first to get me a towel, determined to dry every inch of my body. Blood stained the towel when he wiped between my thighs, but I didn't have the energy to be embarrassed.

He retrieved a pad from beneath the sink and gave it to me while kissing my forehead. "I'll go get you some underwear."

My heart swooned along with my knees, and I sank onto the toilet, too tired to even think about his lack of being grossed out.

Rhett knelt and slid a dark pair of my underwear up my

prickly legs, making no mention of the fact I needed to shave.

I stared at him, unmoving, pad clutched in my hand.

No mask closed him off to me as his eyes met mine. "Okay?" he asked, rubbing his hands over my calf muscles.

"Why aren't you grossed out?" I blurted and bit the inside of my lip.

"It's a natural part of life, and you're going to be sharing in ours, so why hide from it?"

"You're strange," I muttered, shaking my head.

Chuckling, he plucked the pad from my hand.

Heat flooded my face. "I'll do it—" I reached to grab it from him, but he yanked his arm back.

"Someday, you're going to bear Ashton a child, and I plan on being beside you both every second, every step of the way. I've done my homework—I know what happens to a woman's body after giving birth."

He peeled open the wrapper, removed the tabs, and stuck the pad onto the inside of my panties stretched between my thighs.

"I'm going to die," I muttered, hiding my hot face in my hands.

Rhett grabbed my wrists and pulled them down, making me meet his gaze. Warmth filled his dark eyes along with a bit of laughter.

"You're insufferable," I stated with a huff, and he leaned in to kiss me soundly on the mouth.

"And you're delicious." He grabbed some toilet paper.

"Nuh uh. Nope. No way." I clamped my knees together and held out my hand. "Give me that."

He allowed me to wipe myself but didn't move away from where he knelt in front of me.

I shifted to get up, and he helped me pull up my panties before standing.

We brushed our teeth side by side, him gloriously naked, me in diaper-like stuffed undies. Whatever embarrassment I'd felt earlier had dissolved, and once we crawled into bed and he shoved a thigh between mine to rest against my padded core, I couldn't find a single care to give.

I closed my eyes, and all thoughts shut down.

———

Ashton stayed in the hospital for two more nights, and the morning Rhett went to bring him back to us, I took the day off from bagging groceries to clean our home from top to bottom. It was more nervous energy than anything that had me scrubbing the kitchen floor on my hands and knees even though the cleaning ladies were set to arrive on Friday.

I changed our sheets since we'd messed them up the night before. My period had pretty much faded to nothing, and I looked forward to having both men inside me without barriers of any sort.

Rhett had given me plenty of romantic loving in Ashton's absence, but I couldn't get enough of his touch, his kisses, his delicious dick.

Just the thought of him finally having my ass again when Ash filled my pussy dampened my panties. I wanted it. Craved it. Knew having them like that would be nothing but pleasure since Rhett had taken down those walls that had kept us from emotionally connecting.

Grinning and giddy, I washed myself into the kitchen corner by the garage door. Laughter snorted from me when I realized what I'd done.

"Moron." Shaking my head, I considered resting where I

sat until the floor dried, but excess energy denied me that idea. I crawled back over the floor, wiping up my knee and hand prints as I went until the dining room's hardwood lay beneath me. "There." I dropped the rag and stood, eyeing my work—then the island Rhett had bent me over the morning before, disturbing our coffee.

Not that I'd minded.

My face heated along with the rest of my body, but the doorbell shut down all thoughts of my two favorite men, their dicks, and how well they would satisfy the ache growing inside me.

A quick scurry toward the entryway, and I saw the unwanted visitor through the side windows.

Nora.

"What the..." Scowling, I wrenched open the door. "I'm all done with your negativity, so if you're here to treat me like trash, you can go suck a duck egg and choke!"

Law laid down, I lifted my chin and glared as she glanced over my shoulder.

"Can I come in?" she asked quietly, her gaze as closed off as Rhett's old one when she met my eyes.

"Why?"

"Because Mom and Dad didn't send me this time. I'm not going to try to get you to go home or anything like that."

"Then what's the point of driving all the way down here? I know it's not just for a friendly chat."

"I came to apologize."

My mouth dropped open, my mind blank.

"I've been a miserable bitch and taking it out on you my entire life," she rushed the words, sounding so much like my dumpster spew that I blinked back to reality.

I closed my jaw and narrowed my eyes while leaning forward to sniff at her. "Are you drunk?"

She huffed a soft laugh and shook her head. "I finally started to see a therapist, and she told me jealousy and envy would only continue to fester inside me if I didn't let it go."

Jealousy. Envy...

"*What*?" I whispered, my idiot brain not following.

"Can I come in?" Nora questioned again, and I didn't think, simply stepped back and allowed her entry.

She glanced around the house, a soft, sad smile on her face when she turned to face me where I stood in front of the open door. "Your home is lovely."

"I share it with two men, and we have unnatural sex," I reminded her, my chin lifting.

"Do they make you happy?" she surprised me by asking.

"Extremely."

Nora nodded as though pleased, her focus once more flitting around the kitchen off to her right.

"What do you mean by jealousy and envy?" I asked, needing to get to the bottom of her visit because I was clueless. She *must* be drunk. Or maybe she'd smoked some pot. I hoped she hadn't driven...

My sister clutched her purse in front of her pencil skirt like armor. "All our life, I had to compete with you."

I snorted a bark of laughter, wondering which twilight zone I'd meandered into without meaning to.

"I'm serious, Skylar," she insisted, her green eyes imploring me to believe her. "You were always so carefree, untouched by expectations placed on us by Mom and Dad. You didn't care about how they drove us toward perfection —you did your own thing. You chose the way your dreams took you every single day while I fought tooth and nail to gain our parents' approval."

I stared, dumbstruck.

Nora reached out and pressed up on my once more unhinged jaw.

"Wh...what are you t-talking about?" I sputtered. "I-I simply gave up because I couldn't compare to *you!*"

Sadness filled her eyes as she once more clutched her purse. "Do you have any idea what I would have given to be allowed a moment to live in the clouds? How many nights I cried myself to sleep because I couldn't bear the thought of letting Mom and Dad down? Yes, I've been gifted an amazing mind, but the expectations that come with it..." Nora shook her head and swiped at the tear trickling down her cheek. "I have no freedom," she whispered, breaking my heart. "I'm stuck in a world of my own making with no way to escape."

I wanted to apologize although I had no reason to do so —nor did I understand why. She'd chosen her path, same as I'd done mine, but courses could always change.

Anyone could fly free if they truly wanted to.

"Switch jobs," I blurted the first thought to come to mind.

"Huh?" She blinked.

"If you're miserable working for NASA and under too much pressure, quit. Find something you love, whatever you dreamed about as a kid."

"I-It's not that easy."

I shrugged. "For someone like you, it definitely is. Give your two weeks' notice. You have enough money in your savings account to travel the world and live a little. Ride the tallest roller coasters. Stand on the shores of every ocean. Visit the Eiffel Tower and that leaning one in Italy. See the pyramids. Take a camel ride. Oh! A gondola through that other Italian city. Kangaroos! You've always loved those bouncy little creatures."

Nora snickered. "They're hardly little, Skylar."

I shrugged, grinning from the bubbliness inside me. "I wouldn't know, but how about you head down under and take a few selfies so I have something to compare them to? Because I'll probably never get there—and you can have all the freedom in the world. No lovers, no spouse, no responsibilities but finding your happy."

Nora dropped her purse and threw herself into my arms, causing me to stumble back a step. Sniffles sounded in my ears, and I hugged her for the first time since we were around four years of age and still shared a bed.

My throat swelled shut, and tears stung my eyes as a sense of coming home I hadn't realized I'd missed so damn *much*, flooded through me.

"I've been so jealous for so long, pitying myself...I'm so sorry," Nora whispered, hugging me tight.

"I forgive you," I stated simply since there were no other words she needed to hear.

And it was my truth.

She eventually pulled away, her green eyes bright from the tears. "Is Ashton home? I owe him an apology too."

I blew out a huge breath. "He's not right now... it's a long story. Do you have time to sit for a spell? I have some home-made bread. Gram's recipe. I even whipped up some coconut muffins of a sort. Can't promise they'll be any good. Oh, and coffee! We've got lots of coffee."

"Oh my God, yesss," she hissed, sounding so much like me that I burst into laughter.

"I missed you, Nora Jane."

She grabbed my hand. "I've missed you too, Skylar Anne."

"Come on." I finally pushed the front door shut and tugged her toward the kitchen, thankful to see the floor had dried while we'd blubbered about like little kids. "Let me tell you all about my life the past couple of months."

"I'm not sure I want to hear *all* the details..."

I snickered. Nora wasn't one for sex, so I took pity on her and edited out the juicer bits that would curl her lips down in a grimace. Sharing those parts would have definitely turned me on and made me more anxious for my men to return home.

45

ASHTON

I felt far from invigorated but ten times better than I had in weeks as Rhett drove us away from the hospital. The process of being discharged had taken hours, and the lunch Skylar had planned for us at home would end up being an early dinner, but I didn't care.

I still had a few days left of oral antibiotics but no more drugs since the pain had faded from my upper abdomen. The lump on my head had gone down, and I'd been given the green light to finish resting up at home with plans to follow up with my PCP.

A few things in my life needed to change though—no more wine, unfortunately, but I could live without it. Red meat, all things deep-fried, and pastries were also off the list, but Skylar had been over the moon the day before while visiting, sharing dozens of recipes she planned on making. Her excitement and commitment to help eased the sting of losing out on some of my favorite foods and flooded my heart with love.

The doctor assured me that eventually I would feel healthy enough to splurge on occasion, but having suffered through the previous couple of weeks, I had zero wish to put anything inside my mouth that might make me sick again.

"So how are you feeling?" Rhett asked while reaching over to hold my hand atop my thigh.

"Tired. Happy. Relieved. You?"

Rhett didn't answer right away, and I gave him time to sift through his thoughts. He'd been nothing but candid since my accident, telling me all about his breakdown, his and Sky's talk to clear the air, and everything he and Skylar had been up to while alone in our house.

The pictures he painted in my head while Sky sat on the other side of my bed, red as a beet, had turned me on. At least pancreatitis hadn't gotten the best of my dick.

The lack of walls between them while gazing at one another was what did it for me the most though. The openness, the vulnerability in Rhett, the desire for him to fall for Sky as I'd done...it was everything I'd hoped for.

Even if we never had children of our own, I would be happy they'd found something just as special as she and I had.

"Is it wrong for a part of me to grieve over what we used to have even though I'm looking forward to our future together with Skylar?" he finally asked, his focus on the road ahead of us.

I squeezed Rhett's hand, knowing exactly what he spoke about. "I'm sure there will be moments when I miss having you all to myself too, but Sky wouldn't ever deny us if we wanted to leave town together for a few days."

"I don't think I would be so thrilled about the two of you going off without *me*," he admitted with that new candor I expected would catch me off guard for weeks to come.

"Because you're a possessive asshole who likes to be in control." I gave him the God's honest truth.

"And you love me," he shot back with complete confidence.

I lifted our clasped hands and kissed the back of his. "Without question or condition."

"It's the same with me." Rhett glanced over at me briefly before giving his attention to the road, and the rawness of his gaze stole my breath. "And my feelings have grown for Skylar. She's not what I thought I wanted—wasn't what I expected to share in our life."

"You needed her."

"Need," he corrected me. "She shows me how to live to the fullest extent every day, even in the small, mundane things. There's no hiding, no way for my trained brain to stifle emotions around her. She draws them out of me so damn easily—and strangely, I *want* to give them to her."

"Are you in love with her?" I asked, imagining my fingers crossing.

He let out a slow exhale, his cheeks puffing slightly. "Well on my way, yes."

Lightness rose inside my chest—more than happiness, more than hope. "I'm already there," I admitted.

"I've been aware of that for some time."

"And you're okay with sharing my heart?"

"If it means making said heart happy, then I'm all in, Ash —you have to know that."

Tears clogged my throat—but they didn't spill until I walked through the garage doorway into the kitchen and a whirlwind of colorful sundress and coconut-scented skin filled my arms.

"You're home!" Sky squealed and kissed my face all over, giggling and squirming against me like a puppy who hadn't seen its master for a week.

The chuckle behind us warmed me through.

"I'm home, angel," I murmured against her hair, breathing her deep into my lungs.

"Are you hungry? You must be starved since Rhett texted me that you didn't get lunch from the hospital, and it's almost dinner time." She stepped back as quickly as she'd thrown herself at me, tugging me toward the island while I swiped my face dry. "I grilled some chicken breasts after Nora left, made some quinoa in chicken bone broth, and roasted a few different veggies—easy ones to digest for you, promise—"

"Wait." I halted her forward motion. "Nora?"

"She...um, visited earlier this morning?"

I sat on the barstool and tugged her close between my thighs. "What happened?"

Rhett tossed his keys onto the island and crowded her backside, resting his chin on her shoulder, his arms wrapped around her waist.

I expected tears or a scowl, but her face shone like the sun.

"Would you believe she's jealous of me? I mean, really. I don't get it—it makes no sense whatsoever. She shows up prattling on about how she never could measure up to me, and I just couldn't understand a word. She. Said."

Laughter flowed from Skylar, and I grinned at Rhett.

"How about you tell us all about it?" I suggested, loving how she wiggled in Rhett's hold.

"How about you—" she elbowed Rhett "—let me go so I can get you both some dinner, and I'll randomly spill everything I can remember about her visit this morning even if it isn't in order and doesn't make any sense?"

Chuckling, Rhett kissed her cheek and settled onto the stool beside me. We both watched Skylar flit around the kitchen like a gorgeous butterfly, hands fluttering as she attempted to recount the conversation she'd had with her sister.

What I understood from her rambling while making us three plates?

She'd gotten the closure she desperately needed to find complete happiness in her new life.

Skylar set our food in front of us and flopped onto the third chair, eying her dinner. "I'm too jittery to eat, but I'm going to need my energy for tonight. Rhett said we have to take it easy for a while, but I really want you both—the sooner the better. Since, you know, everything is good down there now?"

I bit back my snickering but couldn't keep a grin off my face.

"Shit. I can't believe I said that—I blame Rhett! He's so open about...that stuff. He even washed me in the shower and—you know what? Never mind."

Pink flushed her cheeks, making her the most beautiful creature on the face of the earth.

"Oh! I forgot! Nora wanted me to offer you her apologies. She asked to wait for you to get home, but I said no way. Nuh uh. I fed her some toast and allowed her two cups of coffee but then kicked her out because I had to get ready for you. There are rose petals on the bed. A new bottle of lube —but no condoms. Nope. Done with those. I shaved my legs too—"

Skylar snapped her mouth shut, and both Rhett and I laughed.

"I'm an idiot," she muttered.

"None of that," Rhett stated sternly.

She straightened. "If you heard *half* the thoughts racing through my head, you would agree," she argued, a bit of heat in her eyes.

"Like?" I prompted, wanting to know them all—every last one down to the point she exhausted her vocal cords.

She bit her lip, glancing between the two of us.

"Do any of them include things *outside* the bedroom?" Rhett asked while forking up a piece of the grilled chicken Skylar had sliced in precise angles and thickness.

"Playing in the ocean," she blurted and stabbed a roasted brussels sprout that had a dried cranberry hanging onto its side for dear life. "Making sandcastles. Long walks through lapping waves. The three of us holding hands wherever we go and ignoring the looks we'll get. Going out to dinner and sharing about the shit of our day—or the good things. Watching movies all cuddled up in a pile of tangled limbs. Grocery shopping. Cooking together. Enjoying the sunset over the horizon while sitting in the pool—but without the wine. Nope. That's no longer on our menu. What would you think about a kitty? A white fluff ball with cute little toe beans. But when I get pregnant, one of you will have to clean the litter box since that's a no-no for a mother-to-be."

"Okay," Rhett inserted when she paused for breath. "You've convinced us that you want more than just our delicious dicks." His mouth twitched as he attempted to hold back a smile.

Lower lip between her teeth, Skylar reached over and mussed up his hair, losing that bite of roasted vegetable to her plate as the brussels sprouts tumbled free. "There. You were looking too...robotic to match your happy voice."

"My happy voice?" He raised an eyebrow, a smirk still on his mouth as he popped another bite of chicken between his lips.

"You know the one." She glanced at me and nodded as though I'd agreed with her and her waving, empty fork. "All content and pleased like you just finished..." Red flushed her face as her words trailed off.

"Finished what, angel?" Rhett pushed, leaning onto the table with heat flickering to life in his eyes.

"Um...spilling your cum over my back or belly?" she squeaked. "That last little curse you always groan out sends shivers down my spine—like you're the king of the world and flying higher than any bird in the sky."

I rubbed a hand over my scruffy jawline, eyeing Rhett. I knew that voice—craved it. Missed it. But I wasn't jealous she'd gotten to enjoy him while I'd been in the hospital by myself every night.

I would gladly have suffered countless more days, over and over, to see my desires come to fruition exactly as they had done.

The bond between them had fully sprouted to life.

46

———

RHETT

We hadn't actually discussed the future, hadn't mapped out what it would look like with Skylar included in our daily lives, but I couldn't imagine anything different than what I enjoyed playing out in front of me.

I lounged on the living room chair within eyesight of the kitchen while Skylar busied herself cleaning up our dinner mess—without help, she'd insisted after I'd offered.

Ash leaned onto the island, chin propped in his hand as he watched her. He wore his heart on his sleeve, but I imagined I appeared the same.

Skylar hadn't put a name to the emotion I felt at having Ash home safely with us, but it did match that sense I had after ejaculating with either of them. Complete, utter satisfaction, that everything was right in the world for that moment.

The problem?

I didn't want the three of us to last a mere blip of time. Yes, I expected I would miss having Ash to myself, but I couldn't imagine going back to the way things had been before Skylar had arrived.

My uptight reservations dampening the feel of our home. Stoicism and childhood trauma dictating how our evenings would go. Dinner parties with similar-natured acquaintances who didn't soak in every moment like I'd learned to do since Sky had slammed into our lives.

I had shed that skin, and even though I sometimes found myself automatically going to enter robot mode at times, I recognized it for what it was.

Shutting that shit down came easier than turning off my emotions like I'd thought I had mastered. I'd bottled up so many for dozens of years, never allowing myself to truly enjoy the deeper meaning in life.

My three days of off work, visiting Ash in the hospital with Skylar, taking *her* to talk to a doctor about her ADHD, and sleeping with her wrapped around my body all night had filled in the empty parts of my heart I hadn't realized I'd kept closed off.

So much unconditional acceptance. Freedom to express —being encouraged to do so and *heard* without scorn—gave me a new outlook on my existence.

Skylar was so much more than sunshine, but I didn't have words to adequately describe how she made me feel.

I just knew I didn't want her moving out, moving on, or moving in a direction that didn't include both me and Ash by her side.

She finished wiping down the counters, hung the rag to dry, and ambled over to Ash.

"How are you feeling?" she asked him, rubbing her hand down his arm from shoulder to wrist.

He twined their fingers together and straightened in his chair. "I'm not in pain. No more nausea. Still tired though."

Skylar smoothed his hair off his forehead, and he closed his eyes, leaning into her touch I knew soothed him on a deeper than skin level. Her gentle, feathering fingertips always did the same for me.

I smiled, more than content to sit back and watch the two of them interact. They would make beautiful babies, I imagined, a little redheaded boy with big hazel eyes or maybe a brown-haired girl with her mom's green ones.

Sudden longing shot through me so damn hard that my breath caught.

I yearned for both visions to come true with a deep hunger I'd never felt before. No longer did I worry about noise and chaos. I needed to see a visual manifestation of our love—*their* love—more than I cared about my sanity.

For the first time since Ash had brought up the idea of inviting a woman into our lives to bear his children, I got it.

Thoroughly.

And I wanted the same without a single reservation.

I stood and approached them, my nearness drawing them out of their own little world.

A smile lit Skylar's face when our gazes caught.

"I think it's time to put our boy to bed."

Her lips parted, pupils starting to swell. Another gorgeous thing about Skylar—her body revealed every feeling inside her just as freely and uninhibited as her mouth did.

"Bed sounds divine," Ash muttered, pushing to his feet as though exhausted.

I tamped down my desire to get him hard and watch him fuck our angel, filling her with his cum.

We had time.

He snuggled between us in that tangle of limbs Skylar had said she wanted, and it was his front pressed against mine—his choosing.

Love swamped my blood to the point I blinked back

tears, and I kissed his minty-fresh mouth with slow gentleness, having no wish to stir up our dicks.

"I love you," I murmured to him while grasping Skylar's hip and pulling her closer against his back. If she took those words to mean more than just intended for him, I wouldn't have corrected her.

But we all closed our eyes without another word and drifted off.

———

The sky outside our window had begun to lighten when I woke. My brain set to planning out the free day we had ahead of us since neither Sky or I had to work.

After her little want-list spew, I changed up what I'd already figured on filling our hours with on Ash's first day back home.

We would take enjoy a walk on the beach through the lapping waves. Sit in the sand when Ash needed a rest and build a sandcastle while he watched.

If he felt up to it, I would take them out for lunch.

The night could end with a movie and cuddling—or more if either preferred. I knew I would. My morning wood was already set on getting some action.

I slid from bed to keep from temptation, allowing my lovers to sleep.

A few minutes later, hot coffee dripped into my mug, and I swiped my cell to life.

Colton had texted, and I grinned.

So I switched up my profile and what do I see? Tons of little red hearts just for me!

I snorted at his little rhyme and shot back an eye-rolling emoji.

Colton: **I didn't think I wanted anything serious, but I'm tired of hookups.**

Me: **Finally looking for love like you should have been doing all along, huh?**

Colton: **Fingers crossed this app gives me what I want.**

Me: **It worked for us.**

Missing Link had finally gifted us with what we'd intended her for. Satisfaction welled up inside me, puffing me up with a sense of pride I'd never felt before.

Grinning, I sipped my black coffee, loving its unmuted bitterness while reveling in our success.

Colton: **Get the fuck out! Really? Goddamn, I'm jealous. You aren't going to shut the app down or anything, right? Cuz I've got a few dozen pokes to return.**

I snorted a laugh and hit the voice-to-text button since I didn't want to put aside my coffee. "Enjoy, my friend."

I returned to our bedroom a few minutes later to find Ash awake and on his back, hands clasped behind his head.

Skylar had spread over his chest, a vision of pale skin, freckles, and a river of auburn hair. The sheet barely clung to the rounded swell of her backside and revealed every inch of Ash's stiff dick he ignored.

I propped my shoulder against our doorjamb and sipped my second cup of coffee I'd brought along, simply enjoying the sight of them together.

Ash lifted his head slightly as though feeling my stare, his hair a wild mess and hazel eyes still sleepy. "Come here," he whispered.

Fuck, I loved when he got bossy, especially with that raspy morning voice.

I obeyed because I couldn't deny the man whatever he wanted. Setting my mug aside, I slid back onto the bed beside him, propped up on my elbow.

"Do you feel rested?" I whispered, and he nodded while reaching for my face with the hand closest to me.

I leaned in and pressed my lips against his, his palm against the back of my neck holding me there briefly.

"Love you too," he murmured against my mouth and released me. "I passed out last night before I could tell you."

I settled in beside him, leaning on my elbow and resting my chin in my hand.

Skylar's lips still parted in sleep, and I tucked wayward strands of hair behind her cute, rounded ears. A frown creased her forehead as though I'd disturbed her sleep, but she didn't move from where she draped over Ash's chest.

"She looks good on you," I murmured.

"Feels good." Ash closed his eyes, a smile on his lips. "So soft and sweet."

I eyed his hard cock, my mouth suddenly watering for a taste. Figuring Skylar wouldn't care if I woke her up by turning Ash on beneath her, I slid down the mattress and leaned into his groin.

A steady inhale filled my lungs with his familiar musk, and I groaned as my own dick thickened, and I filled one hand full of his warm balls.

"Rhett," he moaned, spreading his legs slightly.

I took him into the back of my throat in one go, and his hips bucked.

"Fuck."

"Mmm," I hummed around his length and slowly sucked upward, lathing around his glans.

Ash groaned his approval.

"Oh, that's so. Damn. Hot," Sky breathed the words with a sleepy moan, and I grinned around my mouthful of cock, reaching for her with my free hand.

Taking Ash deep into my throat once more, I found the

apex of Sky's thighs. Wet warmth met my fingertips, and I all but growled at the need aching my shaft.

"Rhett." Ash spoke through gritted teeth, but I didn't want a mouthful of cum.

I backed off, tugging down on his balls. "Bring that sweet pussy over here and stuff yourself full of his cock, Sky."

"Oh God." She scrambled to obey with clumsy movements, and I held Ash's dick upright as she straddled him. "You're okay for this?" she asked him as I rubbed the swelled head of his cock along her slit.

"Yes."

She sank onto him without another word, both of them moaning.

I lay back and lazily stroked my length as she moved over him, but I didn't join in wholeheartedly since I had plans for my dick.

Ash wound his fingers in my hair, and Sky grabbed my free hand.

While I didn't fuck with either of them, I still felt connected, a part of what they shared.

Ash let out a hiss as she ground her hips in a circle.

"Want to fill her up with your cum, baby?" I asked, watching his face as she lifted and lowered, lewd, wet sounds of their fucking tempting me to jerk off harder.

"Yes—fuck, yes," Ash bit out through clenched teeth.

"Play with your pretty little clit, Sky," I told her, rolling to my back fully to get a better view. "Smear your cum over his dick until he fills you with his."

"Filthy..." she panted, her head tipping back as she snaked a hand down over her chest and belly to the swollen bit of flesh at the top of her slit. "Love it—all of it. God, you feel so good, Ashton."

She moved without a hint of insecurity or self-consciousness, soft belly jiggling, breasts bouncing. A gorgeous siren hell-bent on finding her release, Sky chased after it with parted lips and furrowed brow. She panted and moaned, pulling curses from Ash left and right.

"So fucking close—please, Sky...angel...need you to come first." Ash begged, whining in his pleading for her to find her release before he let go.

"Yes. Oh God, yes." She slammed her hips down and cried out, shuddering through her climax.

"Fuck." Ash grabbed hold of her hips and fucked up into her with short, harsh thrusts. "Sky—" A grunt tore from his lips, which caused my dick to jerk in my hand.

Hissing, I squeezed the base of my cock, fighting off my need to erupt with him.

A shiver slid over Sky's body, pebbling her skin, and she slumped forward against Ash's chest. "Jesus and Joseph," she murmured and giggled.

Ash lifted his knees, trapping her against him and his spent dick inside her.

I understood his wanting to linger went beyond enjoyment of her wet warmth. He remained buried deep, hoping sperm would find their way into her womb and give us what all three of us longed for—same as he'd done every time they'd fucked before the accident.

We lay in silence, and I allowed them a few moments to come down from their high.

The second Ash let out a groan I recognized from his slipping free from a tight hole, I rolled Sky onto her back, lifting her hips high before a drop of his cum slid from her body. Kneeling and shoving my knees beneath her, I slowly sank my throbbing dick into her sloppy pussy and went still, refusing to move.

"Need to keep you like this just a little longer," I explained, and she wrapped herself around me as I fought to keep from fucking into her until my dick went useless as a plug for Ash's seed.

47

ASHTON

"Christ, Rhett." I sprawled on my back, not even bothering to clean up the mess smeared over my groin as I realized what he did.

Firmly lodged inside her body, he held still, smoothing Sky's hair from her sweat-damped face.

She stared up at him in wonder, his action and words probably having blown her mind, same as it had done to mine.

They'd gone without a condom while I'd been in the hospital, but he always pulled out before coming. Rhett didn't want to father kids, but he would move heaven and earth to make sure I got the ones I'd dreamed of since childhood.

"You're keeping his cum inside me," Sky whispered, a smile growing on her face.

"I hope it works," he said.

"Worth a try," she added sass to her tone and glanced over at me. "What do you think, Ashton?"

"His self-control is unreal. How can you just stay buried

like that in her perfect pussy and not want to rut away like an animal?"

"It's hard," Rhett stated, not sounding nearly as calm as seconds before.

"Hard." Sky giggled, and Rhett cursed, burying his face in her neck.

"Stay still, woman," he grumbled, his feet digging into the mattress as he attempted to push into her deeper. "Fuck!"

Sky laughed again, clutching his backside with her heels and wiggling.

"Christ, woman!" Rhett lifted off her, his hair a wild, dark mess, eyes half-feral. "Don't. Do. That!"

Still smirking, she lifted an eyebrow.

Rhett hissed, his stomach contracting along with his backside flexing. "Fuck!"

I chuckled as I realized how she teased him. "You're clenching around his dick, aren't you?"

"Mmm hmm," she hummed an agreement—and Rhett cursed again.

"I'm trying to help you out here," he grumbled, his arms starting to tremble, sweat beading on his brow.

Rhett suffered with his dick wrapped in decadent, wet heat. Such a selfless lover, he deserved to enjoy himself too.

A thought struck my head, and I went for it without hesitation.

"I know a sure way to set him off," I said, rolling to get between his legs.

"Fuck—Ash," Rhett moaned but sank back onto Sky's body, snaking his hands beneath her ass to lift her as he did the same with his own backside in offering to me.

I spread his cheeks and ran my nose over his drawn up

balls, along his taint, and over his puckered hole. A flick of my tongue sent a shudder through him.

"Squeeze around him, Sky," I said and shoved my tongue into his ass.

"Ah...Jesus *fucking* Christ—goddamnit!"

He pulled out of her body with a jerk, shoving me backward, pulsing his spunk all over her belly.

"*Fuuuck...*" He went lax after one final shiver, that happy contented tone of his painting a smile on my face.

"*That's* the voice right there," Sky said with a sigh, and I kissed up Rhett's spine, caging him between the two of us.

"Success." I smiled down at my green-eyed lover, the heat of Rhett soaking through my chest.

Sky giggled, and I leaned down to kiss her, trapping his hard body between us.

"I think we killed him," I told her while pushing up onto my hands again.

Rhett grunted but didn't move.

I reached between his spread legs to find his softening cock and a mess of my cum dripping from Sky's core.

"We've got nothing but time, baby," I told Rhett and kissed his shoulder. "But I appreciate the effort in helping make my dreams come true."

I slumped down beside Sky, and Rhett rolled onto his back on her other side.

"Christ. I've never gotten off like that. Not one goddamn thrust—like I was seventeen and owning Ash's ass for the first time," Rhett muttered, an arm tossed over his eyes. "Fucking hell, that was hot."

Chuckling, I leaned over Sky, grabbed Rhett's scruffy jaw, and kissed his mouth with a press of my lips—same as I'd done after he'd filled me with his cum that day all those years ago. "Love you," I whispered.

Sky sighed and palmed my ass cheek. "Next time, I'm watching," she said, her voice dreamy like her head was in the clouds.

"Sounds like a good plan to me," Rhett said.

We enjoyed a lazy shower together after downing a cup of coffee each, taking turns in washing each other.

Rhett and I both got hard again from Skylar's wandering hands and roaming fingers but denied her, promising to care for her that evening.

Saltwater lapped at our bare feet as we walked along the beach. Sky in the middle, both her hands firmly clasped in ours, she drew attention.

But she laughed and chatted, completely naive to the looks she got, clueless about her stunning beauty.

We went out for a late lunch, and I napped on the couch while we watched a movie, Sky's fingers in my hair, Rhett's hands kneading over my feet.

Mom called that night, making sure my first day home had gone smoothly, asking yet again if she should fly across the country to care for me.

"I understand your concern, Mom," I assured her, "and I don't want to upset you, but I don't need you hovering over me. I'm going to be fine."

"I-I just want to see my son," she whispered, her tone flooding with tears.

I clicked over to FaceTime, giving her what she wanted. "There," I stated when her face came into view. "See? I'm fine. A little pale still, tired, but the doctor said I've got plenty of years ahead of me. Other than gallstones causing pancreatitis, I'm healthy as an ox."

Mom huffed a heavy sigh. "If you need me— anything—you make sure that second son of ours calls me."

"He will," I said, snickering and eyeing Rhett who still rubbed my feet.

"Hi, Mrs. Blackwood," Sky said, leaning down to get her face onscreen.

"Mom," my mother corrected her.

They'd met on FaceTime during one of the hospital visits, and Mom had smiled nonstop at Skylar's nervous chatter and expressive face.

Dad had pretty much done the same and offered us the best of luck for our future.

Yeah, he still wanted those grandsons, and with how on board Rhett had become, I didn't doubt we would be successful in fulfilling my dreams.

"I gotta go, Mom," I stated abruptly, cutting her off mid-sentence while climbing from the couch. "Call you in a few days." I hung up, tossed my cell onto the couch, and grabbed Sky's hand.

"Where are we going?" she asked with a soft giggle, scampering after my quick steps toward the stairs. "To bed."

"I thought we were waiting until later—and you don't seem sleepy anymore."

"Because I'm not." I glanced over my shoulder. "Rhett—you coming, or what?"

"Only if it's in your ass like Sky said she wanted!" he hollered back.

"Yes, please!" Sky squeaked as we hurried up the stairs.

His footsteps thundered behind us, and we fell to the bed in a tangle of body parts, hungry mouths, and grasping hands.

Yeah, Rhett and I had every intention of giving Sky what she desired, but she proved too much of a temptation.

When the three of us came together in a soul-satisfying symphony of moans and curses?

I decided as long as I had my lover and my angel for life,
I would be content if that was all fate gifted us.

48

EPILOGUE

RHETT - A FEW MONTHS LATER

I stood across from Skylar, listening as she solemnly swore before the small group of friends around us and the Justice of the Peace to love us until death.

We'd sent an invitation to my dad, but he'd declined without offering an excuse. It had been the first time I'd reached out to him since Mom's death. He hadn't done so at all, but that fact didn't hurt me. Ash's parents—and Sky's as well—had accepted me as their own. They were the only family I needed.

Ash and I had discussed marriage a few times over our years together, but neither of us had felt the need for a piece of paper to declare us legal partners. We belonged to each other, and nothing and no one would ever change that.

Thankfulness for never taking that step swept through me as my two lovers exchanged vows as she and I had done.

Sky would have my name, and thanks to the state of California recognizing multiple-partner civil unions, so would Ashton—and the baby we hoped would one day grow in her womb. A few months had passed without success, but Ash had his sperm count tested, and everything appeared good and in working order, so we continued to keep our fingers crossed.

But even if we never conceived, even if Missing Link failed in providing us with children, she'd given us the angel Ash had desired to bring sunshine into our lives, the woman I needed on a daily basis.

She completed us in ways I never recognized we'd lacked in, and I would choose her all over again, every single day for the joy she'd brought to every moment.

Skylar took medication to help with her ADHD, and even though her ability to focus and hyperactivity had gotten better, her chattering hadn't slowed one bit.

So yeah, I still needed my silence some days, but both of us understood because I opened my mouth and communicated so as not to hurt feelings.

And Sky, being the angel she was, never once tried to invalidate my emotions or say I was the one with a problem. Relationships sure as fuck weren't easy, but listening and trying to understand how the others felt made for a more peaceful existence.

Swells and waves played over the ocean behind us in soothing, rhythmic motions, and same as the last time I'd considered life while glancing over her beauty, I contemplated what lay beneath, hidden from sight.

Restless depths full of the unknown, unnamed creatures that didn't have a chance of surviving outside their hiding places.

I'd done exactly as the Pacific once upon a time, and I breathed in the freedom Skylar had helped me find. No longer did I fear the depths of unidentified feelings. Learning to appreciate each and every one, allowing proper responses, had offered me personal growth I never would have attained otherwise.

I was no saint, and all three of us had plenty of areas we could grow in, but it came easier when we set aside our selfishness and chose love.

The official ceremony concluded, setting the first part of my plan in stone.

But I had to let go of my control and leave the rest of our future and possible children up to fate since they were out of my hands.

And I was actually okay with that fact.

———

SKYLAR

Long after our small group of friends and family left the reception we'd had at our house, Ash, Rhett, and I sat out on the patio, watching stars wink in and out between the clouds.

My parents had flown in for the wedding and were staying with Nora who'd come back from a weeklong mini vacation to Australia to visit the kangaroos. She hadn't fallen in love like I'd dreamed about happening, but a healthy flush had made her appear happier than I'd ever seen her.

As for our mom and dad, neither complained about my loving two men. Dad had puffed up with pride while walking me down the sandy makeshift aisle, happy that the two men he handed me off to saw me as an angel rather than annoyance like my ex had.

Mom had sat with tears in her eyes while we'd said our vows, but I knew that smile on her face came from the fact we were trying for babies and lots of them.

Okay, so just three, but still.

Nora didn't want love or kids, so it was up to me to relieve her grandkid itch. Something I couldn't wait to do.

Ashton rubbed his thumb over the band on my ring finger, and I snuggled deeper into Rhett's chest, thankfulness swelling inside my heart.

We'd bought a huge lounger for beside the pool, wide enough for two, perfect for my sprawling atop them both. That seat saw more action than any furniture in the house besides our bed.

There wasn't much better than making love out in the open air where only nature—and possibly drones—might see us. But all it ever took was a toe-curling kiss from either Ashton or Rhett to cause my inhibitions to flee.

"So I have one more wedding present," Ashton said, "and it's for both of you—upstairs. In our room."

I snickered even as arousal rose to life between my thighs.

Rhett stood, keeping me in his arms. "Lead the way, baby."

Red stained Ashton's cheeks when we stepped into the brightly lit living room. The man definitely had something up his sleeve since he rarely flushed like I did on a daily basis.

A million ideas flew through my mind, each and every one I ticked off my list, same as we'd done for all my real-life fantasies. Whatever I'd wanted, blurted in suggestion about our sex life, they'd been happy to satisfy.

What had been left untouched? What had I forgotten?

I puzzled as Rhett's sure steps climbed the stairs, the added weight of my body seeming no matter to him.

God, he had such thick thighs. I loved grasping hold of them whenever he thrust into me. Even better was watching the muscles ripple beneath his skin every time he made love to Ashton.

Rhett set me on my feet beside our bed, and Ashton went to their closet.

"What do you think it is?" Rhett asked.

I shrugged. "No clue."

Ashton came out, hands behind his back.

Rhett lifted an eyebrow and waited while shivers licked over my skin.

"Remember that day all those months ago when I teased about taking Sky to a sex store?" Ashton asked.

I didn't know what he referred to and glanced up at Rhett.

Brow furrowed, he shook his head.

"She said something about your coffee choice not surprising her," Ashton offered and bit his lip.

Realization dawned on Rhett's face, but I remained in the dark. "You said she had me pegged," Rhett murmured. "Fuck."

"Yeah—and I want to watch." Ashton pulled his hands from behind his back, and I studied the strappy thing in his grasp. Leather...cinches...and—

"Oh God." I gulped. "That's a...a..."

"Strap on." Ashton supplied what I couldn't find the word for, coming closer to show me the contraption. "And you're going to own Rhett's ass with it."

My gaze shot to Rhett, who studied the thing in Ashton's hands. He flicked his focus to me as though feeling all the questions rushing through my brain.

"Put it on, baby," Rhett ordered, ripping at his button-down as though suddenly desperate for me to fill him with that...thing dangling from the harness.

Heat rushed through my body, sending rippling need through my center with heavy pulses. "Oh God."

The men stripped in record time, but it took all three of us to rid me of clothing, and arousal smeared the inside of my thighs until they got the damn leather connected around my waist.

The dildo swung a bit with every step I took toward the bed, and I had to bite down on my tongue to keep from giggling.

Rhett knelt on the bed, Ashton's face in his ass, rimming the hell out of him—one of Rhett's favorite forms of play I'd enjoyed seeing a few times.

Once Ashton lubed and stretched him to the point Rhett begged for relief, I replaced Ashton between Rhett's spread legs. Back arched, ass in the air, Rhett clutched at the sheets above his head.

I rubbed my hands over his backside, spreading him like he did to me before having my ass—his antsy movements ceased same as always whenever I offered a soothing touch.

"You're sure?" I whispered, my focus on the glistening hole he offered me, something even Ash didn't get to enjoy too often.

"Yeah, angel. Feed me that dick."

Another rush of heat swept over me, and I fought to keep steady. "Ash...h-help me," I whispered, holding the lube-covered piece of silicone in my trembling hand.

Ash crowded against my back and positioned the tip at Rhett's hole. "Bear down."

Rhett pushed back, impaling himself, his hole stretching to take the dildo into his body. He let out a hiss, and my heart thundered inside my chest, watching as he rocked his body over and over, slowly stuffing himself full.

"That's so hot," I whispered, moving my hips forward to

meet him when he slid back over the length strapped to my hips.

"*Fuuuck...*" Rhett moaned, his spine arching deeper.

"That's his happy voice, angel," Ash said with a chuckle against my ear. "I think you got it." He left me then, but I couldn't tear my focus off Rhett's ass, couldn't relax my grip on his cheeks as we moved together, and he let loose with moans and grunts that made me want to leak from my core.

"Hands and knees, baby," Ash told him, and groaning, Rhett lifted his chest off the bed.

"Fuck...what are you..." Rhett's voice faded as Ash maneuvered beneath him in a sixty-nine position, his hips faltering in our rhythm.

"Fuck my throat," Ash murmured from beneath him.

Rhett moved forward, groaning a deep curse.

Ash hummed appreciation, and I bit my lip to keep from whimpering as Rhett backed onto the silicone dick.

Mirrors! My mind screamed, dozens of them—on every surface of the bedroom. I could watch my slick dick being sucked into Rhett's body but couldn't see the mouth he sank into when pushing forward.

Next time, I told myself, because I was *so* doing Rhett's ass again.

And Ash's—Rhett would share. I knew he would.

I stayed still, trembling like a leaf in a rainstorm, letting Rhett take what he wanted from the thing cinched tight around my waist. Every grunt and curse spilling from his lips heightened my own need for release. Ashton's pre-cum dripped onto his tight abs, and when Rhett leaned down to taste him, I grabbed hold of his hair.

"No—that's mine," I whispered, my voice wrecked with lust.

"Ah fuck." A shudder ripped through Rhett, and his hips slammed forward.

The sound of Ash gagging tightened my nipples, and I eased out of Rhett's ass the second he sagged, panting and head hanging.

My hand shook, and I cursed a few times, but I got the damn straps undone and tossed the leather and silicone bits away. A quick scamper, and I knelt over Ash's dripping tip, so damn needy I couldn't focus on anything but his dick. In me.

Now.

"Fuck yeah," Rhett said, slumping onto the bed, his dark, sated eyes on me.

Ashton grabbed my hips and slammed my swollen lips and soaked core down over his rigid length.

I cried out, arching back as he fucked up into me hard and fast, hitting my cervix with every thrust. The pleasure bordered on pain, but I needed him deeper—I wanted to feel him for days.

"Make a mess all over his cock, angel."

I did as Rhett told me, yapping absolute nonsense as I came undone in Ashton's grasp.

ASHTON - TEN MONTHS LATER

Sky's shriek fucking killed me—I swore, babbling the same as she'd been doing for hours on end about how I was never touching her again. I would never let another single sperm of mine anywhere near her poor, wrecked vagina.

"One more push, Skylar," her doctor said, and I gritted my teeth just as hard as she did, holding her trembling thigh as she curled her upper body and bore down, snarling like a rabid animal.

"That's it, Sky," Rhett murmured as though in complete control, gently rubbing her other thigh where he perched beside the hospital bed. But his eyes were wide, hair a wild mess from running his hands through it while Sky had labored. She'd finally gotten to the pushing part, and both of us bracketed her, watching our child be born.

"Okay...relax for me for a minute," the doctor murmured, and Skylar flopped back, a sweating, red-faced gorgeous mess.

Bright auburn hair covered the baby's head sticking from my lover's body, its tiny face scrunched up, eyes clenched shut as the doctor turned its head. Half in, half out of my poor, sweet angel's entrance—my stomach churned, but I wasn't going to miss that moment for anything.

"This is the worst part, I promise," the doctor stated in his annoyingly calm voice—I wanted to rip his goddamn throat out with how he maneuvered that head, those shoulders...one popped free...two—the baby came out in a rush of liquid.

Penis...

"It's a boy!" I cried, tears erupting from my eyes. I tore my focus off his little mouth being suctioned to find Sky smiling, eyes closed, her flushed face finally at rest.

"I'm *so* doing that again," she murmured as the baby's shrieks filled the room.

"The fuck you are!" I trembled, so damn overwhelmed I couldn't move. Couldn't decide where to look—baby. Rhett. Sky. I sobbed, snot running from my nose and everything.

Warm arms wrapped around me from behind. "Ash."

I sank into Rhett's embrace, handing off Sky's limp leg to a nurse who stepped in to replace me.

The doctor laid our crying son on Sky's chest, and she cradled the tiny body like he was made of the most precious gold.

"Hi, baby," she crooned, lifting him higher to press her lips against his forehead. "Aren't you just the cutest thing? I love you so much already—you have no idea. Your daddies do too, you know."

Rhett and I moved forward as a single unit, both of us reaching with shaky hands to touch our boy who quieted, blinking as though trying to see his mommy who continued to whisper to him with soft chatting about how she would endure giving birth all over again to see his precious face.

"He's so damn perfect," I choked out and rubbed my leaking nose against my hospital gown. "Look at all that hair." I laughed and met Sky's watery gaze.

"I love you so damn much, angel." I kissed her soundly, the warmth of Rhett's firm hand on my lower back keeping me grounded when my heart wanted to soar. "And I love you, little man," I told our son, kissing his button nose.

He started shrieking again, and more tears rolled down my face as I laughed.

Rhett leaned around me, and I shifted to make room for him alongside the bed. "Well done, love," he murmured against Sky's hair. "You're the strongest woman I know, and I can't tell you enough how much I adore you."

"I love you," Sky whispered, her eyes still watery and full of radiant joy as she peered up at Rhett.

An hour later, Rhett and I sat beside each other on a couch in Sky's private room as she breastfed our son.

I leaned my head onto Rhett's shoulder, still grinning like a fool, beyond content. I'd thought I'd known what happiness was before, but having my twin's namesake being given a clean bill of health and watching him nurse like a champ...

That dream come true completed me in ways I'd never imagined. There was no single word for the well of emotion inside me.

Fate had intended for us to meet. The three of us—no, four—were meant to be.

"Love you both so damn much it hurts," I whispered, rubbing a hand over my aching chest.

Rhett kissed my temple while squeezing me tight, and the tired smile Sky gave us across the room spanned the distance between us, filling my soul to overflowing.

THE END

ABOUT THE AUTHOR

USA Today bestselling author Lynn Burke is a CrossFit and coffee addict. Her three spawn and two fur babies dictate how often she can be found hunched over her Mac, typing as fast as her fickle muse cooks up hot stories.

You can find more about Lynn at her website: www.authorlynnburke.com

ALSO BY LYNN BURKE

Abel's Obsession

Divulging Secrets

Healing Storms

In Between

Reluctant Lumberjack

Resisting his Mate

The Playboy Bachelor

Billion Dollar Love Anthology

Blood Born Series

Bonds of Worship Series

Dark Leopards MC

Darkest Desires Series

Devil's Outlaws MC

Elite Escort Series

Fallen Gliders MC

Forbidden Obsession Duet

Found by Fate Series

Midnight Sun Series

Missing Link Series

Risso Family Series

Sandy Ridge Series

Sinful Nature Series

Vicious Vipers MC

www.ingramcontent.com/pod-product-compliance
Lightning Source LLC
Chambersburg PA
CBHW070239200726
48293CB00005B/1699